Praise for *SPINNAKER*

"Perspective from a woman… I was fully captivated by the storyline and characters. I quickly found myself feeling I was Katarina playing a part in the outcome of WWII. I felt her pain, her joy, her sadness, and her desires. ('What would I do to surprise Karl?') I would find myself thinking about the couple's story when I put the book down. (Which was only two times, as I read it in one day.) It certainly was a page turner for me, full of suspense and wonder. The author had an ingenious way of taking you far enough in the love scenes allowing you to create your own level of passion… leaving it to your imagination and your personal comfort level. I truly felt the couple's ever trusting love. I found myself in tears at times as I walked with them through the blissful moments and the times of misfortune. This book will arouse your emotions on every level. It is full of ecstasy, joy, anticipation, excitement, surprise, sadness, and fear. As an added bonus you will walk away with a few historical facts about WWII."

—Diane N.

"This is a World War II love story about a young German farm girl and a corporal American Air Force pilot on his first bombing raid into occupied Germany. The story is full of suspense and surprises throughout. I liked the fact that you never knew what was going to happen next, it left me sitting on the edge of my chair. I found myself hoping for the best yet always waiting for the worst to happen. At the very end you'll see how history repeats itself in a surprisingly different way."

—Charlie N.

"A romance like no other. Follow an American soldier as he falls in love, turned undercover operative in a life of espionage, Karl, on his love-conquers the mission-all journey during the most trying times of World War Two."

—Nichole M.

"A beautiful love story with family intrigue during wartime drama. It kept my interest throughout. Well written, lots of visuals in my mind as I read. The novel is very detailed, and the author did a great job making the reader feel the characters. The end was good, sad. I see a sequel, two of my favorite movies are Schindler's List and The English Patient."

—Joan N.

SPINNAKER

An Endearing Romance Novel
Entwined With Suspense and Espionage

SABATO diVINCENTI

This is a work of fiction. All of the characters, names, incidents,
organizations, and dialogue in this novel are either the products
of the author's imagination or are used fictitiously.

Archway Publishing books may be ordered
through booksellers or by contacting:

Archway Publishing
1663 Liberty Drive
Bloomington, IN 47403
www.archwaypublishing.com
844-669-3957

ISBN: 978-1-6657-0543-1 (sc)
ISBN: 978-1-6657-0541-7 (hc)
ISBN: 978-1-6657-0542-4 (e)

Library of Congress Control Number: 2021907212

Print information available on the last page.

Archway Publishing rev. date: 07/31/2021

DEDICATION

Spinnaker has been years in the making. I wish to dedicate this novel to my wife Paula and daughter Nichole for their inspirations that helped me create this story. A lifetime of personal and joyful memories along with countless special occasions have been intertwined in the novel. As the story unfolds, so do the memories of our love together. Although not part of our family background I built in many surprising series of events, often with grim details of murder and revenge to make the war plot come to life.

The creation of this novel stemmed from years of thoughts churning in my mind inspired from countless hours watching old vintage weekly TV wartime series, WWII movies, and espionage films.

In writing this novel I often thought of the thousands upon thousands of brave men and women who served, and currently serve, in the United States military branches and those of our Allies. They have risked and continue to risk their lives daily for our freedom. For those I dedicate this novel to all of them.

ACKNOWLEDGEMENTS

Writing a novel is more challenging than I imagined, and more rewarding than I could have ever imagined. None of this would have been possible without my dear family members and friends, my deepest acknowledgement, appreciation, and thankfulness goes out to them.

I must start by thanking my loving wife, Paula, and for putting up with me for over forty-seven of the best years of my life. From reading early drafts to giving me advice on the cover to keeping me focused on edits to write the best novel I could. Thank you so very much, Tibs.

To my daughter Nichole, along with her crazy work schedule and tending to three little ones, our beloved grandchildren, found the time to read and provide valuable and heartfelt comments.

To my brother Pat and sister-in-law Joey, and longtime and dear friends Charlie, Mark, and Tom for their endless hours of reviewing. They each contributed to this novel and provided honest and genuine reviews and edits. Their very different perspectives and approach to reviewing and editing provided a host of opinions, all of which were very helpful.

Thank you all for your part to bring this novel to its final chapter.

ABOUT THE AUTHOR

Sabato diVincenti is a husband, father, and grandfather whose writing is inspired from various vintage television wartime series, World War II movies, and espionage films. He resides with his wife Paula in Florida. By day Sabato enjoys a successful career as an executive in heavy civil construction. He is self-taught and prides himself on mentoring and sharing his knowledge with others. By night his mind drifts into the world of fiction. Join Sabato as he debuts his first novel, intertwining personal and memorable experiences into a story of romance, drama, intrigue, espionage, and suspense. He meticulously and thoughtfully created this exceptionally written love story. His creativity takes the reader beyond expectations with a page turning plot set during World War II. As his love story unfolds, diVincenti's mind wanders with immense imagination narrating the lives of Karl and Katarina. Eerie events occur which changes the path of the young couple's lives forever. Turning the pages becomes infectious as the reader follows their journey to its conclusion.

CONTENTS

INTRODUCTION

Spinnaker: a thrilling romance novel of adoring love, weaving fiction and fact in an intriguing mystery adding drama and suspense while intertwining espionage within the characters' lives. Chapter after chapter you will join in on a journey of incredible and bizarre turn of events and follow a passionate love affair along with grim details of murder and revenge.

As the story unfolds in war-torn Germany, 1943, the plot takes many unexpected turns with unpredictable suspense. Joyful surprises with unparalleled sadness and glorified fulfillment, coupled with bone chilling and harrowing twists. A young American pilot's plane crashes and the story begins to unfold. A young German farm girl discovers his battered and broken body. With evidence of his origin to Allied alliance, she hides him until she can get him to safety.

A U.S. Army Air Force pilot Karl, and a beautiful young woman Katarina; the daughter of a German officer who stands against Hitler, his regime, and the Third Reich. She cares for Karl and nurtures him back to health. Their kind-heartedness and friendship turn to love. As they endure falling in love in occupied Germany, Karl is entangled in a bitter sibling rivalry with Katarina's toxic brother, a Nazi SS officer. They fall in love and their journey together unfolds.

The author's imagination reveals suspense and espionage. The surprising turn of events will keep you fully engaged to see where the story takes you, and how the story ends. The author braids multiple plots into one compelling story. Page after page, chapter after chapter, the suspense continues, the reader finds themselves unable to put this novel down.

Eerie events occur changing the path of young Karl and Katarina's lives forever. The novel often takes the reader back to normalcy, then jumps out and seizes you with more unexpected occurrences. Spinnaker is a love story of Karl and Katarina, a passionate and endearing love affair. The novel will take you through their journey of the young couple's lives. The ending will leave you with a question, astonishment, and disbelief. You will be literally taken back. A novel unlike any other, one you will not soon forget.

PROLOGUE – A YOUNG AIRMAN

A hot June afternoon in Milwaukee, 1939. A young seventeen-year old stands in line at the United States Army Air Corps recruiting station. Just graduating high school, the young seventeen-year-old is about to fulfil his desire to become a pilot, and enter the Aviation Flying Cadet Program. As he awaits his turn, he reminisces of his childhood years. His train of thought is interrupted by a recruiting officer. "Next, you young man, come sit down."

An hour of completing his paperwork and application passes. He learns of his assignment. The U.S. Army Air Corps Training Center, Randolph Field, San Antonio Texas. He has two weeks to report for duty, basic flight training. As the weeks pass, he reflects on what led him to his decision to enlist. *Perhaps I will make a difference.*

Thirty-nine hundred miles away, in London England, June 1939; a young nineteen-year-old girl embarks on a new journey. She arrives from Germany to attend the University of London and begin her studies. The young maiden is alone.

On March 16 1935, Adolf Hitler announces he will rearm Germany, in violation of the Treaty of Versailles. Hitler reveals that Germany has begun to construct an air force and unveils plans to reinstitute conscription and create a German army of more than half a million men. Hitler directs a large-scale rearmament. On September 1 1939, Hitler invades Poland, resulting in Britain and France declaring war on Germany. In June 1941, Hitler orders an invasion of the Soviet Union. As the unrest further develops in

Europe, the U.S. Naval Command resurrects and organizes the Atlantic Fleet in February 1941.

On December 11 1941, four days after the Japanese attack on Pearl Harbor, Nazi Germany declares war against the United States. The United States Eighth Army Air Force is deployed to England with a daunting mission; to destroy Germany's ability to wage war, and gain command of the European skies to pave the way for an Allied land invasion. To accomplish this, thousands of American airmen face the constant threat of death.

The Eighth Army Air Force is established as VIII Bomber Command on January 19 1942. The advanced detachment of VIII Bomber Command is established near Royal Air Force Bomber Command Headquarters at Royal Air Force Daws Hill England on February 23 in preparation for its units to arrive in the United Kingdom from the United States. The first combat group of VIII Bomber Command arrives in the United Kingdom and is the ground echelon of the 97th Bombardment Group, which arrives at RAF Polebrook on June 9 1942.

This is the start of offensive operations against Nazi-occupied territory. Regular combat operations by the VIII Bomber Command begin on August 17 1942, when the 97th Bombardment Group flies twelve B-17E bombers in the first VIII Bomber Command heavy bomber mission of the war from Royal Air Force Polebrook, attacking the Rouen-Sotteville marshalling yards in France.

The United States and its Allies, England, and France, quickly develop a strategy plan to respond to Nazi Germany's aggression. A planned turning point is a strategic attack to be launched on the Wilhelmshaven Port in a plan to stop Germany from advancing attacks on England and France from the sea.

The novel begins with this mission but quickly takes an unexpected turn. The mission takes months to plan. This initial wave is planned for an air assault to be carried out in January 1943, a strategic bombing mission that will catch the Nazis off guard. The second wave is planned by sea and land, from the northern part of the Netherlands and the North Sea to blockade the seaport, giving the Allies a stronghold in northwest Germany.

As the chapters unfold, so does the suspense, drama, and intrigue. The suspense builds, chapter to chapter. Surprises and uncanny turn of events continue right to the last chapter. Turning each page becomes infectious.

THE MISSION

On this night, January 27 1943, the Eighth Army Air Force dispatches a squadron of B17 bombers from Royal Air Force Bomber Command Headquarters at Royal Air Force Daws Hill England, flying the first American bombing raid into occupied Germany. The mission is targeting the Wilhelmshaven Port. Wilhelmshaven is a coastal town in Lower Saxony, Germany and is situated on the western side of the Jade Bight, a bay on Germany's North Sea coast. The port is a strategic target that will cripple the Kriegsmarine, the German navy, based in Wilhelmshaven.

Karl Schellenberg is a twenty-one-year-old corporal, a scout pilot in the Eighth Army Air Force. Karl is an exceptional airman and rose quickly through the Army Air Force. He is on a reconnaissance mission into northwest Germany from England. Karl is piloting the lead scout aircraft ahead of the initial wave of bombers, which is preceding the main bombing mission. Karl's mission is to keep a lookout for the Luftwaffe's counterattack, the German Air Force.

Karl's heading takes a more southern route over Amsterdam, away from the main squadron's flightpath. He is flying a very hi-tech aircraft with a new technology, an airborne radar system called H2S. The H2S is the first airborne, ground scanning radar system able to identify enemy targets for night and all-weather bombing, allowing attacks outside the range of radio navigation aids. It is immune to conventional tracking systems. The plane is also equipped with a new technology called WINDOW, or chaff. It was developed by the British. It is a radar countermeasure system designed to overwhelm and confuse an enemy radar system with false echoes. The night is clear as Karl heads over the border into Germany.

"Bogey; Spinnaker checking in." Bogey is Command's code name, from the Humphrey Bogart's character in the 1941 movie, *The Maltese Falcon.* Spinnaker is Karl's code name, named after the lead sail on a sailboat, on the windward way. "I see heavy bombing from coalition forces on the horizon with substantial return ground fire. Crossing the German border now."

"Roger that, Spinnaker," Bogey replies.

"Bogey, I see the city of Wilhelmshaven with heavy bombardment. Explosions and fires erupting in the distance." Karl reaches for his dog tags, where he always carries his mother's locket.

Karl's mother died when he was very young. On the night of her death, Karl was at his mother's bedside. They were holding hands. With her last breaths, Hazel opened Karl's hand and placed her locket in his palm. As she closed his hand over her locket, she said, "Keep this with you forever, it will always protect you." He smiled and nodded. Looking into each other's eyes, his mother took her last breath.

There is slight turbulence. The plane rocks to the left. Karl corrects the roll and adjusts the flight path as planned, he eases the controls to correct the yaw of the plane. The plane corrects itself to the planned flight path. He settles back and continues his focus on the mission. He focuses on the northern horizon. He sees the enemy's artillery fire focused to the westerly skies, toward the incoming Allied aircraft. He radios command. "Bogey, they have reconnaissance. The German's know we are approaching."

"Spinnaker, abort the mission, I repeat, abort the mission."

Suddenly a severe flash of bright light encompasses the sky. "Bogey, an unusually bright light has just enveloped the sky around me. I lost track of the earth for a moment. A type of flash I have never experienced before."

"Spinnaker, we have no reports of any abnormalities in your area."

"Bogey, I feel vertigo. I have dizziness. It feels as the sky is moving abnormally, like it is spinning. I am having a problem focusing. My eyes are blurry. My hearing, I cannot hear. I have severe ringing in my ears. My balance is off. I am beginning to sweat profusely. I feel nauseous. Something from the flash of light." Karl passes out for a moment.

"Spinnaker; try to collect yourself."

The radio is silent. "Spinnaker, do you read me? Come in Spinnaker."

"Bogey, yes, I read you. I must have passed out briefly. The symptoms are subsiding. That was very strange."

"Glad you're back with us, Spinnaker."

"Bogey, I am experiencing electrical problems. Bogey, my electronics are failing, my engines are failing. I am aborting the aircraft."

Before ejecting, Karl distinctly turns the airplane to a westward heading in hopes of avoiding crashing into occupied Germany and giving the Nazis the new aircraft technology. Karl ejects. He can see the airplane fall from the sky in the distance, exploding as it hits the ground. He fears it crashed in Germany. As Karl descends, the waning moon gives enough light for him to see the ground approaching. He is within several hundred meters of landing. He sees a small clearing next to the woods, about fifty meters away from the trees. He is heading toward the trees. He pulls the steering cords to steer his parachute away from the trees and toward the clearing. He prepares for a normal touchdown. He feels a strange abnormality in his parachute, some sort of a malfunction. The parachute is wandering aimlessly, Karl has no control. Suddenly, his parachute fails. He plummets helplessly.

Early morning, the temperature is three degree Celsius. Karl awakes. He is cold and shivering. He is unsure how long he has been unconscious. *Am I in Germany?* he wonders. It's just becoming daybreak. He landed next to the clearing in a heavily wooded area. The remains of his parachute are tangled in the trees and brush. Unclear of his injuries and location, he has the wherewithal to gather his chute so as not to be seen by German patrols. Karl is in severe pain. As he tries to move, he feels excruciating pain from his leg, abdomen, and arm. He cries out from his injuries. Karl somehow musters the energy and overcomes the pain to gather the remains of his parachute knowing it will draw the attention of German patrols. He hides the tangled and torn parachute under branches and dried leaves alongside his battered body. Karl hears what he believes to be an American plane. *I wonder if they are looking for me.* As daybreaks, he can see a farm over the ridge, a farmhouse, and a village in the distance.

Karl begins to assess his injuries. He knows they are grave. His right leg and left forearm are broken. His head is hurting. He feels the back of his head, it is wet. He looks at his hand and realizes he is bleeding from his head in multiple places. His abdomen is punctured, apparently from a tree branch during the fall, and he has numerous cuts and scrapes. He is unable to see from his left eye.

His adrenalin and survival training kick in. He knows he must tend to the most severe injuries quickly. He uses his parachute for bandages and the cords as lacing to bind the bandages around his wounds. He gathers tree branches and uses them to splint his forearm and leg. The pain is excruciating. Karl passes out.

HIDING

Karl is groggy, he slowly opens his eyes. It appears to be midafternoon as he looks at the sun in the blue sky. He covers himself with brush and dried leaves to hide himself until nightfall, until he can develop a plan. He is cold. He has no idea if Command knows where he is, especially since he sent his aircraft on a reverse heading. He hears a vehicle coming toward him. He can see it as it crests the hill. Karl hunkers down as the road is only one hundred meters from him. He can barely see a Nazi patrol car passing by, but they keep going. He knows now he is in Germany. Night approaches. Karl hears the bombing in the distance. He dozes off.

At daybreak he is awakened by the sound of another vehicle. A Nazi patrol car and numerous other vehicles in a convoy, mostly halftracks with troops. The motorcade stops a few hundred meters from him. Karl, barely awake, dizzy, cold, and in pain from his injuries watches in horror. He sees the troops exit the vehicles. They appear to be discussing something and pointing in his direction. He feels they know he dropped in the vicinity. Karl, fearing he will be captured or killed, looks around the area. He begins to crawl toward a more secure and covered area in the woods. He reaches the crest of a hill. The pain is unbearable. He sees a hollow log in a ravine, laying in a slight depression. He desperately struggles to get to the log, and does, dragging the remains of his parachute with him. Once inside the log, he pulls in leaves, sticks and twigs to cover the opening.

The soldiers now dispersed into groups of four, begin searching the woods and approaching his location. In German, they say, "The American must be here, we will find him. We have air searches on going as well." Karl, very fluent in German, understands them. He hears them as they get closer. The cold leaves are crackling under their feet. Suddenly, they are there, standing directly over the log. One sits down on the log. Karl can barely see through the end of the log. He sees three maybe four men: legs and boots only. Thankfully Karl does not see nor hear any dogs. He lies and listens.

"The American must be close. Why should we capture him? We should kill him and spare Germany the prison camp expense; we do not need more prisoners; we need dead Americans." They laugh! A cigarette drops to the ground and begins smoldering in the dried leaves. They seem to be devising a plan to continue the search. Karl hears them say they found the wreckage of the plane, but no pilot.

"The plane was completely destroyed," Karl hears one say. Karl is pleased to hear that, as he was concerned the Germans would get the new H2S aircraft technology. As they shuffle through the leaves, looking onward into the distance, the patrol walks directly over some remains of the parachute under leaves, but do not see it.

He hears them say, "We will come back tomorrow with the dogs, and we will find him."

Escaping a close call, Karl settles in for another long night, his pain is getting worse. He is warmer inside the log. Karl falls asleep. He awakes and peers from the log to a fresh fallen snow. He reaches out from the log and gathers snow for a drink of water, as he is severely dehydrated. He hears crackling of footsteps, and fears the Germans are back. He is still groggy and cannot see clearly. He hears bombing in the distance and dozes off again. The Germans come back, this time with dogs. They decide to begin the search on the opposite ridge. Karl hears barking dogs. The Germans consume the day and find nothing. Karl sees them leave. He believes the Germans will search his current location next. By this time Karl is losing track of time; hours pass. *Is it the second day or third?* He knows he must move out of this area as it is only a matter of time until the Germans find him. He decides to move at night.

As the sun finally sets, a front rolls in. Karl painfully crawls from the log and over to the ridge where the Germans had searched. He is careful to crawl in areas under pine trees not to leave tracks in the snow. The trees shaded the ground from the snow. Karl drags pine branches with him to mask his scent from the dogs. He nestles himself in a heavy brush area. Karl hears the Allied bombardment in the distance. He smiles and dozes off. Snow begins to fall.

HELP ARRIVES

January 31, Karl is suddenly startled and awakened to a wet cloth on his forehead. "Shh, do not say anything." Karl can barely make her out but sees an image of a young woman. His vision is blurred from his head injuries and blood. "Here, drink some water. I have been with you for a few hours. You have grave injuries. Let me help you. I saw the Germans here yesterday and today, there are many patrols looking for you, including air patrols. We heard an American plane had crashed. My mother and I were curious, and we began looking after the soldiers left. My mother is looking in the woods. I saw partial remains of a parachute in the trees on the other ridge. The Germans must have missed it. I gathered it so the soldiers would not find it. As I was walking to this area, I happened to spot some white cloth in the bushes. I found you. Let me help you get better settled for now. What is your name?" she asks.

In a painful and muttered voice, "Karl."

"Ah, a German name." Karl nods. The girl struggles to get him in a comfortable position. She tends to his wounds the best she can. "I have a blanket. Let me wrap you up to stay warm." Karl looks into her eyes. "Rest for now," she says. "I will come back at nightfall with my mother and a wagon. I will take you to our stone barn in an outfield on our farm, you will be safe there."

"Who are you, what is your name?"

"Not to worry about that right now. My father is a German officer and leads the Resistance, an underground movement against the Nazi regime; you must trust me, we can help you."

"Fräulein, you speak good English."

"Very good English indeed. My mother is English, my father is German. Take my coat. You are still shivering. Try not to talk, you need to rest, you will need your strength tonight. I must leave now. I will be back."

An hour or so passes. Karl hears the patrol return, with dogs. They begin searching the area where Karl was days before. "We know the American is in the area." The heavy snow throws off his scent from the dogs.

Karl can only lay and watch, listen and pray. He clutches his mother's locket. The sun begins to set, the Nazi soldiers leave again. Karl knows they will eventually find him if he stays. Nightfall approaches. Karl lays in waiting. The sky is clear, and the moon is a waning crescent moon. He is cold, in severe pain, and it appears the bleeding has subsided from the dressings the young girl applied. He hears air-raid sirens in the distance, planes, bombing, and German anti-aircraft fire, or flak. He can see the tracers off in the distance.

Nightfall approaches. Karl has trouble resting from the cold temperature, and his pain intensifies. He finally dozes off. Katarina and her mother return, it is late, 23:00. The sky is lit by a waning crescent moon. Karl is awakened by the clomping of a horse, and the wagon wheels rolling through the rocks in the woods. The girl and her mother return to take him to shelter. The young girl ties the horse to a tree. Karl opens his eyes and sees a silhouette in the moonlight.

"Hi Karl, it is Katarina. I was with you earlier. I have come back to take you to a safe place." She kneels down and asks Karl, "How are you doing? We are here to take you now. My mother, Anna is with me, you can trust her."

"Where are you taking me?" he asks.

"To our farm, on the outskirts of Aurich. Remember I told you my father was a German officer. The Nazis will not think to look for you on our farm. We will get you settled. You can heal until we can get you well and help you escape. Are you ready to get in the wagon?"

Karl can barely utter a word yet says, "I am ready." Karl is lying on his back.

"We are going to get you stood up." My mother will hold your good arm; I will get behind you and lift. Keep your weight on your good leg. Do you understand?" Karl nods. "Let me sit you up Karl, this will hurt. We will be careful. Ready?"

"Yes," in a meek voice.

Katarina and Anna begin to pick Karl up, and a shivering scream erupts from him. "Just a little more Karl, almost up," Anna says. Karl is crying it is so painful. They finally get him to his feet next to the wagon. "Are you ok?" Karl nods.

Suddenly they hear a vehicle. Katarina looks off in the distance and sees headlights flickering from the horizon. They know the sound. "Karl, it is a German patrol car, be still and quiet." As the patrol vehicle approaches, they see a search light combing through the trees. Katarina is frantic as they did not hide the wagon well. The patrol is canvassing both sides of the road, sweeping the light from one side to the other. "Mother, tend to the horse so he is not spooked, Karl, lean on the wagon and be very still, I will hold you." The patrol vehicle is only a few hundred meters away. The light flickers through the trees on their side as the vehicle approaches them. Just as light is almost upon them, it moves to the other side of the road. The vehicle passes by.

The women regroup. "Karl, we need to get you in the wagon." The bed of the wagon is low. "Try to sit down, on the wagon. We can slide you back then. I have straw for you to lay in to soften the ride back." He nods. "Lie back in the straw. We need to slide you into the wagon more." Karl shrieks with pain but is finally settled in the wagon. Katarina askes, "Karl, are you comfortable?" Karl nods. "The ride back will be a bit bumpy. It will take thirty to forty minutes. We will travel slowly and as easy as we can, I will stay with you in the back." Anna gathers the remains of the parachute. Karl lays and gazes into the moonlight sky. He falls asleep and dreams of his childhood. He dreams of playing in the neighborhood streets, cooling down at the fire hydrant on hot summer days and playing in the snow in the winter.

Katarina has the wherewithal to remove the tracks from the wagon and horse. She ties a log to the back of the wagon. She also sprinkles garlic to distract the dogs. It is a slow, long ride to the barn. They arrive at the barn in the early morning hours. Earlier that day Katarina and Anna prepared a bed for Karl in the fruit cellar of the barn. Katarina and Anna wake Karl. "Karl, wake up, we are here. I backed the wagon close to the barn for you. When you are ready, let's get you in and settled."

"I am ready."

"First, we will slide you forward, then sit you up." As they slide him, he again shrieks with pain. Sitting him up is worse. "You must have broken your ribs as well," Katarina says. "Let us stand up and we will get you inside." Karl takes a deep breath and stands up. Katarina and Anna struggle but manage to get him in the barn. They remove a few floorboards to get Karl in the fruit cellar. "Karl, we are going to lay you on this board and slowly slide you down to the cellar. Mother help me get him in the fruit cellar, then tend to the horse and wagon. I will get him settled in and change his dressings." Katarina lights a fire in a small wood stove to keep him warm. She has a candle burning.

"Will I be safe?" Karl asks.

"Yes, this barn has an underground shelter. The original stone barn did not have a basement, only a wooden floor. My father dug out a basement and built this fruit cellar for shelter. Here, sip this."

"What is it?" Karl asks.

"It is schnapps. It will help the pain and help you sleep." She spends the next hour with him until he falls asleep. She leans down and whispers, "Sleep well, I will be back in the morning." Katarina stokes the fire, extinguishes the candle, and replaces the floorboards as she exits the cellar. It is 3:00 AM, Katarina walks to the main farmhouse, about one-half mile away. The moon has traveled halfway across the night sky.

Katarina settles in bed, but cannot sleep, she keeps thinking of Karl. She goes to her mother's room, and softly knocks. "Mother, are you awake, can we talk?" Katarina is crying.

"I am awake, I cannot sleep either thinking of that poor boy."

"I want you to hold me for a while Mother." They fall asleep together. Katarina is up at sunrise and notices the snow has melted. *That will help remove the tracks from the fields,* she thinks to herself. She gathers fresh bandages, ointment, oranges, bread, cheese, walnuts, and water and places them in a basket. As Katarina begins the walk to the barn she looks off in the distance and sees a patrol searching the area where Karl was the night before. She faintly hears the dogs barking. They seem to have picked up a scent, she sees they are running in circles, disoriented. Her plan to use garlic worked, Katarina smiles.

Katarina arrives at the barn. She gently enters and whispers, "Karl, it is Katarina, are you awake?" She hears nothing. She quietly removes the floorboards and descends the ladder to the fruit cellar. She is mindful to replace the floorboards in the opening. Karl seems to be comfortably sleeping. Katarina gently places a damp compress on his forehead. Karl makes a mumbled sound and continues sleeping. Katarina stays by his side. After a couple of hours, Karl wakes up. "Good morning Karl." He looks at her, into her eyes, and smiles. He can see she is wearing a blue dress and a white apron.

"You are the girl, the young girl who helped me, thank you."

She smiles back. "Yes, I have water and food for you. You need nourishment. She helps him drink a little water, eat part of an orange, and a small piece of bread with cheese. Let me get your dressings changed and get better splints on your leg and arm. I found some sticks in the barn. I have bandages to wrap your ribs as well. I am going to begin with your dressings. Are you able sit up?" He nods. Katarina helps him sit up. She unbuttons his tattered and torn shirt and notices a locket on his dog tags. There are more injuries than she anticipated. From his labored breathing, she thinks numerous ribs are broken and can see a branch has punctured his side. She is concerned about internal bleeding. "Karl, a branch has penetrated your side, it will need to be removed." Katarina carefully wraps his ribs, staying away from the branch stuck in his side. Karl, in pain, tightly holds her arm. "Lay back down Karl, I need to roll you over a bit. I also have clean clothes for you." Karl slowly lies back and painfully rolls over. Katarina cleans the wounds on his back. She finishes dressing his wounds and helps get new clothes on him. She can see his leg has a compound fracture and can tell Karl is in extreme pain.

"I am going to change the splints now." The arm splint went better than she expected. As she removes the old splint from his leg, he screams from the pain, and passes out. Katarina gently places the new splint on his leg and lets him sleep. Katarina knows she needs a doctor for Karl. Karl is very unrested, in and out of sleep and consciousness. She stays with him until nightfall. Katarina leans down and kisses Karl on his forehead and departs for the farmhouse. The next day at daybreak, after a sleepless night herself, Katarina scurries to the barn to check on Karl. She is petrified when she sees him. He is soaking wet from a very high fever and seems to be unconscious. Katarina places a wet compress on his forehead. In astonishment, she runs back to the farmhouse to get help. As she runs over the crest of the hill to the farmhouse, she immediately stops in her tracks. Katarina sees a German SS staff car in the driveway and knows it is her brother Wilhelm.

The SS are the German Secret State Police formed out of the existing state police after the Nazis took power. Wilhelm Keitel has extreme alliance to the German Army and to Hitler. He has been the black sheep of the family from a very young age. Wilhelm became obsessed with the Third Reich and their propaganda. He joined their Army at the age of seventeen.

Frantic and frightened, Katarina hides behind a tree to gather herself. *He rarely comes to our home; he is too involved with Hitler and never has time for us. Why is he here this early? It is barely daybreak*; she asks herself. Wilhelm and her father argue all the time between the Motherland's Army and what Hitler has turned it into. Startled, Katarina hears a noise in the tree, she looks up and sees an owl. Precious time is being wasted. Her plan is to send her mother to get the doctor while she goes back to Karl, to be with him. *Shall I go to town myself? How long will Wilhelm be here?* she wonders.

The front door opens, Wilhelm walks from the house with Anna at his side. He seems calm, again unusual. As they get to the car, Katarina can see Anna give her son a hug, he has no response. Wilhelm gets in the car and his driver takes him away. Katarina runs to Anna.

"Mother, Karl needs help, he became very ill last night and needs Doctor Vandenburg now. Will you go to town? I need to get back to Karl. What was Wilhelm doing here? Did he mention the American pilot? He has to know."

"I will go now; Katarina, go be with Karl. I will tell you about Wilhelm later, everything is fine, he wondered where you were though. Go now, be with him." Anna walks into town, somewhat guarded. The people in the town of Aurich are disgusted with Hitler and his regime. Anna, Katarina, and her father have trusted connections within the Underground Movement. Anna walks to Doctor Vandenburg's house. As she knocks on the door a German patrol vehicle passes through town. She says to herself; *They are still looking for Karl.* She steps behind a trellis. As she steps from behind the trellis Anna can hear another car approaching, she immediately ducks behind the trellis again. She can see it is a German officer's staff car. As the car passes, she sees Wilhelm. He glances over toward the house. No eye contact though Anna is now petrified if he saw her. She runs down to the street and can see the car drive out of town.

The doctor opens the door, "Anna, why are you here so early, what is wrong?"

"Doctor Vandenburg, let us go inside, I need to talk with you. Have you heard about the American plane that crashed?"

"Yes Anna, I have. The German soldiers have been searching the countryside for days. I heard the soldiers found the plane but not the pilot."

"The pilot, he is with us," Anna's shaken voice mutters. "Katarina and I found him a few days after the crash in a field not far from our farm. We were curious and went out riding and came across him. Come with me, he needs your help, I will give you the details as we go."

"Anna, tell me about his injuries so I can take the necessary supplies and instruments."

"Katarina came to me this morning frantically and hysterically crying. She went to check on him and found him with a very high fever, sweating profusely. He was unconscious. When he ejected, it appears his parachute did not open. His chute got tangled in the evergreen trees and slowed his fall. He would be dead otherwise. He has a broken arm and leg; the leg is a compound break. A puncture in his side, and maybe broken ribs. We are concerned about internal bleeding. Many cuts and scrapes, and he has been in severe and unbearable pain. We rescued him from the woods, otherwise the Germans would have found him. We have him in the out barn at the rear of the farm, a thirty to forty-minute walk from the house."

"Let me gather what I need, I will take pain medication and something to help him sleep."

"Doctor, let us go to the farmhouse first. Would you feel comfortable taking the horse and wagon to save time?"

"Yes, let's hurry."

"Katarina is with him. Wilhelm was here today, at the house."

"Do you think he knows Anna?"

"No, I do not think so, he would have done something right then. He told me he was on his way to one of the concentration camps and was passing through town."

"Do you believe him?"

"No, nor do I trust him, we must go now Doctor." Little do they know Wilhelm did have another motive and reason for the visit.

As they approach the barn, they hear air raid sirens in the distance. Katarina hears the wagon and runs out to help the doctor. "Doctor Vandenburg, thank you for coming so quickly, come with me, he is in the fruit cellar. His name is Karl." The three go to the cellar. The Doctor immediately sighs when he sees Karl. He begins to examine the pilot. Karl is still unconscious. The Doctor first takes his temperature. His temperature is over forty degrees Celsius. Doctor Vandenburg further examines the wounds, and the puncture.

"This boy is in very bad shape, first I need to remove the branch that punctured his side and close the wound. I fear he is bleeding internally. Katarina, Anna, I will need your help." The women begin to cry more.

"Stay strong," he says. "I need to operate and see the extent of the internal injuries. I am glad he is unconscious. Help me roll him over. Steady him so he does not move." Doctor Vandenburg sterilizes his scalpel with alcohol. He makes the incision, blood pours out. "Anna, use the towels to sop the blood so I can see. I now see what is causing the bleeding, Karl has a ruptured spleen. Katarina, in my bag, get the forceps and the container with sutures. Sanitize the forceps with the alcohol, and hand me the sutures." Karl rolls a bit and groans, then relaxes. "I need to get his spleen repaired and get him stitched up. Thankfully the rupture is contained within the splenic capsule. If the bleeding broke through the splenic capsule, he would have gone into hemorrhagic shock and bled out in a very short time. Katarina, this boy would have died had you not got help." Katarina is trembling.

"Since that is finished, I will tend to his other injuries. You did a good job with the splints Katarina. You are correct, his leg is a compound break that will need set. Help me roll him on his back. Steady him and hold him down if he tries to move, this will be very painful. I need to cut the pant leg."

"No," Katarina hurriedly says. "They are the only clothes I have for him; his uniform was bloody, torn, and ruined. I burned his American uniform, his boots, and remains of the parachute so the Germans would not find them."

"Ok Katarina, I understand. Help me remove them, easy though. His leg is in bad shape. Ladies, get ready." He grasps Karl's upper leg and sets the lower leg back into position. Karl jolts out a painful reaction, but fortunately stays unconscious. "The worst is over for now." The doctor places a double splint on Karl's leg. "Now let us look at his arm. This is not bad, a slight fracture. I will replace the splint." The doctor examines Karl's rib cage. "He does have broken ribs, three I believe. The only thing we can do is wrap them." As Doctor Vandenburg finishes tending to Karl's wounds, Katarina stays by his side and comforts him. "That's all I can do for him now. I brought morphine for his pain. Once he wakes, give him as needed, but not too much, it can be very addictive."

"What about his unconsciousness?"

"That was a blessing Anna, his unconsciousness. The fever caused that and eased his internal bleeding. Give this penicillin to him every four hours to fight the infection. I have a new drug that will help him stay calm and sleep. It is called Blue 88; the American soldiers use it to battle fatigue. It will induce sleep. Give him one to two in the evening if he cannot sleep. I will be by daily to check on him and change his dressings. Should his ailments, condition, or fever turn worse, come get me immediately. His fever should come down in a day or so since we stopped the bleeding, the other injuries will take time. Katarina, you have done a remarkable job in saving this boy's life."

"We are ever in your gratitude as well. Mother will take you back, thank you Doctor."

———— ❦ ————

REMINISCING

Hour by hour pass, day by day. As time passes, Katarina begins to see improvement. Katarina has been by Karl's side daily, tending to him and giving him his medication. She has been sleeping in the barn. By the third day after the surgery, Karl is resting better and his fever is down. Sitting by his side on a crisp winter morning, it's been nearly a week since she found him, she leans over as she does every morning, "Good morning Karl, it is Katarina."

Karl opens his eyes. He looks at her. "You are Katarina."

Katarina holds his hand as she looks into his eyes. "Yes, you remember me," and smiles at him.

"Katarina, I love your blue eyes, so soothing and relaxing to me. Your dark braided hair is lovely."

"Karl, I like your dark hair as well; it is like my father's."

"How do you know my name? Where am I? How long have I been here? I do not remember anything."

Katarina begins to tell the story. Karl lies and listens. "You are in occupied Germany, a small town called Aurich. I live here, on our farm with my mother and father. Our farm is just on the edge of town. I have a brother; we have disowned him from the family, he is a Nazi. My father is a German officer." Karl becomes agitated, Katarina sees he is frightened. "Do not be concerned, he is very involved with the Underground Movement against the Nazi regime; trust me, we can help you. He is against the aggression of Hitler and does not want to disrupt our life. He keeps his anti-German feelings and involvement in the Underground Movement a secret between my mother and me. He knows how pro-Hitler and brainwashed my brother is, and how violent he can be. The Underground Movement here can be very trusted.

"Your plane crashed. You must have ejected yet your parachute did not open. Fortunately, the chute got tangled in trees and saved you. You are badly injured." Katarina can see Karl is struggling to remember."

"I am recollecting that now."

"You almost died. I found you a few days after the crash, in the woods. My mother, Anna, and I brought you here. That was nearly a week ago. A doctor friend from our village helped you. He can be trusted; he is part of the Movement as well. Take a drink of water, you need to rest now, I will stay with you."

"I remember now," he softly says. I remember seeing a landing area, away from the trees. I remember steering the parachute away from the trees and toward the clearing. I then remember the parachute out of control. That is all I remember about the fall. I remember waking and hearing German soldiers."

Katarina smiles. Karl closes his eyes and falls asleep.

The next morning Katarina is at Karl's bedside. Karl awakes. "Good morning Karl. Did you sleep better?"

"Yes," he says in-sluggish voice. "Katarina, tell me more about you, and your family." Katarina sits next to him and holds his hand. She senses something, a funny feeling, though a good feeling, in her heart as she holds his hand.

"I was born here in Aurich, on August 16 1920. I was educated in London. I left Germany in June 1939 for the University of London. As the war intensified, I returned to Aurich last year to be with my parents. My father met my mother at the same University, they were in university together." Karl smiles. "What is it Karl?"

"June 1939, that is when I enlisted in the Army Air Corps."

"How ironic Karl. June 1939 will be special to us then." As soon as Katarina says those words, she gets a that feeling again. "After graduating, my parents returned to Aurich, always wanting a modest life. My father became a prominent German businessman before the war. He worked in Wilhelmshaven, a about three hours from here. He traveled during the week and was home on the weekends. He ultimately joined the German Army. Not by his choice! My father's business was in automotive fuels. He was very instrumental in leading technology with fuels, fuel development, fuel consumption, utilization, and expulsion. As his business grew, the Third Reich, particularly Hitler, observed his research and gained interest. As we later found out, Hitler himself had personal interests in fuel development. The Nazis saw an opportunity to capitalize on his expulsion technology to develop a long-range war plan for missiles, to defeat the Western World.

"The Third Reich approached my father and presented an opportunity for him to advance his research in fuel development, to better the world, they said. Little did my father know they were setting him up to steal his knowledge and research. My father accepted the position and opportunity, and he went off to Berlin to initiate the plan. My father always had our family's best interest in his heart. The year was 1939.

"Over the course of the next four-years, my father, Gerhardt Keitel, developed a fuel that was very efficient and burned longer, giving a missile a much longer flight distance. During the last two years, the research and development period, my father was led to believe the research was for the betterment of Germany. He later found out through exhilarating research, it was only for the development of the Third Reich, Hitler, and Hitler's Army. My father was horrified and felt humiliated! It was at that moment he vowed to help defeat the Third Reich and turn against the Nazi movement, Hitler, and Hitler's Army. My father knew he could make the Third Reich pay for their terror, while protecting his family. He had to be patient.

"He met a prominent German businessman named Oskar Schindler, from Sudetenland. Sudetenland became incorporated into Nazi Germany in 1938. Through Schindler's business associations, he became a member of the Nazi Party. In October 1939, he moved to Krakow and took over an old enamelware factory and began to build himself a fortune. By the end of 1942, the factory had expanded into a massive enamel and ammunition production plant, employing almost eight hundred men and women. Three hundred and seventy were Jews from the Krakow ghetto. As my Father understood the story, Schindler seemed to be no different from other Germans who had come to Poland as part of the industrial occupation. The only thing that set him apart from other extortionists of the war was his humane treatment of his workers, especially the Jews. Schindler observed how the Nazis treated the Jews. He developed a plan to use his factory to protect the Jews from the Nazi Party, a safe haven if you will from Auschwitz. Schindler began a transition of hiring less Polish workers and more Jewish workers. Schindler was very close to the SS, so he was able to persuade them in certain ways. That is when my father met him. My father was on a tour of his factory, because of the ammunition side of the business." Karl listens intently.

"Schindler never developed any ideology or motivated resistance against the Nazi Regime. His growing disgust and horror of the Nazis brutality and senseless persecution of the helpless Jewish population brought a transformation in him. His once egoistic goal of accumulating wealth took a back seat to the all-consuming desire of rescuing as many of his Jews as he could from the clutches of the Nazi executioners. Schindler was not only prepared to spend his money to help this effort, but also to put his own life on the line. His passion and main effort were refocused to bring his Jewish workers safely through the war.

"Schindler's most effective tool in this privately conceived rescue campaign was the privileged status his plant enjoyed as a business essential to the war effort, as afforded him by the Nazi Regime in occupied Poland. This not only qualified him to obtain lucrative military contracts, but also enabled him to draw on Jewish workers who were under the jurisdiction of the SS. He is now helping the Underground Movement in Poland. I somewhat got sidetracked, sorry Karl."

"Not at all, that was interesting."

"My father is not home much. He spends most of his time in Berlin. My mother and I tend to the farm."

"You mentioned a brother."

"We do not talk of him much."

"Why?"

"He has betrayed us, our family and the German people. Wilhelm is his name. He is older than me, by three years. He developed an extreme alliance to the Third Reich, Hitler, and Hitler's Army; and has been the black sheep of the family from a very young age. Wilhelm became obsessed with Hitler, the Third Reich, and their propaganda at the age of fifteen. He joined the Hitler Youth and unified his militancy and allegiance to Hitler. He then joined Heer, the German Army at seventeen. He has been progressing through the ranks since."

"I joined the U.S. Army Air Corps at seventeen. I too am of German descent," Karl says with excitement. My father was German, my mother French-German, mostly German."

"How nice, tell me about you Karl."

"I speak fluent German. My parents fled Bavaria in January 1917, during World War I, months before the U.S. declared war on Germany. My father was from Kriestorf and mother from Walchsing. They traveled to America by steamship, as did many Germans of the time and settled in the Grover Heights neighborhood of Milwaukee. I was born in Milwaukee, January 15 1922."

"I am seventeen months older than you."

He smiles at Katarina. "Life was simple, yet tough. Being German immigrants, my father had trouble getting work because of the effects of World War I. My father was very disciplined. He was very proud of his German heritage. He and my mother raised us in a German household. I obviously learned English, yet when at home, we spoke German and lived the German culture."

THE CHILDHOOD
[THE DEPRESSION ERA]

K arl continues telling his story to Katarina. "The war years
were difficult for Milwaukee. Many Germans that fled to
Milwaukee had relatives and friends fighting in Europe, many those
who were left in the Motherland suffered from an anti-Germanism
sentiment that was a by-product of the war. It continued with Hitler
during his reign, he demanded all Germans join his campaign, and
fight for Germany and the Nazi Regime.

"When the United States entered the war in April 1917, tensions
reached a peak. Anti-German sentiment was stoked further by
attacking the local German language. Spouting disloyalty and
hatred for the U.S. Government. As the war continued, nearly
anything that smacked of Germanism was held up for derision by
many Milwaukeeans. Some Germans themselves tried to hide their
Germanism by changing their names and avoiding anything that
made them appear too German.

"Initially, my father worked at a beer manufacturing plant.
Prohibition impacted that industry dramatically. During prohibition,
he worked on and off at various manufacturing facilities that
supported the automobile and war effort. However, those jobs were

sparse. My father was a fighter; he took on odd jobs as a carpenter for additional income. Although he was proud of his heritage, he and my mother learned some English, with my help. We were getting by, until the great depression hit in 1929. Milwaukee's economy fought the depression but in a few short years, that battle was lost.

"It was a cool fall evening in September 1931, the thirteenth. We lived in a German neighborhood on the north side, in an old and dilapidated apartment building. Although it needed a lot of work, it was home to us. The plaster was falling from the ceilings, we had hot water maybe once every few days if we were lucky. I remember the apartment was always cold and drafty in the winters. The hallways were always noisy with people coming and going, and the family above us had several small children. A good thing, but you can imagine the noise from them playing. A train track was behind the building. It seemed trains were rumbling all day and night. Our playground was next to the tracks. The rats ran rampant in the neighborhood. I remember coming home from school, my mother made me finish my homework before I could play. I worked on a small kitchen table, the only table we had. We would listen to the radio at night. In the summertime a baseball announcer's voice filled the room with excitement and cheers. My favorite team was the New York Yankees. In the winter months I would listen to the Green Bay Packers when I could."

"Who are the Green Bay Packers Karl?"

"A professional football team, in the town of Green Bay Wisconsin. Not like English football, we call that soccer. One night in particular I will never forget. I remember as if it was yesterday, and I will remember it for the rest of my life. My mother Hazel was preparing supper, beans, and rice. She had made a loaf of bread earlier that day. My father had just come home from work. He was sitting in his chair, pretending to read the paper. I could tell his mind was elsewhere though, the place it usually was this time of day. He was a strong and proud man, yet I could imagine and feel his worry and concern for his family. '*Will I be able to feed my family tomorrow, where will my next pay come from?*'

"We had a quiet evening; my father Joseph played his harmonica to relax. We gave each other hugs and kisses and went to bed. While we were asleep, our apartment building caught fire." Katarina tenses up. "We lived on the fifth floor. I awoke to my mother screaming. My room was off the kitchen; my parent's room was opposite the parlor. I opened my door and saw nothing but flames."

Oh, my Lord Karl."

"The flames and heat had engulfed the entire floor. I could hear other people screaming for help, shrieks of screams, screaming like I have never heard. My father was screaming, I will get you Karl. I could not see him. He never did come. I passed out from the intense heat. I was revived on the street amidst firefighters in the arms of a nurse. I was nine-years old and placed in the hospital with second degree burns. I was hoping and praying my parents survived." Katarina stares in horror.

"The next day a nurse came to my bed and told me the firefighters found my mother, she was in the hospital, badly burned. I begged to see her. I was told she had to have complete isolation for one week. Where is my father? I asked repeatedly. The nurse did not know or would not tell me. On the fifth day, a nurse came to take me to see my mother. I went to my mother's bedside. I did not recognize her. I held her hand, it was very lifeless. She opened her eyes, saw me, and began crying uncontrollably. She squeezed my hand. 'Karl,' my mother, trying to tell me through the tears, 'your father died in the fire.' I began to cry and scream. Why did this happen? With her last breaths, my mother opened my hand and placed her locket in my palm. As she closed my hand over her locket, she said, 'Keep this with you forever, it will always protect you.' I could see she was having trouble breathing and was crying very hard. 'Karl, when your father and I escaped Germany in World War I, I had this with me. It was my mother's. She told me it would always bring me good will. Please keep it with you always.' I was trying to control my crying, I sobbed, smiled, and nodded. I wanted so much to be strong for my mother. We looked into each other's eyes. I held her. She took her last breath in my arms."

"Karl, I am so sorry for you," Katarina says with tears in her eyes.

"I was a very young boy and alone in America. I was very scared that day. I eventually was placed in a foster home and I enrolled in the Army Air Corps at seventeen. Since that day I always carried her locket with me, I have it on my dog tags." Karl reaches for it. "Where is my locket?" he frantically asks.

"Calm down Karl," as she holds him. "I have it. I had to burn your clothes and parachute so the Germans wouldn't find them. That's when I saw the locket on your dog tags. I saved your medals and papers as well. I also have this of yours. I found it interesting, yet odd. The words on the front I mean. 'If Found Return To'" Katarina struggles to say it, "'COMNAVAIRLANT'. Did I pronounce it correctly? What does that mean and what is this box for?"

Karl chuckles. "COMNAVAIRLANT is the acronym for the Commander, Naval Air Force, U.S. Atlantic Fleet. COMNAVAIRLANT was formed last month, January 1943. The Navy developed this box; it is a survival kit. This was given to all U.S. Navy pilots. The Atlantic Fleet shared these with the U.S Army Air Force. I received this one just before my mission."

"What is it for Karl?"

"In case we are shot down, or stranded behind enemy lines, we could use this for bartering, for food, shelter, and safety. Even perhaps safe passage to Allied territory. Let me show you inside. It has five gold coins and three gold rings. One Great Britain Sovereign coin, two half Sovereigns, and a ten and twenty Francs."

"Why the rings? Two of them have patterns."

"For something different, other than using the Great Britain and French coins, more universal. See, this one has a diamond pattern and this a leaf pattern. The other is a plain band. Gold has power everywhere."

"Very interesting, Karl. Get some rest now. I need to go to the farmhouse to see Mother, I will be back before nightfall to care for you."

THE SS SEARCH INTENSIFIES

Little did Katarina and Anna know Wilhelm did have another motive and reason for his visit. The Germans know Karl is in the area, and they suspect he is being helped. They found no traces of him nor his parachute after searching ten square kilometers from the crash. The patrols continue to search. The Germans suspect the Underground Movement has been strengthening for months in western Germany. Wilhelm is on a scouting mission but is very discreet at first. He knows his family's feelings toward him and Hitler. He must gain their trust back. Wilhelm also suspects the American pilot could be in the area and is in search of information. Some clue, some slip-up, anything.

As Katarina crests the hill toward the farmhouse, she sees Wilhelm's staff car in the driveway, again. She says to herself, *something is up, he never visits, and now twice in one week.* She pauses, *should I wait until he leaves? I was gone the last time he was here and question my mother as to whereabouts.* Katarina decides to continue. As she approaches the house, she can hear her mother arguing with him. When she opens the door Anna abruptly stops talking. Katarina stares at Wilhelm, a cold and piercing stare.

"You look surprised to see me Katarina."

"Wilhelm. Why are you here?"

"Just passing through on my return from Neuengamme Concentration Camp to the north, heading to Berlin. I was just leaving, by the way, where were you? I was here earlier in the week and you were gone as well." Katarina is silent. As he walks toward the door, he slowly turns, looks at them, and displays a smirky smile. "Take care ladies."

"He knows Mother, he knows," Katarina says trembling. "I heard you arguing with him, why and about what?"

"He was being very inquisitive as to where you were. I told him you were taking a walk. He insisted on waiting for you. I told him I did not know how long you would be. He raised his voice and accused me of lying, that I did know where you were. That is when you walked in."

"We need to be careful Mother. He has been here twice; I do not trust him. The German patrols are increasing. Mother sit down. I want to tell you something." Katarina holds Anna's hand. "I am falling in love with Karl, I need to be with him. I came for water and supplies. I will wait until nightfall and go back to him."

"Katarina, as a mother, I can tell you love Karl. I have known for a while. I sense your feelings toward him. I had a strong and keen instinct for some time, you have found your true love, and you have given your heart to Karl. I see your love and affection in your eyes, how you both look at each other. I genuinely feel he loves you as well."

"I love him Mother, I do not want to lose him." They hug each other, ever so close.

"I will help you gather your things Katarina." As night falls, Katarina returns to Karl. Her daily routine continues, as do the patrols.

A week later the Waffen SS set up an outpost in Aurich. They takeover a storefront in town. The Underground Movement schedules a secret meeting. Hans Houseman, the Resistant's leader, owns a local market. The Movement has developed a way to safely communicate messages through the town. Hans communicates one-on-one with people coming to the market. With the SS setting up an outpost in town, and the increased patrols in the area, Han's gets word to the Movement to meet in the church, at Sunday service.

Sunday morning arrives. The town's people begin to gather inside the church, Saint Ludger. Hans makes sure he has folks in the bell tower, and at the windows to watch for any German activity. Anna and Katarina arrive as they normally do for morning service every Sunday. Doctor Vandenburg joins them. Before the meeting starts, Katarina asks if she, Anna, and Doctor Vandenburg can speak privately to Hans.

"Hans, I am sure you know the Germans have been looking for a pilot, the one his plane crashed in January."

"Yes." The four of them walk to the front of the church to be alone.

"I must tell you something in strict confidence and secrecy Hans. I found the pilot shortly after he crashed. He ejected from his plane before it crashed, he has been with us on the farm since. He has very grave injuries, Doctor Vandenburg helped him. No one else knows."

"I understand Katarina and will keep it that way. Doctor Vandenburg did tell me though."

"Oh, that's good. Please get word to my father, we need to see him, soon."

Hans holds Katarina's hand, "I will."

Fifty-five people gather in the church. Most of those are involved in the Underground Movement. The others can be trusted, however. Once all are settled, Hans begins. "I know all of you have seen the heightened German activity in town. Through our Intel we have learned they are suspect of our Movement, we must be very careful, even more so since they are here all the time. Many of you may have heard they have been searching for an American pilot since January. That has increased their patrols as well. Moving forward, we must not be seen in groups gathering in public spaces. We will communicate only at the market, individually. If anyone sees or suspects anything, no matter how small or insignificant you feel it is, you must tell me. Wilhelm has been in town twice this past week, the Germans and SS are up to something and suspect something is going on here. Be smart, be vigilant, and stay safe. I suggest we lie low for a while to see if and when this situation calms down. I will let you all know what Intel I receive."

HEALING

The days turn into weeks, weeks into months, and the war continues. Springtime, April 19. Katarina brings Karl food every day, spending all day with him. His wounds are healed, and he is doing much better. His leg still gives him pain. He is up and walking with a cane; yet has a limp. In the mornings they venture out of the barn together to enjoy the fresh air and listen to the birds chirping. The feel of morning dew is fresh, the fog is lifting from the valley. One morning Karl is walking alone and notices a patrol vehicle in the next field over. He knows they are looking for him. Katarina is due to come by anytime. Karl is afraid they will see her but cannot warn her. Katarina has breakfast with her mother, it is Anna's birthday.

"Happy birthday Mother, I am going to see Karl now." Katarina leans over and gives Anna a kiss.

"Thank you, Katarina, be careful." As Katarina strolls through the field toward the barn, she sees the patrol as well. She tries not to be conspicuous, yet she is noticed. The soldiers turn and drive toward her. Katarina slowly turns and walks in another direction, away from the barn.

A sergeant steps from the vehicle, "What are you doing here?"

"I live here, my father is Captain Gerhardt Keitel."

"Yes, we know him, and your brother, Major General Wilhelm Keitel."

"May I help you with something?" Katarina curiously but cautiously asks.

"No," he abruptly says. "We are looking for an American pilot whose plane crashed a few months ago, I am sure you have heard." The sergeant turns and points to the stone barn. "The barn over there, what is in it?"

"That is an old outbuilding. We have not used it for years." As soon as those words leave Katarina's lips, she knew she made a huge mistake. The sergeant immediately orders his troops to search it. As they drive toward the barn, Katarina begins trembling, she has no way to warn Karl. Little does she know Karl has been watching. He has already gone back to the barn, and into the fruit cellar. He closes the boards over the opening and stays very quiet. He is not sure if they have decided to search the barn.

Karl hears the patrol vehicle approaching, his question is answered. He hears the Soldiers. One says, "You search the outside, go around back; the rest come inside with me." As they enter the barn, dust falls through the floorboards onto Karl's forehead. Katarina, in the field, watches in horror. The soldiers walk through the barn, saying they would love to kill the American. "The SS will be very pleased and proud of us if we find the pilot and kill him. Nothing here," Karl hears them say. They leave. Katarina sees the patrol drive away and is sure they did not find Karl.

Once the patrol is long out of sight, she immediately runs to the barn, "Karl, Karl, are you here, are you ok?"

"I am fine Katarina."

She frantically removes the floorboards, as the last one comes off, she sees Karl. She hurriedly climbs down the ladder into the cellar and embraces him, "I was so scared, the soldiers stopped me in the field, asked who I was, then they saw the barn. I did not know what to do, how to warn you, I was so scared. I thought they would find you, I thought you would be taken from me, I thought I would lose you!"

"It's fine, it's fine Katarina, calm down. I happened to be outside getting some fresh air and saw the vehicle as well. I immediately came back in, went into the cellar and hid. We were lucky today, but I have seen and heard the patrols are intensifying."

Katarina thinks of his mother's locket, '*it protected him today.*'

"Katarina, I need to leave. It's not safe for you, for your family, or for the town's people."

"No," she shouts. "We need your leg to be well, for you to be well, it will not be much longer. We can protect you. The Movement is smart, smarter than the SS." Katarina begins crying. Karl holds her tight. He knows he has feelings for her, he is growing very fond of Katarina. Katarina spends the rest of the day with Karl. "You need to rest Karl; I will be back tomorrow, good night." She gives him a kiss on the cheek. Karl smiles, gazes into her eyes, and she to his.

"Good night to you as well Katarina, thank you for helping me, and being with me. You saved my life. Stay with me a little while longer." He looks into her blue eyes. "I am growing very fond of you Katarina. At first, I thought my feelings were coming from the care you gave me, now I know they are more than that." They kiss. The air raid sirens begin, again. Nearly every night recently. Karl and Katarina hold each other, Katarina knows they are falling in love. Katarina is in Karl's arms. The moonlight is shining through the cracks in the floorboards. She steps back, her dress drops. Katarina draws her waist length hair back. Karl can see the silhouette of her breasts in the moonlight glistening through the cracks in the floorboards. He embraces her, they lay down on his bed. "I love you Katarina. I am falling in love with you." Uncontrollably, a stream of tears runs down her cheeks.

"I love you Karl, and I am falling in love with you. I never want to leave you. I will talk to my father, mother, and Hans. The Underground will help us. We will plan to leave Germany together."

Their passion unfolds, they make passionate love, Katarina spends the night.

The next morning, Karl awakens, Katarina is in his arms, and staring into his eyes. "Karl; last night was wonderful. You made me feel so good, so special. I saved myself for you."

"Katarina last night was wonderful. I saved myself for you, you are my first as well." Karl kisses Katarina. "Katarina, when you first brought me here, I listened to the thunder rolling over the hills, at least I thought it was thunder. Then I learned to tell the difference between thunder and the bombing. Some nights I could not tell the difference. Unfortunately, as the war grows on, so does the bombing."

KATARINA'S FATHER

Katarina walks into town, to the market to see Hans. Hans greets her and guides her toward the back of the market to talk in private. "I sent word to your father. I heard back; he will be here in the next few days."

"Thank you, Hans." Katarina returns to the farm, it's nightfall. The next morning, at daybreak, Katarina goes to see Karl. She has a special way of entering the barn, so Karl knows it is her. Three knocks on the barn door. She enters, removes the floorboards, and climbs down the ladder to the cellar.

"Good morning Karl, it is Katarina. I brought you a basket of fresh flowers. Red roses and white lilies, my favorites. How are you feeling today?"

"I missed you Katarina, I am feeling better and stronger each day."

"I miss you as well, I think of you all the time."

Just as she is ready to tell Karl the news of her father, they hear someone enter the barn. They hold each other. Karl can tell it's a man with heavy boots. The man walks to the opening and stares down at Karl. Karl looks up, he sees a German Officer peering down at him. Katarina forgot to cover the opening. Karl struggles, he tries feverishly to get up, to escape, but cannot due to his leg injury. Frantic and scared, he screams at Katarina, "You lied to me, you set me up!"

"No Karl, this is my father, relax, relax Karl. Remember I told you of my father, he is a German officer, he is in the Underground Movement. He will help you." Anna then appears next to him.

"Hello Karl, my name is Gerhardt. I am sorry I frightened you, I should have announced myself. May I come down?" Karl collects himself and nods.

"I am so sorry I screamed at you Katarina; I was scared. I did not mean what I said. I love you," he whispers to her. She smiles and holds his hand.

Gerhardt sits next to Karl, "Let me explain."

"Father, Hans told me it would be a few days before we saw you."

"Yes, then I heard Wilhelm was coming back, with more troops. The SS killed a couple in a nearby town last week for suspicion of affiliation with the Resistance. I had to come now to warn you. Karl, the Resistance is very strong in this region. Aurich is a strategic location for the Resistance. We are close to Wilhelmshaven, a major port for the Kriegsmarine, and there are many concentration camps in the region. I have been aligned with the Resistance since the war started. I despise Hitler, and what he has done to Germany."

"I know of Wilhelmshaven Gerhardt. It was January 27, I was flying a scout plane, on a reconnaissance mission when my plane had some sort of mechanical trouble and crashed. I parachuted and Katarina found me, she helped me, and saved my life."

"Karl, that mission failed, many American planes were lost. The Luftwaffe knew of the attack."

"Then I failed as well."

"No, Karl. The Luftwaffe has good reconnaissance in that region. They have lookout posts in the Netherlands. Northern Germany is a very strategic front for Hitler and the Third Reich. Wilhelmshaven must be protected. We can combat that; I will help you. The reason the SS is here is they have been suspicious of the Underground Movement in this region for many months now, and now believe they are hiding you. My son is leading that effort for the SS."

"Katarina told me of Wilhelm."

"He is a very ruthless and terrible man; we have disowned him; he is not my son anymore. We act cordial to him though, as to not draw attention or concern from him. We need to stop him and Hitler's regime. I am going back to the farmhouse with Anna. I will be in touch. I do not want to draw any attention though. I will be in town for a while. Stay safe and rest Karl. It was very nice to meet you. We'll get a plan together to get you back to England." Katarina and Karl look at each other and smile, they know of a slightly different plan.

THE OLDER BROTHER

Wilhelm Keitel was born March 10 1917 in Aurich. Unlike Katarina, he did not attend University. He developed an extreme alliance to the Nazi Party, the Third Reich, to Hitler, and to Hitler's Army. He has been the black sheep of the Keitel family from a very young age. Wilhelm became obsessed with Hitler, the Third Reich, the Nazi Party, and their propaganda at the age of fifteen. He joined the Hitler Youth and unified his militancy and allegiance to Hitler. He then joined the Heer at seventeen. He has been progressing through the ranks since.

After the Nazi rise to power in 1933, one of Adolf Hitler's most overt and audacious moves was to establish the Wehrmacht, a modern offensive and-very capable armed force, fulfilling the Nazi Régime's long-term goals of regaining lost territory as well as gaining new territory and dominating its neighbors. This required the reinstatement of conscription, and massive investment and defense spending on the arms industry. The Wehrmacht defense force was the unified armed forces of Nazi Germany from 1935 to 1945. It consisted of the Heer, the Kriegsmarine, and the Luftwaffe. The designation Wehrmacht replaced the previously used term Reichswehr and was the manifestation of the Nazi Regime's efforts to rearm Germany to a greater extent than the Treaty of Versailles permitted.

Wilhelm was placed in a fast-track military school, masterminded by Hitler. At the age of nineteen he was promoted to lieutenant. The Nazi Regime, particularly Hitler himself, saw Wilhelm as a very intelligent and talented young man, he had promise. Promise for the greater master plan which Hitler had. His training was accelerated. He was being prepared for senior officer training. Hitler needed trained leaders that were loyal to him and only him. Hitler sought Lebensraum or living space for the German people in Eastern Europe. His grand plan was to overthrow the neighboring countries. This, along with his aggressive foreign policy is considered the primary cause of World War II in Europe.

Six months after his twentieth birthday Wilhelm is promoted to Hauptmann; a Captain; and begins having one-on-one meetings with Hitler. At the age of twenty-two, Wilhelm's rank reached Major in charge of the Tenth Panzer Division, which fell under the control of the Waffen SS. The SS: the Schutzstaffel, is an elite force within the Nazi Party. It is the foremost agency of security, surveillance, and terror. The Tenth Panzer Division was a formation of the German Army during World War II. It was formed in Prague in March 1939, to serve in the invasion of Poland. Hitler began directing large-scale rearmament and on September 1 1939 and invaded Poland. Wilhelm led a masterful, well planned invasion. In May 1940, Wilhelm oversaw the conversion of the Auschwitz I from an army barracks, to a prisoner of war camp. Auschwitz I became the main camp in Oświęcim; Auschwitz II-Birkenau, a concentration and extermination camp built with several gas chambers; and Auschwitz III-Monowitz, a labor camp created to staff a factory for the chemical conglomerate IG Farben. All under his watchful eye. Wilhelm is one of Hitler's masterminds that developed the heinous punishments, the torture and death techniques used in these camps.

After Poland, Wilhelm was assigned to various concentration camps in the Neuengamme network of Nazi concentration camps in Northern Germany, close to Aurich where Wilhelm was born. Neuengamme, established by the SS in Hamburg, Germany, became a massive Nazi concentration camp complex using prisoner forced labor for production purposes in World War II. It consisted of the main camp and ninety-nine satellite camps. Established in 1938 near the village of Neuengamme in the Bergedorf District of Hamburg, the Neuengamme Camp became the largest concentration camp in Northwest Germany.

In June 1941, now an Obrest or Colonel, Wilhelm faced his most important assignment to date. The invasion of Russia. He led the Seventeenth Panzer Division. This was a formation of the Wehrmacht in World War II. It was formed in November 1940 from the twenty-seventh Infantry Division. It was a key division for the top-secret Operation Barbarossa, the invasion of the Soviet Union in June 1941. Hitler trusted Wilhelm so much and applauded his leadership, Wilhelm was also placed in command of a Special Forces frontline elite attack group, the Brandenburg Special Forces. Their mission was to infiltrate the Russian front lines and camps and assassinate the soldiers and officers. They were very well trained. Hitler also had another motive, to see if those within the Special Forces could survive. Wilhelm remained in Russia for the next year.

Wilhelm became a trusted member of Hitler's Inner Circle. In May 1942, he was transferred to the Waffen SS, and promoted to SS-Oberführer, Senior Leader. The Waffen SS, or the Schutzstaffel, was created in 1925 originally to serve as Hitler's personal bodyguards. The SS became the foremost agency of security, surveillance, and terror within Germany and German-occupied Europe. The SS is an elite group within the Nazi Party's paramilitary forces.

On September 30 1942, Wilhelm was promoted to the rank of Lieutenant General and appointed Chief of the Reich Ministry of War's Armed Forces Office, the Wehrmachtsamt, which oversaw the army, navy, and air force. After assuming office, he was promoted to Major General on April 1 1943.

THE RAID ON THE FARM

Wilhelm returns to Aurich for an update. Hans sees him drive in. Wilhelm drives directly to the SS outpost. He confronts the sergeant on the street. Wilhelm gets out of his car. "Did you search all of the houses, the town, the fields, and the countryside?" Hans can hear Wilhelm's stern voice.

"Yes, Herr Keitel."

"Everywhere?" Wilhelm asks. "I know the American is here somewhere, close by. We have had roadblocks setup for months, we have conducted exhaustive searches in the region, and we find nothing! He could not have escaped."

"Yes sir, everywhere," the sergeant hesitates, "except for your farmhouse."

Wilhelm erupts in furry, "I told you everywhere! That means my house as well! Search it now!" He also orders a raid on the town. "I want all of the village searched again. I will send more troops. I want guards posted on every corner, all day and night. No automobile enters or exits without being searched. I want the American found!" The small town of Aurich is paralyzed. Hans needs to get word to Katarina, but how. Hans devises a plan to befriend the soldiers, a plan to deliver food to them as a cover so he does not draw attention delivering groceries around town. This is his way to pass messages throughout the town.

Anna can see the German's activity from the farmhouse and hurries to tell Katarina. She carefully but quickly walks to the barn. Katarina and Karl hear three knocks. Anna enters, "Katarina, it is your mother." Katarina removes the boards from the cellar opening, Anna climbs down. "Hello Karl, how are you feeling today? I brought some food and water for you, and fresh flowers to cheer you up."

"Much better, thank you Anna."

"Katarina, something is going on in town, there is much activity with the German soldiers. You should come back with me."

Katarina looks at Karl, "I should go, Mother is right. I will come back as soon as I can."

Katarina and Anna arrive at the farmhouse just in time. The Germans arrive at the farm, knowing an American soldier is hiding nearby. Wilhelm bursts in the door and immediately sees his father. "What are you doing here?"

"I ask the same question to you?" says Gerhardt.

"Get out of our way. Search the house top to bottom," screams Wilhelm to the soldiers." He pushes his father to the side. Then turns toward him, "Why are you here I asked?"

"You remember I live here," Gerhardt says in a sarcastic way. "I had this trip planned for weeks. Being in Berlin, as you know, I do not get home much."

Anna pleads to her son, "Please do not hurt us or break anything, do your business and leave."

The sergeant returns, "We have found nothing, no one is here."

Wilhelm stares at Katarina, "Get out of my way. I should give you to my men, they would have fun with a little German virgin, or are you?" Katarina spits on Wilhelm. Wilhelm slaps Katarina, knocking her to the floor. Gerhardt lunges at Wilhelm. Wilhelm turns with his luger drawn. Anna pulls Gerhardt back; they run to help Katarina. Anna cradles her.

Wilhelm stares at Gerhardt. "Do not be a fool Father, the difference between you and I is I am loyal to the Third Reich, to the Fuhrer. I will take a bullet for Hitler and you will not." Wilhelm storms out of the house. He and his troops get in their vehicles and leave. Wilhelm is suspicious. Too many coincidences.

"He will not stop; he is insane and will stop at nothing. He needs stopped." Gerhardt looks at Anna and Katarina, "We need to get Karl to safety. I have an idea; it is bold though. It may accomplish both objectives."

"What is it Father?"

"Let me think a bit more on it, I will talk with Hans."

"Father, I need to be with Karl and warn him." Katarina slowly opens the door and peers out. It is becoming dusk. She slowly walks down the path toward the road. It appears all is clear; she can see the activity of soldiers in the village. Katarina runs to the barn. She knocks three times yet hastily enters and sees Karl on the main level.

"I saw you coming and could tell something was wrong."

"Karl, the Germans were at the farmhouse. They were led by my brother, demanding to search the farm. He had our house searched then left. I feel he will be back; he is obsessed with finding you. He knows you are in the area."

"Katarina, what happened to your face?" Karl can see her cheek is reddened; he caresses Katarina's cheek.

"I am fine, it was Wilhelm, I am okay." Karl hugs her.

"He and I will meet some day; I will have my way with him." Frantically, she begs him to hide in the abandoned fruit cellar. Karl holds Katarina, "Calm down Katarina, we will get through this." Katarina stays with Karl that evening.

The morning sun is rising. The night seemed endless. "Stay in the cellar Karl, I must get back to the farmhouse, I love you."

After Wilhelm left the farmhouse, he orders additional troops for a surprise raid. As daybreak evolves, Anna and Gerhardt see the activity of additional troops entering the town. Gerhardt tells Anna, "This is a full platoon, four ten-man squads. This is not good. I need to see Hans." A German platoon has a platoon commander and four squads of troops; each comprised of a squad leader, an assistant leader in an armored car, six soldiers in a troop truck, and a half-track armed with a machine gunner and an assistant gunner.

Wilhelm gathers his troops. Gerhardt walks into the village to see and hear what is going on. He sees Wilhelm with the platoon commander, talking and pointing in various directions of the village. Wilhelm climbs on the back of a half-track. He is barking orders. "I want each squad to go separately and search the town and perimeter. Group one, go to the east outskirts and begin searching the town. Group two, you begin at the stream to the south. Group three, you begin at the western edge of town. Group four, you are with me." Wilhelm gets in his vehicle and drives to the farm.

"Where are we going?" asks the sergeant.

"We are going to my farm and search the northern countryside. Sergeant, you and two of your men come with me." Gerhardt is speechless but can do nothing. He hopes Katarina and Karl will be safe but must take this opportunity to see Hans. Wilhelm and the troops arrive at the farm. "Go to the main barn," he says. Anna hears the vehicles and peers out the window. She sees the soldiers drive past the house toward the main barn, led by her son. Dust rolling from beneath the trucks. She is petrified and begins trembling. *How can I warn Katarina and Karl?*

Katarina and Karl, hold each other, not wanting the night to end. Sunlight is glistening through the cracks in the floorboards. They hear bombers in the distance, not too far. Dust is falling from above. The bombers pass, the risk has passed. Suddenly they hear vehicles approaching. Then voices of the soldiers, and then she hears the voice of her brother.

"Search the barn."

The sergeant looks at Wilhelm, "With all due respect, I was here a few days ago and searched this building myself."

"Search it again," Wilhelm screams.

"Shh, stay quiet Katarina." She is trembling. Karl tightly holds her. They hear footsteps of the Nazi soldiers as they enter the barn. They begin searching. Katarina begins to sob. "Shh, be strong Katarina," Karl holds her tighter. The dust is falling on Karl and Katarina.

Wilhelm says, "I know they are here. My father is behind this." Katarina and Karl hear their boots clunking on the floorboards. They hear another voice.

The sergeant reports back to Wilhelm, "We have searched the barn, the stalls, and loft."

"I know they are here somewhere," screams Wilhelm." The voices go silent for a few seconds.

Karl whispers to Katarina, "What is that noise?"

"What noise Karl?"

"Listen, that clicking noise."

"Oh, that's my brother's jaw, he does that when he gets extremely frustrated and angry, he clicks his jaw."

Being very obedient, the sergeant repeats, "We found nothing Herr Keitel."

Another soldier asks, "What is beneath this wooden floor?"

"Nothing," Wilhelm answers. "I helped my father build this barn; it is only dirt below the floor." A statement he will regret. "We placed the wooden floor for the animals, so we did not have the mud." Little does he know his father dug it out for a fruit cellar and shelter. Gerhardt strategically placed the floorboards for access in a stall, so they would go wall to wall and blend in. That way the outline of the opening would not be evident. Wilhelm notices a fresh flower petal on the floor. He thinks to himself, *why is a fresh flower petal in here?*

Suddenly, the air raid sirens go off in the village. Allied aircraft are approaching the area, British Hawker Typhoon single engine fighter/bomber planes capable of high speed and quick attacks of a target. Wilhelm hears the planes approaching and runs out of the barn. He sees them flying very low, just above the trees. The planes begin a barrage of machine gun fire at the German troops in the field. Wilhelm sees the path of bullets as they trace across the ground toward the barn. He runs inside the stone barn, knowing he will be safer. As the planes pass, he immediately orders his soldiers to retreat to safety. He knows Karl is close, and now suspects his father and sister. On their way back to the village, Wilhelm stops his staff car at the farmhouse and motions the soldiers to continue. He storms to the farmhouse and bangs on the door. Anna opens it, she is extremely frightened knowing how crazy he gets. "Where is Katarina?" Anna stands silent, trembling. "Where is Katarina I ask?" screaming at Anna.

"She went to town to get your father."

"We shall see, she is always gone when I come here." Wilhelm storms off, slamming the door behind him.

Katarina knows she cannot go back to the farmhouse, Wilhelm will know something is up, perhaps even where she was. Katarina plans to stay with Karl for the rest of the day. Anna bursts in the barn, and startles Katarina and Karl.

"Katarina, come, come quickly. Wilhelm was at the farmhouse again and was furious. He knows something is going on."

"Yes Mother," as she climbs from the cellar. "He and his soldiers were here also but did not find us. The attack scared them off. We heard him say he suspects Father and me."

"Katarina, you must come back to the farmhouse and lay low for a while, otherwise he will catch all of us."

"Ok Mother, I will be back shortly, I just want to be sure Karl is settled in." Katarina climbs back down to the fruit cellar. "Karl, I must go," she pauses, "I must go for a while. At least until things calm down."

"Yes, my Love, I heard. Things are not going to calm down until they find me, I must be the one to go." Katarina begins to cry. Karl embraces her, they passionately kiss. "Go now my Love, be safe."

"You must stay Karl; do not do something you will regret. I will talk with my father. He will figure something out. We will be back soon. I love you." Katarina is crying hysterically as she leaves the barn.

As Katarina approaches the farmhouse, she slows, and looks to see if things are clear. No sight of the soldiers or Wilhelm. She sees her father walking up the path. She runs to be with him, still crying. Gerhardt hugs her. "What happened Katarina? I saw Wilhelm head this way with his troops. I was scared they would find you and Karl."

"Father, they were at the stone barn, searching it. Karl and I were in the cellar. Allied planes flew over and attacked their convoy. Wilhelm was furious and left. They did not find us. I heard him say he suspects you and me. What are we going to do? We must protect Karl; I love him father, he loves me." Gerhardt was caught off guard a bit with that statement.

"I have a plan Katarina; I had a chance to talk with Hans since the soldiers left the town to search for Karl. Let us go inside, I will tell you my plan."

"Gerhardt," Anna says trembling, "Wilhelm was here this morning; he searched the farm. He stormed in the house. While he was leaving, he demanded to know where Katarina was. He was furious. I told him she went to town to get you."

The door slams open, Wilhelm is in the doorway. He sees Katarina. "Where were you? Again, I came, and you were not here."

Katarina boldly stares at him, and strongly says, "I went to town to get your father, we saw all of the activity. Mother and I were scared." Wilhelm raises his hand to slap Katarina. Gerhardt steps in and grabs his arm.

"Wilhelm, if you ever harm my family, I will kill you." Wilhelm jerks his arm away from Gerhardt.

"You all are liars; I will find that American. I will find him and kill him, and anyone who is helping him." Wilhelm storms out.

"Father tell me your plan for Karl," pleads Katarina.

"Sit down please, both of you. This is a bold plan. We need Karl's help more than he needs us right now. I talked with Hans about this. Katarina, you told me Karl's parents were native Germans and immigrated to America."

"Yes, from Bavaria."

"In doing so, they kept the German traditions," continues Gerhardt. Karl speaks fluent German."

"Yes, fluently."

"Karl can help us overthrow the Third Reich, the Nazi Regime, and Hitler. I need to ask Karl to be a spy for us. I can get him papers to show he is a German soldier. Hans can create papers for his citizenship."

"Father, I am afraid for Karl."

"Katarina; let's talk with Karl and lay out the plan. I promise I will honor his decision."

The next day, a calm Monday morning, Katarina tells Anna and Gerhardt she is going into the village, to the market. "I need to pick-up some food for Karl. When I return, we can tell him of the plan." Shortly after she leaves, the air raid sirens sound. Katarina can see the Allied coalition bombers in the distance. This was unusual for an early morning bombing run by the coalition. There is heavy bombardment in the distance. Fearful for Karl, she runs back to the farm. She meets her father, and they go to Karl. In the village, Hans' plan is working. He has been able to gain the German soldier's trust. He continues to bring them food and water and can mingle throughout the village uncontested.

Katarina and Gerhardt, knowing it is dangerous to be out in the daytime, arrive at the barn. Katarina knocks her three times. She enters with her father, "Karl I am here, Father is with me."

"Good morning," he says from the cellar. Gerhardt removes the floorboards; he and Katarina climb down. Katarina hugs Karl. Gerhardt replaces the boards.

"Karl, you have a unique opportunity to help your country, and the people of Germany."

"Karl, my father has a plan, listen to him please."

THE PLOT

"Karl, first things first, how are you feeling?"

"Much better, time heals, I am feeling much stronger."

"Karl, I have a plan, and I want you to listen to it. It is risky but it will help your country and mine." Karl nods his head. "It will involve you and the Underground. We have established a plot to defeat the German Army, the Third Reich, the Nazi empire, put an end to Hitler's regime, to help the people of Germany, and most importantly get you to back to the States." Gerhardt pauses and gathers himself, "We must stop my son, he is evil." Katarina holds Karl's hand. "It will mean you cannot go home for a while; you must stay in Germany. Karl, what I am about to ask of you is of great importance. You have a unique opportunity. I want you to become a spy, an operative, and pose as a German soldier, a German officer. You will be a tremendous asset for our plan since you speak German fluently. The Germans will not detect any deviation in your dialog."

Karl sits back, pauses for a moment, "Tell me more of how I can help. My parents fled Germany in WWI due to the war and regretted that. I want to help end this with Hitler. Gerhardt, how can I infiltrate the German Army as an officer, they will know I have no roots here, no records, no family. How will you document that, and establish my past to prove who I am, that I am an officer? More so, how will I prove I am a citizen of Germany?"

"Karl, we have a very deep and entrenched Underground Movement, one that is suspected by the Germans but is much stronger and united than they realize. I have strong alliances and a network within the German Army, not the Third Reich or Hitler's regime, but with Germans who also want him stopped. Many of us have been trapped in a vicious and seemingly helpless time where, as Hitler rose to power, ordered men and boys to join his Army. If we didn't, he would have harmed or killed our families. Now we are strong enough to help stop him. That is where you come in. Through these alliances, you will be able to furnish very strategic intelligence to the Allies; to once and for all overthrow and stop this terrible atrocity that has crippled our Motherland.

"To answer your question, Hans Houseman is a principle and founding leader of our local Underground Movement. He lives here in Aurich and owns the local market. He has connections that will produce your authentic documents and ensure they are registered as if you were born and raised in Germany. You will have a new name, a new identification papers, a birth certificate, parents, an address where you were born and lived, where you went to school, everything you need. If the Germans check on you, which they will, you will be authenticated. Through my alliances in the German Army, they will authenticate your enlistment papers, all your assignments and rank, your commanding officers, and, you will have earned some medals along the way."

"But Gerhardt." Karl interrupts. "What if my records are checked back to a certain platoon or a certain commanding officer? How will that be substantiated?"

"Not to worry Karl, we considered that would happen. We will link you to platoons that have been, say essentially lost in war, and commanders that have died. No one will be able to track any inconsistencies. On paper, you will be a naturalized German citizen and an authentic German soldier. Karl, think about this overnight, we will talk tomorrow."

Karl nods, "Thank you Gerhardt."

"Get a good night's sleep Karl."

"I am going to stay a while Father." Gerhardt kisses Katarina on the forehead, and leaves.

"Be safe my little one."

"Karl, thank you for listening to my father, he loves Germany, and is very genuine. With the activity in town, especially with Wilhelm, I should go back to the farmhouse tonight."

"Yes Katarina, we need to be careful and stay safe for a while, I love you."

"I love you Karl." Katarina kisses Karl. She leaves and walks home in the moonlight. Karl lies in his bed, thinking of Gerhardt's plan.

The next morning, before daybreak, Gerhardt and Katarina walk to the barn. "Good morning Karl."

"Good morning. Gerhardt. I have thought about your espionage plan and proposal. I will help you; I will help Germany. It was an easy decision." Katarina hugs her father.

"Karl, thank you, this is fantastic news." Gerhardt embraces Karl. "We have a lot of work to do. We need to introduce you to Hans. That will be difficult with the German soldiers in town. I have an idea. We need to get you to the farmhouse. Hans has free rein of the town. It will be risky though. We will plan on you coming to the farmhouse tonight, well after dark. Katarina will come and help you. I will make arrangements for Hans to meet us there. We must go now; we need to get back before sunup."

"I will see you tonight Gerhardt," Karl says with a firm smile. Katarina gives Karl a kiss on the check and whispers, "Sleep well my Love."

Katarina and Gerhardt walk to the farmhouse. The crescent moon is beginning to set, the sun is beginning to rise, they hear bombing in the distance. "Father, I need to talk with you."

"Yes Katarina, what is it?"

"Father, I love Karl; and want to be with him. Not only now but forever. I have fallen in love with him, and he with me."

Gerhardt stops in the path, turns toward her, and holds her hands. "Katarina, I can tell. I see the sparkle in both yours and Karl's eyes. Does your mother know?"

"Yes Father." Katarina begins to cry and hugs her father; he holds her tightly. They hold hands as they walk to the house.

THE PLAN

It is mid-June 1943. Katarina and Gerhardt arrive at the farmhouse just as the sun rises. Katarina, Anna, and Gerhardt are sitting at the kitchen table. "Anna, Karl will be here tonight to talk with Hans. Katarina, stay with your mother, I need to tell Hans." Gerhardt leaves for town. As he approaches the town and enters the village square, he can see a flurry of unusual activity, more so than the flurry of activity over the past few weeks. Gerhardt walks slowly, so he can strategically observe everything going on. It appears the platoon is gearing up to leave. As Gerhardt approaches the market, he can see Hans stocking supplies for a few soldiers. They make eye contact. Gerhardt walks into the market, the soldiers turn and see him, and salute him. He responds. Gerhardt nonchalantly strolls through the market looking for fruit and vegetables. After the soldiers leave, Hans walks to Gerhardt.

"How can I help you captain?"

"Come with me to the back of the market Hans," Gerhardt says in a soft voice. They walk to the produce stand in the back of the market intentionally to have their backs toward the street.

"Hans, what is going on, the troops appear to be leaving?"

"Most of the soldiers are leaving, they have been ordered back to Hamburg I heard."

"That is good news, perfect timing. Karl will be at the house tonight; can you meet with him?"

"Yes, I can, I will be there."

"Good, I will see you at 22:00. Be careful Hans, as I know you will."

Gerhardt returns to the farmhouse. "Katarina, we are set for 22:00 tonight to meet Hans and develop the plan. That will give ample time for darkness to get Karl here. Plan on having him to the house at 22:00 sharp, you will need to help him. Anna, you will be on guard. Turn the light on in the second-floor bedroom. Leave it on if Katarina and Karl have a clear path. They can see it from the trail. If not a clear path, turn it off."

The flurry of activity continues in town. Hans sees that as an opportunity since the soldiers may not be so focused on movement, especially at night. He can travel the back alleyways and side streets. Night falls. Katarina leaves for the barn, watching for any movement, and listening for any sounds. The moon is somewhat covered by clouds. As she approaches the barn, she suddenly hears a noise in the woods. Startled and frightened, she stops, and ducts behind a tree. The noise seemingly is coming toward her, she is trembling. Then on the path, in the moonlight she sees a deer. Still shaking, she sighs with relief.

Katarina arrives at the barn and knocks three times. "Karl, it is Katarina, I am here to take you to our farmhouse to meet with my father and Hans."

"I am here," he removes the floorboards. "I was anxiously waiting for you, I thought you would never come, I thought something bad happened."

"I am here for you now. I will help you get you up and on our way. It will be a long walk; we will go slowly." Karl walks with a distinct limp from his injuries, his fractured leg. He still uses a cane. They stop often to give Karl a rest. This is the first venture he has had since his crash. As they approach the crest of the hill Katarina can see the light is on, meaning all is clear. She also looks into the distance, into the village and does not see any vehicles approaching the farm. "We can go Karl, all is clear." They arrive at the farmhouse; Anna sees them coming and opens the door. Hans is in the room.

"Hello Karl. How are you doing, how was the walk?"

"We went slowly Anna; Katarina was a great help. I was anxious to get here, things are good."

"Karl this is Hans." Gerhardt introduces them.

"Karl, very nice to meet you."

"Come, we will sit in the kitchen." Gerhardt turns to Anna, "Anna, watch the road, stand by the window." Anna goes to the window.

Hans tells Gerhardt what he has learned about Wilhelm's and the soldier's departure from town. "Gerhardt, my people have learned Berlin is upset with Wilhelm's rant and his obsession in finding Karl. In that he should leave it to local command. The SS believes the pilot parachuted close to the border and fled to the Netherlands. What they do know is their radar had no trace of his plane entering Germany, only a small trace heading back to the west and a blip when it crashed. The wreckage of the plane was found close to here, but too destroyed to extract anything."

Karl looks at Hans. "Hans, my plane was equipped with special technology, I am glad it was destroyed. As I was having mechanical problems, I turned a heading to the west, hoping it would make it across the border."

Hans nods. "Berlin has ordered Wilhelm back to Berlin and the troops back to Hamburg."

"Ha." Gerhardt slaps his hand on the table. "Good for him, he will be upset though. I have seen him when he does not get his way. Very well, on with business."

Just as they sit down, Anna screams, "Someone is coming, someone is coming!"

"Karl, Hans, get in the pantry, quickly. Go to the back of it and stay low," Gerhardt says in a hurried voice. "Anna, can you see anything?"

"Yes, it is Wilhelm, he is coming up the path."

"Katarina, Anna, come sit at the table, quickly, act surprised when he enters." The door bursts open. Katarina and Anna scream, to pretend they are suddenly startled by Wilhelm, but in fact he truly did startle them, with his bold and loud entry. Gerhardt jumps up.

"Now what do you want?" They all are fearful he was here for a surprise search.

"I must return to Berlin. I am leaving in the morning and you are coming with me!"

Gerhardt says in a calming voice to throw Wilhelm off, "I was leaving tomorrow as well."

"You will ride with me then. We leave at 6:00, sharp. My business is not done here." He storms out.

Anna runs to the window, "He is gone."

"Gerhardt, do you need to leave tomorrow?"

"Yes Anna. I need to get back and I do not want to cause any more suspicion with him. Keep watch, just in case he returns, I do not trust him. Karl, Hans, you can come out now, he is gone. I need to return to Berlin tomorrow morning. Let us get back to discussing the plan with Karl." Karl, Katarina, Gerhardt, and Hans sit at the table. Katarina holds Karl's hand for a few minutes, then leaves the table. The sound of clattering plates and silverware clangs fills the room as Katarina clears the table. "Karl, Hans and I have developed a masterful plan to infiltrate and disrupt the Germans."

Hans begins to explain and roll out the plan for Karl to become German spy. "Karl, you have no idea what this means to me, your family, and the people of Germany. Wilhelmshaven, north of here, is a major military port, and Hamburg is a strategic city for the German's planning and intelligence."

"Yes, Hans. I am aware of the port. My mission was to fly reconnaissance for a bombing mission to Wilhelmshaven, of which I now know failed."

Hans continues, "Here is how we will first create and establish the paper trail to prove who you are. We will establish your birthday, place of birth, family, and your name. We will locate a village; I would suggest Oldenburg. It is a small village, not far from here, and a good location to Wilhelmshaven and Hamburg. We have people there that can help us with your records. We will use a name from a family who has died and has no living relatives, thereby nobody can dispute who you are. The schools will have your records, through graduation. We will fabricate your papers and place them in the village records. Karl, how old are you, when is your birthday?"

"I am twenty-one, I was born on January 15 1922."

"Perfect, we will find a couple in their fifties. From there, Gerhardt will establish your existence in the German Army."

Gerhardt chimes in, "Yes Hans, that is correct. My people will have Karl's enlistment papers, his training, assignment records, and progression through the Army. We will locate a battle on the Russian front where nearly all the entire platoon was killed, including the commander and officers. From there you will be reassigned to Hamburg. Do you understand Karl?"

"Yes, Gerhardt; how long will that take?"

"It will take some time, perhaps a couple of months." *Hans agrees.* "It must be done right. Until then, you will stay here. Hans will give you information as we develop it so you can learn your new identity. You must learn it as it was always true. You will be questioned, and your answers must be quick, accurate, and most of all, natural. Karl, there may be times you will need to put your comrades and Allies in harm's way. For the good of the war you must forge on. We have a lot to do. We need to get some sleep. Katarina will help you back to the barn. It was nice to meet you Karl."

"Gerhardt, Hans, I will not let you down, thank you both and good night."

"Everything is clear," Anna says as she peers through the window.

Katarina walks with Karl to the barn. The clouds have cleared, it's a beautiful moonlit night. They talk of their future together. "Karl, when this is over, and we leave Germany, we will have children. I want to have your children my Love." Once at the barn,

Katarina hugs Karl, they kiss. "I will be back in the morning, I want to see my father off, I love you Karl."

"I love you Katarina." They kiss one another.

The next morning, Gerhardt leaves, kisses Anna and Katarina. "Be careful, I do not know when I will see you next, Wilhelm is up to something. I need to keep an eye on him."

"Be safe as well Father." They both have tears in their eyes. "We will walk you to the road."

As Gerhardt walks into town he can see the platoon vehicles lined up in formation, ready to leave. He sees and hears Wilhelm barking orders.

Wilhelm sees Gerhardt. "Get in my staff car Father."

Gerhardt can hear the soldiers ordering the villagers to the street. He sees the sergeant bring an elderly couple to the center of the village. *I know them,* he says to himself. *They are the Mullers, a very nice couple. What does Wilhelm want with them?*

"Bring them here," shouts Wilhelm. "Get on your knees." Wilhelm goes behind them. "If I find any of you are helping the American, this is what will happen to you!" He draws his luger from his holster and shoots them both in the back of the head. He gets in his car and drives off.

Gerhardt looks at Wilhelm, "Why did you do that? You are a monster. They did nothing to you."

"Shut up."

The townspeople are mortified. They all see Gerhardt is with Wilhelm, *is he a traitor?* Did Wilhelm stage this intentionally? Hans gathers the villagers. He must be careful; some do not know his allegiance to the Underground Movement. Katarina and Anna, hearing the shots, run to the village. "Hans; why was Gerhardt in Wilhelm's car," asks one of the villagers. "Has he turned SS?"

"No! Absolutely not. Wilhelm ordered him to return to Berlin with him. As you all know, he, like many other Germans, was ordered to join Hitler's Army. Gerhardt is a good man; he can be trusted. He had nothing to do with these shootings. He was just as astonished as we were. Wilhelm is a vicious man." Katarina and Anna arrive. Anna sees the bodies and collapses in tears. These were good friends of hers. "Wilhelm did this, Anna," as Hans comforts her. Katarina stands in awe.

THE NEW IDENTITY

Two weeks have passed. The war wears on. A pleasant summer day in Germany, the first week in July. Karl is thinking of the Fourth of July celebrations in the States. The war continues, the bombing continues. Katarina has been with him daily. She told him of the brutal shootings in the village, by Wilhelm. Since the soldiers have left town, Katarina and Karl have been getting out more, taking walks in the woods. They are careful not to let the townspeople see them. Karl is getting stronger. Katarina and Karl are falling more and more in love. Katarina and Karl are in the field, enjoying the day. She sees her mother walking up the path.

"Good afternoon Karl, how are you feeling?"

"Much better Anna, every day I get stronger."

"Katarina, Hans wants to talk with Karl tonight."

"Okay Mother, we will come to the farmhouse tonight, after dark. We will be there by 22:00."

That evening Anna hears a knock on the door. She looks out the window. It is Hans. Anna opens the door. "Have a seat Hans, Katarina and Karl will be here shortly." They arrive at 22:00, just after dark.

"Hello Karl, the plan is in motion. Here is what we have so far. We have searched the records in Oldenburg. We found a couple with no children that were killed in a recent bomb attack. Your name will be Karl Pfisterer, a German citizen. You were born January 15 1922. I will keep some of your information the same to help you. Your parent's names are Elsa and Fritz Pfisterer. Your mother was born in Brokhausen in 1901. Your father was born in Bloherfelde in 1898. They were married September 17 1920." Karl reminisces of his parents. "We will alter the town's records to show they had one child. Your father was a machine builder in Wilhelmshaven. Your school's records will show you attended the Oldenburg Volksschule four-year elementary school, and the Oldenburg Mittelschule six-year middle school. Oldenburg also has a school called the Oldenburg Gymnasium, a secondary university prep school for boys. You did not attend that school; you chose to enlist in the German Army. Understood Karl?"

"Yes Hans, so much information. Thank you. How were you able to gather all of that information so quickly?"

"We have a tremendous network here, as you will continue to learn. Your papers are being developed as we speak. I will bring your identity credentials soon."

Two days later, Katarina walks to the barn and sees Karl in the doorway. He is wearing the sleeveless undershirt she gave him, and her father's suspenders. Karl turns and sees her coming. "Good morning my Love."

"Good morning Karl, what are you doing?"

"I am tightening this hinge on the door. I noticed it was loose and squeaking. I found tools in the back of the barn."

"They are my father's tools. It is nice to have a man around to tend to things."

"Yes, it is," he looks into her eyes, smiles, and lightly touches her nose with his finger. "It is nice to have a woman around to tend to things."

Katarina looks into Karl's eyes and smiles, "I love tending to certain things." She takes her finger and lightly touches his nose.

Karl gazes into Katarina's eyes, "Katarina, I too love tending to certain things that need tended to."

Karl and Katarina are walking in the field next to the barn. "Karl, are you up for a longer walk?"

"Yes Katarina, if you can put up with my gimpy leg," he laughs.

"Good, I want to take you somewhere."

"Where Katarina?"

"It is a surprise, come with me." Katarina takes his hand, and they walk down the path. Karl thinks they are going to the farmhouse.

"I know where we are going Miss Katarina."

"No, you do not Sir Karl." Just before the top of the hill, Katarina turns into the field, they walk toward the woods. "Karl, I love taking walks in the woods, especially with you now." They continue the walk for another forty-five minutes; and arrive at a small clearing in the woods. "Karl, this is where I found you, this is the exact place."

"Oh Katarina, this is very special, thank you for bringing me here." They reminisce for a while, and hug.

Karl stares into the woods. Katarina can see from the look on his face his mind is trying to process and comprehend something. "Karl you seem puzzled."

"Yes, I am beginning to remember, to remember the days here in the woods before you found me. My memories are coming back."

Holding Katarina's hand, Karl looks around, scans the woods, and walks toward the crest of a hill. He peers down into a ravine. "Katarina, look, see that log. I remember that log. The Germans were searching for me. I crawled into that log to hide."

Katarina hugs Karl. Karl is choked up. A tear runs down his cheek. Katarina gently wipes it away. Karl takes a deep breath.

"I heard soldiers approaching. I remember them standing over this log. One soldier sat on the log. I could barely see through the end of it as I camouflaged it so well, yet I remember seeing legs and boots only of three or four men. I then, fully not remembering when, crawled to another area after they left. The area where you found me. I remember that as being thicker brush."

"You must have been petrified."

"I remember wanting to survive."

"Karl, I am sorry I brought you here."

"No, do not be, I needed this closure, thank you."

"It is good you have released those memories. You now have closure."

Karl looks into Katarina's eyes, and holds her hands. "Thank you, Katarina. The place we met, this is special for me, and always will be."

"Karl, I have one more place to show you, come with me." They walk back toward the barn; but take a different path. As they approach a small ravine in the woods, Karl can hear running water, he sees a small stream. "When I was a little girl, I would come here all the time, this is my most favorite place. Sit with me and enjoy this beautiful place. See the little waterfall, see that rock, the one shaped like a kettle? I love how the water runs off the flat rock, into the kettle rock, then overflows back into the stream. I call this place the Kettle. Look over there, see where the steam flows into the pond. My father dammed the stream to create a water supply for the farm. We would ice skate on the pond in the winter. Karl look on the other side of the stream, those buttercups come up every year."

"I will be right back Katarina." Karl walks to other side, stepping on rocks.

"Be careful you do not slip."

Karl begins to pick the buttercups. He leans down. Katarina can see he is doing something on top of the rocks. When he is finished, he comes back to Katarina.

"Karl, you wrote I Love You with the buttercups, how sweet."

They sit on the bank, take their shoes off, place their feet in the cool running water, lay back, and stare into the blue sky through the trees. There is a gentle wind blowing the leaves. Karl, I love the sun glistening through the trees." Katarina lays her head on Karl's chest. "Listen to the sounds Karl, the stream, the breeze blowing, the tree leaves shuffling. It is so peaceful here."

"What other sounds do you like, Katarina?"

"Let me think. Oh, I know Karl. You will think this is silly," she says giggling.

"What is Katarina?"

"A cuckoo clock, I love the sound a cuckoo clock makes."

"Do you have one Katarina?"

"No, I wish I did."

They lay there for hours. They hear rumblings off in the distance. "Karl is that thunder? It does not sound like bombs."

"I think it is"

The wind picks up. Suddenly a series of thunderstorms roll in, quickly. "Karl, we will never make it back to the barn." No sooner she says that the skies open up, they get drenched with rain. Laughing and holding each other, they lay in the rain.

"Katarina, I dream every night this war will be over, and we can be together forever."

"I love you Karl." Katarina looks in his eyes; the rain is running down their faces. They sit up. Karl slowly unbuttons Katarina's blouse. The rain is dripping from her breasts. She unbuttons his shirt. Karl gently lifts Katarina up in his arms, he softly kisses the water droplets from her breasts. They fall to ground; they make passionate love in the rain. After the rain stops, they lay there, seemingly forever. Katarina in Karl's arms. On their way back to the barn Karl picks Katarina a bouquet of wildflowers.

Two weeks pass. Hans has another meeting with Karl. Karl comes to the farmhouse, again at night. Anna meets him. Karl, Katarina, and Hans sit in the kitchen, Anna stands guard from the window. "Karl, I have heard from Gerhardt, the plan is coming together. His people are getting your army enlistment papers and credentials together from the information I gave him. Your rank will be documented starting as an army recruit, then advancing to a private, corporal, sergeant, then to a Second Lieutenant, and now, a First Lieutenant.

"You will be assigned to the Army Group North, outside

Hamburg in the Neuengamme region. That is a German strategic echelon formation, commanding a grouping of field armies. This is a group that has valuable information about the military movements and strategies of Hitler's Army. It will be very important for you to gather as much Intel as possible to help the Allies. The German Army Group North is subordinated to the Oberkommando des Heeres (OKH). The OKH is the High Command of the German Army. It is a key part of Adolf Hitler's remilitarization of Germany. The German Army's high command coordinates the operations of attached separate army corps, reserve formations, rear services, and logistics, including the Army Group North Rear Area. In Northwest Germany alone, these field armies have upwards of three hundred thousand troops."

"What is the Army Group North Rear Area Hans?"

"It is an area of military jurisdiction behind the Wehrmacht's Army Group North. The Group North Rear Area's outward function is to provide security behind the fighting troops. Gerhardt has learned of a battle on the Russian front, just nearly two weeks ago. Ironic enough, it started on July 4, your Independence Day Karl. A perfect storm, if you will, for our plan. The Battle of Prokhorovka, part of the wider Battle of Kursk. The Russian battle at Orel salient is to the north of Kursk in the Soviet Union. The entire German 9th Army was redeployed from the Rzhev salient into the Orel salient. The Russian Red Army then launched a counter-offensive. The Red Army battled through the demarcation line between the 211th and 293rd infantry divisions of the 2nd Panzer Army on the Zhizdra River and steamed towards Karachev, then onto Orel. The Red Army joined the reserves of the Soviet 5th Guards Tank Army outside Prokhorovka. I heard over one thousand tanks were engaged. A very bloody battle for both sides. The Red Army prevailed. Gerhardt has learned many German platoons were obliterated. That is where your most recent assignment would have been, your papers will document that. As a matter of fact, your limp can play into this. You were injured in the battle. Karl that is all I have for now; the time is getting closer. I will keep you posted and start organizing the logistics for your travels. Thank you. Do you have any questions?"

"No, none for now. Thank you, Hans, this is a lot of information to digest and comprehend."

"Study it and learn it well. The details are very important Karl. Your life and this mission will depend on it."

Nearly two weeks pass, Tuesday July 27, Hans sees Anna in town. "Anna, I need to see Karl tonight, we are ready. I will be at the farmhouse at 22:00."

"I will let him know, Hans."

Katarina brings Karl to the farmhouse, it is 22:00, their normal meeting time. "Hans is coming," Anna says. "I will stand watch." They sit in the kitchen. Katarina clears the table.

"Karl, things have moved quicker than we thought, we are ready. Gerhardt has things in place. Here are your credentials." Karl looks at his new identity, Karl Pfisterer. "I have your uniform, gun and holster, and boots here also. Katarina was kind enough to help me in sizing everything. You are First Lieutenant Pfisterer. Sunday morning August 1, before sunrise, a German staff car will meet you behind the church. The driver, a German soldier, is part of our Underground. His name is Klaus, Sergeant Klaus Schmidt. He will take you to the Army Group North Command in Hamburg. He is stationed there. The Commandant, Georg-von Kuchler will be expecting you. Nobody comes into his Camp without him knowing it and knowing who they are. Kuchler will want to meet you. Katarina, your father did a very good job infiltrating the Army and North Group Command's Organization's files. Karl, your history with the German Army is embedded in their records, you will be fine. You have a top classified clearance level. Gerhardt sent your transfer papers to the North Command. You are being transferred from Kursk, Russia. Your trail in Kursk has been protected. As I mentioned, your platoon was defeated and nearly all killed or captured. You were found injured, displaced from your unit. We have you released from the hospital a week ago. Everything is in place. I have brought all your files, papers, and records for you Karl, your family history, your new life. Study them, know them well.

"Once you arrive in Hamburg, you will meet with Kuchler. You will be assigned to Captain Helmut Straughen in the Strategic Command. We have arranged for a Sergeant Hoffmann to be your direct report. He is not aware of your mission, nor the Underground. He is a true Nazi. Hoffmann has access to all the Base, and a lot of information. He has the clearances to get information, he knows a lot. Remember, Kuchler will be expecting you. He will, well interrogate you in his own way. Do not allow him to intimidate you, he does this with everyone. He has a very commanding demeanor. Klaus will take you to him. I am confident he will assign someone to you to help you to get settled in, and help you navigate the Camp, probably Hoffmann."

"What will my assignment be Hans?"

"All of the missions for the Western Front and North Atlantic are planned and developed from the Army Group North. You are being assigned as a tactical technician."

"What is that position, and what will I be doing?"

"Karl, as a tactical technician, you will have access to all of Command's missions, information the Allies desperately need. Gerhardt structured your orders so you will have the necessary credentials and clearances. Your training and background as a pilot will help you understand their missions and strategic positions. You will provide input and advice, all while protecting your identity. Your assignment, as I understand it, will be a liaison and courier between the Wehrmacht armed forces, the Heer, the Kriegsmarine, the Luftwaffe, and most important, the Waffen SS.

"There are certain things, missions and strategic plans we have heard about, yet we know little. The Germans have increased security and more so have refocused their efforts on the Western Front, equal to the Eastern Front. We need you to find out the details of these missions and strategies and get us the information. In recent months, the Germans have installed new radar systems across the Reich territory from Norway to the border with Switzerland. Since then that territory has been impenetrable, the Allied bombing missions through that territory have failed. We have learned the Luftwaffe has developed some type of new camouflage scheme for night flying, we do not know what it is. There has been a lot of radio chatter of the German Kriegsmarine strengthening the North and Baltic Seas in an effort to blockade, intercept, and destroy Allied war and merchant ships."

"I understand Hans."

"We also have learned the German Army is struggling on the Eastern Front, and the Red Army is gaining ground, and the advantage. That may work to our advantage. Even though Sergeant Schmidt is with us, you will pass your Intel to one of our people in the village of Kirchdorf, just outside the command in the Neuengamme Region of Hamburg. Her name is Ingrid Schneider. She owns a small tailor shop just outside the Base. She launders, tailors, and sews for the officers; she is in and out of the Base often. The soldiers know her, she can come and go as she pleases. You will use one of her garment bags for the transfer of information, you to her and her to you. Ingrid will come by each night between 22:00 and 23:00, for the pickup or drop off. Sergeant Schmidt will arrange that. Your bag will have a secret compartment in it. Use the words, Classified Intelligence; Covert Mission 1, 2, etc. on your messages. Do you have any questions Karl?"

"I am all set. Thank you, Hans."

"Karl, be very careful not to speak any English whatsoever, do not let anything slip out."

"I understand Hans."

"God be with you, Karl."

Karl and Katarina spend the next few days together, every minute of every day. They have picnics in the woods, take walks through the pastures and spend unforgettable, passionate nights together. Saturday evening arrives, Karl and Katarina spend their last night together for the unforeseeable future. Gazing into each other's eyes, Katarina falls asleep in Karl's arms. Karl awakes to quietness, not even the sound of bombs in the distance. It is 3:00 in the morning and Karl knows he must get ready and prepare himself for his new mission, his new journey. "Katarina, my Love; wake up." He kisses her forehead. She slowly and gently opens her eyes, sees Karl and smiles. Then realizing the time, she begins to cry.

"Karl, I do not want this night to ever end."

"I know my Love, but the time has come. I must go." Karl holds her ever so tightly, Katarina sobs more. "Katarina, I do not know when or how we can talk once I leave. I will communicate through Hans."

"I will do the same Karl."

"Be strong Katarina, this time will pass quickly." She nods and continues to weep. Karl gets dressed, in his German uniform. Katarina helps him.

"You look very handsome Lieutenant Pfisterer." They leave the barn, walk down the path, holding hands ever so tightly. It's a crystal-clear night with a full moon. "Karl, look at the moon, how full and bright it is. Karl, when you are away, look at the moon and know I will be as well, we always will be looking at the same bright moon together. Think of me and I will of you." Karl stops in the path, they kiss. Anna meets them at the house.

"Karl, please be careful, be safe, and come home to my Katarina."

Karl and Katarina hold each other, and kiss. Katarina gives Karl a butterfly pin. "As with your mother's locket, keep this with you my Love, it was my grandmothers. I love you very much Karl, come home to me."

"Katarina, the butterfly is blue, like your eyes. I will keep this with me always. I love you my sweet dear Katarina, I will come home to you, I promise." Karl takes off his dog tags, unclips his mother's locket, and places his dog tags over Katarina's neck. "Keep these for me my Love." They kiss and hold one another one last time. Karl turns and walks to the church. He has a distinct limp. He can see Hans and Sergeant Schmidt waiting. Karl knows he must be strong and begin this mission. He turns one last time to Katarina who is being held by Anna, crying uncontrollably.

THE SPY MISSION - NEUENGAMME

Sunday afternoon, August 1, 14:30, a sunny day in Kirchdorf. Karl arrives at Army Group North Command in Neuengamme, outside of Hamburg. Sergeant Schmidt drives Karl to the gate. The guard walks to the car and asks their business. Sergeant Schmidt informs the guard of Lieutenant Pfisterer's purpose. The guard requests Karl's papers. He reviews the papers, looks at Karl, and says, "Commandant Kuchler is expecting you lieutenant." He tells Sergeant Schmidt where to go and motions them to continue through the gate. Sergeant Schmidt pulls up to the Commandant's headquarters' building.

He leans back to Karl and says, "Good luck sir. Be mindful to always speak German."

"Yes, I will, thank you Klaus."

Karl gets out, the two guards at the door salute him, "Heil Hitler!"

"Siege Heil." Everything, so far, seems to be in order, the Camp expected him. Now the next test. Karl enters the headquarters building, walks to the receptionist. "Good afternoon, I am Lieutenant Karl Pfisterer, Commandant Kuchler is expecting me."

"Go right in lieutenant, he is expecting you."

Karl enters, "Heil Hitler Herr Commandant Kuchler!" Karl sizes him up quickly. Kuchler is a large man, and as Hans mentioned, Karl can tell he has a commanding demeanor.

"Heil Hitler Herr Pfisterer. Please, have a seat. Welcome to Neuengamme. I have heard good things about you lieutenant. I see you just came from the Russian Front."

"Yes Herr Kuchler, I was assigned to the battle of Prokhorovka. Nearly three-weeks ago, our platoon came under heavy fire, most of my comrades were killed or taken prisoner."

"How did you escape lieutenant?"

"I do not know sir. I was knocked unconscious from a mortar blast. The Russians must have presumed I was dead and left me behind. The next thing I remember was waking up in the field hospital."

"I see you have a limp."

"Yes, Herr Kuchler, from my injuries."

"Lieutenant Pfisterer, tell me about yourself, your life up to now?" *Karl wonders if he really wants to know or is this trap.*

"Commandant Kuchler, how much detail would you like?"

"Everything about you lieutenant, I like detail. It helps me get to know my officers better."

"I was born in Oldenburg, on January 15 1922. My parent's names were Elsa and Fritz Pfisterer. My mother was born in Brokhausen in 1901, and my father was born in Bloherfelde in 1898. They were married September 17 1920. I was their only child."

"Why do you say, was the only child, lieutenant?"

"My parents were killed in a bomb attack."

"I see lieutenant, carry on."

"They had a small farm; my father was a machine builder in Wilhelmshaven. I attended the Oldenburg Volksschule four-year elementary school, and the Oldenburg Mittelschule six-year middle school. I chose not to attend the Oldenburg Gymnasium; I chose instead to enlist in the German Army. I have served in various units of the Heer, and as you know, I recently was assigned to the Russian front."

Kuchler sits back and smiles. "I know all of that lieutenant. I thoroughly check everyone that comes to my command." Karl is tremendously relieved and thinks to himself, *test one passed.*

"I understand you have tactical training lieutenant."

"Yes Herr Kuchler."

"Good, that's all for now lieutenant. My corporal will see you to your quarters. He will direct you to our uniform supply building, you can get additional uniforms and anything else you need. Report to Captain Helmut Straughen at 5:00 tomorrow morning. He is in the Strategic Command building."

Karl arrives at his barracks. Since he is an officer, he has his own private room. Karl enters the room and studies it. He sees a fireplace, a bed and nightstand, a small desk, a table and chair, a private bathroom, and a closet. He unpacks and gets settled in. Karl takes a walk around the Base to get acclimated and comfortable with navigating through the streets and pathways. He also wants to locate the building he is to report to in the morning. As he is walking, he is very observant of specific features of the Base, locations of buildings, and general layout. He makes mental notes. When he returns, he finds a garment bag from Ingrid's Tailor and Seamstress Shop, hanging on his door. Karl thinks to himself; *Hans has a remarkable underground organization.* Karl remembers Hans saying any notes and messages would be placed in a secret compartment. He searches the bag, looking for the compartment. Inside a zippered compartment, he locates another interior flap, with a zippered compartment as well. Opening it he finds a note.

'Hello Karl, this is Ingrid, welcome. Use this bag to communicate between us. Be sure to include clothing and some notes as to the tailoring, laundering, or pressing needed. It will be searched. We know, based on your Gerhardt's papers, you are assigned to Captain Helmut Straughen in the Strategic Command. This is the group that plans and organizes all the movements and missions for the Army Group North Operations for the Western Front and North Atlantic.'

Karl settles in. He lays his mother's locket and Katarina's butterfly pin on his nightstand. Lying in his bed he is thinking of Katarina, *my first night away from my Love,* he reminisces of her gentle hugs and kisses, the romantic times, and memorable times they have between them. Karl reaches for Katarina's butterfly pin and his mother's locket. He falls asleep holding them.

Monday morning, 5:00. Karl, feeling a bit nervous but strong in his will for the mission, reports to Strategic Command, to Captain Straughen. "Good morning Captain Straughen, Heil Hitler, I am Lieutenant Pfisterer."

"Ah, yes, Heil Hitler, I have been expecting you. Have a seat Lieutenant. I understand you have a tactical background."

"Yes, Herr Straughen." "My Heer's training and missions on the Eastern Front were tactical and recognizance in nature."

"I see that from your records. Good, we can use you. Let us get you settled and to work. You will be working with First Sergeant Peter Hoffmann; he will be your assistant and will report to you; he will help you. I will introduce you, come with me lieutenant. Sergeant Hoffmann."

"Yes, Herr Captain Straughen."

"This is First Lieutenant Karl Pfisterer. He has been sent from Berlin and has top security clearances. He will be taking over the strategic planning for the Western Front. Get him acquainted with everything, our staff, equipment, data, and our missions. Start him with the Kammhuber Line."

"Yes, Herr Captain. The sergeant turns to Karl, "Very nice to meet you Lieutenant Pfisterer. Where are you from lieutenant?"

"I was recently at the Russian Front, the battle of Prokhorovka. It was part of the wider Battle of Kursk. My platoon was attacked. Most were killed, others captured. I was injured, knocked unconscious, presumed dead I believe, and left behind."

"Oh, I am sorry for your Platoon, lieutenant. Welcome, let's get to work. Lieutenant Pfisterer, our group's activity has been accelerated for the Western Front. Hitler is livid that Stalin and the Russian Red Army are advancing their movement into Poland, and the Heer and the Luftwaffe are struggling. We would never publicly admit that, but it is the truth. Not many people within the Nazi Regime know that either, understood?" Karl nods. "Mostly everyone in our group knows though. Hitler is increasing his propaganda to show the German Army and the German people the Third Reich is winning the war effort on the Eastern Front; and gaining control into Europe on the Western Front. Hitler wants to reinforce the Western Front for two reasons. First is to continue the stronghold we have here. We know the Allies are ramping up their forces; and second, we do not want to show we are redirecting troops to reinforce the Eastern Front. The plan is to do both."

"What can I do to help sergeant?"

"Herr Lieutenant, let me show you our new radar system we have in place, it is called the Kammhuber Line."

"How does it operate, why is it new, where is it located?" Karl asks very inquisitively.

"Lieutenant, come with me." Sergeant Hoffmann takes Karl to the central control room. Karl sees a series of main control stations. "These are the Himmelbett's. Up until now, the British bombers have been very effective in their attacks toward us, and to specific targets. We have been unable to detect their raids until it was too late. For months we have been working on a new radar system for early detection of the Allied aircraft. We have established a chain of new radar stations across the western edge of the Third Reich territory, stretching from Norway to the border of Switzerland. The code name is the "Kammhuber Line. This system is an undetectable nighttime air defense system. It consists of a series of control sectors, each sector is three deep, and equipped with radar and searchlights to illuminate the enemy bombers.

"The stations overlap one another, and each has a range of thirty kilometers. There are a series of control centers we call a Himmelbett zone, consisting of a Freya radar system with a range of about one hundred kilometers. For each control center, the Himmelbett also has a master searchlight directed by the radar, and several manually directed searchlights spread through the cells. Each cell is assigned one primary and one backup night fighter. The fighters we are using are Dornier Do 17Z-10's, Junkers Ju 88C and Messerschmitt Bf 110's. This new technique of ground-controlled interception, or GCI. It was preceded by our older technology, using single-engine non radar-equipped Bf 109 aircraft that were guided to the attacking bombers by the illumination of searchlights, termed; Helle Nachtjagd or illuminated night fighting. The entire system is tied into our central command here at the Army Group North Command, and to our gunnery stations and Luftwaffe air bases. We have the technology for early detection of the Allies' air raids. We can attack from the ground, and we can scramble our Messerschmitt Bf 110's and Junkers Ju 88 aircraft from the Luftwaffe fighter wing Nachtjagdgeschwader."

Karl makes a mental note. *Classified Intelligence; Covert Mission 1, Kammhuber Line.* "Incredible," Karl says. "Where are the stations actually located?"

"Here, sit down Herr Lieutenant, you can monitor for yourself, we have hundreds in place now."

"Can they be seen from the air?"

"No lieutenant, we have camouflage paint on them, the same as our field artillery."

"Very interesting, and well planned." Karl takes a seat and begins to study the system. He has an idea to gain trust with Captain Straughen, something Hoffmann said. Karl knows he must gain the trust of these people so he can continue to gain intelligence, even if it means helping the Germans short-term as Hans mentioned.

"Lieutenant Pfisterer, come here. I would like you to meet Second Lieutenant Rolf Webber. He joined us three weeks ago from the SS, under Major General Wilhelm Keitel. He will be working with you Herr Pfisterer." Karl's stomach gets a knot in it.

"Lieutenant Webber, this is First Lieutenant Pfisterer and has been assigned to our team today, he came from the Russian Front."

"Nice to meet you Lieutenant Webber."

"Likewise, Lieutenant Pfisterer," he says with a stern and unemotional voice.

Karl continues his tour with Sergeant Hoffmann. Day one ends. Karl returns to his room. He is suspicious of Webber and knows he must keep his guard up. Karl immediately begins reconciling his day, making notes in his journal to send to Hans. Karl whispers goodnight to Katarina. He falls asleep thinking of her. Tuesday morning Karl goes straight to Captain Straughen's office. He knocks, a voice says, "Enter."

Karl enters his office, "Heil Hitler. Herr Captain Straughen, may I speak to you?" The captain nods. "Herr Captain, Sergeant Hoffmann was showing me the Kammhuber Radar Line yesterday."

"Yes," says Straughen.

"Well, I asked how they are camouflaged. He told me they have camouflage paint, the same as our field artillery."

"Yes, that is correct lieutenant."

"Herr Captain, may I suggest, to supplement the camouflage at their positions. We should use camouflage netting to further mask them with the countryside. Without the netting, any movement would show from the Allied aircraft." In true German form, Straughen slams his fist on his desk and jumps up, startling Karl.

"I am extremely upset." Karl wonders to himself, *what did I do wrong, what will happen?* "I have people dedicated to working on nothing but protecting our equipment, and you come in, after one day, and tell me of this idea. Well done, lieutenant. That is a very good suggestion. I will see to it immediately." A sigh of relief resonates within Karl.

"Thank you, Herr Captain, Heil Hitler." Karl leaves. On his way to his office he knows this was an ingenious plan; a plan to gain the captain's trust. Karl smiles to himself. This plan to help the Germans was not a concern in Karl's mind to impede his mission, but to help the Allies. Remembering something Gerhardt and Hans told him, *sometimes you may need to help the German's in order to help the Allies. There may be times you will need to put your comrades and Allies in harm's way, for the good of the war you must forge on.* When Karl was studying the Kammhuber Line information yesterday he noted all the stations had location coordinates.

The next few days are very informative for Karl. Sergeant Hoffmann, although following orders, is very talkative. Karl takes it all in, asking questions and providing suggestions. Every night Karl thinks of his dear Katarina, how he so deeply misses her. Karl writes his detailed notes in his journal. He knows his cover could be blown at any time. Karl needs to keep Hans updated frequently, and his journal hidden. He notices a ventilation duct in his room. *That is where I will hide my journal.*

NEUENGAMME – THE FOLLOWING WEEKS

I t is Sunday morning, August 15, week two of Karl's mission. Karl plans to send information to Hans this week, and to let him know things are progressing well in Neuengamme. Karl begins his note to Hans. 'Hans, I have settled in and have been accepted here. Enclosed is my first update for you. You and Gerhardt did an amazing job with my records and papers. I have been assigned an assistant, a Sergeant Hoffmann. He is very knowledgeable of the systems and missions at the Army Group North Command. He also is very talkative, which is very helpful. I feel he is trying to impress me, ha ha. I met a Second Lieutenant Rolf Webber; he was sent here a few weeks ago from Wilhelm Keitel's SS command. I will keep an eye on him. Ask Gerhardt to check him out. Let me know what you and Gerhardt find out about him, how close he is to Wilhelm, and what he is doing here. I am concerned that coincidently a lieutenant from Keitel's SS was sent here. Hans, here is what I have learned so far.

'I learned of the German's new radar systems that were established across the Reich territory from Norway to the border with Switzerland. This was one of the concerns you and the Allies have, I have valuable information for you. It is called the Kammhuber

Line. I am including a map of the locations and coordinates.' Karl continues with detailed information of how the system works. 'Hans, a note for Katarina, please see she gets this.'

Karl lays her butterfly pin in front of him on the table. 'Katarina my Love. I miss you and very much love you. These past two weeks without you have worn heavy on my heart. I think of you every minute of every day, and dream of you every minute of each night. You are what keeps me going and focused on my mission. Tomorrow is your birthday; I wish you a beautiful birthday. One more thing my Love, it is a clear night. I am looking at the moon and thinking of you. I love you, sweet dreams Katarina.' Karl finishes his notes and seals the information in the compartment in the garment bag. Karl places a uniform in the bag with a note.

'Please clean and press.' He hides his journal in the ductwork and hangs the garment bag on the door. Karl lays down, thinking of Katarina. Holding her pin and his mother's locket; *Good night my Love,* he says to himself; and falls asleep.

Monday, August 16. Karl arrives at the Command Center. He knows he needs to be more active, take more initiative and control. He must act the role. Karl knows he must stay close to Webber and listen to what he knows and says. "Sergeant Hoffmann," Karl barks out.

Sergeant Hoffmann immediately stands and salutes, "Heil Hitler Herr Pfisterer."

Karl plays on the words Hoffmann told him on his first day, to get Hoffmann to bite. "Sergeant, you told me the Luftwaffe is struggling on the Eastern Front, and we need to ramp up operations on the Western Front."

"Yes sir."

"Tell me what the Luftwaffe is doing to plan attacks and missions for the Western Front initiatives. The Luftwaffe is greatly feared by the Allies, we need to use that to our advantage."

"Yes, Herr Pfisterer."

"Lieutenant Pfisterer, the Luftwaffe has been unable to

successfully attack London at night. Our Luftwaffe bombers are all black. We were convinced that was the best color for night attacks, blending in with the night sky. What we learned through our Intel is the English could see our night fighter planes and bombers from the reflection of the sky glow over the cities at night. The reflections light up the underbellies of our planes, they become sitting targets to their anti-aircraft guns. Late last year, December 1942, we began developing a new paint scheme. We have devised a new color scheme to mask our bombers. A light-color camouflage scheme that takes advantage of the sky glow over the cities we are attacking. We also have learned our bombers are creating silhouettes over the target areas from the fires below and searchlights, which would make them vulnerable to aircraft attack from above.

"Our testing finished last month. Code name Big Week. Our new color scheme also prevents that silhouette effect on our planes. We have tested the color scheme over German cities at night that were on fire. The result is our planes now are much more camouflaged. We now have the upper hand again for night attacks on western cities."

"How does the color scheme work, sergeant?"

"It was quite simple actually; a Luftwaffe bomber pilot, Major Hajo Herrmann came up with the idea. We used the colors of the Luftwaffe's diurnal, or daytime aircraft. It was ingenious. The color scheme comprises the use of the Luftwaffe's Hellblau light blue undersurface color, and a light gray base coat over the upper surfaces to match the sky glow over the cities we attack, and the German cities we defend. The light gray base color has irregular patterns of darker gray splotches or irregular wavy lines spread over the light gray areas to increase the camouflage effect. We also are experimenting on some Luftwaffe night fighters, the Kampfgeschwader He 177A heavy bombers in particular, of switching back to a black coloration for the undersurfaces and vertical sides of the aircraft. For now, we kept the new light gray with dark gray-color disruptive patterns."

Karl continues to ask questions; he gains valuable Intel; and Hoffmann's trust and respect.

Karl makes a mental note. *Classified Intelligence; Covert Mission 2, Code Name Big Week.* Sunday evening, August 21, Karl is in his room documenting his journal. He hears a knock on his door.

Karl looks at his watch, 22:30. He opens it, no-one is there, except his garment bag with his clothes. *Ingrid was here,* he says to himself. Karl locks the door; and checks the bag. A note is in the compartment. Karl opens it, it is from Hans.

'Karl, the information you provided on the Kammhuber Line is immensely vital to the Allies' air campaign. I have passed this onto our people in Britain. I did give Katarina your message. There is a note from her for you.' Karl burns the note from Hans in the fireplace in his room. He sits back and opens Katarina's note.

'Karl, I think of you every day and look forward to your letters. I am always very happy to hear from you. The past three weeks have worn heavy on my heart also. When I received your note from Hans, I got butterflies inside of me. Thank you for remembering my birthday, you are so sweet. I cherish seeing the moon on clear nights and think of you seeing the same moon, our moon Karl. I ask Hans about you every day. You are in my thoughts and my prayers always. I deeply miss you and I send my Love to you. Mother sends her love as well. Forever yours, Katarina.'

Monday morning, Karl arrives at the Command Center. He says good morning to Sergeant Hoffmann. Weeks have passed. No one is suspicious of Karl, or his movements. He sees Lieutenant Webber and decides to have a conversation with him. "Lieutenant Webber, I recall you saying you worked under Major General Wilhelm Keitel."

"Yes sir, he took me in as his protégée. I am on a fast track in the SS. This is one of my assignments."

Karl maintains his composure. "I have heard many good things about Herr Keitel; you are fortunate to have his tutelage. Where were you assigned prior to Neuengamme?"

"I spent six months at Auschwitz," Webber says with a glee in his eye, as if he enjoyed it. Karl has an eerie feeling about this man.

"How long will you be assigned here Herr Webber?"

"I do not know exactly; I do not think too long. Herr Keitel has plans for me to be engaged in many of our units for training, including learning to speak English."

"Why English?"

"For more effective interrogation purposes, and perhaps, I may become a spy," he says and laughs.

Karl nods, turns, and walks toward Sergeant Hoffmann. "Sergeant Hoffmann, our advancement on the Western Front relies heavily on the success of the Luftwaffe. You told me of the color scheme for our planes. For me to help with the effort, tell me what other strategies we are planning, or technology we are developing."

"Lieutenant Pfisterer, Berlin is convinced the Third Reich will win this war through our Luftwaffe's air campaign. We are developing a new radar detection system for our aircraft. Recently, we outfitted three Jagdgeschwader fighter wing planes, a JG 300, a JG 301, and a JG 302, with these devices. Code name is Wilde Sau. The units are equipped with the new radar systems. The FuG 350 Naxos-Z detector is under development. We have two prototype versions; one version is the Bf 109 G-6/N and the second version is the Fw 190 A-5/U2. Both aircraft versions are modified for night use and are fitted with a Naxos passive radar detector. The FuG 350 Naxos-Z detector can track the enemy's H2S radar transmissions from a range of thirty kilometers, which enables our German fighters to home in on British Bombers. We also have adapted our Duppel radar system into this new technology."

"Sergeant, when will these be active?"

"Herr Lieutenant, the prototype testing is nearly finished. The planned date to be fully functional is mid-September, just a few weeks from now. The Luftwaffe will be outfitting additional planes beginning then. The Luftwaffe is planning major simultaneous raids on London on the nights of October 7 and 8 of this year."

"This is good news sergeant, thank you." Karl makes a mental note. *Classified Intelligence; Covert Mission 3, Wilde Sau.*

The weeks continue. Karl's infiltration is going well. Sergeant Hoffmann continues to share information with Karl and Lieutenant Webber. Webber seems to have accepted Karl as well, although they do not have much interaction, as they have different assignments. Karl needs to get close to Webber to learn what his exact role and assignment is. Karl continues to fill his journal with top secret German information. It is Friday, August 26, Karl prepares his notes to Hans.

'Hans, I continue to gain valuable information, the Command trusts me. Two pieces of critical information, Covert Missions two and three, I am writing about tonight. The first, code name Big Week. The Luftwaffe is changing their color schemes on their bombers to mask and camouflage their bombers and fighters from the reflection of the skyglow over the cities at night on the underbellies of their planes. The new color scheme also prevents the silhouette effect on their planes from overhead.' Karl continues with the details, the testing and the German's plan.

'Hans, the second piece of information I have for you is a new radar detection system the Germans have developed, called The FuG 350 Naxos-Z detector. Code name Wilde Sau. A nighttime version is also under development. It has the ability to track the Allies H2S radar transmissions from a range of thirty kilometers, leaving their aircraft vulnerable to attacks, sitting ducks. The planned date to be fully functional is mid-September. The Luftwaffe will be outfitting additional planes beginning then. The Luftwaffe is planning major simultaneous raids on London on the nights of October 7 and 8 of this year.' Karl finalizes his details. 'Hans, please give Katarina this note.'

'Katarina, I dearly miss you and I love you very much. The longer we are apart, the more my love grows for you. You are in my heart and my dreams always. I love you. Karl.' He then seals the notes in the Garment bag. As directed by Ingrid, Karl places two uniforms in the bag, with a note, 'Please clean and press.' Sunday evening, Karl places the garment bag on his door for pickup by Ingrid. Shortly thereafter he hears a knock on the door, and smiles. Karl settles in, again thinking of Katarina, and falls asleep.

Nearly a week later, Saturday September 3, Hans responds. Karl wakes to a knock on his door. He opens it and finds his garment bag. Inside a message from Hans. 'Karl, your messages were received. I have passed them onto London. London has responded quickly on the radar system. They have studied the information you sent on the new radar technology. The only information they can compare it to is the Wurzburg radar equipment which they captured and brought back to the London last year. Upon examination of that system, and subsequent reconnaissance, it has been revealed to the British and Allies that all German radars operate on three specific frequency ranges. London knows those frequencies. Up until now the Allies could jam those old systems. What we do not know is the new frequency range, or ranges of this new system, the FuG 350 Naxos-Z detector. We need you to find the frequencies of this system. With the raids a month away, we need this information quickly so we can respond. Katarina sends her love, and a note.'

'Karl my Love. As I write this note I am at the barn, thinking of you. I am lying on a blanket, gazing into the blue sky. I look across the field and see the butterflies fluttering through the wildflowers. The leaves are beginning to turn. The town has been peaceful lately. Please be careful and come home to me. I love you. Katarina.'

Karl knows his mission. He summons Sergeant Hoffmann to meet him at the Command Center in the morning. He burns Hans' note.

Sunday morning, Sergeant Hoffmann arrives, "Herr Lieutenant, what do you need?"

"Sergeant Hoffmann, I am concerned with the upcoming October raids on London."

"Why, Herr Lieutenant?" Karl uses his Intel as if he has past knowledge of the German radar systems.

"I know our older radar systems operate on three frequencies. The Allies know how to jam our systems; they are doing it now."

"Yes," the sergeant acknowledges.

"Herr Lieutenant, you do not need to be concerned. We have taken that into account. I failed to tell you the new system operates on variable frequencies."

"How does a variable frequency work sergeant?"

"The new system emits a series of frequencies, from eight to twelve cm bands, making it very difficult to detect. These new frequencies are different bands from our old systems."

"I am glad to hear that sergeant, I should have asked before, thank you."

With time running short, Karl must get this information back to Hans quickly, quicker than through the Underground and Ingrid. He has a bold, but risky idea. Karl goes to the headquarters building. He enters and asks the receptionist if she can contact Sergeant Klaus Schmidt.

"Yes lieutenant, what is the message?"

"Sergeant Schmidt brought me here last month, I believe I left something in his staff car. Have him meet me at my barracks."

"Yes sir, right of way." Karl returns to his room and drafts a message to Hans, with the frequency information. Thirty minutes pass, Klaus arrives, and knocks on Karl's door.

"Herr Pfisterer, you called for me. What do you need?" The sergeant is careful not to disclose Karl's identity.

Karl looks down the hallway, "Come in Klaus. I need you to get some information back to Hans immediately."

"I can go tonight," replies Klaus.

"Good, I told the girl who called I left something in your car. Let's walk outside, and I will pretend to look." Karl hands Klaus an envelope. "Give this to Hans." They walk to Klaus's staff car. Karl opens the back door and pretends to search the seat. Suddenly a third voice interrupts him.

"Lieutenant Pfisterer, what are you doing?" Startled, Karl suddenly turns, it is Webber.

"Lieutenant, Webber, you startled me. Sergeant Schmidt brought me here last month. I thought I left something in his car." Karl continues to search. "Ah yes, I did. Here it is." Karl holds up a pen. "I was taking notes; and lost this pen. It is special to me; my father gave it to me for a present. Carry on Sergeant Schmidt, thank you." Schmidt leaves. Karl thinks to himself, *that was a close call, was this a coincidence, or was Webber alerted?* Karl makes small talk. "Lieutenant Webber, out for a walk?"

"No, I was working, just going back to my room."

"We have not talked in a couple of weeks, what are you working on?" asks Karl. Webber seems standoffish to answer.

"I have been working on strategic planning for the Panzer Division, and you Lieutenant Pfisterer?"

"I have been busy with learning the new radar systems, and some upcoming missions."

"Good, carry on Lieutenant Pfisterer. I am glad you found your pen." Webber stares at Karl for a few seconds. Karl does not want to press on with any more conversation; but he will take this piece of Panzer information and work on gathering more Intel. Perhaps Sergeant Hoffmann knows something.

Monday, September 5, Karl arrives at the Command Center. He wants to quiz Sergeant Hoffmann; but must be astute in his method. He first checks to see if Lieutenant Webber is around. Karl does not see Webber. Karl takes a risk on his next question. He will state that Captain Straughen mentioned something to him, but the captain did not. Karl hopes Sergeant Hoffmann will simply answer the question and move on. "Sergeant Hoffmann, Captain Straughen mentioned a Panzer Division involvement with the Army Group North Command."

Karl no sooner gets the words out of his mouth and Sergeant Hoffmann blurts out, "Yes, Herr Lieutenant." Hoffmann likes to impress Karl with what he knows. "A few months ago, in the summer, the Luftwaffe and Waffen-SS have recently had Panzer divisions assigned to them, each with two battalions. Panzer Battalion IV is assigned to the Eastern Front, and Panzer Battalion V is assigned to the Western Front, reporting through us at the Army Group North for strategic planning missions. The 155th Reserve Panzer Division was assigned to our command in August; and the 179th Reserve Panzer Division was assigned in July. The SS's plan is to reinforce our positions in France, and southern Europe. Lieutenant Webber is organizing the group's positions to mobilize the 155th and 179th to France by the end of September for offensive measures."

Karl makes a mental note. *Classified Intelligence; Covert Mission 4, Panzer Deployment.* "Thank you, sergeant. That is my understanding as well." Karl plays to Hoffmann's description of the events. He now knows why Webber is here, it's because of the SS's involvement with the Panzer Divisions in France.

Karl must get this information to Hans, quickly, so the Allies can prepare an offensive plan before the end of September. He does not want to engage Sergeant Schmidt again so soon. He decides to visit Ingrid's tailor shop. He returns to the headquarters building. The secretary greets him, "Good morning Lieutenant Pfisterer."

"Good morning Fraulein. I need to have some alterations done on my uniform. I understand there is a tailor shop close by. They do my laundering by drop-off at my barracks, but I do not know their location."

"Yes, Herr Lieutenant, that is the same shop. The proprietor is Ingrid, a very nice lady. When you leave the main gate, turn right for one block. Ingrid's Tailor Shop will be across the street."

"Thank you, Fraulein." Karl returns to the Command Center, goes to his office, and prepares a note for Hans. 'Hans, you recall I mentioned Lieutenant Webber, from the Keitel's SS. He mentioned something the other day about his assignment. He said he was working on strategic planning for a Panzer Division; but would not elaborate on it. I got creative and dropped a question to that talkative Sergeant Hoffmann.' Karl lays out the details of what he learned.

'Hans, I need to get this information to you quickly as time is of the essence, so I will go directly to Ingrid's shop today to send this to you. I have placed a note for Katarina with this message, please give it to her.'

Karl's letter to Katarina. 'My dearest Katarina. It has been thirty-six days since we last held each other in our arms, since we gazed into each other's eyes, since we kissed. I have your butterfly pin with me always, and I think of you every day. I miss you so much my dearest love. I miss holding you, I miss kissing you, I miss loving you. Our lives came together in such a unique and special way. I am so grateful we met each other, and of how we met. I am doing fine here in Neuengamme, no one suspects me, and in fact I have gained their trust. Last night the moon was beautiful, so bright. Sweet dreams my Love.' Karl does not want to tell Katarina about Lieutenant Webber and his relationship with Wilhelm. He does not want her to worry. 'Soon my work here will be finished, and we will be together my Love. I think of our new life together, our new family, and our new future together once this war is over. Tell Anna I said hello. I love you, Katarina.'

Karl waits until noon to go to Ingrid's. He takes a coat with him.

"Sergeant Hoffmann, I am going into town for lunch."

"Mind if I join you lieutenant?" Karl must respond with a quick answer and not hesitate.

"Perhaps another time sergeant, I have a few errands to run while I am out." Karl arrives at Ingrid's shop and enters.

"May I help you sir?"

"I am looking for Ingrid."

"I am Ingrid, how can I help you."

"Is anyone else in the shop Ingrid?"

"No, I work alone."

"Ingrid, I am Karl, the one working with Hans."

"Herr Karl, it is very nice to meet you, but you need to be careful coming here."

"I know Ingrid, but I have some very important information that must get to Hans, quicker than the normal route."

"I see, very well. I will send a courier, what do you have?" Karl lays his coat on the table, with an envelope under it. The shop door opens, and a lady enters.

"I will be with you in a minute." Ingrid turns back to Karl. "Now lieutenant, you were saying you needed alterations or something?"

"Yes Fraulein, I need two buttons sewn on my coat."

"I will get right to that Herr Lieutenant; I can bring this to the Base when I am finished."

"That will work fine. Thank you. I am Lieutenant Pfisterer, ask for me."

"Very good," Ingrid slides the note from under the coat and places it in her pocket. Karl tips his hat to the two ladies, and leaves.

Twelve days have passed, September 17. Karl arrives to his room late that evening and finds the garment bag on his door. He enters his room, locks the door, and opens the bag. Ingrid returned his coat. He finds a note from Hans. 'Karl, we have received your information, from Klaus, and from Ingrid. Very good work. I have passed the new radar frequencies on to our Allies in London, and the deployments of the two Panzer Divisions to our Allies in France and Britain as well. We have been gaining ground in France and have suspected the Germans would reinforce their positions, we just did not know when and how. They will be in for a big surprise. Thank you for quickly getting us the Intel. I talked with Gerhardt about Webber; his words were 'do not trust that man.' He comes from the same mold as Wilhelm. He was in Auschwitz before Neuengamme. Gerhardt heard Webber receive praise from Command for his role in torturing and killing Jews. He has been under Wilhelm's mentoring for two years, and is being fast tracked through the SS. He will never say no. Be careful Karl, but we need to continue to know what he is up to.'

Karl burns Hans' note. He finds a second note in the garment bag, from Katarina. A smile comes to his face. He sits back in his chair, opens the note, and reads it. 'Karl, my Love, by the time you get this letter, it will have been at least forty-three days since we held each other, kissed each other, looked into one another's eyes, and loved each other. I miss you very, very much. The love for you in my heart grows deeper and stronger every day that we are apart. I know your work is very important to the war effort, and to our people of Germany. Thank you for doing this. I think of you every minute of every day. You are in my dreams at night, and always in my heart. The moon has been very beautiful the past week. I think of you when I see it, and know you think of me when you look at it, we gaze together my Love. Aurich is somewhat back to normal since Wilhelm and the soldiers left. Wilhelm has not been back since. I still see patrols daily. From what we hear, the Germans have given up their search for you. The Allied bombing campaign is increasing, Aurich has been spared. Mother is doing well, we have been tending to the farm, it occupies our time. I love you, Karl. I cannot wait to hold you in my arms. My love to you forever, Katarina.' Tears come to Karl's eyes, he clutches her letter, and falls asleep in his chair.

Weeks turn into months since Karl first arrived in Neuengamme. It is mid-October; the smell of Fall is in the air. The mornings are becoming crisp. Karl continues his crusade to stop Hitler and his Third Reich. He is busy with his new mission. Karl continues to take control and offers advice, both strategic and tactical within the Camp. The Germans continue to trust his leadership. Karl is mindful to keep Hans informed of any commitments, plans, or missions of the Germans regarding strategy or tactical changes so the Allies can counter. He is careful not to suggest anything that would backfire on the Allied missions. He continues to gather valuable intelligence and information for Hans and the Allies. He thinks of Katarina every day.

KARL IS NOTICED

"Lieutenant Pfisterer."

"Yes, Sergeant Hoffmann."

"Captain Straughen wants to see you." Karl gets that feeling in the pit of his stomach, *are they onto me,* he asks himself.

"Herr Straughen, Lieutenant Pfisterer here. Sergeant Hoffmann said you wanted to see me."

"Yes lieutenant, please sit down. I have been watching you the past couple of months. You have been here over two months now, nearly three." The pit is getting tighter. "You have adapted well and have shown the leadership we need, that of which I expected from you. In addition to your current assignment, I am placing you in charge of the North Atlantic Strategic Planning Group as well. Our Luftwaffe is not making the headway we need in that region, and the Kriegsmarine need to take more control of the North Atlantic. In the past week, from October 8 through the 14, the U.S. Eighth Airforce has had one thousand three hundred forty-two sortie bombing missions that have been very effective, they must be stopped." Karl smiles to himself. Little does Straughen know, those missions will be the turning point of the war.

"Thank you, Herr Straughen, I will not let you down."

"Lieutenant give Lieutenant Webber more oversight and

responsibility for the Western Front initiatives, under your leadership of course. Then you can begin focusing more on the North Atlantic. Sergeant Hoffmann will stay with you, the two of you work well together and he has been involved in the North Atlantic operation as well." A plan develops in Karl's head. *This is perfect,* he says to himself. *With Webber's assignment to the Western Front, I can keep a close watch on him, I can set him up as a spy, and turn the tables on him and Wilhelm.*

Karl returns to his office. "Lieutenant Webber, Sergeant Hoffmann, I need to talk with you. In addition to my duties on the Western Front, I have been assigned to the North Atlantic Strategic Planning Group. Lieutenant Webber, you will take over my responsibilities for the Western Front Strategic Planning Group, and report to me. Lieutenant Webber, I will meet with you separately to brief you on my work to date on the Western Front. Sergeant Hoffmann, you and I will strategize today on our plan for the North Atlantic."

"Yes, Herr Lieutenant," they both say in unison.

"Sergeant Hoffmann, tell me where we are with the North Atlantic Operation, and how I can help."

"Lieutenant Pfisterer, this is a plan we have been working on since earlier this summer, the Army Group North Command, in concert with the Kriegsmarine, began planning the Battle of the North Cape, as we are naming it. The targeted time frame to launch the attack is two days after Christmas Day, December 27 1943. The German's strategy is that perhaps the Allies may be distracted with Christmas."

"Why is this battle important?"

"This attack is part of our Arctic campaign. The campaign is to block war materials from the western Allies being sent to the Soviet Union."

"How much traffic, and how many supplies and materials."

"The traffic has been increasing over the past few months. The western Allies have been supporting the Red Army; and is hampering our efforts on the Eastern Front. We need to ramp up our efforts in the North Atlantic and Arctic regions. They are very strategic regions for us, for our water attack campaigns against Europe and Norway's north coast. We also need supplies. Our Armies are consuming our supplies faster than we can replenish them. The British have had blockages setup in the region for months, which have been hampering our merchant runners. The Kriegsmarine's battleship Scharnhorst along with a flotilla of destroyers from our Naval Shipyard Wilhelmshaven just north of here have been assembled to reinforce support in those regions."

Karl makes a mental note. *Classified Intelligence; Covert Mission 5, Battle of North Cape.* "Very good sergeant, show me our plan, deployment strategy, and strategic locations."

That evening Karl retires to his room and prepares a note for Hans. 'Hans, I bring good news and a major piece of information. I have been promoted in a sense; I have been assigned to the North Atlantic Strategic Planning Group. I also remain overseeing the Western Front's Strategic Planning Group. Webber is assigned to that group under me. I will be able to keep an eye on him. I have a plan brewing for Webber and ultimately Wilhelm. Please let Gerhardt know, both of my new assignment and a plan to set Webber up, I will need his help. With Webber having access to this information, and the fact he has been here longer than me, we can plant information with the German's that he is a spy, a British spy.

'Here is what I have learned regarding the North Atlantic Operation. The Kriegsmarine is planning for the Battle of the North Cape as they are naming it. The targeted time to launch the attack is two days after Christmas Day. They feel we will be relaxed with Christmas. This campaign is to block war materials being sent to the Soviet Union. Our support is impacting the German's efforts on the Eastern Front. They are ramping up their presence in this region to assist in getting supplies into Germany for their own needs as well. The German armies are using supplies quicker than they can replace them. We must keep our vigilance in this region.' Karl finalizes his details. 'Han's, please give Katarina this note.'

'Katarina, I love you and constantly think of you. The smell of Fall is in the air. The leaves have turned. I dream of taking walks with you to the Kettle. I must go now, my Love to you. Karl.' Karl notices it's close to 22:00. Karl's arrangement with Ingrid is she always picks up from his barracks between ten and eleven each evening. Karl places the information in his garment bag, along with five shirts and a note to Ingrid, 'Please launder and press,' and hangs it on the door. The next morning it is gone.

October 19; there is uproar in the Command Center, Karl is called to Captain Straughen's office. Karl knocks and enters. The captain is pacing back and forth. "You want to see me sir?"

"Yes lieutenant. I just came from a meeting with Commandant Küchler. He has been in discussions with Berlin. Our new tactics on the Western Front have not been effective. The Allies have begun a bombing campaign on our Kummhuber radar sites. Our strategy of the camouflage paint scheme has not helped our bombing missions over London, and today I have learned our Wilde Sau Radar Detection technology is proving ineffective. In July and August, the Army Group North developed a plan to mobilize the 155th and 179th Panzer Divisions to France by the end of September for offensive measures, to solidify our positions in France and Southern Europe. Today I have learned, after a three-day battle, both Panzer Divisions, the 155th and 179th, were defeated before they entered France. We were taken by surprise. We deployed Luftwaffe fighter jets and bombers to assist the Panzer Divisions, but those efforts were countered by Allied air defenses prepared for these measures.

Berlin is concerned, as am I. There are too many coincidences with the Army Group North's missions failing. Our Intel acknowledges top secret information is being leaked, somewhere from one of the high commands in Germany, but we do not know from where. Could be coincidence, but I do not believe in coincidences." Karl gets that lump in his throat, *are the Germans on to me?* "We here at Army Group North take extreme pride in screening our officers, both commissioned and noncommissioned. We know who is here and where they came from. I do not believe we have a spy." In typical Nazi form, Straughen blurts out, "We do not make mistakes." Karl thinks to himself, *first, obviously you do not do a good enough of a job checking people, and second, Gerhardt is a mastermind.* "Get with Lieutenant Webber and make sure he stays on top of these developments, find out what is going on, am I clear lieutenant?"

"Yes, Herr Captain."

A summary of results from Karl's first wave of intelligence.

'Classified Intelligence; Covert Mission 1, Kammhuber Line: *Karl's Intel proves invaluable. The Allies are amazed the Germans have installed this many radar stations so quickly, and learning of their range, must develop an unconventional plan to destroy them. Prior to this knowledge, the Royal Air Force Bomber Command exerted no discipline on how pilots were flying their aircraft to their target. The boxes of the Kammhuber Line were well set up to deal with the broad approach paths of these individual bombers.*

The initial phase of this plan, since Karl provided the maps and coordinates of the radar stations, was an intense artillery long-range bombing and air campaign against the stations. Phase two of the plan, the Bomber Command reorganized their attacks into streams of bombers, rather than sporadic individual bombing attacks for four or five hours. They carefully positioned the bomber stream to fly down the middle of a single cell. Data provided allowed the British scientists to calculate the bomber stream would overwhelm the six potential interceptions per hour that the German night fighters could manage in a Himmelbett zone. It was then a matter of calculating the statistical loss from collisions against the statistical loss from night fighters to calculate how close the bombers should fly to minimize Royal Air Force losses. This allowed the British bombers to fly by a common route and at the same speed to and from the target, each aircraft being allotted a height band and a time slot in a bomber stream to minimize the risk of collision.

To further add to this plan, the British introduced the "WINDOW. The WINDOW is a radar jamming technology that drops strips of foil, or chaff, from the lead bombers. The German radar operators see what appears to be a stream of aircraft entering their box, each packet of chaff appears to be a bomber on their displays and confuses them. Night fighters are sent to attack this stream, only to find empty airspace. Just as the night fighters reached the false stream, the Allied bomber stream appears hundreds of miles away, too far away to be attacked. Karl's Intel provides spectacular results. The German radar-guided master searchlights wandered aimlessly across the sky. Their anti-aircraft guns fired randomly or not at all and the night fighters, their radar displays swamped with false echoes, utterly failed to find the Allied bomber stream.

Classified Intelligence; Covert Mission 2, Code Name Big Week: *Learning of the plan to change the color scheme of the Luftwaffe aircraft to disguise and camouflage the planes from Karl, the Allies developed a bold plan to counter that measure. They will allow the interim plan of the Nazis to unfold, much to the detriment of Allied casualties, for the betterment of a much larger plan. The plan is the implementation of a sequence of raids by the U.S. Army Air Forces and Royal Air Force Bomber Command in a strategic bombing campaign against Nazi Germany. The plan intends to attack the German aircraft industry to lure the Luftwaffe into a decisive battle where the Luftwaffe could be damaged so badly the Allies would achieve air superiority which would ensure success of the invasion of continental Europe.*

Although the color scheme was a great plan, it was short lived. The Allies used very bright and long-range search lights to aid in seeing the aircraft at night. However, the Big Week plan was bold, but the German's color scheme initiative never gained much ground as the Luftwaffe was thrown into defense mode. The joint daylight bombing campaign was also supported by RAF Bomber Command operating against the same targets at night. The Royal Air Force Fighter Command provides escorts for U.S. Army Air Force bomber formations, concurrently as the Eighth Air Force began introducing the P-51 long-range fighter as part of the plan as well. This offensive will overlap the

German Operation Steinbock, the Baby Blitz, which lasted from January to May 1944.

Classified Intelligence; Covert Mission 3, Wilde Sau: *The Wilde Sau was developed on July 24 1943, after the British developed an airborne radar countermeasure immune to WINDOW. Karl's plane had this new technology radar system, WINDOW. The British previously captured German Würzburg radar equipment during Operation Biting, a raid in February 1942. Upon examination of the Würzburg radar equipment brought back to the UK, subsequent reconnaissance revealed to the British that all German radars were operating on no more than three frequency ranges, making them prone to jamming. Not knowing if the Germans changed their frequencies for the new Radar System, Hans requested Karl to get the frequencies. The findings were the new German radar system operates on variable frequencies. The new system emits a series of frequencies, from eight to twelve cm bands, making it very difficult to detect. The Allies' plan is to use these new frequencies ranges at once to counter the attacks. The Luftwaffe, on their first mission, was encountered immediately by Allied aircraft. These encounters continued every subsequent Luftwaffe mission. The Luftwaffe suffered severe losses. Their new system was short lived and abandoned by the Luftwaffe after three weeks.*

Classified Intelligence; Covert Mission 4, Panzers Deployment: *Immediately upon receiving the information from Karl, the Allied forces in Southern Europe and France began mobilizing additional ground forces and aircraft to locations where the Panzer Divisions would enter the region. The Allied assets were in place by September 17 1943. Although the Panzer convoys were traveling by night, Allied air reconnaissance scout planes verified their locations and routes while still in Germany. The Allies established key locations to ambush the Panzer convoys. Long-range ground artillery and tanks were positioned by the Allies. As the Panzer convoys approached, the Allied heavy bombardment campaign began, supplemented with air campaigns carried out by the Free French Air Force, the British Royal Air Force, and the U.S. Army Air Force in concert. The Germans were taken by surprise. The Luftwaffe deployed fighter jets and bombers to assist the Panzer Divisions,* *but those efforts were immediately countered by Allied air defenses prepared for these measures. The battles lasted three days. Both Panzer Divisions, the 155ᵗʰ and 179ᵗʰ were defeated before they entered France. The Germans suffered heavy losses. This also reflected failures of Lieutenant Webber and SS Major General Wilhelm Keitel. The German forces in France remained unsupported, and now more vulnerable with the additional Allied forces present.'*

Karl believes his cover is safe, but he knows he must be more careful and more scheming. This was the perfect timing to begin to set Webber up. Karl returns to his office and meets with Lieutenant Webber. "Lieutenant Webber, I just met with Captain Straughen. He tells me our new strategy on the Western Front is proving ineffective. The Allies have begun a bombing campaign on our Kummhuber radar sites, our strategy of the camouflage paint scheme has not helped our bombing missions over London, and today we have learned our Wilde Sau Radar Detection technology is proving ineffective."

"Lieutenant Pfisterer, I have been watching the Kummhuber Radars the last two days. It appears only a portion of the line has been attacked. The Allies are flying in a bomber stream, flying down the middle of our single cell locations in the Himmelbett zones. Three cells have been compromised so far. It appears this bomber stream is overwhelming our six interceptions per hour that our night fighters can manage in a Himmelbett zone. The Royal Air Force has had losses, but not as many as we have had in the past when the Kummhuber Line was fully functional. I have heard our camouflage paint scheme has not helped our bombing missions over London, and just today as well, I have learned our Wilde Sau Radar Detection technology is proving ineffective. I was on my way to update you Herr Lieutenant Pfisterer."

"Good, carry on Lieutenant Webber and keep me posted."

Karl returns to his office and calls for Sergeant Hoffmann. "Sergeant, our recent missions on the Western Front are proving ineffective. When we are finished get with Lieutenant Webber and see what you can do to help, you are the most knowledgeable. Sergeant, what is next for us to discuss with the North Atlantic?"

Sergeant Hoffmann responds. "Herr Lieutenant Pfisterer. Last month, in September, the Kriegsmarine deployed the battleship Scharnhorst from Wilhelmshaven to join our Bismarck class battleship Tirpitz, patrolling in Norway."

"I have heard of the Tirpitz Sergeant Hoffmann."

"Yes lieutenant, she was the second of the Bismarck class warships built for the Kriegsmarine and re-outfitted in 1941. She, together with the Scharnhorst, are two of our largest and most deadly battleships. The Tirpitz was patrolling the Soviet Baltic Sea before her reassignment to Norway. Her assignment is to intercept and attack Allied convoys in route to the Soviet Union. To combat the Tirpitz, the British sent significant naval forces to the region. We have countered that with the addition of the Scharnhorst. Three weeks ago, the Tirpitz and Scharnhorst had successful attacks on Allied positions in Spitzbergen. The addition of the Scharnhorst to our North Atlantic Fleet is part of the plan I mentioned to you, the Battle of the North Cape on December 27."

Karl makes a mental note. *Classified Intelligence; Covert Mission 6, Scharnhorst.* "Very good sergeant. Go and spend time with Lieutenant Webber."

"Yes sir."

October 21; Karl retires to his room. His garment bag is on the door, Ingrid is early tonight. He enters his room and locks the door behind him. Karl checks his bag, no note from Hans, not unusual though as it often takes a week or two for Hans to respond. He needs to alert Hans on the addition of the Scharnhorst to the German North Atlantic Fleet. He gathers his journal and updates it first, then prepares the note for Hans. 'Hans, the Kriegsmarine have two Bismarck Class Battlecruisers deployed in the North Atlantic to intercept and attack Allied convoys heading to the Soviet Union. The Tirpitz was assigned to the Norway Region, but with the British sending additional naval forces to the region, the Kriegsmarine deployed the Scharnhorst from Wilhelmshaven to join the Tirpitz. They are two of Germany's largest and most deadly battleships. The addition of the Scharnhorst to supplement their North Atlantic Fleet positions is part of the plan I sent you a few days ago, the Battle of the North Cape on December 27. I also have been thinking of a way to set Webber up and destroy Wilhelm.

'Hans, my plan is to use the same setup for Webber as you and Gerhardt did for me. Here is the story we will create for him. Have Gerhardt establish papers that Webber was born in Bavaria on November 7 1921. A simple farming family from a small town, Bad Griesbach, close to the Czechia border. The Czechs were divided in WWI, some chose to fight for the Allies. In a fierce battle between the Germans and the Czechs, German artillery kills Webber's mother. He and his father fled to England where he learned English. We will need to establish his life in England. When Hitler and the Third Reich came to Power and WWII began, it brought back the memories of WWI and his mother. Webber is against Hitler's agenda and vows to bring the Third Reich down. He will become a spy from England. Have Gerhardt set this up. I will need some papers, a birth certificate, orders from England, his assignment, and anything else you think would be appropriate. Have Ingrid bring them to me, and I will plant them in his room. I will think of a plan to have his room searched at the right time. We can bring Wilhelm down as well for not discovering this and providing Webber with sensitive information. The fact that Webber played him will not be viewed well in Wilhelm's career.' Karl finishes his update to Hans. 'That is all for now Hans. I also included a note for Katarina.'

'My dear sweet Katarina. It is cold, the winter weather has set in. I so long for you. Every minute of every day I think of you. I cannot wait to hold you in my arms. Things are going well here. The Germans do not suspect me. I have been able to provide Hans much needed information to help the Allies. Be strong my Love, we will be together soon. I love you.'

Karl seals the messages in the garment bag, with some clothes and a note, 'Please clean and press', hangs it on the door and goes to bed. Shortly after 22:00, he hears a light knock on the door. Karl smiles and goes to sleep.

WINTER IN NEUENGAMME

Three weeks have passed, the War goes on. It's the middle of November, winter weather has arrived early in Northern Germany. Karl reminisces of his childhood, Thanksgiving, the Holidays, sled riding. Karl continues his mission. Webber comes to Karl's office,

"May I have a moment with you lieutenant?"

"Yes, come in Lieutenant Webber."

"Herr Pfisterer, I have been studying our missions, and the counterattacks by the Allies. May I be candid sir?" Karl nods. "I know you are a trusted leader here," says Webber. "You are well respected by our command, and I have come to respect you as well Herr Pfisterer. I am confident our missions and strategies are being given to the Allies by someone in this Camp."

"Why do you say that lieutenant, what proof do you have?" Karl has that lump in his throat.

"I have no proof, yet. There is one thing, one commonality that I can point to. Sergeant Hoffmann is the only person that has access to all of our information."

"Lieutenant Webber; we need to keep this to ourselves for now, until we know for sure. These are very serious allegations. I have not sensed anything from him about him providing information to the Allies." Karl plays along. "You have a very valid point though, thank you lieutenant. I will keep a close eye on him as well."

"Herr Pfisterer, I have a plan. We will set him up with false information, only we will know. We will see if it gets to the Allies."

"Very good idea Lieutenant Webber. That will be a good test. What do you have in mind?"

"Nothing yet sir but let me work on something and I will get back with you."

Karl takes this as an opportunity, a way to set Webber up. Karl will develop his own plan against him. Karl thinks to himself. *I know my days may be numbered here, and my mission may be coming to an end. I need to make as much progress as I can; and I must be prepared for a quick exit at any time. I must get a plan in place and let Hans and Sergeant Schmidt know.* Karl retires for the evening. Upon entering his barracks, he sees the garment bag on his door. He takes it into his room, locks the door, and finds two notes. One from Hans, and one from Katarina. Karl sits at his table and opens Katarina's note first, with a smile on his face.

'My dearest love. I too spend every minute of every day thinking of you and when we will be together, to begin our new life. I love the smell of Fall. I often think of the evening we first made wonderful love. I spend many days in the woods, the woods where we made love at the Kettle by the stream, just lying, gazing into the sky, thinking of you. Somedays when in the rain I remember getting caught in the thunderstorm and us laying in the woods, gazing into each other's eyes. The cool rain falling on us. I think of you gently kissing the raindrops from my breasts, and the bouquet of wildflowers you picked for me that day. I think of those amazing feelings I have, ones I have only with our passionate love making. Hans mentioned you, he, and my father are devising a plan to end Wilhelm's evil reign, once and for good. That is wonderful news, the sooner the better. Winter has arrived here as well. I want to cuddle with you at the fireplace. Stay safe my Love. I long to hold you in my arms. I love you. Katarina.' By the end of her note, Karl is sobbing nonstop. Tear drops fall on Katarina's note.

Karl gathers himself and opens Hans' note. 'Karl, we were aware of the Tirpitz being in the Norway region. But now since the Germans have two warships, the Scharnhorst, and the Tirpitz, working in tandem is concerning to us. This information is perfect timing from your last update of the December 27 planned attack. Knowing this now will help us counter the Luftwaffe and Kriegsmarine offensives. Karl, I have provided Gerhardt your plan, he thinks it is a great idea and plan, your vision to stay one-step ahead of the German's is remarkable. Gerhardt is preparing the documents you suggested, and we are working with the Allies to plant Webber's life in England. I will keep you posted on timing, but Gerhardt said this will take some time to get everything in place. Perhaps three to four weeks.' Karl burns the note from Hans and prepares another note to Hans to inform him of Webber's suspicions.

Karl prepares his note for Hans. 'Hans, Webber came to me today. He knows their missions and strategies are being given to the Allies by someone in this Camp. I challenged him on how he knows that to be true and asked what proof he had. If he suspected me, he would have gone to Captain Straughen. He may have but I do not believe that to be true, at least not yet. Webber tells me he has no proof, yet; but has concluded one thing. He said there is one commonality that he can point to, and that is Sergeant Hoffmann. Webber has concluded Sergeant Hoffmann is the only person that has access to all our information. He wants to develop some false information to plant with Hoffmann, to see if the Allies receive it, and wait to see if it comes back to the Camp full circle. I asked him to keep this between the two of us for now, that he and I will develop the plan together. We will use his own plan against him, with our false information. Please give this note to Katarina.'

'My Love. Your letter is very tender, it brought tears to my eyes. My tears fell on your note. Watermarks of love forever. I long for the day we can walk together to the Kettle and make love. Perhaps another thunderstorm will roll in. We will cuddle in front of the fire, someday very soon Katarina. Our plan here at Neuengamme is coming together. I so miss you, and I so miss holding you in my arms. Tell Anna I said hello. I must go now. My love to you. Karl.'

Karl places his journal and Katarina's letter in the air vent, along with her other letters. Karl seals the note in his garment bag, and places it on the door, again with clothing and a note, 'Please launder.'

To head off Webber, Karl develops a plan to share with him, and with Straughen collectively. This will develop further trust of Karl in the Camp and will solidify Karl's plan for Webber, when Webber is accused, only three people will know. A week goes by, Karl arrives at his office.

"Lieutenant Webber come into my office. I have been thinking of your accusation of Hoffmann. I have been more alerted to him and his actions for a week now and have drawn similar suspicions. I believe you may be correct. He talks a lot to many of the different section leaders in the Camp, he gets around to every Group, and he has much information. I also have noticed he disappears for long periods of time. When I confront him, he always has an excuse. He says he was doing an assignment, running errands, just seems to always be bullshit." Karl knows none of this is true with Hoffmann but needs to convince Webber and hook him. "Due to the nature of these atrocities of treason, I have asked Captain Straughen to join us, he will be here momentarily."

The end of November is approaching. It is a very cold day with winter like weather in Germany. Straughen enters Karl's office. "Lieutenant, you asked to see me?"

"Yes, Herr Straughen. A week ago, Lieutenant Webber came to me after I talked with him with your concerns of our information being leaked, the so-called coincidences as you put it."

"Yes, go on lieutenant."

"Lieutenant Webber has a suspicion of one of our sergeants, Sergeant Hoffmann."

"Nonsense, I do not believe that. Hoffmann has been here a long time. He is a good man, loyal to the Third Reich."

"My point captain, he has been here a long time."

"After some investigation of my own, I now concur with Lieutenant Webber's suspicions that our missions and strategies are being given to the Allies by someone in this Camp."

"Why do you say that lieutenant, what proof do you have?"

"As of now, we have no proof, but we both agree, there is one thing, one commonality this points to. Sergeant Hoffmann is the only person that has access to all of our information."

"Herr Captain, Lieutenant Webber and I have decided to develop a plan, a plan which will either confirm our suspicions, or prove Hoffmann innocent. We need your concurrence. We will set him up with false information, only the three of us will know, we will see if it gets to the Allies."

"What do you have in mind Lieutenant Pfisterer?" Karl makes it a point to control the discussion, to have Straughen remember Karl's control of the meeting. "Herr Captain, I want to plan a false mission, where the Luftwaffe and the Kriegsmarine are planning an attack on Western Europe, and specifically England, but from the west. A full force attack from the Atlantic Ocean side. We know the Allies are very focused on stopping us in the North Sea. A region we need to regain control of for the many reasons we discussed."

"Yes lieutenant, carry on."

"We will make the Allies believe we are assembling a fleet of destroyers and aircraft carriers in the Mediterranean, from South Europe and the north coast of Africa. If they bite, they will focus their efforts and assets to stop this plan. This so-called attack, code name Deep Sea, will be conveyed to be launched concurrent with our North Cape attack on December 27. I believe they will move assets to the Atlantic Ocean to counter this fake offensive. If this works, we will catch the Allies off guard, and they will be vulnerable for our North Cape attack."

"Lieutenant Pfisterer, this is a wonderful and masterful plan; how will we communicate it?"

"I will lay the plan out to Hoffmann in this manner. He will not be aware of this new mission, obviously. I will tell him orders came from Berlin, from Hitler himself, and you have only told Lieutenant Webber and myself."

"Wonderful plan lieutenant, I hope you are wrong, in a sense. I have always liked Hoffmann, but to your point, we can trust no one at this point. Put your plan in place." *You are so right; you cannot trust anyone;* Karl thinks to himself. "Lieutenants, due to the severity of this I need to advise Commandant Küchler and the SS, Major General Wilhelm Keitel."

"Absolutely Herr Captain." Karl expected that and knows this will work into his plan to set Wilhelm up as well.

The next morning, Karl and Webber call Hoffmann in Karl's office. "Sergeant Hoffmann, we have just met with Captain Straughen. Berlin is planning a very top-secret mission, one that will change the direction and outcome of this war. It will be led from here, the Army Group North. A plan is being developed to invade Western Europe, and specifically England from the west, from the Atlantic Ocean. We want you to be engaged in assisting us to lead this mission Sergeant Hoffmann. We believe this will draw the Allies attention from the North Sea, and they will focus their efforts on countering the Atlantic offensive."

"That is an amazing strategy, how can I help?"

"Sergeant Hoffmann, you have been very involved with the North Cape attack plan."

"Yes sir."

"Well you have just become more involved."

"Sergeant Hoffmann, the Atlantic offensive, code name Deep Sea, will be launched concurrent with our North Cape attack on December 27."

"Wonderful Lieutenant Pfisterer, the Allies will never expect that. They will be forced to send assets to the Atlantic from the

North Sea." Lieutenant Pfisterer and Webber look at each other, and Karl thinks to himself, *you think you are so right Hoffmann, but dead wrong.*'

"Precisely sergeant. That's all for now sergeant."

Webber turns to Karl, "Lieutenant Pfisterer, that was an act from the theater, you did a very nice job, you almost had me convinced." *If you only knew Webber, if you only knew.*

Karl must get this plan to Hans and Gerhardt. That evening, Karl prepares his journal and the message to Hans. 'Hans, the stage is set. I came up with a plan, a great plan, actually. You know, if the Germans were smart, they would use it against us. I met with Captain Straughen and Webber today and laid the plan out to set up Hoffmann. Webber and Wilhelm will fall into our trap. Here is the false information to plant, and the message to relay. I will tell you my thoughts on that. The Luftwaffe and Kriegsmarine will be preparing an attack on Western Europe, and specifically England from the west, the Atlantic Ocean. The deployment will be from the Mediterranean region and their forces in North Africa. It will be carried out on December 27, the same day of their North Cape attack. As I have conveyed the plan to them, the Allies will believe this, and will draw our, meaning the Allies attention from the North Sea to the Atlantic, to counter the German Atlantic offensive.

'For the plan to work, we need reputable and detailed radio communication from Allied Command confirming this attack, and we need to be sure the Germans pick this information up, and relay it to Berlin. Berlin needs to be convinced the Allies believe this information is reliable, and that we, the Allies, are beginning to move assets from the North Sea to the Atlantic to prepare for this offensive, even to the point Britain hears the U.S. will send additional warships from the U.S. mainland. I suggest we send this communication in two waves. The first wave: We, the Allies, have received information from our trusted source inside the Army Group North the Germans are planning an offensive from the Atlantic Ocean, code name Deep Sea, on December 27. The second wave is:

The Allies have requested additional support from the U.S. Navy, and the Navy is moving assets from the North Sea and Naval Station Norfolk. Be very detailed in exactly what we say, what we know, and when. We must be very specific, so the Germans know this is factual and an authentic communication from the Allies. They need to believe this information came from the informant at Army Group North Command. I would send the second communication one week before December 27. Hans, please give this note to Katarina.'

'Katarina my dearest love. It is November 25, Thanksgiving Day in the states. Soon we will be together. I feel my mission here is will be ending soon. I am planning my escape should I need to move quickly. We have devised a plan to cause suspicion on a sergeant here in Camp, but the trail we leave will lead the conspiracy to Lieutenant Webber, Wilhelm's protégée, and ultimately to Wilhelm. With winter arriving early, my dreams have shifted to sled riding in the fields with you, taking a moonlight horse drawn sleigh ride, and snuggling up to a warm fireplace at the end of the day, you in my arms, and we fall asleep. I must go now. Sweet dreams my Love, I love you with all of my heart.' Karl places his journal in the vent and secures the notes in the garment bag. He hangs the bag on the door. A few minutes pass, and light knock.

December 3, Karl is working at his office. A knock at the door. "Enter," Karl says.

It's Lieutenant Webber. "Lieutenant Pfisterer, I have received information from Berlin of a new series of planned attacks against the Allies, of which we need to strategize the logistics. I have kept this information from Hoffmann, he is not aware of the plan or our discussion. Berlin has ordered us to plan a series of air attacks, a continued bombardment of London. The British Bomber Command began a campaign against Berlin last month. Operation Steinbock will be a strategic bombing campaign commencing on January 1 and continue through May 1944 against the Allies."

Karl makes a mental note. *Classified Intelligence; Covert Mission 7, Operation Steinbock.* "It is a systematically organized and executed attack from the air which can utilize strategic bombers, long or medium range missiles. The Luftwaffe is assembling four hundred seventy-four bombers for this campaign against London. This offensive will be the largest-scale bombing campaign against England to date, and we believe will be the turning point of the war in Germany's favor. We will wear the Allies down."

"Lieutenant Webber, the Luftwaffe has attempted many air campaigns against the Allies; and although most were effective, the Allies seem to always withstand them. How will this be different?"

"Herr Pfisterer, in addition to the conventional aircraft, which will be Phase 1, the Luftwaffe will be using our short-range cruise missile, the V-1 flying bomb."

"Yes, I know of those, lieutenant."

"But what very few do not know Herr Pfisterer, we have developed a long-range guided ballistic missile, the V-2 rocket."

"Wonderful Herr Webber."

"Yes, it is the world's first long-range guided ballistic missile. We can launch it from deep within Germany. The missile is powered by a liquid-propellant rocket engine. It will be our vengeance weapon."

"Lieutenant Webber; we must immediately begin planning the dates, launch locations, and flight paths for the missions, January is not far away. I suggest most attacks to be at night." Karl suggested this due to the new night radar systems the Allies developed from his past intelligence, and the fact the guided missiles will give a very red glare; the *hey Allies, "come and get me" type of glare.*"

December 6, the feast of Saint Nicholas. Karl and Webber have a preliminary strategy developed, with dates, launch locations, and flight paths. They present this to Captain Straughen and the Commandant of the Army North Command and receive a green light. Karl has been busy drafting his message to Hans; but wanted to wait for this information and confirmation. Karl returns to his room. The garment bag is on the door, with a message from Hans. That evening Karl finishes his message to Hans. Karl opens Hans' message. He also sees another small envelope. As he opens it, he smells the fragrance of a flower. It is a white lily petal with an image of Katarina's lips in red lipstick, and a note; 'Karl, my Love, to a new beginning and budding love. The sweet and innocent beauty of the lily symbolizes the purity of our love. The Christmas season is upon us. Mother and I went to the woods today to get our Christmas tree. I wish you were here to help trim it. I love you, be safe my Love. Katarina.' Tears run from Karl's eyes.

Karl then reads Hans' note. 'Karl, the papers for Webber are finished, Sergeant Schmidt has the necessary documents to plant in Webber's room. His new name will be Heinz Fischer. Ingrid can help you with that. They need to be hidden in a place where he will not find them, but upon a thorough search, they will be found; perhaps hidden and attached to the underside of his bed. His life in Bavaria and England has been established, the plan is all set. The Allies are ready to begin the false communications, as you outlined. Very good work Karl.' Karl prepares his response to Hans.

'Thank you, Hans, I am sure I will hear about the Allies communications. Keep me posted. I have additional and critical information for you. This is very time sensitive. I learned today the Luftwaffe is planning a series of systematic air bombardments on London over a period of five months, beginning January 1 through May, in two phases. They will be running this concurrent with Britain's campaign against Berlin. The mission, Operation Steinbock will be utilizing strategic bombers, medium and long-range missiles. The Luftwaffe is currently assembling four hundred seventy-four bombers for this campaign. They say this will be the largest-scale bombing campaign against England to date and believe it will be the turning point of the war, in Germany's favor. Their strategy is to wear the Allies down. In Phase 1, the Luftwaffe will use their conventional aircraft and short-range cruise missiles, the V-1 flying bombs. However, for Phase 2 of the campaign, they have developed a long-range guided ballistic missile, the V-2 rocket. I am told it is the world's first long-range guided ballistic missile. They have the ability to launch from deep within Germany, making it less vulnerable from our air attacks. The missile is powered by a liquid-propellant rocket engine. They have named it their vengeance weapon. Ask Gerhardt what this is? I will provide the attack dates, launch locations, and planned flight paths to Klaus when I see him to get Webber's papers. I suggested to the captain and commandant for most attacks to occur at night, they agreed. In addition to our newly developed night radar systems, we will see the Krauts coming. Hans, I feel my mission may be coming close to ending. I have developed a quick escape plan in case I need one. Klaus will be helping me. I will fill him in when I see him. Hans, a short note to Katarina is included.'

'My Dearest Katarina. The lily petal, with your kiss, is very touching, so loving and tender. It brought tears to my eyes. I have it in my wallet. Merry Christmas if we do not talk before then. I love you.'

Karl seals the messages in his garment bag along with five shirts. He hangs it on the door with a note, 'Please clean and press.' It's 20:30, Karl hears voices of soldiers in the hallway. They are checking garment bags. They come to his and open it. Karl listens intently.

"It is fine," one says, and they move down the hall. This gives Karl an idea, *I may be able to plant information in Webbers bag, but I can't draw attention to any connection with Ingrid. I will talk with Ingrid.* He hears a light knock on the door, it's 22:45, it's Ingrid.

The sting is set. Another week passes in Neuengamme, December 13, twelve days to Christmas. It started snowing yesterday and has accumulated fifteen inches, it's pretty. Karl wishes Katarina could see it. Karl is formulating his false note to the Allies to plant in Webber's room. Hoffmann again was very talkative. The Allies have had a stronghold in Italy from their invasion in 1943 but have progressed only as far as the Gustav Line south of Rome. The German Army must stop the Allies from advancing further. Their plan, the Invasion of Anzio was put in motion. January 30, the German Army will send additional forces to invade Gustav to surround the area and push the Allies back to the southern beachhead. This mission was handed to the Army Group to develop. Karl will type this message in detail and have it placed in Webber's room, along with his false credentials.

Karl returns to his barracks and finds the garment bag. A short note from Hans. 'Karl, this will happen quickly, the first communication will be broadcast by London on December 15, and the second on December 22. Karl, I agree with you, the time has come to get you out of Neuengamme. I heard from Gerhardt. He has had enough of this war, of Hitler, the Third Reich, and of Wilhelm. He is planning for him and Anna to defect from Germany. With the coordinates you furnished on the fuel plant and missile sites, he will use those bombings of his fuel plant as a decoy to escape. Assuming the Allied planes succeed. The last straw was the final development of the V–2 missile, a very gruesome weapon. Gerhardt did not know the Luftwaffe perfected this missile so quickly, he knew they were close. Karl, your efforts have changed the path of the war, thank you.'

Karl documents his journal and burns the note from Hans. *We all will flee Germany together;* Karl says to himself.

SUSPICION – THE STING

December 14, Karl prepares to implement his plan. He must see Klaus. Karl calls the Camp communication center; a lady answers the phone. "Fraulein, this is Lieutenant Pfisterer, will you have Sergeant Schmidt call me?"

"Yes sir."

A few minutes later Klaus calls, "Herr Lieutenant Pfisterer, you called for me."

"Sergeant, can you talk?"

"Yes sir."

"I understand you have some information for me, from Hans. Meet me at Ingrid's at noon today."

"Yes Sir."

Noon arrives. Karl and Klaus meet at Ingrid's. They arrive at separate times. Ingrid locks the door and places a sign in the door, 'I will return at 13:00.'

"Lieutenant Pfisterer, I hear the plan is in place to set up Hoffmann."

"Yes Klaus, but we will clear him, the ultimate catch is Webber and Keitel. They must be stopped. Hans says you have been briefed on our plan."

"Yes sir, Ingrid has been as well."

"Good. Ingrid, we have papers, false identity papers that need to be hidden in Lieutenant Webber's room to set him up as a spy. We need to do this quickly."

"My cousin Theresa is the housekeeper for the officer's barracks. She routinely works with us; the Underground I mean. She will do it."

"Good, I have this message that needs to be included."

"It will happen tomorrow lieutenant."

"Have her place the papers in the bed slats, under the bed."

"Yes Herr Karl. She will leave a garment bag with tissue in it on your door when completed."

"Klaus, things are ramping up here. I am working on a plan to depart quickly if I need to, or should I say escape. Ingrid, when I feel the time has come, I will place a note in the garment bag for Klaus."

"Understood Herr Karl."

"If I feel it is happening quickly, I will attempt to call you directly Klaus, the message will be, 'have you found my pen?' I will have two plans in place. Plan A, Ingrid, you will have an independent person ready, a villager, one you trust, to take me back to Aurich. I am not sure of a date yet. I feel soon though. I need to work that out."

"I can arrange that, not to worry sir."

"Plan B will be with you Klaus. If I need to exit quickly, I will call you; we will meet behind my barracks."

"Understood."

December 15, Karl hears of the first communication from the Allies. Webber enters Karl's office. "Lieutenant, our intelligence has picked up radio communications from British command alerting the Allies of the Invasion, Operation Deep Sea. This is the message. 'We have received information from our trusted source inside the Army Group North the Germans are planning an offensive from the Atlantic Ocean, more to follow.' Hoffmann is our spy; this confirms it. We need to get him, take him into custody and question him."

"Not so fast lieutenant, was this all of the message?"

"Yes, Lieutenant Pfisterer."

"We need more information, more of the facts we planted with him. We will wait a few days."

December 23, Webber storms into Karl's office. Hoffmann is not in the building. "Lieutenant, we have him, we have Hoffmann. We just picked up a second communication from London. This is the message. 'The Luftwaffe and Kriegsmarine have been assembling a fleet of destroyers and aircraft carriers in the Mediterranean, from South Europe and the north coast of Africa. This activity has been confirmed by the Royal Navy destroyer HMS Wallace stationed in the Mediterranean; by her First Lieutenant Philip Mountbatten. This attack, code name Deep Sea, will be launched concurrent with the German's North Cape attack on December 27. We have contacted the U.S. Atlantic Naval Command for reinforcements. They are deploying a convoy of aircraft carriers and destroyers from the North Atlantic and Norfolk Navan Station in the U.S. We will deploy British destroyers to rendezvous with them. More to follow.' We have him lieutenant, the message is word for word what we gave Hoffmann."

Karl smiles, "Yes, Lieutenant Webber, it appears so. We need to take this information to Captain Straughen."

The two go to see Captain Straughen. They knock on his door.

"Come in lieutenants, I have been expecting you."

"Herr captain."

"Yes, Lieutenant Pfisterer."

"We have confirmed Hoffmann is the spy, Berlin has received two radio communications, verbatim to the false information we gave Hoffmann."

"Yes, lieutenant, I just received confirmation as well. Take him into custody, but do not interrogate him, do not tell him anything, no one talks with him. Commandant Kuchler wants the SS to do the interrogation, specifically SS Major General Keitel. He will be here in a week or so. Major General Keitel has been called to the Russian Front to deal with a serious matter there."

"Yes, Herr captain."

Lieutenants Pfisterer and Webber summon the Camps SS soldiers. They enter Hoffmann's office; Webber leads the way. Hoffmann jumps up, "What is going on?"

"Take him away," screams Webber.

Hoffmann is taken into custody. He is screaming as he is taken away. "I demand to know what this is about, what is going on?"

Webber looks at Karl, "Good work lieutenant."

Karl thinks to himself; *it is only the beginning for you my friend.*

Karl returns to his room that evening and finds the garment bag, with the tissue. Ingrid's cousin Theresa has planted the documents in Webber's room. The stage is set. It is Christmas Eve tomorrow, it's snowing. Karl is thinking of Katarina, *I wish I could be with my Love; it will be soon.* Karl goes to sleep.

Christmas day comes and goes, no emotions with the Germans, just another day in the war. Form his prison cell, Sergeant Hoffmann demands attention. He has been pleading to speak with Commandant Kuchler or Captain Straughen. He is being ignored. Nothing else has been said about Hoffmann, they are waiting for Wilhelm. Karl goes about his business. December 28, Wilhelm arrives. Lieutenants Pfisterer and Webber are summoned to Captain Straughen's office. As they enter Karl gets his first face to face look at Wilhelm. No introductions today. Karl stays strong. *Your day is coming you monster,* Karl says to himself. Due the serious nature of this, Commandant Kuchler; Reichsfuhrer Heinrich Himmler, the SS Commander of Waffen SS & Commander of Gestapo; Herman Goring, the Commander/Chief of Luftwaffe Airforce, Hitler's successor, and three other SS officers are present.

"Have a seat," Straughen says.

Wilhelm begins, he looks straight at Karl.

"I have heard and know a lot about you Lieutenant Pfisterer. In a short time here at Army Group North Strategic Command you have done very well. Your plan for Hoffmann was very well orchestrated. You will have a great future with the SS."

"Thank you, Herr Major General Keitel." Karl says to himself; *you will wish you would have gotten to know me better.*

"Let's get to business. Captain where do you have this Hoffmann fellow?"

"We have him in our prison, under twenty-four-hour guard. I have an interrogation room ready at the prison Herr Keitel."

"Take me to him, I want to see this traitor."

The group arrives at the integration room, Hoffmann is handcuffed to the table, his legs chained to the chair. Hoffmann immediately demands to know why he has been taken into custody, and is struggling in the chair, trying to get up. Two of the SS guards restrain him.

Wilhelm walks around Hoffmann and stops in front him. He looks at Hoffmann with a bone chilling, cold and evil stare. Hoffmann begins to speak. "Shut up, shut up you traitor."

"Traitor, what do you mean?" screams Hoffmann as he struggles to get up.

"Shut up, I said. You are a spy, a traitor. We have evidence you have been providing our secrets to the Allies." Again, Hoffmann becomes irate.

"That is a lie, that is not true, who told you this. I am loyal to Hitler and the Third Reich." Wilhelm motions to one of the guards. The guard strikes Hoffmann with the butt of his rifle, Hoffmann slouches onto the table. Karl cringes. The guards set him back up in his chair.

"I will not tell you again to be quiet. Tell me who your contacts are, tell me everything you have told the enemy." Hoffmann begins his screaming again, his denial to these accusations.

"I am not a traitor; I do not know what you are talking about." The guard strikes him again, this time rendering Hoffmann unconscious.

"Leave this worthless traitor lie, I will be back tomorrow. We have ways to make him talk."

A staff sergeant enters the room, "Herr Captain Straughen, I have an urgent message for you." He reads the message. "Gentlemen, come to my office, we need to talk." At his office, the captain shares the message with the group. "As you know, our so-called surprise attack, the Battle of North Cape began on December 27, yesterday. The Allies knew of this surprise Battle, they were waiting for us. Coincidently, the day before, our battlecruiser Scharnhorst came under attack and was sunk by the Royal Navy's battleship HMS Duke of York. Also, yesterday, a heavy bomber from Czechoslovakia's Coastal Command attacked our cargo ship Alsterufer. It scored five hits on the Alsterufer and the ship immediately caught fire. She sank yesterday afternoon."

"What about the false Atlantic Invasion we set up, the Deep-Sea mission that Hoffmann communicated to the Allies?" asks Karl. The captain goes on to read the message.

"As our intelligence confirmed, it appears none of the Allied ships were fully redeployed from the North Sea to join with the U.S. Navy's Atlantic Fleet to intercept our false mission. The Navy fleet never showed for the Deep Sea mission, they were deployed to reinforce the Allies in the North Sea."

Karl knows this is true. To convince the Germans the Allies did in fact believe in Operation Deep Sea, the Allies did redeploy some ships toward the Atlantic, but were called back once the bait was in play. The U.S. Naval Command also directed their ships toward the site of Operation Deep Sea; but had to travel in the direction to arrive at the North Sea for reinforcement. The plan worked perfectly for the Allies.

Wilhelm slams his fist on the table, "Hoffmann is behind this; we need to find out what he has told the Allies." He storms out of the room.

December 29, Karl knows he must get things in place quickly to depart. 1944 is almost upon him. Before meeting with the group, Wilhelm meets privately with Captain Straughen and Commandant Kuchler. "I want all of the barracks searched, especially anyone who has arrived in the last six months. Something is going on here, I know it."

"Yes sir," they both say.

Karl, Webber, Straughen, Kuchler, and Wilhelm arrive at the interrogation room, another day of intense interrogation by Wilhelm. Hoffmann stands firm in his denials. The next two days bring no change in Hoffmann's position. "Herr Keitel, please believe me, I am not the only person here that knows our secrets. Lieutenant Pfisterer and Lieutenant Webber do as well." Wilhelm pauses a minute and retains that piece of information.

"I will be back tomorrow Hoffmann; we will continue this fun." Wilhelm stands and leaves the room, slamming the door behind him.

January 1, Wilhelm meets again with the commandant and captain. "I want to know who recently transferred here. I want to interrogate them myself." One by one Wilhelm eliminates suspects, including Karl. Karl stood strong and convincing of his German past, his life in the German Army during a one-hour intense interrogation. His paper trail developed by Hans and Gerhardt holds up. Karl recalls Wilhelm's jaw clicking during his interrogation. Karl remembers Katarina telling him about Wilhelm clicking his jaw when he is agitated.

Wilhelm does not interrogate Webber which raises suspicions from Captain Straughen. Straughen mentions this concern to Commandant Kuchler. Kuchler ensures Straughen he has nothing to be concerned about. "Captain, Webber is Major General Keitel's protégé." Wilhelm continues to become further frustrated but vows he will find and kill the spy. January 2, the interrogation continues, and the torture begins again. Wilhelm sits across from Hoffmann and looks into his beaten face.

"Tell me who your contacts are, tell me what all you have told the enemy." Hoffmann lays helpless from his beatings. Wilhelm takes a pair of pliers from his jacket and grabs Hoffmann's hand. The SS soldiers hold Hoffmann's arms down. "Hold his hands also," bellows Wilhelm. The two SS soldiers firmly hold Hoffmann to the table as he tries to pull back. Wilhelm opens a pocketknife. He grasps Hoffmann's right hand. He slides the knife under Hoffmann's index fingernail. Hoffmann shrieks. Wilhelm grabs the fingernail with the pliers and tears off his fingernail. Hoffmann screams with excruciating pain, a scream like Karl has never heard. Tears of pain are pouring from Hoffmann's eyes. "Tell me, tell me who your contacts are!" Hoffmann continues his denial; Wilhelm continues the torture. One by one Wilhelm pries up Hoffmann's nails with his knife, and one by one he tears off Hoffmann's fingernails until Hoffmann passes out. "He will talk, trust me." Karl feels for Hoffmann, as a German soldier he was doing his job here at the Camp, but he is a German soldier, and aligned to Hitler. Wilhelm is a ruthless monster.

Two days pass, Hoffmann does not disclose any information, because he has none to disclose. He is near dead from the days of continued torture. Wilhelm knows if he dies, the SS will never get any information. January 4, Captain Straughen calls Karl and Webber to his office. As they enter Karl sees the Commandant, two SS Soldiers, and Wilhelm are present. Karl has a feeling, perhaps this is the day Webber falls.

Captain Straughen is pacing back and forth. "Gentlemen have a seat. We have another unfortunate development. Operation Steinbock has failed. The British established a new series of air defenses of anti-aircraft guns and fighter aircraft, to intercept the Luftwaffe's planes before they reached London. They used the same air defense systems to intercept our V-1 bombs before they reached their targets. As an offensive part of their campaign, concurrent attacks were made on our missile launch sites, our liquid propellant fuel factories, our underground fuel storage depots, and our missile plants. These were underground sites." Karl hears Wilhelm's jaw clicking. "The Allies had our plan, they had our plants and factory locations, and they knew we were coming, again!" He slams his fist on the table with such force he cracks the wood. You know the problem I have with this gentlemen, you two are the only ones who knew of this mission. It was your idea to keep this from Hoffmann."

Webber jumps up and in true fashion of Wilhelm's protégée, he flips the table over and immediately accuses Karl. Karl, in keeping his composure, slowly stands up.

"You are wrong Lieutenant Webber, who says you are not the spy."

Captain Straughen is beginning to have his own suspicions. In a surprise move he stands and asks Wilhelm, "Why did you not interrogate Webber, you said you interrogated all recent transfers."

"Webber is one of mine," Wilhelm says in a very agitated voice, his jaw is clicking.

"Interrogate him," screams Reichsfuhrer Heinrich Himmler. In his defense, knowing the answer, Karl asks a question to Captain Straughen.

"Herr Captain, I know the SS conducted room searches, what did the searches uncover?"

The captain turns to Wilhelm, "Herr Major General, please answer the lieutenant's question."

In Wilhelm's normal loss of composure and fit of rage, he screams, "Webber is one of mine!"

"Search his room, now, search Pfisterer's again also," screams Reichsfuhrer Heinrich Himmler. Two SS Soldiers depart to Webber's room.

"That is not necessary," Herr Himmler, he can be trusted," screams Wilhelm.

"Shut up," screams Himmler.

Karl knows this is his time. He also knows nothing will be found in his room. A few hours pass. The SS Soldiers return, with envelopes. Webber is intently observing. They take them directly to the senior officers; Straughen, Wilhelm, Kuchler, Himmler, and Goring, at a table in the front of the room.

"You two stay where you are," says Captain Straughen, directing his order to Karl and Webber. Webber begins pacing while

Karl maintains his composure. Karl can see them reviewing the documents, and sees Wilhelm getting agitated. Fifteen minutes pass; seems like an eternity though. Karl sees Wilhelm getting further agitated by the minute. The officers return to Karl and Webber. Webber has a smirk on his face as he stares at Karl. He knows nothing could have been found in his room.

"Sit down Webber," Wilhelm screams. "Do not say a word." The SS Soldiers force Webber into a chair. Webber is astonished. Wilhelm begins laying down information. Webber scans the documents with his eyes. Wilhelm gathers himself; his jaw begins clicking again. In a somewhat calming voice, "Lieutenant Webber, or shall I call you Heinz Fischer? How do you explain this birth certificate, how do you explain this address where you lived in London?"

Webber immediately jumps up and cuts him off, "They are lies."

"Shut up and sit down." The SS Soldiers restrain him and gags his mouth. Webber now struggles more. "How do you explain these pictures of you and your family, your service records in the British Army? And lastly Herr Fischer, how do you explain this message we found, one you were preparing to send to your Allied friends." Karl sees a sort of pleasure in Wilhelm as he is reading Webber's demise. 'The German Army is planning the invasion of Anzio. It will be put in motion January 30. The German Army will send additional forces to invade Gustav to surround the area and push the Allies back to the southern beachhead. The Luftwaffe will be providing air support.' How do you explain any of this Herr Fischer?" In a burst, Webber tries to stand, but before he can get a word from his mouth, Wilhelm draws his luger and shoots him between the eyes. Webber falls to the floor. Wilhelm walks over him, and spits on him. Karl is taken back, and realizes he has blood spatter on his face and uniform. As cavalier and brutal Wilhelm is, actions like this with no emotion, just taking care of business immediately, regardless with whom, keeps him in good standings within the SS.

Wilhelm turns to Karl, "Lieutenant Pfisterer, do not take offense for me not trusting you, I do not trust anyone. I had to find the truth. I will say I had suspicions of you." He stares at Karl, a cold stare. "You are dismissed." Karl retires to his room, it is ransacked. He immediately goes to the air vent; his journal and Katarina's letters are there. As Karl straightens his room, he begins to plan for his departure from Neuengamme. *I need to send Hans and Gerhardt a note. I heard Straughen say the German fuel factories were bombed, I hope Gerhardt is ok.*

A summary of results from Karl's second wave of intelligence.

'Classified Intelligence; Covert Mission 5 & 6, Battle of North Cape and Mission Scharnhorst: *From the intelligence gathered by Karl, the Allies preempted the planned German attack of December 27 1943. Beginning the week before Christmas, the Allies moved additional assets into the North Atlantic. On December 23, aircraft from the U.S. Navy escort carrier USS Card sighted a suspected runner. Other air reconnaissance reported a flotilla of German destroyers, led by GRT Osorno, escorting another merchant fleet east from France. The HMS Gambia, HMS Glasgow, and the HMS Enterprise were in position and formed a cordon to intercept the flotilla. Allied aircraft attacked the flotilla and reported a direct hit on the GRT Osorno. The light cruiser HMS Penelope, minelayer HMS Ariadne and four Free French destroyers were dispatched and joined the patrol to intercept other German runners. The RAF Coastal Command aircraft were on standby for support.*

On December 26, off Norway's North Cape, the German battlecruiser Scharnhorst, on an operation to attack Arctic Convoys of war materiel from the Western Allies to the Soviet Union, was brought to battle and sunk by the Royal Navy's battleship HMS Duke of York along with cruisers and destroyers including an onslaught from the HMS Stord of the exiled Royal Norwegian Navy. The results of Karl's intelligence paid huge dividends. Britain believes this battle became the turning point in the war between Britain and Germany, and solidified a massive strategic advantage held by the British.

On December 27 a heavy bomber from Czechoslovakia's Coastal Command spotted the cargo ship Alsterufer. The Liberator attacked the cargo ship with semi-armor piercing rocket projectiles, scoring five hits. The

Liberator also dropped a five-hundred-pound bomb which hit the ship aft of her funnel. The ship immediately caught fire. The Alsterufer defended herself with anti-aircraft fire and rockets but sank on the afternoon of December 28.

The Allied Intel learned the Kriegsmarine destroyers and torpedo boats were sent to meet and escort Alsterufer in an operation code named Bernau. The Glasgow and Enterprise were redirected to intercept them. Guided by shadowing aircraft, the Allied cruisers intercepted eight Kriegmarine destroyers early in the afternoon of December 28 and exchanged fire with them. Despite accurate German gunfire and torpedoes, effective German evading action and an attack with guided bombs by a Luftwaffe aircraft, the Royal Navy's ships maintained their advantages. The Battles of North Cape failed the Germans. As a result of Karl's Intel of the Battle of North Cape, and the German's fake plan Code Name Deep Sea, to invade Southern Europe from the Atlantic, the Allies did not take their focus from the North Atlantic campaign. It did not distract them. The false communications, sent by the Allies acknowledging the Germans were planning the Deep Sea invasion, and intercepted by Berlin, set the Nazis up for failure as well.

Classified Intelligence; Covert Mission 7, Operation Steinbock: *Only Karl and Webber knew this, Hoffmann did not. The British bombing campaign against Berlin continued and proved effective. The Luftwaffe had to retain forces to combat those attacks and could never fully engage in Operation Steinbock. Steinbock later became known as the Baby Blitz by the Allies, thanks to Karl's work. The use of Luftwaffe aircraft in Steinbock was called off when the V-1 rockets became available for the retribution attacks and after the loss of three hundred twenty-nine Luftwaffe bombers. From Karl's Intel, the Allies were well prepared for the so-called invasion. Another key factor, the lack of night flying experience of the Luftwaffe, contributed to the losses.*

Eventually, the Luftwaffe's revenge attacks gave way to attempts to disrupt preparations for the impending Allied invasion of France. The British bombing campaign against Berlin and the effort spent for Steinbock had worn down the offensive power of the Luftwaffe to the extent it could not mount any significant counterattacks. Karl's Intel provided the Allies with an offensive plan against Operation Steinbock, rather than a defensive one. As part of operations against the V-1, the British operated an arrangement of air defenses, including anti-aircraft guns and fighter aircraft, to intercept the V-1 bombs before they reached their targets, while the launch sites and underground storage depots became targets for Allied attacks, including strategic bombing of the V-2 plants and liquid fuel plants.

This coincided with the ongoing Battle of Berlin which began in November 1943. That began with a series of attacks on Berlin by RAF Bomber Command along with raids on other German cities to keep German defenses dispersed. The new strategy, from Karl's Intel, was to use this campaign to destroy the Germans V-Weapons plants, which were underground locations. The Allies would strategically continue their bombing campaign against Berlin. The British bombing campaign was chiefly waged by night so large numbers of heavy bombers could use the cover of darkness. Karl provided the Allies the plant locations, launch sites, and launch dates. Gerhardt provided the fuel plant locations, which were also underground. These sites were bombed and severely damaged, greatly reducing the Luftwaffe's ability for missile attacks.

The Allies continued the campaign with the Big Week Plan. During the Big Week bombing campaign of late February 1944, the Eighth Army Air Force flew bombing missions from bases in Britain and Southern Italy, carrying out raids against the German aviation industry throughout Europe. To bolster this offensive, the U.S. changed its policy and required escorting American fighters to remain with the bombers at all times.

The American fighter pilots assigned to fly the bomber defense missions were ordered to fly far ahead of the P51 bombers, in combat box formations for air supremacy mode, literally clearing the skies of any Luftwaffe fighter opposition heading towards the target. This strategy fatally disabled the Luftwaffe's twin-engine Zerstörergeschwader heavy fighter wings and their replacement, the single-engine Sturmgruppen of heavily armed Fw 190As, clearing each wave of Allied bomber destroyers for their turn in Germany's skies throughout most of 1944. This game-changing strategy, especially after the bombers had hit their targets, the U.S. Army Air Force's fighters were then free to strafe German airfields and transports while returning to base, contributing significantly to the achievement of air superiority by Allied air forces over Europe.'

THE HUNT

Karl sits at his table. 'Hans and Gerhardt, this will be my last note to you from Neuengamme. Today, our plan was partly accomplished. Webber is dead. Wilhelm killed him, shot him in front of me and the SS Officers. Wilhelm is still in the picture though. I am preparing my departure. My preference is Plan A. I will have Ingrid set up an independent person, a villager, one she trusts, to bring me back to Aurich. I am not sure of a date yet. I need to work that out. Plan B will be with Klaus, if I need to exit quickly, I have mentioned this to him. We have a plan in place, but I want to keep him clear if possible. Gerhardt, when Webber was confronted, I heard Captain Straughen say the German fuel factories were bombed, I hope you are okay. I have a note for Katarina as well, please give it to her.'

'My dearest sweet Katarina. It is January 4. My mission here is finished. Wilhelm scathed the setup, but his man, Webber, is dead. I am planning my return to you. I do not know what day exactly; I need to plan it right. I want to be with you on my birthday for certain, to spend that day with you, to hold you and love you. Our anniversary is also approaching. I first saw you when you found me in the woods, January 31. The best day of my life. I remember gazing into your eyes and you helping me.'

Karl seals the notes in the garment bag along with a shirt, and a note, 'Please clean and press quickly,' and places it on his door. He goes to bed. Karl knows Ingrid will understand this note needs to get to Hans quickly. He is anxious to see Katarina, thinking of the very minute he sees her, the very minute he holds her again in his arms. He falls asleep.

The next morning the garment bag is gone. Karl arrives at his office. Sergeant Hoffmann is at his desk, a beaten man. His fingers are bandaged and taped from the torture, he has many cuts and bruises on his head. Karl is proud of Hoffmann, in a sense, that he stood strong.

"Sergeant," Hoffmann looks up at Karl. "I am glad you were not the spy; I have always liked you and could not believe it when Webber brought this falsehood to Command."

"Thank you, lieutenant, I heard Webber was confronted and killed. Things are changing here. Commandant Küchler and Captain Straughen were relieved of their command this morning, heads are going to roll. Major General Keitel is in command, for now. That man is terrible." Karl places his hand on Hoffmann's shoulder. Karl knows the time has come.

Karl no sooner sits down at his desk, his phone rings. It is Wilhelm. "Lieutenant come to my office at 13:00." Karl gets that lump in his throat again.

Karl calls for Sergeant Schmidt. "Fraulein, this is Lieutenant Pfisterer, will you have Sergeant Schmidt call me?"

"Yes, Herr Lieutenant." Twenty minutes pass, Karl's phone rings, it is Klaus.

"Sergeant, can you talk?"

"Yes sir."

"Tonight, is the night. I want to keep you clear of this. Will you get word to Ingrid, see if she can have a driver ready tonight, we will plan on 22:00? I will come to her shop."

"Yes Karl; if she can I will have her place your garment bag on the door. The only thing in it will be a piece of tissue paper."

"Perfect, thank you Klaus."

"One more thing Karl, I have heard what has happened to Sergeant Hoffmann."

"Yes Klaus, he has been cleared. I have a meeting with Keitel this afternoon, not sure what he wants. Stay safe Klaus and thank you for all you have done. Perhaps, when this war is over, we can have a beer together."

"I would like that Karl, Godspeed."

Precisely at 13:00, Karl arrives at Wilhelm's office. Karl knocks on the door. "Enter. Have a seat lieutenant. Lieutenant Pfisterer, I want you to meet Captain Wagoner, he is SS. I have relieved Commandant Kuchler and Captain Straughen of their command today. They are being reassigned to the Russian front. I want you to stay here at Neuengamme. You will report to Captain Wagoner."

"Yes sir, Herr Keitel."

"I want you to continue your strategic planning for our campaign, only now you will oversee the Russian Front operations as well. Captain Wagoner will fill you in, that is all lieutenant."

Karl stands, "Heil Hitler." Karl spends the afternoon, into early evening with Wagoner. The end of a long day Wagoner invites Karl to dinner, at the Camp's dining hall for officers. Karl, knowing tonight is the night he leaves is concerned with time. He agrees to go, to not raise suspicion.

They arrive at the dining hall at 19:30, the two are seated at a table. "Lieutenant Pfisterer, I am told you have done a wonderful job here."

"Thank you, sir."

They order dinner and have small talk. Karl tells him of his career in the German Army. At the end of dinner, Wagoner asks Karl, "Tell me more about yourself, where did you grow up?" It's going on 20:30, Karl looks at his watch, and he is anxious to get back to his room to see if Ingrid can help him leave tonight.

"I was born in Oldenburg, not far from here. My parent's, Elsa, and Fritz were simple people. My father was a machine builder in Wilhelmshaven."

"Tell me more lieutenant."

"I schooled at the Oldenburg Volksschule and the Oldenburg Mittelschule six-year middle school. I then enlisted in the Army, sir."

"Very good lieutenant. It is getting late. I will see you in the morning." The two stand up, Karl gets his coat on.

"Excuse me sir." Karl turns to see a young officer, a Second Lieutenant.

"My name is Becker, Second Lieutenant Becker. I could not help to overhear you. I heard you say you are from Oldenburg."

"Yes, lieutenant, that's correct. Good night lieutenant." Karl did not want to get into a conversation about Oldenburg. Karl and Captain Wagoner leave the dining hall.

It is 21:15, Karl returns to his room, the garment bag is on the door, with a single piece of tissue inside. *It is time, and perfect timing. The young lieutenant compromised my alias,* he says to himself. Karl knows it's a matter of hours, if that, that his cover will be exposed. Karl reaches in his pocket, pulls out his mother's locket and Katarina's butterfly pin. *You protected me tonight ladies, thank you both.* Karl gets his journal and Katarina's letters from the air vent, gathers his personal things, and leaves. It is a cold night as he walks to Ingrid's shop. Karl walks through the gate, the guard salutes, and says nothing. As he approaches Ingrid's shop, he sees a car on the side street next to the shop. It's windy, the snow is lightly drifting across the cold pavement. He hears the motor running; the lights are off. He approaches the car; the lights blink once. The window rolls down. Karl sees a woman.

"Herr Karl?"

"Yes."

"Ingrid sent me, get in. My name is Gerda. I am here to take you to Aurich." As they drive off, Karl turns and looks out the back window, thankful to finally leave. "Herr Karl, I am to tell you Ms. Katarina is expecting you. She will be at the barn."

Karl smiles, "Thank you, Gerda."

"Herr Karl, I am going to take back roads, so we are not conspicuous. It will take us about three hours."

I will be with my true love in three hours.

They finally arrive at the farm, January 6, it's nearly one o'clock in the morning. Karl sees a light in the farmhouse, in Anna's room. "Gerda, drive up that road please." Karl points to the dirt road leading to the small barn. It is a clear night. As they approach the barn, Karl can see a stream of smoke rising from the chimney. *Katarina has a fire going, how romantic,* he says to himself. Karl gets out of the car and smells the wood smoke in the air, "Thank you, Gerda." Karl enters the barn. He knocks three times, as Katarina always did. He can see the light of a candle burning from the cellar, between the floorboards. He sees the opening is uncovered. "Katarina my Love, I am here for you."

Katarina's voice from below, "Come to me my Love, and do not ever leave me." Karl first sees a bouquet of fresh flowers, red roses, and white lilies. He then turns to see Katarina, lying in the bed, partially covered with a sheet, but unclothed. Karl embraces Katarina, they passionately kiss.

"My dearest Katarina, I missed you so much."

Katarina looking intensely into Karl's eyes gently whispers, "As did I my Love. I dreamed of this day since you have been gone."

"I had you in my heart everyday Katarina. I missed you so, every minute of every day. I missed your blue eyes, and your lovely smile. Your smile is one of a kind, so unique. I always kept your butterfly pin with me. I have your lily petal with your lipstick kiss in my wallet. I am back now Katarina, and I will never leave you."

Katarina cups her hands around Karl's face, "Karl, I do not want this night to ever end, I do not want our life together to ever end." Katarina takes Karl's dog tags off her neck and places them around Karl's neck. "These are yours I believe. I have never taken them off until now." They make endless love into the early morning and fall asleep in each other's arms. They awake in each other's arms, gazing into each other's eyes.

That morning at Army Group North, the young Lieutenant Becker requests to see Captain Wagoner. "What can I do for you lieutenant?"

"Herr Captain, the man you were with last night at the dining hall."

"Yes, he was Lieutenant Pfisterer."

"Well sir, you recall I told him I overheard him saying he was from Oldenburg."

"That's correct lieutenant, I do remember."

"I need to tell you sir, with what has happened here at the Camp with treason recently, Lieutenant Pfisterer did not live in Oldenburg."

"What!" Wagoner jumps out of his chair.

"I am from Oldenburg. There was only one family named Pfisterer, and they had no children."

"Come with me lieutenant." Wagoner tells his sergeant to call Major General Keitel and meet him at the officer's barracks. Wagoner takes two SS guards with him. Wilhelm arrives outside the barracks the same time as Wagoner.

"What is going on captain?"

"It is Pfisterer, he is the spy."

"What do you mean captain?"

"He lied to us; Lieutenant Becker lived in the town Pfisterer said he lived in. His so-called parents never had children." They storm into barracks, and break Karl's door open only to find an empty room.

"Where is Pfisterer? Find him captain. Search his office, search the Base."

"Yes Herr Keitel."

"I want that bastard found. He played us, he set Webber up for the fall. Only a small group knew about the Hoffmann plan. Find him!" Wilhelm returns to his office. He begins thinking, *how was this able to happen, and how were the details intertwined in our systems? We even checked his personal credentials, birth records, everything. Someone else is behind this, someone in the German Army or Third Reich who has access to manipulate our records.* Wilhelm receives a phone call from Berlin.

"Herr Major General Keitel."

"Yes, this is."

"I am Captain Richter of the SS."

"Yes, I know who you are captain."

"I regret to inform you of bad news."

"What is it captain?"

"It is your father. We believe he was killed in the Allied bombing mission on January 4. We have searched the rubble and have not found any recognizable remains." Wilhelm in his cold, unemotional way, hangs the phone up. *I do not believe this; this is not another coincidence. Ha! I never trusted my father; he has access to confidential records for his work. He is behind this treason. I always believed the American pilot was hiding in Aurich, now I believe my father, mother, and sister were behind it.*

Captain Wagoner enters Wilhelm's office, "Herr Keitel, we have searched his office, the Base, and found nothing. The guard at the main gate told me he saw Pfisterer walk through the gate last evening, around 21:40. He simply walked away. He is gone." Wilhelm slams his fist on the desk.

"Captain; get two platoons ready. We are going to Aurich."

"When Herr Keitel?"

"Now," shouts Wilhelm.

The convoy leaves just before noon; and arrives in Aurich just after three in the afternoon.

THE CAPTURE

Mid-afternoon of January 6, Hans hears trucks rumbling toward the village. He looks and sees a large German convoy coming and is immediately alarmed. *Something is going on;* he says to himself. He then sees Wilhelm in the lead staff car. *I must warn Gerhardt, Anna, Katarina, and Karl. I must warn them now.*

Wilhelm's convoy stops in the center of town. Wilhelm yells to his troops, "The American pilot is here, find him." He motions for one platoon to go one way, he takes the other with him, toward the farm. Katarina was in the market earlier buying food for Karl. Hans knows she is at the barn. He needs to get there quickly. Not being able to take the direct route, he takes his motorcycle, with a sidecar, and heads through the woods to the barn.

Wilhelm bursts into the farmhouse and sees Gerhardt. "Father, what are you doing here, I was told you were killed in the bombing of your factory."

Gerhardt jumps up and begins to yell at Wilhelm, "I escaped the explosions and wanted to be with Anna and Katarina." Wilhelm cuts him off.

"You are a liar and a traitor." Anna begins crying uncontrollably. She knows Katarina and Karl are at the barn, but how can she warn them? "Shut up Mother, stop your crying!" Wilhelm's jaw is clicking. The interrogation continues. "Where is Katarina?"

"Get out of my house Wilhelm," screams Gerhardt.

"Shut up, I said. Where is Katarina? Every time I come here; she is gone. The American pilot is here. She is helping him, along with you. I will find them." Wilhelm hits Gerhardt on the side of his head with his luger. Gerhardt falls to the floor. Anna immediately cradles him.

Anna looks up at Wilhelm, "Get out Wilhelm."

Wilhelm turns to two SS Soldiers, "Stay here with them." He goes outside to the other troops. He notices the smell of wood burning. He looks up the trail toward the barn and sees the trail of smoke rising from the small barn. *That should not be, that barn has been abandoned for years.* He then remembers the fresh flower petal he saw on the barn floor; he remembers he was curious about that. Wilhelm gets in his staff car and heads toward the barn with one halftrack following. The sun is beginning to set.

Wilhelm hurriedly jumps from his staff car before it stops screaming to his troops, "Surround the barn." Wilhelm enters the barn; he can see candlelight between the floorboards. *I have the American*, he says to himself; *I finally have him.* With his flashlight he notices an opening in the floorboards. Wilhelm has a flashback, *I had him months ago, he was right here beneath my feet.* In frustration, he kicks a bucket to the back of the barn. He orders his troops to prepare their guns. Wilhelm jumps down to the cellar and finds it empty. He sees the bed, and a German uniform, a lieutenant's uniform with the name tag Karl Pfisterer. Frustrated he begins kicking and throwing things. He then sees a journal. He opens it and finds detailed notes of the activities and missions from Army Group North, dates, coordinates, all classified information. The Underground Movement is mentioned as well. Karl is now confirmed as the spy. In a rage, he exits the cellar and notices a reflection on the floor. He reaches down and picks up a set of dog tags. Karl Schellenberg; U.S. Army Air Force, 19555773, T13 17A; Joseph / Hazel Schellenberg; Milwaukee

WI, 1939; Eighth Army Air Force. In Karl's haste to leave, his dog tags got caught on the ladder, and the chain broke.

Ten minutes earlier, Hans arrived at the barn and calls for Katarina. "Katarina, it is Hans, come quickly." Karl and Katarina appear at the door. "Katarina, Karl, you must come with me quickly, Wilhelm is here with two platoons. He is searching the town for you Karl. I saw him heading to the farmhouse. I have never seen him so furious and committed."

"Hans, what are you saying?" asks Karl.

"We must go and hide; Wilhelm will find you otherwise. Come, we must go."

"But where?" asks Katarina. It is January and gets dark early.

"I need to get a few things from the cellar. Katarina, get in, I will be right back."

"We do not have time Karl, get in," says Hans.

"I will only be a minute." Karl quickly gets his mother's locket, Katarina's butterfly pin, the letters Katarina wrote to him, his wallet, and his survival kit. They leave through the woods.

"Where are we going?" asks Katarina.

"I will take you to Saint Ludger Church, you can hide in the bell tower." As they approach the village, Hans stops his motorcycle. "We will need to walk from here. Come with me." The town is dark. The villages keep all lights off at night so Allied bombers cannot see the towns and cities.

Hans looks up and down the street. He can see the soldiers about one hundred meters away, at both ends of the streets. They are going in and out of the houses, ransacking them as they go. "It looks clear, quick, follow me across the road, we will get you in the church." Hans gets blankets from the vestibule. "Take these, it will be cold in the tower." Karl and Katarina climb to the tower. "I will be back when the Germans leave, stay safe you two."

Karl and Katarina hear the soldiers on the street below. They peer through the louvers and can see the soldiers going house to house. They hear the soldiers screaming at the people, they can hear the women of the village crying, screaming, and the men arguing with soldiers. They tightly hold each other. The soldiers are getting closer. Katarina and Karl hear them enter the church.

"Stay quiet my Love," Karl holds Katarina tighter. They can hear the soldiers raffling through the pews.

One of the soldiers says, "There is no one here." Katarina and Karl breathe a sigh of relief. Still startled, they hear one of the soldiers say, "This is what I think of this building." Suddenly a burst of gunfire erupts as a soldier pellets the altar with bullets. They leave. Katarina, shaking and scared, holds Karl.

Wilhelm continues to search the stone barn, then the main barn. It is nearly midnight. Saying nothing Wilhelm storms from the barn with Karl's dog tags and his German uniform in hand and drives back to the farmhouse. He orders the guards to take Anna and Gerhardt to the center of town. They enter the village, Anna is crying. Karl and Katarina hear the commotion and look out of the bell tower louvers. On a loudspeaker, Wilhelm announces to the town, "Everyone outside." A few minutes pass. "I said everyone outside," he fires his luger into the air. "I told you before what would happen to traitors." A few villagers venture out.

Hans comes to his porch, and sees Anna and Gerhardt, and thinks to himself, *oh my God, he is going to kill them.* The flashback of Wilhelm killing the Mullers in this very street races through Hans's mind.

"Get to your knees traitors," screams Wilhelm. The church bells strike midnight. Katarina and Karl, cover their ears. They can see from the headlights of the staff car; it is Anna and Gerhardt. Katarina begins to scream and cry. Katarina is shaking frantically. Karl helps her stay quiet as now the bells are still.

"Shh, they will find us."

The SS Soldiers force Gerhardt and Anna to their knees. Wilhelm walks in front of them, "Where is Katarina and the American pilot?" he screams. Anna and Gerhardt remain silent. Gerhardt stares into Wilhelm's eyes, Anna to the ground. Wilhelm holds Karl's uniform in front of them. "I found this in the stone barn, where is Katarina and the American pilot?" he screams again, this time louder. "You have been hiding him!"

Anna now stares at Wilhelm, "You are too late, you missed them you stupid fool, they fled last night, they are in France by now."

"You traitors do not deserve prison." Wilhelm looks directly into Gerhardt's eyes and shoots him in the head. He immediately turns to his mother and does the same. He then spits on them. Their lifeless bodies lay in the middle of the road. Katarina passes out. Hans is in disbelief. Wilhelm orders two soldiers to stand guard at the farmhouse, gets into his staff car and drives off.

Karl sees the soldiers drive off, and he can see Hans and other villagers run to Anna and Gerhardt. Katarina regains consciousness and screams, "Oh my God Karl, what just happened." As she stands to leave, to go to her parent's, she wails hysterically. A sea of tears erupts. Karl embraces her. Katarina is distraught, she looks through the louvers again, in disbelief. She runs to the street and falls on her parent's bodies. Karl pulls her off and helps her to her feet. Her clothes and hands are bloody. He embraces her. Katarina is infuriated. "My brother will pay for this, I hate him."

Hans covers the bodies. Hans turns to Katarina and Karl, "We must leave, it is not safe for you to be here in the open. The soldiers are still here."

"Why did this happen, why? I will kill him for this," Katarina says to Karl. The villagers take the bodies away, Katarina's crying is overwhelming.

Hans embraces Karl and Katarina, "Karl, Wilhelm has posted guards at the farmhouse, stay with me tonight. I have a loft above my market. You both will be safe there for a while. Katarina, I will get clean clothes for you. You can get yourself cleaned up." Karl helps Katarina to the market.

"Lie down Katarina, please try to get some rest." She eventually cries herself to sleep, Karl is at her side consoling her. Karl puts his hand on his chest and suddenly realizes his dog tags are missing. He grabs his pocket; he can feel his mother's locket and Katarina's butterfly pin, but not the dog tags.

THE ESCAPE

Several days have passed, Katarina has not left the loft. Karl has been by her side comforting her. "Karl, I cannot believe this happened. I cannot believe that monster would kill his own parents," Katarina begins crying again.

"Katarina, Hans has been helping with the funeral arrangements. The service is tomorrow morning."

She lays her head in his arms, sobbing and falls asleep from exhaustion. Karl takes a walk to the barn to look for his dog tags, through the woods to not be seen. When he arrives, he does not see any soldiers. He is thinking of all the memories he and Katarina had in the barn. *Katarina cared for me and nursed me back from my injuries, the special moments we had together. The first time I met Anna and Gerhardt was here, I have been here nearly a year.* Karl climbs down to the cellar, and finds it ransacked, everything is destroyed and broken. Karl notices his uniform is gone. He looks for his dog tags, uncovering everything, but does not find them. *I must get back to Katarina, it is getting late.* Karl arrives he sees Katarina is up, sitting at the table.

"Hello, my Love, I am happy to see you up."

"Hello Karl, I need to get myself composed, but it is difficult. I am so blessed I have you, my life has been turned upside down."

"I know," as he hugs her. "I will always be here for you my Love.

"Where were you?" she asks, sobbing.

"I realized I lost my dog tags, I thought it happened in our hurry to leave the barn, I went to look for them," Katarina jumps from the chair.

"What about your mother's locket?"

"I have it. Remember when you put the tags back around my neck?" She nods. "I never put her locket back on them, I had the locket and your butterfly pin in my pocket, as I did every day at Neuengamme. As I do now."

"That makes me happy Karl."

Karl continues, "My dog tags must have fallen off during the motorcycle ride to town. Hans told me the soldiers left the farm this morning."

"Karl, can we go to the farmhouse, I need to get some things for my parent's funeral?"

"Yes, we can go tonight." They arrive at the farmhouse in the cover of darkness. Karl stands guard outside while Katarina gathers the items. He turns and looks toward the kitchen and notices jewelry on the table. "Why do you have the jewelry out, Katarina?"

Teary eyed Katarina replies, "These were my mother's rings and pins, and my father's rings and cufflinks. The Nazis would not allow my father to wear rings, or anything personal. It had to be their stuff. I want my parents to wear some of these tomorrow. Karl, can we stay here tonight?"

Karl looks at Katarina lovingly, "We should not my Love, we need to be sure Wilhelm and his soldiers stay away, I do not trust him." Katarina and Karl leave and go back to the loft above Han's market. "Katarina, Hans and I have been talking about a plan to flee Germany, we will talk tomorrow after the service. We have a big day tomorrow; we should go to bed and get some rest." As they lay in bed, Katarina begins to weep. Karl holds her.

In her sobbing voice, "I remember every night when I went to bed, I would wait for my mother to peek her head in the door, and say good night Katarina, I love you. I would say, good night Mother,

I love you. God bless you. We did that every night of my life. And my father, he would come in and give me a kiss on my forehead, he even did that the last time I saw him. Before," Katarina pauses, she can barely say the words, "before he and Mother went to heaven."

Katarina and Karl prepare for the service. It is a sunny and cold day in January. They are up early that morning; Katarina was up most of the night. They disguise themselves the best they can. They bundle up with coats and scarfs. Katarina and Karl walk to Saint Ludger. They see hundreds of mourners standing outside the church, they came from neighboring villages. Hans is waiting at the doors for Katarina and Karl.

Hans whispers to Katarina and Karl, "Katarina, I am so sorry for you, for your loss. Karl, I have people watching for the Nazis, at the edge of town and here at the church. Let us go inside." As they enter the church, they see it is completely full, not even standing room. Hans walks to the front of the church. Karl and Katarina, with her head wrapped in a shawl, sit at side pews in the front of the church remaining inconspicuous to the townspeople. Karl sees the remains of the damage from the gunfire. Windows broken, statues shot up and broken, bullet holes in the walls. *The Germans can break the relics and statues, shoot up the walls; but cannot change the purpose and soul of this Church*, Karl says to himself. Flowers adorn the church. Katarina looks at the two coffins and sobs. She is struggling to keep her composure. Karl puts his arm around her and consoles her. Father Root walks to the altar. The service begins. At the end of the service, the bodies are taken to a horse drawn wagon. They all follow to the cemetery. Katarina and Karl stay inconspicuously remain to the back of the villagers. Again, Katarina is struggling to control her emotions yet manages. After the service they return to Hans' house for a small reception. Hans talks with Karl and Katarina.

"Hans, Karl tells me you and he have been making plans for us to flee Germany."

"Yes Katarina, I did not want to bring it up now."

"Let us talk tomorrow Hans. I want to leave this war-torn

country soon. I need to make preparations for the farm, and for my parent's belongings, that will take some time."

Hans places his hand on Katarina's shoulder, "I will see you tomorrow, and again Katarina, I am very sorry for you."

"Hans, I want to stay at the farmhouse tonight." Karl nods in agreement.

"I will send a few of my people to stand guard outside."

"Thank you, Hans."

Karl and Katarina get to the farmhouse after dark. They are sitting on the sofa in front of the fireplace. Karl has a fire going, the wood is crackling. Katarina is snuggled tightly to Karl; her cold nose is pressed against his neck. "Karl, this fire smells like the night you came back to me."

"Yes, it does my Love."

"Karl, Saturday is your birthday."

"You remembered, how sweet, yet that is not important."

"Karl, we both know we want to spend our lives together. I want to have children with you. I want to take care of you." He kisses her forehead. "Karl, we will get married on your birthday. You know Germans have a tradition of Saturday weddings." She smiles. "I want to leave Germany as Mrs. Schellenberg."

In true old-world form, although in reverse roles, Karl gets down on one knee, and says, "Yes, I will, and yes I want to be your husband. Well Miss Katarina, we have a wedding to plan." With that he picks her up in his arms, they kiss, and retire for the evening.

January 13, early the next morning Katarina and Karl walk to the church to plan for Saturday. As they enter the church, Katarina is taken back by the damage.

"Karl, I didn't realize the German soldiers did this much damage, I was so focused on the funeral service."

"Yes Katarina, they will pay for this someday."

"Good afternoon Father Root."

"Good afternoon, Katarina, what can I do for you?"

"Father, this is Karl, Karl Schellenberg. He is the American pilot."

"Yes Katarina, Hans told me of him, and of your love for one another."

"Karl and I want to be married; will you marry us Saturday?"

"I am happy for you both, yes, I can, and will be honored to."

"We would like a 15:30 wedding, a small ceremony, will that work?"

"Yes, it will. I will arrange to have someone here to play the organ, it was not damaged by the soldiers."

"That will be very nice Father, thank you."

"I will see both of you then."

On their way back, they pass Hans' market. They exchange good mornings.

"Hans, we have news for you, Karl and I are getting married Saturday."

"That is wonderful news, I am happy for you both. This was inevitable, you were meant for each other. Do you and Karl have time to discuss your departure plan?"

"Yes Hans, walk with Karl and I to the farmhouse. The wedding service will be 15:30. Hans, Karl and I want you to be in our wedding." Katarina gets extremely choked up. "I want, I want you to," she begins crying intensely, "to walk me down the aisle."

Hans hugs her, "I will be honored, thank you Katarina." He and Karl both begin crying.

"Hans, will you also ask Ursula Muller to attend, we have been friends since we were children. I want her to be my maid of honor. In fact, ask her to come to the farmhouse Saturday morning, she can help me get ready."

"Katarina, I will talk with Ursula. She will be happy to be with you, with what Wilhelm did to her parents, and now Anna and Gerhardt. I will be at the farmhouse in the afternoon, at 15:00 Saturday, I would like to walk with you to the church."

Teary eyed Katarina responds, "Thank you, Hans."

The three of them sit at the kitchen table. "You two love birds, I have been thinking of the best route to get you safely to London. I have talked with my comrades in the Underground, they have communicated with London. They will help you along the way, it will be clearly and precisely mapped out. London will be expecting you as well, and get you, Karl, reunited with your unit."

"I am excited," Katarina says, she turns and smiles at Karl.

"We looked at three routes where we, the Underground, have the best resources to help you. The first route heads south through the Black Forest, into Switzerland, then into France. You are in Germany longer, and the Allied bombing is intensifying in those regions. Switzerland is neutral but Germany is increasing their campaign in France, as we know. The second route is through Belgium into France. The German occupation of Belgium is unstable, and again, you go through France. We think the best route is through the Netherlands. We have a good number of safe houses there. The border is very close. Although the Netherlands is occupied by Germany, most of the war involving the Netherlands has been in the North Sea, the mainland has not been a fierce battle front. We can get you to London easily from there. Since you speak fluent German Karl, it will be best to travel on small country roads rather than cross country where planes and patrols can spot you."

"We understand, thank you Hans."

"Our route will take you south through the border town of Bad Nieuweschans. There will be checkpoints, so stay calm. From there you will head west to the town of Gronongen. We will change drivers there, at a small café that is run by one of our Underground members."

"Why?" asks Karl with a puzzled look.

"On a mission like this, we do not want our drivers susceptible to any more interrogation than needed if captured. Neither driver knows where the other has come from or is going. It is better this way."

"I understand, that is a good plan."

"Then you will travel south to the town of Lelystad. The last leg of your journey you will cross the Markermeer Sea to Enkhulzen, north of Amsterdam. We want to stay out of Amsterdam. From there, you will be traveling northwest to the small coastal town of Egmond aan Zee. If things go as planned, you will arrive late afternoon. It should be a four to five-hour trip. There is an old abandoned small grass airstrip there. We will arrange for a small plane to take you and Katarina to London that evening under the cloak of darkness."

"Thank you very much Hans. I am excited but nervous."

Hans pats Katarina's hand, "We will get you both there safe."

"Karl, do you still have your German papers?"

"Yes Hans, I have them with me. Fortunately, Wilhelm didn't find them."

Katarina looks at Karl, "Find them in Neuengamme?"

"No, I didn't want to tell you with everything going on. "Wilhelm was in the barn after we escaped; he ransacked the cellar. I had the papers hidden; he found my journal but miraculously not my papers."

"I understand, thank you Karl, nothing we can do about that."

"He had to see my uniform; my Pfisterer name tag was on it. That is what put him over the edge that terrible night." Katarina holds his hands.

"Karl; do not think that, he already was over the edge. Remember what Hans told us at the barn the day Wilhelm arrived, that he has never seen Wilhelm so upset."

"Yes," says Hans, "Wilhelm had his own agenda and mission that awful day. Klaus told me of the young lieutenant at the dining hall the night you left, that he coincidently asked where you were from. The next morning, he went to Captain Wagoner and Wilhelm; that is what exposed you. Your timing to leave the Camp was spot on. Karl, you mentioned Wilhelm has your journal. Is there anything in it that can expose our Underground Movement?"

"No, Hans, I kept the details to the missions, however our names were in code."

"Very good Karl. Regarding your German papers and documents, do not worry about those anymore. Wilhelm will have the name Karl Pfisterer all over Germany, the Nazis will be on the lookout for you. I have arranged for new papers for you, for both of you. Karl and Katarina Schellenberg. How perfect. I should have them in a few days."

Katarina looks at Karl, "I love how that sounds."

"Hans, we are in your hands and we trust you. We will do what you think is best," Katarina agrees.

"Good, this will take a week or two to get the plan in motion. You both need to travel light, choose what you take wisely."

Katarina smiles, looks at them both, "I will need the time to get my affairs in order here. I need to deal with my parent's farm, I know what I want to do but I need to talk with you Karl."

Hans nods, "Katarina, I understand. When you leave Germany, your life will change forever, for the good. I am happy to help you with that." Although Katarina is in a very good and happy space, she misses her parents immensely, and cries herself to sleep that night. Karl holds her and comforts her.

Friday morning, it's snowing. The fields and trees are covered with a beautiful wet snow. The snow is clinging to the evergreen trees. Katarina wakes to Karl holding her. "I love waking up with you Karl. I want to share my thoughts with you on what to do with the farm, and my parent's personal items. I want to give the farm to the Church, and my parent's personal items to Hans. He has been such a great person, a great friend; and has helped us to no end."

"That is a very nice plan Katarina."

"Karl, we can tell Father Root tomorrow after our wedding. I am excited, I love you. I want to wear my mother's favorite dress, and Karl, you are the same size as my father. The clothes I gave you when we found you seemed to fit you fine. I would love for you to wear his favorite suit," Katarina says with excitement in her voice.

"I would love to and be proud to, in his honor." Karl smiles.

Katarina adds, "One more thing Karl, by tradition, you cannot see the bride on her wedding day before the wedding. You will have to sleep in the spare bedroom." Katarina kisses her two fingers and places them on Karl's lips, looks into his eyes, and smiles. "You get ready in the morning and wait for me at the church."

Karl chuckles, "Yes, I agree, you're absolutely correct. Thank you, Katarina, I love you."

"Karl; I want to go outside and play in the snow," Katarina says in a playful voice. "We can go to the stone barn, so we are not seen." As they walk to the stone barn, Katarina makes a snowball and throws it at Karl. He tries to duck, it hits him, he slips and falls in a pile of snow. He rallies and returns a snowball. It is cold, the fresh snow is clinging to the trees. They have fun in the snow for hours. The snow is clinging to their clothes. It's dusk, they lay down and make snow angels. Staring at the sky, the stars and moon are becoming visible. Katarina is giggling, thinking of their new day tomorrow, the beginning of their new life. They return to the farmhouse; Katarina prepares a meal for them. Karl slices a fresh loaf of bread. After dinner, Katarina kisses Karl good night. "We have a big day tomorrow my Love, remember I cannot see you before the wedding."

Karl replies, "Yes, I remember. I will see you tomorrow afternoon. You have sweet dreams my Love."

Softly Katarina says, "I most certainly will Karl, I love you."

Karl smiles, "I love you. Katarina, I want you to have this, to wear tomorrow." He hands her his mother's locket. They kiss.

Saturday morning, January 15, their wedding day has arrived. The fresh snow from the day before is a perfect backdrop. Karl awakes. He hears Katarina scurrying in her room. Karl gets ready. Gerhardt's suit fits him well. Karl hears a knock at the door, it is Ursula.

"Good morning, you must be Ursula Muller? I am Karl."

"Yes, very nice to meet you Karl, Hans filled me in."

"Ursula, I am so sorry about your parents." Her lips quiver, as tears runs down her cheek.

"Thank you, Karl."

"Have a seat, I will let Katarina know you are here, although I am not allowed to see her." Ursula giggles. Karl walks to Katarina's door and taps lightly, "Katarina, Ursula is here. I will see you at the alar my Love." As he walks to the church, he stops by Hans' market. Karl can see Hans has members of the Underground stationed throughout the village.

"Good morning Hans."

"Good morning Karl, this is a new day for you and Katarina. You look very nice. What are you doing out in the village? You should be with Katarina. Were you careful no one saw you?"

"Hans, you know, Katarina reminded me a groom cannot see his bride on their wedding day before the wedding ceremony, and yes, I was careful. So, here I am."

"I do know that Karl," a German tradition."

"Hans, I want Katarina to have special flowers today, do you have a nice arrangement of red roses and white lilies? They are her favorite flowers."

"That's nice, and yes Karl, I do have those flowers. Come with me to the back of the shop." As soon as Karl sees the flower display, his eyes immediately go to the red roses and white lilies.

"Those Hans, those are perfect."

"Good, I will get them nicely arranged so Katarina can carry them. Wait up front, I will not be long. There is fresh coffee, help yourself." Karl is gazing into the village, feeling sorry for what these people are going through with this terrible war. He knows he and Katarina will soon be safe. "Here you go Karl."

"They are beautiful Hans, what do I owe you?"

"They are my gift to you."

"Thank you, Hans."

"Wait Karl, I have something for you." Hans pins a boutonniere on Karl's lapel, a red rose on a white lily petal.

"Thank you very much Hans, it is beautiful."

"Karl I will help Katarina to the church."

"Thank you, Hans, but do not let her know we saw each other. I want to surprise her with the flowers." Karl embraces Hans and walks to the church.

Karl enters the church, places the flowers on a table in the vestibule, walks to the front of the church, and sits in the front pew. Father Root greets him.

"I see the old tradition is in place."

"Yes Father," Karl chuckles. "I must wait to see Katarina on our wedding day."

"Be comfortable my son, may I get you anything?"

"No Father, thank you, I just want to reminisce."

"Very well, I will be in the sacristy if you need me." Karl reminisces of his parents and childhood. Thinking of the short time he had with them, and what Katarina must be going through. Karl hears footsteps from the rear of the church. He turns and sees a lady approaching him, "Good afternoon, you must be the groom. I am Ethel. Father Root asked me to come. I will be playing the organ for your wedding."

"Hello, I am Karl, thank you very much for doing this." She gets the organ and sheet music ready. It's 15:00.

Hans arrives at the farmhouse early. "Good afternoon Katarina and Ursula. You both look very lovely. Where is Karl?" as if he doesn't know.

"Hans, you know a groom cannot see his bride before her wedding. It is time to go to the church Hans, I am very anxious to see my husband to be. Hans, one thing before we go. I have something for you. Here take this, it is my mother's wedding ring, give it to Karl. I want Karl to give it to me, at the exact time we exchange our vows. I have my father's ring for Karl. It will be a nice surprise."

"How appropriate Katarina."

Karl hears a noise in the back of the church, he hears Katarina's and Hans' voices. Katarina sees a bouquet of flowers on the table. "Those are for you Katarina, from Karl."

"So beautiful, I love red roses and white lilies, Karl remembered."

"Here Katarina, I have something for you. He takes a small boutonniere from inside his jacket. One red rose and one white lily. I want you to wear these in your hair."

"Perfect Hans, thank you, will you help me Ursula?"

The bells of Saint Ludger begin to ring at 15:25 and echo through the village. Precisely at 15:30, the organ begins playing Canon in D. Father Root comes to the Altar with an Altar boy. Karl stands and turns to the back of the church. He sees his soon to be bride walking down the aisle. Ursula leads the way. Hans looks very happy walking with Katarina. *Katarina looks so beautiful; part of her brown hair is braided; and has a red rose and a white lily in the braids.* Karl remembers the braid from the days he first met Katarina. Karl gazes into her blue eyes, her smile, that special smile. *She looks so elegant in her mother's lavender dress. The roses and lilies are so lovely in her arms.* Karl sees his mother's locket draped from Katarina's neck, and smiles, *Mother is with us.* Karl can see Katarina is weeping. A tear rolls down Karl cheek, a happy tear. Katarina arrives at the Altar with Hans.

Karl takes her hands, and says, "Hello, my Love, you look very beautiful."

"I love your boutonniere Karl," she then notices her butterfly pin on his lapel, pinned next to the boutonniere. "Thank you for wearing my butterfly pin Karl." They turn and face Father Root. Hans stands next to Karl, and Ursula next to Katarina.

"Dearly beloved, we are gathered together here in the sight of God, and in the face of this company of witnesses to join together this man and this woman in Holy Matrimony; which is an honorable estate, instituted of God, signifying unto us the mystical union that is between Christ and His Church; which Holy Estate Christ adorned with His presence and first miracle that He wrought in Cana of Galilee, and is commended of Saint Paul to be honorable among all men; and therefore, not entered into unadvisedly or lightly, but reverently, discreetly, soberly and in the fear of God. Into this Holy Estate these two persons present come now to be joined. Please state your vows to one another." Katarina and Karl face one another, gazing into each other's eyes.

"Karl, God sent you to me from heaven, since the day we first met, I had a strange, but good feeling, about you. The feeling was love. My mother noticed as well. As our time together grew, so did my endless love for you. You have made me the happiest woman on earth. I want to spend my life with you. I want to have children with you. I want to take care of you. Happy Birthday Karl, I love you."

"Katarina, my dearest, my Love. My time with you has been remarkable. God truly did send me to you, and you to me. My love for you has grown equally. I want to have children with you. I want us to grow old together. I will spend the rest of my life with you. I love you, Katarina."

"Katarina Caroline, will you take Karl to be your lawful wedded husband, to live together after God's ordinance in the Holy Estate of Matrimony? Will you love him, cherish him, honor and keep him in sickness and in health; and, forsaking all others keep you only unto him as long as you both shall live?"

"I will."

"Karl Nicholas, will you take Katarina to be your lawful wedded wife, to live together in God's ordinance in the Holy Estate of Matrimony? Will you love her, cherish her, honor and keep her in sickness and in health; and, forsaking all others keep you only unto her as long as you both shall live?"

"I will."

"With these symbols of wedlock, these rings will forever be a symbol of your love." Karl's is a bit nervous; he has no ring. Hans takes his hand and gives him the ring. Karl turns, surprised, smiles; and nods a thank you. "These marriage rings seal the vows of marriage and represents a promise for eternal and everlasting love."

"Karl, please repeat after me: I Karl, take thee, Katarina, to be my wedded wife, to have and to hold from this day forward, for better, for worse, for richer, for poorer, in sickness and in health, to love and to cherish forever, according to God's Holy Ordinance, and thereto I give thee my pledge." Karl repeats the verse, takes Katarina's hand, and places her ring on her finger.

"Katarina, please repeat after me." Tears of joy are running down Katarina's cheeks. "I Katarina, take thee, Karl, to be my wedded husband, to have and to hold from this day forward, for better, for worse, for richer, for poorer, in sickness and in health, to love and to cherish forever, according to God's Holy Ordinance, and thereto I give thee my pledge." Katarina repeats the verse, takes Karl's hand, and places his ring on his finger. Karl is surprised with his ring as well. They continue to hold hands.

"Those whom God hath joined together, let no man put asunder. Forasmuch as Katarina and Karl have consented together in Holy Wedlock, and have witnessed the same before God and this company of witnesses, and there to have given their pledge, each to the other, and have declared the same by giving and receiving a ring, and by joining hands; by the power vested in me, I now pronounce you Mr. and Mrs. Schellenberg. You may kiss your bride."

Katarina and Karl embrace in a deep and loving kiss, the organ music continues to play.

"Katarina and Karl, a Marriage Blessing for you." Father Root raises his hands over them. "May the Lord be in your marriage. May He bless your life anew with the joys of heaven as you begin to walk as two. And as you join together just know the strength in life is having God within you as you live as husband and wife. God's blessing be upon you. His grace to you impart. Find joys in every day and keep Him in your heart."

"Thank you, Father, that is a beautiful blessing." The ceremony ends. "Thank you, Father Root for a very lovely ceremony. I felt as if my parents were here with Karl and I, as were his, looking down from heaven," Katarina begins to weep. "Father, I have something I want to talk with you about. Hans please stay as well. Father, Karl and I, with the help of Hans, are going to flee Germany to begin our new life together in America. In order to do that, I need to tend to my parent's estate. Father, I want the Church to have the farm, you can put it to good use."

Father Root hesitates in a moment of surprise. "Katarina, I am taken back, I cannot believe this, that is so gracious, thank you ever so much. We will do the farm proud for your parents," Father Root embraces Katarina.

Katarina continues and turns to Hans, "Hans, I want you to have all of their personal belongings, those that you want, the remaining items can go to help families in need." Hans hugs Katarina, "Katarina, I am very humbled, thank you." Just as they begin to leave, one of Hans' Underground members runs in the church.

"Hans, a German patrol car has just entered town." Father Root turns to Katarina and Karl, "Quick go in the sacristy, I have a back room there. You can hide safely in there until we see what they want." Ten minutes pass, Hans comes to the sacristy.

"Katarina, Karl, the patrol vehicle appears to have gone, they were passing through and did not stop."

"Father Root, Ethel, Hans, Ursula, please come to our house, join Karl and I for a celebration dinner this evening." They all depart to the farmhouse.

"Katarina, I will keep my people posted at the farmhouse and throughout the town to stand guard until you safely leave Aurich."

"Thank you, Hans." When they arrive, Karl picks Katarina up in his arms, and carries her through the doorway. Katarina prepares a simple dinner. Father Root, Hans, Ethel, and Ursula leave after the reception.

"Karl, wait here, I will be right back." Katarina goes to the bedroom. Ten minutes pass, the door opens. "Come to me my Love." As he walks toward the bedroom, he can see candles flickering throughout the room. Karl sees his new wife. Katarina is wearing a white lace robe. She opens her robe to a shear, see through white silk nightgown. "Karl, I have had these for years, waiting for this special night. I bought them in London."

"Katarina my Love, you are astonishingly beautiful, absolutely breathtaking." Karl takes Katarina in his arms. They kiss, slowly at first. In a heated display of passion, they fall onto the bed.

A week passes and Katarina has the final paperwork to deed the farm to the Church. Hans comes to the house. He knocks, Katarina answers the door. "Good morning Katarina," Karl comes from the back room.

"Good morning Karl. I have good news. Everything is in place. You will leave Germany next week, on January 31. We will have your new papers on the thirtieth. Father Root has also prepared a marriage license, it is authentic." He chuckles. "If everything goes as planned, you will be in London late on the evening of the thirty-first."

Katarina looks at Karl, "Karl that is our anniversary." Hans looks confused, thinking they were just married last week. Katarina smiles, "Oh, Hans, without January 31, we would not be together, that is the day we met, the day God sent Karl to me."

Karl and Katarina lie in bed that evening. They hear the bombing in the distance, it's so surreal but numbing. "Karl, it will be so nice to get away from this war-torn country and start our new life together." They fall asleep in each other's arms. The next morning, they begin to prepare for their journey.

"Katarina, we need to gather what you want to take, your thoughts?"

"Yes Karl, I have been thinking of a few things. I know we need to travel light."

"Well, I do not have much of anything so that will help, just the few clothes you gave me. There is something else. Remember when I fixed the hinge on the barn door."

"Yes, I do. You looked so hansom and strong in that tee shirt"

"I used your father's tools. I would like to take some. Perhaps his hammer, the screwdriver and pliers I used."

"He will like that Karl. I want to take my wedding dress, and your wedding suit, a few of my favorite dresses, and Mother's apron.

The apron I was wearing when mother and I took you to the barn. I would like my parent's jewelry, my mother's rosary, and our family bible. It has all the holy cards from relatives who have died, our family tree. I need to note Mother and Father in it." Katarina weeps. "I also want my doll, I have had her since I was three, my mother bought her for me. I named her Christie. I want to dry our wedding flowers and take them. And pictures Karl, I want to take our family pictures and our letters we sent each other when you were in Neuengamme. Our family beer steins, Mother's, Father's, and mine. They have been handed down for generations. Karl, I want my baby fork and spoon, and a special bowl I used when I was a baby. Let me show you. The last items I thought of, my parents and I had special Christmas ornaments for our tree. I will take those. Oh, one more thing, I want my mother's cookbook. Oh Karl, I am sorry, this has grown into quite the list."

"No worries my Love, these are all important items, we will get them safely to the States, I promise."

January 30, the day before they depart Germany Katarina utters, "Karl, I want to go to the cemetery, to see my parents one last time." It's a cold and crisp January day as they walk to the cemetery. The crunchy snow is crackling beneath their feet. Katarina sees the headstone is in place. Hans arranged for that. Katarina and Karl kneel at the grave. Katarina, as she weeps, reads the head stone. 'Anna Margarete Keitel. April 19 1896 - January 7 1944. Gerhardt Samuel Keitel. April 27 1895 - January 7 1944. May they rest in peace together.'

"Karl, Mother and Father fell in love with each other at a very young age; and loved each other every day thereafter. Just like us, forever." Katarina places rose petals from her wedding on the grave. They stand. "Goodbye Mother and Father, Karl and I are beginning our new life together."

January 31 arrives. Katarina and Karl wake early. As Karl opens his eyes, he sees Katarina gazing into his. "Happy Anniversary, Karl."

"Happy Anniversary to you my Love."

"Karl, last night, our last night in this house was amazing with you." She begins to weep. "I was lying here this morning thinking of my parents. Why did they need to die such a brutal and cruel death?" She pauses a monument to collect herself. "I grew up in this house. I remember playing dolls with my mother. I remember my father taking me, putting me on his back and running through the fields. I remember our Christmas mornings; I was always so excited. I remember my grandparents coming for visits. I remember the seasons, how beautiful the winters were, just like now, the springtime, summers in the village, and the fall. I so loved the feeling and smell of fall. Our time here has ended, I will always have those special memories; and now, our new life begins."

Hans and the driver meet Katarina and Karl at 11:00. Ursula is with Katarina.

"Good morning Katarina and Karl. Good morning Ursula. Your new life together begins today. This is Heinrich, he will be your driver for part of your journey."

"Pleased to meet you," he tips his hat to them.

"Karl, here are your new documents and identification, and most important, your marriage license."

"Look Karl; 'Karl and Katarina Schellenberg.' It is official."

"Katarina, if you are stopped, you are traveling to Amsterdam to see a very sick relative, your Aunt Irma, Irma Bauer." Hans looks at both of them, and holds their hands, "I am going to miss you both very much. Katarina, I have enjoyed watching you grow up and I will cherish those memories for ever. Karl, even though our time together has been short, I will always consider you my friend. If you are ever in this neck of the woods, stop by and see me." They hug one another, Katarina kisses Hans on his cheek.

Katarina hugs Ursula, "Ursula, you are dear friend, I will miss you very much."

Katarina then turns to Hans. "We will miss you very much Hans, thank you for all you have done. I will forever be indebted for what you have done for us, and for Germany. Once we get settled in America, I will write to you. Hans, please give these to Father Root, they are the keys to the farmhouse." Heinrich opens the trunk and lifts a false bottom in the floor; and places their suitcases in the compartment.

"Time to go you two, travel safe, Godspeed." Karl opens the car door for Katarina, they get in the backseat. As they drive away, Katarina turns one last time, waves goodbye to Hans, Ursula, and her life in Germany. Tears run down her cheeks.

Heinrich turns to them, "Our drive to the border will be about an hour."

"Heinrich, I forgot something, please turn back."

"What is it?" asks Karl.

"My mother's cookbook, I left it on the kitchen table?" Heinrich turns the car around. As they approach the crest of a hill just before Aurich, Heinrich immediately slows the car and pulls over.

"What is it Heinrich?"

"Miss Katarina; look, a German convoy. I am sorry Katarina; we must leave."

"Yes Heinrich, I understand. We need to be on our way." They approach the border town of Bad Nieuweschans shortly after noon. Heinrich turns to Katarina and Karl, "We are arriving at the checkpoint. Let me talk unless the soldiers ask you a question." Katarina and Karl nod. As they approach, they see three guards, one guard looking at the license plate. A barrier-gate is down so they need to stop. Heinrich rolls the window down.

A guard approaches the car. "What is your business in the Netherlands?" as he leans in and looks at Katarina and Karl. Katarina smiles at him.

"I am taking these people to Amsterdam."

"Why?" asks the guard gruffly.

"We are going to see Miss Katarina's sick Aunt; she does not have long."

"What is her name?"

"Irma Bauer," says Katarina.

"Let me see your papers, where are you from?" Heinrich turns to Katarina and Karl to get their papers, and hands the guard his and their documents, another guard walks around the car. "How long will you be there?"

"They are from Aurich. We will only be in Amsterdam today; we will return tonight." The guard walks back to his hut.

The other guard shouts, "What is in the trunk?"

Heinrich leans his head out the window, "Nothing but a spare tire."

"Open the trunk," the guard says. Heinrich gets out, walks to the back of the car, and opens the trunk. Katarina squeezes Karl's hand. The guard looks in, probes the tire, and walks away. Meanwhile, the other guard exits the hut and slowly walks toward the car, scanning every inch of the car, Heinrich, and Katarina and Karl. Katarina squeezes Karl's hand harder.

In a moment of brain lapse, or perhaps one of his anxious moments, Wilhelm sent orders to all border crossings to be on the lookout for a Karl Pfisterer, thinking Karl will use his alias. He fails to mention Schellenberg, and his own named sister. Something he now will regret. The guard hands Heinrich the papers, and motions for the gate to be opened. "You can pass." They drive off. Katarina slowly, not to draw attention, looks back.

"Katarina, Karl, the guards are trained to ask very quick and sometimes random questions to see how people react, you both did very well. We will be in Gronongen in less than an hour, welcome to the Netherlands. Are you hungry?"

"Yes, I am," says Katarina. "In our scurry to get ready for today I did not eat."

"Good, I know of a nice little café just up the road, in Gronongen. We will change drivers there."

"Yes, Hans mentioned that." They arrive in Gronongen just after noon and have lunch. They see a man walk into the café. He looks around. Henrich motions to him. He slowly walks over and sits down.

"Good afternoon, I am Rudolf. I will be driving you from here."

"Hello Rudolf; pleased to meet you. I am Karl and this is my wife Katarina." Karl thinks to himself; *this is the first time I introduced Katarina as my wife.*

"Pleased to meet you as well."

Heinrich interjects, "Time to go, may I get you anything before we leave?"

Karl replies, "No thank you Heinrich, we are fine." Their suitcases are transferred. Karl notices this car has the same false bottom in the trunk. Katarina and Karl say their goodbyes to Heinrich.

"Thank you, Heinrich for getting us here safely."

"My pleasure and travel safe." Karl opens the car door for Katariina. The three of them get in the car and head south to Lelystad. So far, the journey is going as planned. As they approach the bridge crossing the Markermeer Sea to Enkhulzen Karl sees a German convoy crossing the bridge, in their direction. The bridge is blocked by a Nazi scout vehicle.

Rudolf turns to them. "Just relax, this is normal. They always block the bridges when convoys cross." They patiently wait, about fifteen minutes. Katarina and Karl watch as the troops go by. The bridge is reopened, and they continue their journey. Rudolf informs them, "We are heading around the north side of Amsterdam now; we will arrive in the coastal town of Egmond aan Zee soon. We should be there by 16:00. We will wait until nightfall for the plane, he should be arriving at 18:00."

"How does he know to be here by 18:00."

Rudolf explains, "That's our plan Karl, to keep communication down, we planned for the plane to arrive at 18:00, if we are not there, he waits fifteen minutes and leaves." They arrive at the abandoned small grass airstrip, it is 16:10, they wait under a small grove of trees east of the air strip. The day was just warm enough to melt the snow from the field.

The sun sets. "Karl, the sunset is beautiful."

It is 17:55. They hear a small single engine plane. The plane's lights are off and is flying low to the water. The waxing crescent moon offers just enough light for the pilot. Rudolf flickers his headlights. Katarina and Karl see the plane land. The plane taxis toward the car. Katarina turns to Karl, "Karl, it is happening, it is really happening."

"Hurry," says Rudolf. Rudolf gets their suitcases and places them in a small compartment under the wing. Just as they get in the plane, Rudolf sees a German patrol vehicle racing down the road toward them.

"Quick, get in the plane and stay down," Rudolf yells. The pilot also sees the patrol car; and begins to roll ahead. Rudolf latches the door, the plane accelerates. Suddenly, bullets riddle the back of the plane, Katarina screams, Karl cradles her. *I hope Rudolf is safe.*

The plane lifts off and heads across the English Channel to London. Rudolf is captured.

A NEW BEGINNING
[JANUARY 1944]

As the plane flies over the English Channel, Katarina and Karl watch the reflections in the night horizon to the north from the bombing campaigns. As they are descending, to the south they see fires burning in the London skyline. The plane touches down just before 7:00 in the small town of Colchester, north east of London.

"Karl, we are here, we are free," they embrace each other and kiss. "Karl, London brings back so many fond memories of my schooling at the University." As the plane taxis to the hanger, Karl can see an Army Air Force staff car waiting.

"What a nice sight," Katarina. They exit the plane and are greeted by an Army Air Force Sergeant.

"Good evening Corporal Schellenberg and Mrs. Schellenberg. I am Staff Sergeant McDonald. I've been expecting you." Karl salutes him.

"It has been a long time since I have had that pleasure sergeant."

Staff Sergeant McDonald nods. "Let me get your bags and we'll be off. I'm taking you to the Eighth Air Force Bomber Command in Kettering, Northamptonshire, England. It will be a two-hour drive. We are stationed at the Royal Air Force's Grafton Underwood

Air Station. It is the U.S. Base for the European Theater. Let's be on our way. I heard you have done a wonderful job in helping us while in Germany."

"Yes, thank you sergeant, it was quite an experience."

"Here, I have something for both of you, something to snack on."

"Sergeant, I have not had a Hershey Chocolate Bar in a very long time. Thank you very much."

"I thought you would enjoy it."

Katarina opens it and takes a bit. "Karl this has a unique taste. Like chocolate but not. It is very good."

It is milk chocolate, from the States. Our Government has been sending these to the troops."

"How long were you in Germany?" asks the sergeant."

Karl recalls that night vividly. "One year and four days to be exact." Katarina lays her head on Karl's lap, and falls asleep. "It was January 27. I was on a reconnaissance mission into northwest Germany from England, from the Joint Air Base at the Royal Air Force, in Daws Hill England. The mission had our heading over the North Sea into northern Germany. I was piloting the lead scout aircraft ahead of the initial wave of bombers, and ahead of the main bombing mission, to keep a lookout for the Luftwaffe's counterattack. My flight path was over the mainland, south of the main group's heading. The target was the Kriegsmarine's Wilhelmshaven Port. Suddenly, I saw a strange flash of light and my plane began having mechanical issues and lost power."

"Were you hit by antiaircraft fire corporal?"

"No, it was like nothing I ever experienced. My plane was not hit. I remember Command saying over the radio they saw no strange activity in my area. I ejected, my chute failed, and I was severely injured. Katarina found me one year ago today. She saved my life." Karl runs his fingers through Katarina's hair. It took months to recover from my injuries. The Underground Movement approached me, due to my fluency in German, to help them gain knowledge for the Allies. That mission began in August. We decided to end it earlier this month as the Army Group North Command, which is where I infiltrated, were becoming suspicious of too many coincidental Allied attacks. Katarina's Father, a captain in the German Army and adamantly against Hitler and his Third Reich, was also involved in the Underground. He forged my Army documents and put them in the German's system. The local Underground forged my citizenship documents, my life in Germany up to that point. The network they have is amazing.

"Very interesting corporal, may I call you Karl?"

Karl smiles, "Please do."

McDonald continues, "I'm curious, how were you able to get top secret information Karl."

"That is an interesting question sergeant. My sergeant, a man named Hoffmann, knew everything about everything, and liked to talk and impress me."

"We need more like him helping us Karl." The conversation continues, and Karl nods off. They arrive at the Grafton Base at 21:30. Karl and Katarina wake up to voices. They see they have arrived at Grafton and are at the main gate. Sergeant McDonald is cleared to go through. The sergeant drives Karl and Katarina to their private quarters.

"Karl, General Williams has arranged for you and the Mrs. to stay in our private guest quarters during your time here. Let me take your bags."

"Do you know how long Katarina and I will be here, sergeant? What is the plan for me?"

McDonald replies, "Get some sleep, you have a long day tomorrow, it will all be explained then. You have a meeting with top brass at 0600 hours. It's late, are you folks hungry?"

"Yes, says Katarina," Karl agrees.

"I'll have something sent over; it won't be long. Karl, I will pick you up at 0545 hours in the morning. One more thing Karl. Here is your uniform for tomorrow. I hope it fits, same size as you had before. Good night."

"Thank you, Sergeant McDonald, it has been a very long time since I have had the honor of wearing an Army Air Force uniform." Dinner arrives, they eat, and get settled in for the evening.

Karl is holding Katarina, "Karl, I am so happy to be here, here with you, and out of Germany. We are very blessed. I love you very much. Good night."

Karl smiles, "I am happy to be here, with you as well, to begin our new life together. I love you my dearest, good night to you." Katarina falls asleep in Karl's arms.

February 1, six in the morning. Katarina proudly helps Karl get into his new uniform.

"You look very handsome my Love." Katarina kisses Karl. Karl arrives at headquarters just before 0600 hours. Karl enters General Williams' office and sees three other gentlemen. Karl salutes, they do the same.

"Corporal Schellenberg, I am General Williams; this is Major Douglas, Colonel Baxter, and Captain Fowler."

Karl salutes, "Pleased to meet all of you."

"Have a seat corporal," says General Williams. They sit at a round table. The General begins, "Welcome to London, corporal. How was your journey? How was the flight over last evening?"

"Fine sir, glad to be back on Allied soil. We did have a bit of a scare at the airfield in the Netherlands. Just as we were preparing to take off, a German patrol car came racing toward us. They must have heard the plane. Just as we began to lift off, bullets riddled the plane, it was not badly damaged fortunately. I hope Rudolf, our driver, is ok."

The General continues, "Corporal Schellenberg, many good things have come from your time in Germany, including a new wife I hear."

Karl blushes, "Yes sir. If not for her I would not be here today."

"Tell us why corporal?"

"As you know gentlemen, one year ago, January 27, I was on a mission into Northern Germany to the Kriegsmarine's

Wilhelmshaven Port. My plane suffered mechanical problems, complete engine failure. Just before the engine failed, I remember seeing a strange flash of light, nothing like I have ever seen."

"Yes corporal, I read the report, you had a scout plane with new technology."

"Yes sir."

"When the engine failed, I knew I had to get the plane back over the border, so the Germans would not get our technology. I had crossed into Germany moments before the incident. I turned 180 degrees to a western heading. The plane was descending at a rapid pace. I ejected and hoped the plane would find its way across the border. I later learned it crashed not far from where I landed. I heard it was completely destroyed. It was nearly full of fuel."

The General nods, "Yes corporal, our reconnaissance confirmed that as well. We sent a fighter to ensure that if it was not destroyed, we would finish it off due to the top-secret technology on board. We saw no signs of a parachute though. Until we heard from the Underground, we assumed you had died in the crash."

Karl nods, "Yes sir, I remember hearing an American plane the next morning. When I ejected, my chute failed, and I was severely injured. I did manage to gather the remains of my chutes before the German's would see them. Katarina, my wife, found me the morning of January 31, in the woods. She saved my life. Katarina and her mother took me back to their farm. Katarina cared for me every day; and nursed me back to health. We fell in love."

The General smiles, "We are very happy she did corporal."

A knock on the door. "Yes," as he turns to the door.

Sergeant McDonald, cracks the door open, "We are ready general."

"Good, let's take care of the important things first. Someone will be joining us today, which is not common for this ceremony. Corporal, please stand."

"Hello Karl." Karl turns in amazement.

"Katarina, why are you here?" Sergeant McDonald mentioned

the surprise to Katarina last evening when he opened the car door for her. Katarina smiles, and stands alongside Karl and holds his hand. Karl is wondering what is going on.

General Williams looks at Katarina, "Mrs. Schellenberg, it is a pleasure to meet you." The other officers acknowledge Katarina as well. "Corporal, your efforts in Germany saved thousands of our soldiers and civilian lives. The Allies and the Underground Movement, particularly Hans Houseman, are a tremendous asset to us. Katarina, your father, may he rest in peace, was an immense asset as well. I am sorry to hear of the loss of him and your mother." Tears run down Katarina's cheeks. Karl holds her hand tighter.

"Corporal Schellenberg, it is with great honor, the U.S. Army Air Force is promoting you to First Lieutenant." Karl thinks to himself, *How uncanny, my same rank in the German army.* "On behalf of the U.S. Army Air Force, Lieutenant Schellenberg, I am also very proud to present to you these medals. The Air Medal, our most distinguished medal, the Atlantic Star, the Air Crew, and the Victory Medal for your outstanding service to the United States. Thank you Lieutenant Schellenberg." The General pins them to Karl's uniform. General Williams and the others salute Karl. Each officer, one by one, very proudly shakes Karl's hand, personally congratulates, and salutes him.

Karl is humbled, "Thank you all, I am honored, and surprised, I was doing what I needed to for my country, and quite honestly, for the people of Germany." Katarina hugs Karl; and kisses him.

"I am very proud of you Karl."

"Lieutenant, your new uniform is here as well. If it needs tailored, we will arrange for that, but I did hear you have a tailor in Germany," the General chuckles. He continues, "Have a seat please Lieutenant. Mrs. Schellenberg, please stay as well. Karl, you will be here in London for a week or so for debriefing. We want to learn as much as we can about the Germans, the Army Group North Command, and the SS. Katarina, we are aware of your brother's role in the SS."

"I am sorry General Williams, he is not my brother anymore, and has not been for many years. His day will come, the sooner the better."

"I understand Mrs. Schellenberg. Karl, regarding your assignment after we finish here, you will be stationed at Coffeyville Kansas, the Third Army Air Force Base. The Army Air Force is developing a Strategic Tactical Training Group. From your efforts in Germany, your quick thinking, and your ability to infiltrate the most strategic and secret organization within the Third Reich, you will be heading that group."

"Thank you, General Williams."

The General continues, "You may go now. Lieutenant spend the rest of the day with your lovely wife. We'll begin our debriefing tomorrow. I have invited officers from the British Royal Air Force to join us as well."

Karl stands and salutes, "Thank you, sir, thank you all."

Karl and Katarina return to their room. They have lunch and enjoy the remainder of the day with each other.

"Karl, I am so very proud of you, today's ceremony was wonderful and a great honor for you."

"Katarina, how did you know about it, how did you know to come to the ceremony?"

"Sergeant McDonald, last night when he opened the car door for me, he whispered to me, 'your husband is having a surprise ceremony first thing tomorrow morning. General Williams wants you to join him.' He said he would be back for me right after he dropped you off at headquarters."

"I was very proud to have had you with me Katarina." As they lay in bed that evening, severe thunderstorms roll in. From their window, they can see lightning bolts streak across the sky. The sky lights up with intense lightning, and a few seconds later the walls in their room shake, and the windows rattle from the roar of thunder. Katarina slides over, close to Karl.

"Katarina, I love thunderstorms." Katarina cuddles close to Karl, in a c-position. Her back is tightly against his chest. Karl hugs her. She gently takes his hand; and cups her breast with it. "Good night my Love."

"Good night Katarina." They fall asleep.

The twelve-hour day debriefings begin and last throughout the week, into Saturday. Karl has provided the U.S. and British Royal Air Force valuable information. The debriefings conclude at 1500 hours Saturday. Katarina, and Karl prepare for their journey to the U.S., to Coffeyville Kansas. Sergeant McDonald meets them at 0900 hours to take them to their plane.

"Good morning lieutenant and Mrs. Schellenberg, are you ready to go?"

"Yes sergeant." They arrive at the hanger. Karl sees a military DC-3 transport plane.

"Lieutenant Schellenberg, your journey will require several refueling stops before you arrive in the States. Your flights will take you and Mrs. to a small British airfield in Iceland, then onto Greenland. You will spend the night there, in Ivigtut. You will land at a U.S. Air Base, code named Bluie East Moniker. The next morning you will fly to Newfoundland to refuel at U.S. Army Airfield Base Ernest Harmon. From there you will fly to Army Air Base Dover, in Delaware. You will spend the night there. Your orders will be officially transferred to the U.S. Army Air Force Mainland Command, lieutenant."

"Thank you, sergeant. My first trip to England was a similar route."

February 8. As the plane approaches Dover from the north, they fly over the New York City skyline.

"Karl, New York City is beautiful. I have only seen pictures and read about it." Karl and Katarina touchdown in Dover.

"Welcome to the United States, Katarina." They are greeted by Staff Sergeant Green. He salutes Karl.

"Good afternoon lieutenant and Mrs. Schellenberg. I am Staff Sergeant Green. You are scheduled to depart tomorrow morning at

0700 hours. I will meet you in the morning, 0630 hours. I will take you to your quarters now."

"Thank you, Staff Sergeant Green." Katarina and Karl settle in for the evening.

February 9, Staff Sergeant Green arrives at 0630 hours and drives Karl and Katarina to the hangar.

"We are here lieutenant, wheels up at 0700 hours sharp."

"Thank you, Staff Sergeant Green." Katarina and Karl board the plane for Kansas, a DC-3 military transport. The captain greets them.

"Good morning, I'll be your Captain for the flight. Our flight plan has us arriving at 1430 hours. It's a good day to fly, the weather is clear the entire way. We will be flying at an altitude of fifteen thousand feet. Get seated and we'll be on our way."

"Thank you, captain."

As the plane descends and approaches Coffeyville, Karl can see the Third Army Air Force Base in the distance. Katarina notices the flat farmlands of the Midwest.

"Karl, the land is very flat, many, many farms."

"Yes Katarina, much of our nation's farmland is here in the Midwest. Welcome to Toto land."

Katarina looks at Karl, "What does that mean, Toto land?" Karl chuckles.

"Toto land; Dorothy and the Wizard of Oz, the 1938 movie, one of my favorites."

"I never saw that movie."

Karl laughs, "I will explain that my dear, I am just being funny."

The plane touches down, on schedule. As they approach the hanger, Karl sees a staff car waiting. The plane comes to a stop on the tarmac, Katarina, and Karl exit.

"Karl, it is chilly here."

"Here, take my jacket."

"Good afternoon Lieutenant Schellenberg, Mrs. Schellenberg, welcome to Coffeyville and the Third Army Air Force Base. I'm

staff Sergeant Clarke. I'll be taking you to your quarters on Base. I
trust your flight was good. I'll get your bags and we will be on our
way. You will be living in one of our officer's homes on Base, they
are private homes for married couples. We have stocked the kitchen
with a few supplies until you can shop."

"Very good sergeant, thank you."

"Lieutenant, you have a meeting with General Davis and
Captain Harris at 0700 hours tomorrow morning, the tenth. I'll
pick you up at 0630 hours. After your meetings I'll give you a tour
of the Base, your office, the commissary, the recreation buildings,
and the social hall. During the day the wives meet there." Katarina
thinks to herself and smiles, *hmmm, I will need to get accustomed to this
new life, it will be fun.*

"Thank you, sergeant."

Karl and Katarina arrive at their new home.

"Look Karl, it is a bungalow, so quaint." Sergeant Clarke takes
their luggage in. Karl and Katarina wait by the car.

"Thank you, sergeant, I will see you in the morning." The
sergeant drives away. Karl carries Katarina into their house.

"Welcome to our new life my Love." They kiss. Katarina
immediately tends to the house, unpacking their suitcases. The
beginning of making it their home.

"Karl, I am very tired, we have had a few long days." They retire
for the night. Karl and Katarina lay in bed, hold each other, kiss.
Eventually they fall asleep.

Karl wakes to a wonderful smell. "Katarina, where are you?"

"Good morning Karl, I am in the kitchen, I have made breakfast
for you; eggs, bacon, and biscuits." Katarina comes to the doorway;
she is wearing Karl's unbuttoned shirt, partially exposing her breasts.

"You look very promiscuous, Katarina."

"I like to think I am naughty, yet that will have to wait, you
have an important day ahead of you my dear. This will give you
something to think about today. Last night was wonderful Karl, we
christened this home."

"Hmmm, I thought that was an amazing dream." Katarina throws the kitchen towel at him. They smile at one another.

"Oh, the eggs," Katarina scurries to the kitchen. She hears Karl coming from behind her. Karl gently slips his hands under the front of her shirt, and softly kisses the back of her neck. "Karl, that gives me shivers, I love it." After breakfast together Karl gets dressed into his new uniform and proudly stands in front of Katarina. "Lieutenant, you look very handsome." Katarina straightens his collar, and adjusts the medals on his jacket, and gives him a kiss. "Good luck today my Love."

Sergeant Clarke arrives promptly at 0630 hours. Karl arrives at headquarters at 0650 hours. Karl enters.

"May I help you?" Karl sees a young female private first class. He sees the Women's Army Corps insignia. She salutes. "Good morning, you must be Lieutenant Schellenberg. I'm Private First-Class Baker, General Davis is expecting you. We have you in the private conference room." Private First-Class Baker escorts Karl to the conference room, she knocks on the door and opens it. "General Davis, Lieutenant Schellenberg is here."

"Enter lieutenant, we've been expecting you." Karl enters and salutes. "At ease lieutenant. This is Captain Harris; you will be reporting to him. Have a seat lieutenant. Welcome to the Third Army Air Force Base."

"Thank you, sir."

"We have heard a lot about you lieutenant."

"Thank you, sir, I hope it all is good."

General Davis laughs. "I see you began your career in the Eighth Army Air Force."

"Yes sir, at Barksdale Army Air Force Base, Louisiana. I was then assigned to the Joint Air Base group at the Royal Air Force Base, in Daws Hill England."

"Lieutenant, from what I have learned of your mission in Germany, we are very proud to have you join us. I know General

Williams told you of your assignment here, heading up our new Strategic Tactical Training Group."

"Yes sir."

"Let us tell you of the Group, the purpose, and your role and responsibilities."

"Lieutenant, as you know, the war in Europe has been frustrating for us and the Allies. The Germans have been able, for the most part, to stay one step ahead of us. Until now, though. Mostly in part due to your reconnaissance and intelligence that you collected so quickly. That has been remarkable. Your ability to infiltrate the highest Command in Germany is amazing. We have been working on developing this Strategic Tactical Training Group for months. The timing is perfect for you to join us and head this Group. Your ability to survive in the Nazi environment seems to have come naturally to you."

"There were moments sir," says Karl raising his eyebrows.

"Your role for this Group is to train young Airman, like yourself, to infiltrate the Nazi Organization, engage in their organization, and learn their secrets in time for us to react and respond quickly and effectively. Exactly what you did. Training them to work effectively with the Allies and the Underground Movement will become part of the training program as well. We did not realize that was such an important component before. Any resource you need will be at your disposal."

Karl nods, "Thank you, sir."

"We have hand selected twenty recruits, with the anticipation of, at least ten will become your top choices. You will meet them tomorrow morning. Lieutenant, we need this program to be transparent among the recruits. In other words, the basic training will give them the fundamentals to perform successfully and trained to act on the spur of the moment, to ad-lib if you will, based on current situations. All this while not compromising their cover. We have the Underground Movement to help in developing their German papers, citizenship, birth certificates, etc. We are working with the Underground to identify trusted people within the Nazi Organization like Gerhardt Keitel, to plant their German Army history. I heard Gerhardt was your wife's father."

"Yes sir, he was."

"Lieutenant, something we all need to be aware of, due to your efforts and the intelligence you gathered, the Germans will have their guard up even more. Be cognizant of that and develop your training accordingly. Our plan is to have the first group of recruits available in three months. You have your work cut out for you. This is a very important endeavor for us, and for you. We are confident this program will help drive and steer the outcome of this war in the right direction."

"I understand, thank you."

"Over the course of the next few days, Captain Harris will help you prepare the training. We have quite a few ideas in an outline, I would suggest you prepare the same. The first class will be February 28, 0800 hours. That will give you and Captain Harris two weeks to finalize the program. Any questions lieutenant?"

"I am sure I will have questions at some point, I am fine for now."

"Very good. We have a staff car assigned to you; it will be delivered to your house later today. Let me introduce you to Private First-Class Patrick Owens, he will be your Administrative Assistant." General Davis calls the front desk, "Private First-Class Baker, please send in Private First-Class Owens. Lieutenant Schellenberg, this is Private First-Class Owens. Get to know one another, you will be very busy together." They exchange greetings. "Lieutenant, I'll be leaving you now, Captain Harris and Private Owens will continue from here. Welcome aboard."

Karl stands and salutes. "Thank you, sir." They continue the conversation for the remainder of the day. Karl shares his story of his first mission into occupied Germany, of how Katarina found him, and how she cared for him.

"Lieutenant, we had a very good day. Sergeant Clarke will take you and Mrs. Schellenberg on a tour of the Base to get you acquainted. He will show you your office as well. I'll see you in the morning."

"Thank you, sir. That will be nice."

"Lieutenant let's drive over and get your wife; she is expecting us. I'll show you your office, give you a tour of the Base, the commissary, the recreation buildings, and the social hall." The sergeant and Karl arrive to get Katarina. Karl sees his staff car next to the house. "Good afternoon Mrs. Schellenberg."

"Good afternoon sergeant." They spend the next hour touring the Base, Karl's office, and talking. The sergeant shows them the officer's dining hall. Karl and Katarina arrive home at 1830 hours.

"Thank you, sergeant."

"Katarina let's have dinner at the officers dining hall. It's a bit nippy, but a walk would be nice."

"Yes Karl, I would like that." Karl puts his arm around Katarina to keep her warm, and they walk to the dining hall.

It's Thursday morning, February 11. Karl arrives at his office at 0700 hours. Private First-Class Owens is at his desk.

"Good morning lieutenant," he stands and salutes.

"Good morning Private First-Class. I have a suggestion. We are going to be locked at the arms for a very long time. Although I appreciate the respect, when we are together, in our private setting, you can forgo the official greeting. No need to salute, and please call me Karl."

"Yes sir, I mean Karl. Thank you."

"Very good Patrick."

Karl begins to get settled in his office. Patrick enters.

"Karl, the new recruits and Captain Harris will be here at 0800 hours. I have the conference room reserved."

"Thank you, Patrick, I would like to get to know them, just have a discussion with them to start."

"One more thing Karl, I have a question."

"What is it Patrick?"

"I couldn't help notice on your desk. Is that the survival kit issued by the Atlantic Fleet?"

"Yes Patrick. I was issued this on my first mission into Germany. I have always kept it as a momentum if you will. With Katarina finding me I never had to use it."

The recruits arrive. Karl is waiting for them. They enter and salute. "At ease and have a seat. Good morning gentlemen, I am Lieutenant Schellenberg, this is Captain Harris and Private First-Class Owens. Congratulations, you have been hand selected for this very special training program, the Strategic Tactical Training Group, the first of its kind. Because of this training and your subsequent missions, you have been given the highest security clearance. With that said, you also have been checked out. We are finalizing our program as we speak. One aspect and key feature of you being selected is your ability to speak fluent German. Much of this course will be testing you on that. You must be vigilant in maintaining a German dialog always. One slip will be your demise. The mission, for those of you who graduate, will be to infiltrate yourselves into the German Army as operatives, as a seasoned German officer. You will have a new German life documented, from birth. You will have a fully acknowledged career in the German Army. We will begin the training on Monday the 28.

"First, I would like to get to know each one of you, both personally and your Army Air Force career to date. I will share the same with you. I have one rule, to be candid and honest with one another, do not be afraid to ask me or Captain Harris any questions, nothing is off limits, and I will do the same. This twelve-week training will be intense, the boot camp of Strategic Tactical Training if you will. There will be long days, and I want this to be a very open forum. The goal of this training is for you to become smarter than the Germans; outthink them, out maneuver them, outsmart them, and to always be one, better yet, three steps ahead of them. The result of your training; is for you to survive, not to be captured or killed, and probably the latter if you are caught. If you are successful in the training, I promise you, you will come home to your loved ones. You need to trust me. I just completed an exact mission. I want to know what makes you tick, what makes you get up in the morning, what makes you zig when you should have zagged. Over the next three months we will see what you are made of, if you are ready for this mission, to graduate as an operative. Am I understood?"

"Yes sir." The recruits respond in unison.

"Very well, let's get started." Karl begins to outline the Program he and Captain Harris assembled to date, its goals and objectives. They spend the remainder of the day getting to know one another. Karl tells his story. One recruit particularly stands out to Karl, Airman John Garner. He and Karl share a similar childhood. John was raised in a German family and speaks fluent German.

A NEW ARRIVAL

Saturday morning, a light snow is falling in Coffeyville. February 12 1944. Karl and Katarina sleep in. They play in bed most of the morning.

"I love Saturday mornings with you Katarina."

"Karl, we need to go shopping today. We need food, I want some things for the house, and I would love to get some new clothes, you could use some yourself."

"Yes, great idea, I want to get a few things as well. Let's go into town first and check it out, we can have lunch. I heard it is a quaint town and has nice shops. Maybe take a walk along the Verdigris River. We can go to the commissary afterwards."

"It is a date Karl. I will get ready."

Katarina and Karl spend most of the afternoon in Coffeyville. They have lunch at a small diner on West Eighth Street. After lunch they walk down Maple Street and take a relaxing walk along the river.

"Karl, look at that old warehouse. It needs a lot of repair. I wonder if it is abandoned?"

"Good question, the town seems to be flourishing, but it does look abandoned."

The snow has stopped. Katarina shops and shops, a few dresses and tops, nylons, shoes, a new coat, and handbag. While Karl is elsewhere, she buys a surprise for him, perfume and a sleek, short, low cut silk slip and a pair of lace panties. Karl sees Katarina is very happy; he picks up a few things for himself.

"Karl, I have not been shopping in so long, thank you. I saw a general store down the street, we can see if we are able to find something to make the house more a home." Katarina finds candles, a linen tablecloth, and a few picture frames for the pictures she brought from Germany. "I am ready my Love, time to get our groceries."

Karl spots a florist shop on the way back to the car. As they approach the car, Karl blurts out, "Oh Katarina, I forgot something."

"What is it Karl?"

"Stay with the car, I will be right back." Karl returns to the car with a bag.

"What is it Karl?"

"You will see my Love." They return home after a long day of shopping. Karl and Katarina prepare dinner together. After dinner Karl gets up. "I will be right back." He returns with a dozen of red roses and a dozen of white lilies. "Monday is Valentine's Day, Happy Valentine's Day my Love." Katarina is so surprised, she runs and jumps into Karl's arms, nearly crushing the flowers.

"They are beautiful Karl. You make me so happy. I love you very, very much."

"I love you my dearest Katarina." The next day Katarina is busy nesting the house, Karl is working on his training program.

Karl wakes early Monday morning to that wonderful smell of eggs and bacon again. Katarina brings breakfast in the bedroom. "Happy Valentine's Day Karl."

"Same to you my Love. It is early." Katarina is wearing her new slip. "Katarina, I love that, so beautiful. When did you get it?"

"In town Saturday."

"You smell very nice, and you have that promiscuous look again."

"That is the plan my Love." Katarina flips her slip up; Karl gets a glimpse of the lace panties. She snuggles in bed.

Karl nestles his head on Katarina's breasts. "I love your perfume." Breakfast goes uneaten.

The week begins with Karl and Captain Harris working on their training program; and continues throughout the week. The program is developed to have a different course each of the twelve weeks. Tests and evaluations will be given at the end of each week. Every recruit must maintain an eighty-five percentile average each week or they will be dismissed from the course. Friday arrives. Karl is in his office. It's late afternoon, Patrick knocks and enters. "Karl, I have an urgent message for you from London."

"Let me see Patrick." It's a note from Hans Houseman. 'Karl, I want you and Katarina to know. Wilhelm has been promoted. He is now Chief of the Armed Forces High Command, the office given to the commander and highest-ranking officer of the Nazi Germany Armed Forces. He reports directly to Hitler. He has full reign of the German Army. He came back to Aurich this month, on Saint Valentine's Day. Father Root had a family in need staying in the farmhouse. Wilhelm ordered them out. He destroyed the farm. He burned the farmhouse, the barn, and the stone barn to the ground. The walls are still standing. The animals in the barn escaped the fire, thank God. The Germans are flattening the rolling hills. The SS is building a satellite camp for the Neuengamme Concentration Camp, in Aurich, on the farmland. It is to be completed by October 1944. Terrible to see that. We are all fine though.' Karl leaves immediately and goes home.

"Karl, you are home early." Katarina can see a disturbed look in Karl's eyes.

"Katarina, I have news, bad news. I received a note from Hans today."

"What is it?"

"Wilhelm returned to Aurich earlier in the week. Father Root had a family staying in the farmhouse. Wilhelm ordered them out.

He destroyed the farm. He burned the farmhouse, the barn, and the stone barn to the ground. Our barn Katarina, the walls are all that remain standing." Katarina falls to her knees and begins crying. Karl kneels and comforts her. "The Germans are flattening the rolling hills. The SS is building a concentration camp, in Aurich, on the farm."

"He is a monster Karl, an evil man, he must be stopped. Why would he do that to his own homestead? Is Hans ok?"

"Yes, Hans, Father Root, and the villagers are all fine, he did not hurt anyone this time. Wilhelm has been promoted. He is now the commander and highest-ranking officer of the Nazi Germany Armed Forces. He reports directly to Hitler. He has full reign of the German Army to do what he wants. The Geneva Convention cannot stop him." Karl helps Katarina to the sofa. She falls asleep, crying in his arms. The weekend passes.

Monday the twenty-eighth. The new recruits arrive. Karl and Captain Harris roll out their program. After the first week, one recruit is dismissed. The next week, two more are dismissed. The recruits realize this is serious business and must buckle down. The week of March 14 brings a refreshing attitude to Karl and Captain Harris. The recruits are engaged. John is showing tremendous leadership.

Karl arrives home the evening of March 17. It is 6:30, and dark outside. "Karl, have you been to Shenanigans Pub?"

"No, I have not heard of it. Where is it?"

Come with me you Leprechaun. Katarina has candles burning in the bedroom. "Karl, come with me to the bedroom, or shall I say Shenanigans. I have some news for you." As Karl walks toward the bedroom he sees the flickering of candles. "They enter, sit with me on the edge of the bed. Karl can tell Katarina is happy about something. Her eyes are gleaming. He sits next to her. Katarina takes his hands. She holds one and places the other on her belly. Karl looks into her eyes.

"What news, Katarina." Katarina looks into his eyes. "We are going to have a baby." Karl takes a breath, a breath of joy, excitement, and happiness.

"Katarina, that is wonderful news. I am speechless. When did we conceive, on our wedding night?"

"Karl, we made our baby the night you came home to me, January 6, in the wee hours of the morning."

"Are you sure, I mean I am so happy, I mean, well, I am beside myself."

"Yes Karl, I am sure. I just know, I had a sensational and incredible feeling on that special evening. Butterflies inside of me, just like I do now." Karl embraces Katarina. They passionately kiss each other. They fall back onto the bed.

"You must take it easy Katarina, take care of yourself and the baby. When are you due? I have so many questions." Katarina places her two fingers over Karl's lips.

"Karl, I will be fine."

"May I make you a cup of tea, do you want water, do you need a blanket? You should lay down. I will get extra pillows for you." Katarina laughs out loud.

"Relax my Love. I have an appointment scheduled tomorrow, at 1:00, with the doctor on Base to get a checkup and examination. I wanted to be sure first. I think I am ten weeks along."

"I want to go with you tomorrow. You have made me the happiest man alive; I love you."

"Karl you have made me the happiest woman alive, I love you more."

They celebrate their evening at Shenanigans. Karl is awake all night. He lays and stares at his new bride, his baby's mother, thinking of their new and changing life together. The sun begins to rise, Katarina wakes up, and sees Karl wide awake.

"When did you wake up?"

"I have been awake all night, thinking we just only began our new life together, now we have a bundle of joy coming to join us,

I am so happy Katarina. I need to go into the office. I will be back at 12:30 to take you to the doctor."

"Remember Karl, tradition is we do not tell anyone until we know for sure, even though I know for sure." Katarina kisses Karl.

Karl enters his office. "Good morning Karl, you look very happy today."

"I am Patrick, just happy to be alive. Patrick, my wife has a doctor's appointment at 1300 hours, I need to take her."

"Sure thing sir. No worries, we can cover for you."

"Perfect Patrick, I will let Captain Harris know as well. Most of the afternoon is a reading assignment for the recruits, they will be in good hands."

Karl arrives home at 12:30, Katarina is anxiously waiting at the door. They arrive at Katarina's doctor's appointment early and sign in. Katarina is holding Karl's hand very tight. "Karl, I am nervous, a happy nervous though."

"Me too."

"Mrs. Schellenberg, the doctor will see you now, follow me."

"May my husband come in?"

"Yes ma'am, absolutely."

"Hello, Mrs. and Mr. Schellenberg, I'm Doctor Grabb. I see you're here for a very special examination?"

"Yes Doctor, please call me Katarina."

"Let me take your vitals first. Lay back on the table Katarina." The doctor examines Katarina and sits back in his chair. "You can sit up. Your vitals all are good. How are you feeling, are you tired?"

"No sir."

"How is your energy level?"

"Very high," Katarina says, she looks over to Karl with a smirky smile.

"When was your last menstrual cycle?"

"December of last year."

"Are you taking any vitamins?"

"No sir." The doctor sits a little further back in his chair and cups his chin with his fingers.

"Well, Katarina," he pauses. Katarina and Karl look at him with anxiousness.

"Well what doctor?"

"Well, I would suggest you start taking vitamins, your baby will need to stay healthy. Congratulations to both of you." He smiles. Katarina and Karl embrace each other.

"Thank you, doctor, and thank you for the good news. When am I due?"

"I believe the middle of September; from what I see it could be a week one way or the other. You are in good health; I don't foresee any issues. I want to see you monthly until we get in the last trimester, then every two weeks until the last month, then weekly. My nurse will set the dates."

Karl and Katarina go into town to celebrate. They have a nice relaxing dinner; and return home. As they lay in bed, Katarina turns to Karl. "Karl do you want a little boy or a little girl?"

"I want our baby to be healthy, if I had a choice, a little girl for you Katarina. How about you?"

"I feel the same way about being healthy, but I would love a little boy for you." Katarina lays her head on Karl, they fall asleep.

The next morning, Karl is first at the office. Captain Harris and Patrick arrive within minutes of one another. "Captain Harris, Private Owens, I have very good news." Before they could ask what news, Karl tells them in a very excited voice. "Katarina is pregnant, we're going to have a baby." They both congratulate Karl on the wonderful news.

A week goes by, then a month. Springtime in Kansas has arrived. April 19, a nice sunny and warm day. The flowers are blooming, trees are bearing buds.

"Katarina, do you know what today is?"

"Yes, I do my Love, we first kissed on this day, and we made unforgettable love." They hold each other and kiss, a nice long passionate kiss.

Katarina has her next doctor's appointment, everything is fine, the baby's health is good, Katarina's health is good, her term is progressing well. Seven weeks have passed for the recruits. Fifteen recruits remain. Karl arrives home that evening.

"Karl did you know we have a cherry tree in our back yard. The blossoms are coming out, they are beautiful."

"Katarina, I have been thinking. Let us buy our own home. We can move off Base. We can have a home to make our own. We will paint the rooms, put our own curtains up, a home where our children will have their own rooms. A home we will raise our children in."

"Karl I would love that; we can begin looking this weekend."

As the house hunt continues, so does the Tactical Training. Karl arrives early to the office to send Hans a note. 'Hans, I wanted to write and tell you the good news, Katarina is pregnant. We are having a baby! She is due the middle of September. We are going to buy our own home. I hope you are doing well. I am heading up a training program, the Strategic Tactical Program, training recruits for what I did in Germany with you. I am stationed at the Third Army Air Force Base, in Coffeyville Kansas.' Karl continues his note to Hans.

Week eleven has begun, seven recruits remain. John remains the star recruit. Karl, Captain Harris, and Patrick gather the seven in the training room. "Gentlemen, I want to begin this week by saying you have two weeks left in this training, make the most of them. Those of you that have remained have done well."

Saturday, May 13, Katarina is in her eighteenth week. Everything is fine with her and the baby. She is showing more and more each week. Katarina and Karl have appointments with their realtor for the weekend. Their realtor picks them up at 9:00.

"Good morning Karl and Katarina."

"Good morning Angie."

"How are Mommy and the baby doing?"

"Mommy and baby are doing fine Angie, thank you for asking."

"We have three very nice homes to look at today. Much nicer than those we have looked at before." They drive up to the first one. "I know you wanted a three-bedroom, but I wanted to show this lovely two-bedroom, one bath. The rooms are small though. It is priced very well."

"We should look at it, Angie." They tour the house for about thirty minutes. "Angie, I agree with you, it is smaller than we wanted, and I do not care for the layout. I would like three bedrooms. I am ready to go to the next house."

"Yes, thank you Katarina. This three-bedroom we are going to see next has two baths, a very nice yard that backs up to the woods and has a garage. It is a Craftsman style architecture, very quaint and cozy. It's not much over your price range. I'm excited about this one, it just came on the market. The address is 320 Sycamore Avenue, Sycamore trees line the street." They arrive at 320 Sycamore Avenue.

"Angie, I love the Sycamore trees, and I absolutely love the curb appeal."

"I do as well," says Karl.

As they enter the house, Katarina tugs on Karl's arm. "Look Karl, a porch swing, just like Mother had in Germany. She and I would swing for hours." Katarina begins to cry but composes herself. The owners greet them. "Karl, I love the layout. Look at the fireplace and the built-ins." Katarina notices a vase of lilies on the table. She nudges Karl, and points. They spend the better part of an hour in the house. Katarina is telling Karl her ideas on furniture placement, the baby's room, even where the crib will be. Katarina looks at Karl and whispers, "Karl I love this home, I have a good feeling here." Karl smiles and nods.

"Angie."

"Yes Karl."

"We do not need to see the next house. We love this home. Will you get the offer ready and submitted today?"

"Great, and yes. I will write the offer and I'll get it over to them today."

Sunday morning, Katarina, and Karl wakeup just after 9:00.

"Karl, I dreamt of our new home last night. I hope we hear news today." They have a nice breakfast and leave for morning service at St. Andrews Church. Just as they return, Angie calls, Katarina answers.

"Good morning Katarina, it's Angie. May I come over to see you?"

"Yes, do you have news?"

"I'd rather tell you in person."

"Karl, Angie is coming over with news, but would not tell me over the phone. I hope everything is good, do you think they rejected our offer?" Angie arrives in thirty minutes; and knocks on the door.

"Katarina, Karl. I have news but I wanted to tell you in person."

"Please, have a seat Angie," Katarina says with a somewhat worried/concerned look.

"Well, you recall I thought your offer may have been a bit low, for a couple of reasons. The property is new on the market, and with the neighborhood, I feel the home was priced relatively correct."

"I know," says Karl, "and we understand. We need to be realistic in what we can afford. So, should we start over?"

Angie smiles and hesitates a moment, "No, we start preparing to move. They have accepted your offer." Katarina and Karl look at each other. Katarina hugs Karl, knocking him back on the sofa.

"That is wonderful news," Katarina says with tears in her eyes. "I knew that was to be our home, I just knew it, I had a feeling."

"Katarina, the owners wanted their home to go to a nice young couple. When they saw you, with a new baby coming, and listened to you as you toured the home; placing furniture, they could picture you all in the home. Their mind was made up. They were going to work with you so you would have this home. They can close by the end of June. That gives you about six weeks to close and get settled in." Karl and Katarina settle in for the night. Katarina is nestled in Karl's arms.

"Karl, can you believe it, we have our own home."

"Yes, my Love, I have been dreaming and praying of finding the right home, not just a house." He leans down and kisses Katarina's belly, just as he has done since he learned of their baby.

May 15, the last week for the Strategic Tactical Training. The remaining recruits arrive. Captain Harris, Karl, and Patrick meet them in the training room. "Gentlemen have a seat. As you know this is your last week. As you can see, unfortunately, we lost four more recruits last week. You are the top three, however, this week is just beginning. I want you to know, and as I mentioned to you your first week, we only want to send the best of the best on this mission. Had we arbitrarily sent the original twenty, more than likely seventeen would not have come home. This training has been grueling, it has been tough, and in some ways, humbling to some of you. We structured it that way for a very good reason; for you to be well prepared."

The end of the week arrives. General Davis, Captain Harris, Karl, and Patrick meet the recruits in the training room. "Gentlemen have a seat. Congratulations. I am proud to say we have three graduates. Congratulations Airman John Garner, Airman Philip Stone, and Airman George Steiner. You have done well." The conversations continue. "Your orders are in the envelope in front of you. You will leave for London 0600 hours, Monday May 22. Beginning today, we, the Allies and the Underground Movement will begin preparing your papers, your new identity, your life in Germany. Your career in the German Army will begin soon. Let me give you a piece of advice, from my personal experience. Always keep your guard up. The Nazis are smart, they rarely let their guard down. They are more aware of spies and infiltration than ever before. They are desperate to win this war. We cannot allow that. I have seen that first-hand. Your situation can change in seconds and you must react appropriately, without emotion, and you must stay calm. The information and intelligence you gather will be paramount on stopping Hitler, the Third Reich, and the German Army. I am confident this training has prepared you to serve your country. Godspeed." Karl, the captain, and Patrick proudly salute the graduates, and shake each other's hands.

Once the recruits leave, General Davis, Captain Harris, Karl, and Patrick remain in the room. "Lieutenant Schellenberg."

"Yes, General Davis."

"You have done a remarkable job with this program, especially with the trial training. Captain Harris has kept me filled in."

"Thank you, sir. I have notes on some areas we can improve and enhance the program for the next group."

"On behalf of the U.S. Army Air Force and our Allies, I very much appreciate you not wavering from the standards you set. Three live graduates are much better than twenty dead or captured ones."

A NEW CHAPTER

May turns to June. Karl is enhancing the training program for the next series of recruits, scheduled for June 19. Katarina is busy preparing for the move. June 13 arrives, Katarina's next doctor's appointment. Katarina and Karl arrive at Doctor Grabb's office at 12:45, for her 1:00 appointment.

"Hello Katarina, please have a seat on the table. How are you doing lieutenant?"

"Please call me Karl. I am doing fine, Doctor, anxious though."

"I understand Karl, have patience. Precious little things take time. How have you been Katarina?"

"I have been fine, feeling very well. We are buying a home; we are so excited."

"Will you have it by the time the little one arrives?"

"Yes. We close the end of the month."

"I'll take your vitals first. Now lay back, let me examine you." After a few minutes, "You can sit up now. The baby's heartbeat is strong, everything looks and sounds good. The baby's position feels good. You will be entering your third trimester soon. You will need to keep rested; and stay strong. Are you taking the vitamins I gave you?"

"Yes, I am Doctor Grabb."

"Next month I want to see you every two weeks.

"Yes, I remember you wanted two-week visits."

"Let's wait until mid-July, since you'll be busy moving. If you feel you need to see me in the meantime, we can arrange that, anytime Katarina."

They arrive home, Karl drops Katarina off and heads back to his office. Katarina opens the door to the phone ringing. Katarina barely gets to it. "Hey Katarina, this is Angie."

"Hello Angie, how may I help you?"

"I have good news if it works for you and Karl. The agent for 320 Sycamore called me this morning. The owners can be out next week and wanted to know if you and Karl want to close and move in earlier. They can close June 23, that's a Friday. That will give you the weekend to move in."

"Angie, that is wonderful news. I will call Karl and see if our credit union can have things ready for closing. We are using the Pentagon Federal Credit Union here on Base. I will call you back when we know something. Thank you again, Angie."

Katarina calls Karl. "Karl, Angie just called with wonderful news. The owners of our new home can close on June 23. We can move in that weekend. Will you check with the credit union to see if they can have things ready?"

"Yes, I will call them right now. This is great news Katarina."

The credit union calls Karl back in an hour and confirms the paperwork and funds will be ready. Karl calls Katarina to tell her. Katarina confirms with Angie. Karl arrives home just before 6:00 that evening and sees Katarina at the table, busy with what appears to be, making lists, many of them. "Oh Karl, we have so many things to do, so much we need to buy in ten days. I hope we can afford everything. I have a long list." Karl leans down and kisses Katarina, then sits at the table.

"Katarina, the money we accumulated, my pay, when I was in Germany will help to buy the things we need. The Army Air Force held it for me."

"Yes, I remember you telling me. That was very nice for them to give you your back pay. I think I already spent it though," Katarina giggles. "Look, I have been jotting down things we need for our home. Here, look on the furniture list." Katarina is very excited and happy. "We need bedroom furniture, living room furniture, a kitchen table and chairs, some small tables for lamps, and most of all, a crib, a dressing table, furniture for the baby's room. A rocker will be nice, to rock our little one. We do not need much, just enough to get us started. Here look at the housewares list I started. I have bedding linens for us and the baby's room; oh yes, pillows, I forgot those. I have towels for the bathroom and kitchen, lamps for the rooms. And look here Karl; I did not realize we have nothing for the kitchen; we need kitchen plates, silverware, some pots and pans, cooking utensils, a toaster and coffee pot, a tea kettle, and baking things. I so much want to bake for us. I know you love blueberry pie; I will bake a pumpkin pie also; and I will bake fresh bread."

"Katarina my dear, take a breath. I see you have been busy."

"Karl, can we go into town tonight and start, can we go tonight? I called the furniture store; they are open until nine."

"How can I say no to those beautiful blue eyes and that smile that melts my heart? We will also check W. F. Gable; we could get your whole list there."

"W. F. Gable, who are they?"

Karl chuckles, "Oh, I forgot, you do not know, that is a department store. The guys on Base told me of it. I remembered seeing the first day we went to town. A department store has many departments in one store, like furniture, clothes, shoes, housewares." After dinner they go into town. They shop until the stores close. They have picked the furniture they need and arranged delivery for the afternoon of the twenty-third. Moving day is fast approaching. Katarina and Karl finish their shopping lists the following weekend.

Sunday morning, they sleep in. Karl is fondling and kissing Katarina. "Katarina, I need to get up, I have a big day tomorrow, our new recruits arrive."

"Stay a bit longer Karl, you are making me feel good." They play for another hour. "That was very nice. Are you happy you stayed?" Karl looks at Katarina with a promiscuous smile. She knows the answer.

"I am ready for breakfast my Love. May I help you with anything for tomorrow?"

"I am in good shape but thank you."

Monday morning, Karl arrives at his office at 0600 hours. Captain Harris and Patrick arrive shortly thereafter. The recruits arrive at 0800 hours. Karl begins the same as he did with the first group. After introductions, they spend the day getting to know one another. Two recruits stand apart from the others, Airman David Kiechler and Airman Thomas Helsel. The day ends.

"Captain Harris, may I have a moment."

"Sure lieutenant."

"I wanted to remind you we are closing on our home Friday and moving in that afternoon."

"Yes, lieutenant I remember, I will take the class Friday."

"Thank you, sir." The recruits settle in and begin their training.

Friday arrives. Katarina is up early. Karl hears Katarina in the kitchen. "Good morning my Love. You are up early, what are you doing?"

"Good morning to you my Love. I packed all of our personnel things for the move." They have breakfast together. "Karl, I am excited."

"Katarina, I will clean up, you go and get ready. We need to be at the Credit Union by 10:30. I will put these boxes in the car." They arrive at Pentagon Federal Credit Union at 10:15. They have a seat with the loan officer.

"Good morning Mr. and Mrs. Schellenberg, I'm George Hill. Mrs. Schellenberg, I see you're expecting, congratulations. How far along are you?"

"I am right at twenty-four weeks."

"The timing of the house worked perfectly."

"Yes, it did."

"Let's get started, this won't take long, we need some signatures. Alright, we're finished. Congratulations, you are now proud homeowners."

"Thank you, George." Katarina and Karl stand and hug. As they leave, Katarina sees Angie in the lobby.

"Katarina and Karl, I wanted to personally congratulate you, and give you the keys. The owner's agent dropped them off this morning."

"Would you like to have lunch with us Angie, our furniture is being delivered at 1:00, we have time."

"I would like that, thank you."

Katarina and Karl arrive at 320 Sycamore at 12:45. "Karl, our home is beautiful, let's go in."

As they get to the porch, Karl holds Katarina back, "Wait here my Love." He unlocks the door and opens it. He turns to Katarina, picks her up in his arms, and carries her across the threshold. "Welcome home Mrs. Schellenberg." They kiss.

"Karl, you carried me through the door on our wedding day in Germany." Katarina sees a bouquet of fresh red roses and white lilies on the counter. "Karl, where did those come from?"

Karl smiles, "I had Angie get them this morning."

"They are beautiful, thank you my Love." They hear the delivery truck arrive. "Karl our furniture is here." Katarina stays busy directing the delivery folks in placing the furniture. Karl unloads the car. The furniture is finished. Katarina walks down the hall to the baby's room; a tear runs down her cheek when sees the crib. Karl notices her, walks up behind her and hugs here. "Karl, our little one's room." They begin unpacking and getting settled in.

There's a knock on the door, it opens, and Angie sticks her head in. "Hey you two, I brought you dinner."

"Oh my, I didn't realize it was that time already. "Thank you, Angie, will you join us?"

"No thank you, I just wanted to drop this off. I have a little housewarming gift for you."

"You did not have to do that."

"I know, but I wanted to. We have become good friends over the past couple of months."

Katarina opens the gift, it's a picture. "Look Karl, it is the Praying Man, so sweet, thank you Angie."

"Hang this above your table, let it bring you peace. Do you need any help?"

"No Angie, I want to take my time, we are fine. The furniture is in place, that is the big thing for today."

"I understand Katarina. Well, I need to go and let you two get settled in."

The sun has set. Karl is in the kitchen organizing drawers. Katarina comes from the bedroom wearing her silk slip, lace panties, thigh high nylons, and high heels. "Karl; come to me, let us christen our home. Let's play."

"Oh Katarina, wow you are beautiful."

"Karl, I know you have been a little nervous the past few weeks about making love. You have been very cautious with me, apprehensive, and timid."

"I do not want to hurt you or the baby." Katarina giggles. Katarina cups Karl's face with her hands.

"You will not hurt either one of us. Karl my Love, this is natural, making love is natural, we will be fine. We can be creative; we know other ways to play. Come to me. Be my bad boy. I have the room ready, the candles are lit."

They spend the weekend getting settled in and organized; and playing. Karl is not as nervous anymore. Katarina has the baby's room ready. Everything is white.

"Karl, I want to paint the rooms, freshen things up."

"I like that idea; I will do the painting; you should not be around the fumes. I will start next weekend."

"Karl, can we start with the baby's room, then ours, the living room, and kitchen." Sunday afternoon, after church service Katarina and Karl take a walk through the neighborhood. They meet their neighbors on either side. Ruth and Ed Franklin on their right side, a younger couple; and Carol and Paul Williams on their left side, an elderly couple.

Monday morning, June 26. Karl checks in with Captain Harris. "Good morning captain, how did the recruits do last week?"

"Better than the first group, we still have twenty."

"I am glad to hear that captain."

The weeks go by, the dog days of summer are in full swing. Karl continues his training program. Katarina: day by day, continues makes the house their home. The rooms have been painted. Katarina has planted red geraniums across the front of their porch. She has the finishing touches completed in the baby's room, the crib and changing table are ready, curtains are hung, and a small area rug has been placed in the middle of the room. A rocking chair sits in the corner by the window. Karl walks by the room and see's Katarina sitting in the rocker, staring out the window.

"A penny for your thoughts my Love."

"Oh, hello Karl. I know we have been thinking of a name for the baby. I keep resonating with Nicholas Samuel for a boy, and Caroline Nichole, for a little girl."

"I think those are perfect names, they are my favorites as well." Karl and Katarina begin socializing more and are becoming friends with Ruth and Ed Franklin. Angie stops by at least once a week. August arrives.

"Karl do you remember today?"

"Yes, my Love, August 1, the day I left for my mission in Germany."

"Yes, I was frightened that day, but you came home to me." Summer in Kansas has been very pleasant for Karl and Katarina. Katarina's doctor's visits go from bi-weekly to weekly. The baby is progressing fine.

Monday July 24, six weeks to go, eleven recruits remain. David and Thomas continue to lead the way, showing great promise. The middle of August approaches, week nine begins with six recruits. Karl's program is rigorous, recruits are falling one by one.

Katarina wakes to Karl singing, August 16. "Happy birthday to you. Happy birthday to you." Katarina smiles and giggles. "Happy birthday to Katarina. Happy birthday to you my Love."

"You're silly and so sweet. That is what I love about you, thank you."

"I have something for you. Here, open it."

"Karl, the ring is beautiful. What is the stone?"

"It is a Linde Star; it symbolizes deep love and devotion."

"Karl, it is the perfect gift, thank you."

The weeks go by. September 8, Group Two training finishes. Only two finish. Airman David Kiechler and Airman Thomas Helsel. Katarina is becoming uncomfortable; the delivery of the baby is getting close. Saturday morning, September 9. Karl and Katarina lay in bed. Katarina takes Karl's hand and rests it on her belly. "Karl do you feel the baby?"

"Yes, I do. The little one is getting restless."

"He is getting restless Karl."

"He?"

"Yes, I feel it is a boy."

Katarina rests through the weekend. The week seems to go by quickly. Saturday is a restless day for Katarina. The baby is moving more and more. Sunday, September 17, 5:30 in the morning, Katarina's water breaks. "Karl, wake up, it is time."

"Time?"

"Karl, time to go to the hospital, my water has broken." Karl jumps out of bed in a nervous panic. "Karl, calm down. While you get ready, I am going to shower." Karl gets Katarina's bag ready; they are ready to go to Mercy Hospital. They leave at 7:30.

Minutes turn to hours. Karl is at Katarina's bedside, comforting her and getting her water. Her contractions are beginning to increase. Karl keeps a vigilant check of his watch. The nurses are helping Katarina be as comfortable as possible. Doctor Grabb stops in, it's just before noon.

"How are you feeling, Katarina?"

"I am doing well; the pain is starting to get worse."

"Let me see how you are coming along. Everything looks fine, you have a way to go though. You're still in early labor Katarina, you are just beginning to dilate. Are your contractions regular yet?"

"No Doctor, they are not."

"Just stay relaxed. I'll be back in a few hours to check on you."

"Doctor Grabb."

"Yes Karl."

"Is there anything I can do?"

"Just stay with her and keep her relaxed."

Doctor Grabb returns at 3:00 in the afternoon.

"Hello Katarina, are your contractions beginning to increase."

"Yes, and more regular."

"Good, let me have a look. You're in the second stage of your labor now. This stage is called active labor. You have dilated to six centimeters. Your contractions will begin to pick up now. Everything is looking good though. I'll have the nurse give you something for your pain."

"No thank you Doctor, I want this experience to be natural. For the joy of the result, I can endure a little pain."

"Very good, just relax and breathe steady. I'll check back to check in with you in a few hours." Karl continues to comfort Katarina. Doctor Grabb returns later in the afternoon, it's just before 5:45.

"Hello Katarina, how are you doing?"

"The contractions are closer together, lasting longer, and are becoming more intense."

"That's good. Let me have a look. You're in the last stage of active labor, you're seven centimeters dilated, and everything is looking good. I'll be back. Can we get you anything?"

"No thank you, I am fine." With that said another contraction happens, Katarina clutches Karl's hand.

Doctor Grabb holds Katarina's hand, "I'll see you in a little while, remember, stay relaxed the best you can, and breathe steady during your contractions." It's 7:30, Katarina's contractions and pain are increasing. Doctor Grabb returns. "Katarina, the nurse tells me your contractions have been very regular."

"Yes, regular and with more pain."

"Let's see how the little one is progressing. Katarina, you're getting close, you are nine centimeters, shouldn't be much longer. Stay relaxed." It's approaching 9:30, Katarina's pain is becoming unbearable. Her contractions are lasting upwards of ninety seconds. Doctor Grabb returns. "Katarina let's check you again. My dear, we are ready, you are dilated ten centimeters. Let's get you to the delivery room young lady. Karl, you will need to wait in the waiting room."

"I know, I want to be with Katarina, but I understand Doctor Grabb. This is good where we are at this moment." Karl leans down and kisses Katarina, and her belly.

"I love you both. Be strong my Love."

Katarina looks into Karl's eyes, squeezes his hand, and smiles, "I love you too."

As Karl watches Katarina get wheeled to the delivery room, he checks his watch, 9:45. Katarina looks one more time, waves to Karl and blows him a kiss. In the waiting room Karl is pacing back and forth, praying Katarina and the baby are doing well. He checks his watch, seemingly every minute. A nurse walks by, "May I get you anything Mr. Schellenberg?"

"No thank you, I am fine." The minutes seem like hours. Karl looks at the time, 11:50, just before midnight. Another nurse comes into the waiting room.

"Mr. Schellenberg, would you like to see your wife and baby?" Karl's smile is ear to ear.

"Yes ma'am, how is she, how is the baby, is it a boy or girl?"

"Mrs. Schellenberg wants to tell you herself." As Karl hurriedly walks toward the delivery room he glances up and sees the room number, NSY1. He hears the little one crying, well screaming to be honest, oh so loud. He enters the delivery room and sees their little baby laying on Katarina's chest, swaddled in a blanket, on Katarina's breast. Katarina smiles at him.

"Karl my Love, look, look at your son. We have a baby boy, Nicholas Samuel."

Karl walks over to them, "Katarina, you are beautiful, Nicholas is beautiful. His eyes are blue like yours." He leans down, kisses Katarina, and kisses Nicholas on his forehead. "You have made me the happiest man on earth." He then turns to Doctor Grabb. "Did everything go well?"

"Yes Karl. Your little boy is healthy. He was born at 11:35, he is 7 pounds 3 ounces and 19.55 inches long. Katarina did very well also, especially with this being her first."

"When will they come home Doctor?"

"In three or four days, Karl. We like to keep them under observation to be sure everything is fine." Karl stays with Katarina another hour. Katarina breastfeeds Nicholas.

The nurse comes into the room. "Mr. Schellenberg, Katarina and the baby need their rest, they have had a long day, as did you. You'll need to leave for the night."

Karl kisses Katarina and the baby. "Katarina, I need to go into the office in the morning, I will be in later in the day. Good night Katarina, good night little Nicholas, I love you both."

"Good night Karl, we love you."

Karl gets home and goes to bed. He then remembers his fictitious parents in Germany, Hans had them married on September 17. Monday morning arrives quickly, Karl goes to his office first. Knowing Katarina time was close, Patrick begins to ask Karl how she is doing. Before Patrick can get the words out, "Patrick, I am a proud father."

"I was just about to ask. Congratulations Karl." Captain Harris overhears and comes into the room.

"Congratulations Karl. How are Katarina and the baby? Are they doing well?"

"Yes, very well indeed, thank you for asking. We had a baby boy last evening, his name is Nicholas, Nicholas Samuel."

"So, Karl."

"Yes captain."

"What are you doing here?" Karl looks at him. "Go and be with your wife and baby. Take a few days off, get them settled in."

"Yes sir, thank you." With a smile, Karl leaves. He stops by the house to get Katarina a few things. Then he plans to drive into town for flowers. Karl sees Ruth and Ed when he arrives home.

"Karl, how is Katarina, did she have her baby? We haven't seen much activity the past couple of days."

"Yes, she did. Yesterday, last night, September 17, 11:35, a little boy. His name is Nicholas Samuel."

"That wonderful news, are they doing well?"

"Yes, they are."

"We see you're in a hurry, we'll let you go. Give them our love."

"Thank you."

Karl returns to the hospital that afternoon. Karl walks in, Katarina looks surprised. Karl kisses her and baby Nicholas; and lays the flowers on the bed table.

"Karl, the flowers are beautiful. What are you doing here so early?"

"Captain Harris gave me a few days off, until we get you and the baby home and settled."

"That was very nice of him, he is a sweet man."

"Do not let him hear you say that, it will tarnish his image." Karl chuckles. "Katarina, I brought our camera. I want a picture of you and Nicholas."

"Oh, yes, let me fix my hair. Karl, I thought of something, something we forgot to buy."

"What Katarina, what did we forget?"

"A carriage, we need a carriage for walks."

"Yes, how did we manage to forget that? No worries my Love, I will get one." They spend the remainder of the day together. The day comes to an end. Karl gets chased home by the nurse, yet not before hugs and kisses.

"Good night my Loves, I love you both.

"Good night Karl, we love you, Daddy."

Karl gets a little sleep; but is restless thinking of Katarina and Nicholas. He returns to the hospital the next morning. As he walks in the room, Katarina is feeding Nicholas. "Good morning my Love, did you and Nicholas sleep well?" Karl leans down and gives Katarina and Nicholas a kiss.

"Yes, pretty well, Nicholas did great, and you?"

"I was restless, an excited restless."

"I was too. Look at him Karl, he is so precious." Karl slides the chair next to the bed. He holds Katarina's hand.

"Karl would you like to hold your son?"

"Yes, I would love to. I won't hurt him, will I?"

"You silly man, of course you will not." Katarina places the baby in Karl's arms. They make immediate eye contact. "See Karl, he knows who you are."

"Katarina, he is so beautiful, so precious, and so little." A tear runs down Karl's cheek. Karl rubs his finger lightly down Nicholas' nose. He places his finger in Nicholas' hand. Nicholas closes his little hand around Karl's finger.

Wednesday morning, Karl is at the hospital bright and early. "Karl, Doctor Grabb will be here at 9:00." Doctor Grabb arrives a few minutes early.

"Good morning Katarina, Karl. How are you feeling Katarina?"

"Very good Doctor."

"Good, let me check you and the baby. Everything is fine. The nurses tell me Nicholas has been feeding regularly and seems to be sleeping well."

"Yes, he is a good baby."

"How would you like to go home tomorrow?"

"That would be wonderful, thank you."

"Good, I'll make the arrangements. I'd like for you to stay most of the morning. You can get a couple of feedings in, the nurses will get you ready, and check you out afterwards."

"Karl, I am anxious to go home, for Nicholas to be there with us, to sleep in his own bed." Katarina finishes dinner. 7:30 approaches. The nurse enters the room.

Karl says, "I know, it is time to leave." The nurse smiles. Karl says his good nights and gives kisses.

Thursday morning, Karl is at the hospital bright and early. Katarina is feeding Nicholas. "Good morning Katarina and good morning to you baby Nicholas."

"Good morning Karl." Karl kisses them.

"Today is the day my Love. The day we take our little bundle of joy home. How are you feeling?"

"Good Karl, I am ready to go home." The nurse comes in and checks Katarina's and Nicholas' vitals.

"Are you ready to go home Mrs. Schellenberg?"

"Yes, I am."

"Good, I'll go and get the paperwork ready, we should have you on your way soon."

"Karl, would you get my things ready? I want my flowers also."

An hour passes, the nurse returns with a wheelchair. "Ready Mrs. Schellenberg?"

"Yes, we are."

"Mr. Schellenberg, would you hold Nicholas while I get the Mrs. in the chair?" Karl takes his son in his arms. "Take my arm Mrs. Schellenberg, let's get you up and in the chair." Karl lays Nicholas in Katarina's arms. The nurse wheels them out. "Mr. Schellenberg, would you get your car and meet us at the front entrance?" Karl scurries to the car and drives to the entrance. He sees Katarina and Nicholas waiting with the nurse. "Mr. Schellenberg; hold the baby while I get your wife in the car."

Karl, Katarina, and Nicholas arrive home, it's late morning. Karl takes Nicholas. "May I help you out Katarina?"

"I am fine, just let me have your arm to steady myself." Karl gets them in the house, and settles in. "It is nice to be home Karl. Oh, I see you got a carriage for Nicholas."

"Yes, I was running errands Tuesday. I hope you like it."

"It is very nice, you did good Karl, thank you." Karl helps Katarina to their bed, and lays baby Nicholas in her arms. He is crying. "Karl, Nicholas is hungry." Karl places Katarina's flowers on the dresser so she can see them.

That evening, there is a knock on the door. Karl answers, it's Ruth and Ed. "Hi Karl, we saw you all come home earlier."

"Come in, let me see if Katarina can see you now." Karl returns. "Katarina is in the bedroom with Nicholas, come with me. The baby is sleeping." Nicholas is next to Katarina.

"Katarina," Ruth whispers, "He is precious. Can we do or help you with anything?"

"No, we are fine; thank you."

"We brought a little present for him." Ruth helps Katarina open the gift.

"Thank you both, this is a beautiful blanket. He will love to snuggle with this."

"We'll let you go now; you both need your rest. I made you and Karl dinner. I put it on the table in the kitchen. We are so happy for you and Karl."

"Thank you both, very much." Katarina and Karl are unaware, Ruth and Ed are unable to have children.

The next morning Karl is up early, tending to Katarina and Nicholas. He prepares breakfast for Katarina, as she feeds Nicholas. About 9:00, Karl hears a car door. He looks out the window, it's Angie. He meets her at the door.

"Good morning, Angie."

"Good morning Karl, how is Katarina and the baby? I was by yesterday morning and the Franklin's told me the good news."

"Come in Angie, Katarina is up. She just finished feeding Nicholas."

"Nicholas, that's a nice name, a strong name."

"Katarina, Angie is here."

"Bring her back, Karl."

"Hello Angie."

"Katarina, I heard the news. Oh my! He is beautiful. Look how little."

"Yes, our little bundle of joy."

"Everything went well, I take it?"

"Yes, Nicholas is strong. He was born at 11:35 Sunday night, he is 7 pounds 3 ounces and 19.55 inches long."

"Look at his dark hair, just like you and Karl. I won't keep you. I just wanted to stop by. I have a little something for him."

"You do not need to do that Angie."

"I know, but I wanted to." Katarina opens her gift.

"Angie this is so cute, look Karl, a pajama outfit and little socks. Thank you, Angie. This will keep him nice and warm."

"If you two need anything call me, anytime."

"Thank you, Angie." Karl walks her to the door. Karl returns to the bedroom, Katarina and Nicholas fell asleep. Nicholas is cuddled in Katarina's nightgown. He kisses them both.

THE CHILDHOOD YEARS

Nicholas is growing fast. He is a good baby; he sleeps most of the night. Karl has learned to change diapers. October 28, Katarina, and Karl are sitting on the porch swing. Katarina leans over and kisses Karl. "That was sweet Katarina, and unexpected."

"That is what makes a kiss like that sweet, and I wanted to. Karl, tomorrow is Nicholas' six-week birthday."

"I know Katarina, the weeks went by so quickly."

October 31, it's Halloween night. An unusually warm evening in Coffeyville; fall is in the air. Katarina and Karl finish carving their pumpkins. Karl's Mr. Pumpkin has a top hat and a bow tie, Katarina's Mrs. Pumpkin has a vail, pearls and flowers, and Nicholas' little baby pumpkin has a bonnet. Karl hangs sheets from the trees to simulate ghosts.

"Karl; I want to sit on the porch and hand out candy to the little goblins and gremlins tonight. Nicholas will like the fresh air. I love the smell of autumn Karl. It reminds me of Germany." The Halloweener's begin trick-or-treating. Katarina is on the swing, holding Nicholas, Karl is having fun with the trick-or-treaters.

"Karl, it will be fun to take Nicholas trick-or-treating when he gets older. That is what you call this custom in America, right? I knew it as All Saints Eve."

Karl chuckles, "Yes, my Love."

Karl is in his office, November 3. He just finishes placing pictures of Katarina and Nicholas on his desk. Patrick brings a note in. "Karl, I have a note from London." Karl opens the note, it's from Hans. 'Good morning Karl, well it is morning here. I want to let you know, I met one of your recruits. I should say operatives, John Gardner is his name. We are helping him get into Berlin. John reminds me very much of you, you did good training him. The war is finally turning, it seems. The Nazis are beginning to struggle, and I feel the tide is turning. No time too soon. The SS completed the Concentration Camp on the farm, it is full of prisoners, a real shame. How are Katarina and the baby? In your last note you said the baby was due mid-September. How ironic you mentioned mid-September, Friedrich Kussin, a German Major-General and commander in Arnhem during Operation Market Garden, died in battle on September 17. Have you found a house?' Karl prepares a reply to Hans.

'Hans, it is good to hear from you. I am glad you like and approve of John; he was our best recruit. Much has changed here. We did buy a home, and we moved in at the end of June. The best news, Katarina had her baby, we have a son. Nicholas Samuel. It is odd you happened to mention September 17 in your note. Nicholas was born on September 17, 11:35 at night. He weighed 7 pounds 3 ounces, he was 19.55 inches long, and growing fast. He has dark hair, like Katarina and I, and blue eyes like his mother. Katarina and Nicholas are doing fine, she is a great mother, just like Anna. I have a picture for you, of Katarina and Nicholas. Hans, we miss you, take care and stay safe.'

Winter arrives in Coffeyville. It is Thanksgiving morning. It snowed the night before, seven inches. Karl comes in from shoveling. Katarina is up, and is in Nicholas' room, sitting in the rocker feeding him. Karl comes in and kisses them.

"Happy Thanksgiving, Katarina."

"Happy Thanksgiving to you Karl, our first here in America, and our first as a family."

"The snow is pretty."

"Yes Karl, it is beautiful, the first of the year. Remember when we played in the snow in Germany, the day before our wedding?"

"Yes, I was thinking about that this morning, we had a snowball fight, and made snow angels. We had fun that day. I am going to start a fire in the fireplace. Then I will get the turkey prepared. You will love a traditional Thanksgiving meal Katarina; turkey, stuffing, mashed potatoes, fresh corn, cranberry, gravy, and pies for dessert."

"I will be out shorty to help, I am laying Nicholas down for his nap. I want to bake a loaf of bread today, just as I did the night before our wedding; and I want to make a pie. A blueberry pie for you." Katarina returns, she is wearing her mother's apron. "The house smells good with the fire, like Germany. Remember the stove we had in the little barn. I kept you warm with it. I love the smell of a fire; and to hear the wood crackling."

"Those are great memories, my Love. Wait until you smell our Thanksgiving dinner."

Later that day. "Karl, you are right, the Thanksgiving meal has filled our home with a wonderful aroma, one of a kind." After dinner, Katarina and Karl sit in front of the fireplace. Nicholas is curled up in Karl's arm, Katarina lays her head on Karl's other arm. Karl puts his arm around Katarina. "I love you, Karl. I am so happy we are here."

"And I love you, my Love."

Karl stays busy at the Base. He has taken on more responsibility with internal officer tactical training. His Strategic Tactical Program is gearing up for another group after the holidays. Karl has learned from London, through Hans, all five operatives have been strategically placed within the Third Reich; and are providing valuable information. John Garner is in place in the Oberkommando der Wehrmacht or OKW, the Wehrmacht High Command, the Armed Forces High Command in Berlin. Ironically, Wilhelm Keitel is the Chief of the Armed Forces High Command. This is part of the command structure of the German armed forces. The OKW serves as the military general staff for Hitler's Third Reich, responsible for coordinating the efforts of the German Heer Kriegsmarine, and Luftwaffe. Philip Stone is placed in the Oberkommando des Heeres or OKH, Germany's Army High Command. This group directly commands operations on the Russian front. George Steiner is at the Oberkommando der Marine or OKM, Germany's Naval High Command, the Kriegsmarine. David Kiechler is solidly in place in the Luftwaffe, and Thomas Helsel at the Sturmabteilung or SA, the German Storm Division. The SA functions as the paramilitary organization of the German Nazi Party and continues to play a key role in Adolf Hitler's rise to power. Karl is pleased with this news, and very proud of his operatives. He is keenly aware of their assignments in the very top organizations of the Third Reich, and the risk that comes with that. He is also keenly aware of the rewards to be gained.

"Karl, Christmas will be here in less than one month, let's put the tree up early."

"I would love that Katarina; we'll get the Christmas season kicked off. Let's shop for ornaments and lights this weekend. We need a Nativity crib also. We can get our tree next weekend. That should work well with keeping it fresh and green."

"Karl can we cut our own, like I did with Mother and Father in Germany?"

"Yes, of course."

December 1, Patrick enters Karl's office. "Lieutenant Schellenberg, I have an urgent message from London."

"What is it Patrick?"

"Here you are, sir."

Karl sits back in his chair and opens the telegram, a note from Hans. 'Karl, I received an urgent message from John Garner, your operative who is assigned in Berlin. John needs help and is asking for your advice. Apparently the Third Reich is stepping up their security, new orders from the SS. Since Wilhelm has taken over the Chief of the Armed Forces High Command, he is driving this change. Your name was actually mentioned. The Nazis reference a spy by the name of Karl Schellenberg that infiltrated the Army Group North Command using the name Lieutenant Karl Pfisterer, causing irreputable damage to their war effort. They stated there was forged documentation planted within the Third Reich's system along with village records to confirm the identity of the imposter.

'John said the SS is reimplementing a fingerprint security/ authorization system to verify people with top security clearances. This authorization system has been in place for long time, and for whatever reason, fell by the wayside. Thankfully for you. John has the necessary clearances, just as we did with you. He also has the documentation the Underground created to substantiate his new German identity, military record, birth, childhood, etc. What we do not have is their fingerprints on file. John also learned that due to Gerhardt's loyalists within the German Army that helped plant your information in their systems, the process of gaining access into their systems is more guarded and secure. Wilhelm has many more checks and balances in place now. In addition to the paperwork, files and electronic measures, two people are now required to input any information into the Army's systems under the observation of an SS officer; whether it is related to personal information, military data, or anything else for that matter.

Our concern is how do we get his fingerprint and those of our other operatives in the German Army system without being noticed? We still have people we can trust within the German Army, but we need to be very careful and have a well-established and executable plan. We need to have a back-up plan in place to react quickly if things go awry. Karl, our concern is the identity we used for John and the others. We do not know if any of those men's existing information had fingerprints on file. Please give this some thought and let us know your plan. All your operatives are in danger. London is aware of this and we are awaiting your advice. London originally discussed pulling the operatives out, however they quickly abandoned that idea. We have come too far too quick to make an irrational decision. The information we have gathered is invaluable.'

"Patrick, have Captain Harris join us, tell him it is urgent."

"I believe he is across Base Karl, at the airfield, I'll get him."

Thirty minutes pass, Captain Harris arrives. "Karl, Private First-Class Owens said you needed to see me about an urgent matter."

"Yes sir, have a seat. Read this message from London, from Hans in Germany." Captain Harris takes his time and reads the message carefully.

"This is not good news Karl. Do you have any thoughts or ideas? Do you think Wilhelm is onto our plan, the operatives I mean?"

"No captain, it certainly is not good news. I do not think Wilhelm knows of our operatives either. If he did, they would be dead." Karl stands at his chalk board and begins to write action items down. He makes five columns; 'what do we know, what do not we know, what are our options, who can help, what is the plan.'

"Captain; we need to brainstorm on this and talk through the things we need to verify, the information we need to gather, and a plan to execute. First, as you know, we have three recruits from the first group and two from the second group. All five are in place within the Third Reich. We need to find out, through Hans and the Underground, the identities of the German people that were assigned to our operatives. If we used false names for the recruits, we need to verify any information we may have used from the family, as Hans did with me. You may recall, for my cover, Hans used a family that had recently been killed. I became their son, which they never had. Do any fingerprints exist in the German's, and if so, can we alter those records? Second, we need to know where our recruits are positioned, London has that information. Where do all those fingerprints reside within the German system? We will need to search village records, German State records, birth certificates, death certificates. What else gentlemen, where could they reside? I also have a crazy idea. If fingerprints do exist, can we replicate them or change our recruit's actual prints, or perhaps use a film on their fingers to mimic another fingerprint. That idea is bizarre though."

Captain Harris laughs, "That idea is more than bizarre Karl."

"Next, we need to know when this new system is going to take effect, I am guessing sooner rather than later. We know Hans and his team has the necessary documentation in the German's system, now we need to figure out how to get our recruits fingerprints in their systems with their new processes, and their, call it a three-step verification process; two people and an SS officer. We know the Germans have been using the Kennkarte as the basic identity document inside Germany since 1939. Since 1938 the Nazis required men of military age and Jews to carry identity cards. Shortly after the start of the war, this was extended to apply to all citizens over the age of fifteen."

"Karl, what is a Kennkarte?"

"Patrick, a Kennkarte is a sheet of thin cardboard, measuring about 12 x 5.5 inches. It has two parallel folds, and text on both sides, making it a six-page document. The color of a Kennkarte is based on ethnicity. The Poles have gray ones; Jews and Romas, yellow; Russians, Ukrainians, Belarusians, Georgians and Goralenvolk, blue. Furthermore, letters were introduced to mark each ethnicity, based on the initial letter of the German word for the ethnicity; J for Jews, U for Ukrainians, R for Russians, W for Belarusians, K for Georgians, G for Goralenvolk, Z for Roma, or Gypsies. It was quite ingenious actually.

"To receive a Kennkarte, an applicant had to fill out an application, and provide certain documents such as a birth certificate, pre-war identification, and a marriage certificate in specified cases. Upon receiving the card, applicants were fingerprinted. This was in place when I was in Germany, I had a card, in fact I still have it. The Germans never verified the fingerprints and did not backcheck anything."

"I'm assuming your fingerprints were on your Kennkarte?"

"Yes captain, the same goes with our operatives. The risk is, and question of the day, do any real fingerprints reside within any of the Germans systems. If not, when the Germans verify their actual fingerprints, are they taking the prints and matching those on their card? Or what if, the Germans do not use the card, who's fingerprints are in their systems? We need Hans to verify what information is in the German's systems. Let's get that process started now to save time. Patrick, send a message to London to get to Hans. Have Hans' people investigate what is in the German systems. Also, find out if we have any loyalists in the SS."

"Yes, sir."

"Captain, the best plan is to, somehow, get our operatives fingerprints into the German system. What are our options? One option is we abandon the mission; and we know that is out. Two, do we believe the lack of a fingerprint trail within the German system will not hurt us and not disclose our operatives, and we hope our folks go undetected? No, so that is not an option. Last, our only option as I see it, we need to cover our tracks and get our operatives fingerprints in all the German systems, villages, schools, State, and military. Gentlemen, not an easy task. We need to focus on who can help; Hans will play a big part in this. Regarding the three-step process, we can make the two-person input happen, we need an SS person, hopefully Hans has people in the SS. Let me think about this and get a good night's sleep. Once we piece this information together, we can formulate our plan. Hopefully we will hear from London and Hans in the morning."

It's late, Karl arrives home after 7:00. Katarina has dinner ready. Nicholas is playing on the floor. "Karl, you are later than usual. Is everything ok?" Katarina senses something wrong.

"I am sorry Katarina, something came up today, it is of a very critical nature, and concerning to me."

"What is it Karl?"

"I heard from Hans today. Our operatives in Germany are at risk. Berlin, actually Wilhelm, is implementing a fingerprint verification system to add another layer of security to verify who is who. Hans said the success of my mission prompted it. Our operatives, as did I, have Kennkarte cards, and their identities and past has been documented, but not their fingerprints. Germany has had the fingerprint system in place for years, yet the Third Reich never followed through on the verification, until now. I think they are getting desperate; the war is turning in our favor."

"What are you going to do Karl?"

"Captain Harris, Patrick and I started to develop a plan of action today. I have sent Hans a message for additional information. We will continue tomorrow." Katarina, Karl, and Nicholas have dinner, and retire for the evening. Karl's mind is busy all night.

Karl is at the Base early the next morning after a restless night thinking of the situation and a solution. Captain Harris arrives a short time later. "Good morning Karl, after sleeping on things, do you have any further ideas?"

"The only solution is to get our operatives fingerprints into the German systems, and hope we have all the bases covered. We have five operatives successfully in place in key and strategic areas of the Third Reich. That was not an easy task to do. Hans and his people risked their lives."

"I agree Karl, we have come too far with this effort to turn back. The reward outweighs the risk."

Suddenly Patrick storms in Karl's office. "Lieutenant, captain, I have a message from London." Patrick hands the message to Karl.

Karl stays seated, opens it, and reads it aloud. 'Karl, we have verified the fingerprint records do exist for all German military personnel, and most if not all German citizens, especially since the invasion of Poland. I also have good news for you, we still have trusted people in the Military records office, and we do have a trusted loyalist in the SS. We have had him in place for years. We have kept him inactive in case we needed him to help us in a critical situation. For this very reason he has been dormant and has had no attention brought to him. He is a lieutenant. We believe we can get him re-assigned to Berlin, to the records office in the Third Reich. My people in the Underground can take care of the village records for your operatives. We have all the information we need to make that happen from the false documents and identities we created for the operatives, except for fingerprints on the required German Military forms. Karl, I will work with your five operatives and arrange to have new fingerprints taken. I will await your confirmation and plan. Hans.'

Karl stands, "Well gentlemen, we now have a plan. Captain Harris, Patrick, we will need to move quickly. Patrick, respond to Hans. 'Hans, we have only one plan. Proceed with obtaining our operatives fingerprints and get them documented in the villages and the State's records immediately to match their German documentation. This must happen quickly, please advise when this task is completed. Next you and your people need to get their fingerprints in the German Army Military records. Obviously, we need to input this information very discreetly, along with other batches, as to not raise attention. Once you have your SS comrade reassigned, let the plan unfold. He will need to oversee your two Underground members in the records office and have our operative's fingerprints placed within the German system. Hans, confirm this directive and provide a timeline, this is of utmost importance to the war effort, and to the safety of our operatives. Karl.' "Patrick, send this to London, and expedite it."

"Yes sir."

"What are your thoughts Karl?"

"Captain, this is our only option, we have good people in place. Our network is deep. I have complete confidence Hans and his team will make it happen."

London replies later that afternoon. 'The plan has been relayed to Hans and is in motion as we speak.' Karl, Captain Harris, and Patrick look at each other, with a gleam of hope. "Great job Karl on developing this plan and orchestrating it so quickly."

"Thank you, Captain Harris. This was a team effort, thank you and Patrick as well."

A week passes, Patrick enters Karl's office with Captain Harris following in close step. "Karl, I have a message from London."

Karl reads it aloud; it is from Hans. 'Karl, we have learned the Nazis have begun fingerprint verification, fortunately for us they have decided to start with the outer military establishments. I am guessing Berlin feels they are the most vulnerable, a lesson learned from your stint at the Army Group North Command. We have the first part of the plan in place, we have obtained your operatives fingerprints and have disseminated them in the village's and State's records, and in their corresponding official documents. It was a bit difficult, but our SS Lieutenant has been reassigned to the German military record office and is working with our people. I do not believe we aroused any suspicion. He has been in place for two days and things seem to be operating normally. I await your instructions, Hans.' The three look and one another with joy.

"So far so good gentlemen. Patrick, please respond. 'Hans, great job. Proceed using your best judgement when the most opportune time is to input our operative's fingerprints. The sooner the better. Karl.'

Two days pass, and another message from London. Patrick enters Karl's office. Karl and Captain Harris are talking. "Lieutenant, a message from London, I'm glad you're here as well Captain Harris."

Karl opens the message. "It is from Hans, one word. Done." The three men sigh a breath of relief of a well-executed plan successfully implemented. Karl salutes the American flag, "Once again we outsmarted the Nazis, more importantly, we outsmarted Wilhelm again."

Captain Harris turns to Karl. "Spinnaker, your sail has its wind again!"

Karl arrives home that evening and Katarina can tell by the look on his face he is happy. "Karl, I sense good news."

"Yes, my Love, our plan was successful, our operatives remain safe, and we outsmarted Wilhelm again. Someday, someday soon, I hope and wish for his final day will come. I would love to witness that."

"Karl, his day will come. He deserves what he gets."

NICHOLAS' FIRST CHRISTMAS

Saturday morning, the second week of December, fifteen days until Christmas. Nine inches of snow on the ground. "Katarina, get ready, we are getting our tree today. I have something to show you." He goes to the garage and brings in a sled, with a cradle attached.

"Karl that is so cute, where do you get it?"

"One of the sergeants on Base dabbles in woodworking, his name is David. I bought the sled, a Flexible Flyer, just like I had when I was little, and a small wooden cradle. David reworked the cradle and attached it to the sled. Now we can take Nicholas with us today, and on walks when it snows."

"Karl, that was very thoughtful and sweet."

Katarina, Karl, and Nicholas head for the woods for their tree. "Katarina; look, an old gristmill, we can park here."

"This place is beautiful, where are we?"

"This part of the countryside is called Birmingham."

"Look Karl, the pond at the mill is frozen. Look at the stream, it is partially frozen. It is pretty with the snow." They follow the stream into the woods. The sled is functioning great, Nicholas is enjoying the ride. They find a perfectly shaped eastern red cedar, about seven feet tall. "Karl, I like this tree, we will take this one." Karl cuts the tree, and with a rope slung over his shoulder, drags it to the car. Katarina has Nicholas in the sled. On their way home, Karl finds Christmas music on the radio, I'm Dreaming of a White Christmas was playing. "Karl, so appropriate, I love this time of year. We had a nice day in the woods, it was fun getting the tree. Nicholas seemed to enjoy the day as well. The cold did not bother him a bit."

"I love the holidays as well Katarina."

"Karl can we put the tree up tonight. I will make hot chocolate when we get home."

"I have not had that in forever, that will taste good, and take the chill off. I will build a fire."

They arrive home at dusk. Katarina feeds Nicholas and lays him down for the night. "Nicholas fell asleep while I was feeding him, we wore him out today. Karl, we have a tradition in Germany to place the tree in the middle of the room to enjoy the whole tree."

"I like that, we have never done that, we have always put it a corner." Karl gets the living room ready for the tree.

"Karl, the tree smells so good."

"Yes, it is a red cedar."

"I will get the hot chocolate started." They spend the rest of the evening decorating the tree and drinking hot chocolate. Katarina puts the Nativity crib on the fireplace mantel. "Karl, we are almost finished, I will be right back." Katarina returns with her ornaments from Germany. "Remember I brought these with us?" Katarina places them on the tree. "This was my father's, a miniature church; this my mother's, a handmade snowflake; and this was mine, baby Jesus in his cradle. This was the angel we had at the top of our tree; it was handed down from my grandparents. It has been in our family for many years." Karl places the angel on the treetop. "I love these, and I am happy we brought them with us. I miss my parents." Karl stokes the fire. It's after midnight, he and Katarina lay on the floor in front of the fireplace, the wood is crackling. Katarina is in his arms. "Karl, I love the fireplace. This reminds me of that night at the farmhouse in Germany. The tree is beautiful, our first Weihnachtsbaum. I was thinking of the gristmill today, the pond. We will ice skate there someday."

"Katarina, I do not know how to ice skate."

"I will teach you; it will be fun. The stream we walked by in the woods reminded me of the stream on the farm in Germany, the Kettle."

"I had a great day with you Katarina." They kiss, make love in front of the crackling fire, and fall asleep.

They are awakened by Nicholas crying. "Karl, the little one is hungry. I will get him and feed him out here." As Katarina feeds Nicholas, his little eyes are intently focused on the tree lights. "Look Karl, he loves the lights, he is so precious." Nicholas falls back asleep. "Tomorrow, or I guess it is today, now, can we go and get lights for the outside and hang them? We can make wreaths from the trimmings we cut from the bottom of our tree, actually we will make Advent wreaths."

"You're getting in the Christmas spirit. Yes, I would like that as well."

They fall back asleep. Karl wakes to see Katarina holding Nicholas. Katarina walks over and stands under the doorway. Karl looks above the doorway. "I have a surprise for you, Karl, mistletoe. I brought it from Germany, I dried it many years ago." Karl runs to her, they kiss.

After breakfast, they drive into town to get the outside lights. They return early in the afternoon. "Katarina, I am going to get started with the lights."

"I will lay Nicholas down for his nap and I will be right out."

Ruth and Ed see Karl stringing lights and come over. "Karl, do you need help?"

"Sure, thank you Ed. Katarina is inside Ruth." The decorating finishes late in the afternoon.

"Karl, Ed, you all did a great job, the lights and wreaths look beautiful."

"Thank you, Katarina."

"Ed, would you and Ruth like to have dinner with us tonight? Karl and I have something we would like to ask you both."

"Ruth, are you good with that?"

"Yes, Ed, it will be nice to spend the evening together, and play with Nicholas." Karl builds a fire and lights the tree. They have a pleasant dinner together.

"Have dessert while I clean up, then we can talk."

"Katarina, let me help you."

Later that evening they sit at the table. "Ruth and Ed, Karl and I have grown to love you both very much. You have become dear friends. We have a very special request for you, one we have talked about, one that is very near and dear to our hearts. Here Ruth, hold Nicholas. Karl and I would love you and Ed to be Godparents for Nicholas, we want to have him baptized December 30."

Ruth and Ed look at each other with smiles, "We would love to, and be honored to stand for Nicholas. This is very special, thank you for asking us, thank you very much. We love you both as well, and we cherish our friendship together. We are blessed the good Lord brought us together. There is something we would like to share with you." Ruth briefly looks over to Ed. "Ed and I are unable to have children," Ruth begins to cry. Katarina sits next to her and comforts her. "It's fine Katarina, we've learned to accept it. It is so refreshing to have you two living next to us, and to have little Nicholas as part of our lives. It's late, we should be going, thank you very much, the dinner and time spent with you was wonderful."

"Karl and I will walk you out. Karl, smell the smoke in the air, it reminds me of Germany." Katarina's eyes are closed, her head pointing up, taking a deep breath through her nose. The outside lights reflecting on the snow enhances the Christmas feeling.

Saturday morning, two weeks before the baptism. Katarina and

Karl sleep in and play in bed. "Katarina, I love Saturday mornings with you." Nicholas has kept them up this week.

"Karl can we go into town today, I want to buy Nicholas an outfit for his baptism. We can Christmas shop for him while we are there."

"Good, I have a few things to get as well."

"What do you need Karl?"

"That is a secret, it is Christmas my Love." They spend the afternoon shopping. While Katarina shops for the baptism outfit, Karl slips away to get a few surprises. He finds a Hallmark Christmas card for Katarina. He then has an idea; *Katarina loves Christmas Ornaments. I will start a tradition. Every year they each will get a special ornament.* He finds a Santa for Katarina, and a snowman for Nicholas.

"Where were you Karl?"

"Just looking around," he smiles.

"Look what I found for Nicholas, this little white outfit. It has booties, a hat, and a blanket. It is so cute."

"It is perfect. Katarina, I want to go to the toy store. I want to get some toys for Nicholas."

"That is a great idea, I will shop too." At the toy store, Karl finds exactly what he wanted.

"Look Katarina, I found the perfect gifts for Nicholas. My father bought toys just like these for me when I was a baby, before I could even play with them. A train set, an American Flyer, 4-8-4 Northern #261 steam locomotive, tender and five cars. I found this cardboard city, from Dolly Toy Company. and look here, a Buddy-L dump truck and shovel."

"What is Buddy-L, Karl?"

"A company that makes metal toys, designed to scale and very durable. I had some when I was little, my father bought them for me. I lost mine in the fire."

"I am sorry Karl."

"That's fine, I can enjoy them again with Nicholas."

"Karl, he is too young though."

"That is ok, I will enjoy them myself until he gets older." Katarina chuckles and hugs Karl.

"Karl, I see what I want to get him, this cuddly teddy bear, he will love this." They return home, it's early evening, just after 6:00. Karl lights the tree and turns on the outside lights; and builds a fire. "Karl, I will feed Nicholas and lay him down for the evening."

"Good, I will get something for dinner." After dinner, Katarina and Karl are lying in bed.

"Karl."

"Yes, my Love."

"Tomorrow Nicholas turns three months old; the time has gone by so fast."

The evening ends. Katarina and Karl are in bed. "You smell good, I love your perfume Katarina." Katarina's head is nestled on Karl's chest.

"Nicholas is sleeping, it is nice to have time together Karl." She takes his hand, slides it under her pajama top, and places it on her breast. Fifteen minutes pass, just quiet time. Katarina giggles, "Karl what are you doing under the sheets?" Karl slowly begins to unbutton Katarina's pajama top, from the bottom. He nibbles on her belly. Katarina giggles again. Karl works his way up, nibbling and kissing as he goes, between her breasts, then her neck. Karl then embraces her lips. They kiss. Katarina, with one hand clutches the back of Karl's head, the other around his back, and pulls him closer into a passionate kiss. She wraps her legs around Karl's waist. They look into each other's eyes, and embrace. The night continues ever so slowly, ever so passionately.

Katarina awakes to Karl's eyes. "Good morning my Love, it is Christmas Eve."

"Good morning Karl. Last night was beautiful."

"Katarina, it is snowing. We will have a white Christmas." Katarina gets up and looks out the window.

"Karl it is so beautiful, nice fluffy snowflakes."

"Time to get up, I want to get the train setup for Nicholas, and we have presents to wrap."

"I hear Nicholas, I will feed him while you get breakfast ready." Karl prepares eggs and bacon. After breakfast Karl gets the trainset and the other presents. They hear a knock at the door. "I will get it Karl." Katarina opens the door.

"Merry Christmas Katarina."

"Merry Christmas to you Angie, it is nice to see you, come in."

"I wanted to stop by and see Nicholas. Oh my, he's growing. Your tree is beautiful."

"Karl and I cut it down in the woods, Nicholas helped also."

"I have something for the two of you and Nicholas."

"Angie, thank you. Karl look, Angie made us cookies and brought eggnog."

"Christmas is not Christmas without eggnog."

"You will need to stay Angie; I will get it ready."

"Katarina, keep Nicholas' gift under the tree until tomorrow." Angie stays, plays with Nicholas, and chats for a couple of hours.

Karl is busy setting the train up. He joins them at the kitchen table and begins to assemble the cardboard village. "What do you have Karl?"

"It is a miniature village my Love."

"I never saw one like that."

"I found it at the General Store, it will make the train more realistic. There are five houses, and a church with a bell tower."

"Karl the church looks just like Saint Ludger in Germany."

"Was that your church?" asks Angie.

"Yes, our family church in Aurich. I was baptized there, I buried my parents there, and Karl and I were married there." The sun has set in Coffeyville, Christmas Eve. Katarina and Karl finish wrapping presents and go to separate rooms to wrap each other's gifts. Katarina puts Nicholas to bed and joins Karl. Exhausted, they fall asleep.

Christmas morning, Katarina feels a nudge and awakes with baby Nicholas cuddled in her arms. She smells the fireplace and hears

Christmas music. She gets up and sees Karl in the living room, the tree is lit, and the presents are under the tree. "Good morning Karl, Merry Christmas." She gives him a kiss, and notices the music is coming from the phonograph. Silent Night is playing in German.

"Good morning my Love, Merry Christmas to you. I got up early to get the house ready."

"Karl, where did you find Stille Nacht, heilige Nacht?"

"I found it the day we shopped for our gifts, at the music store."

"I did not see you go to the music store."

"I know, that is the elf in me."

"I will feed Nicholas; and get him ready for church." Katarina returns with Nicholas in a little red outfit.

"Katarina, I did not know you had that, when did you get it?"

"I found it the day we shopped for our gifts also, at Gables."

"I did not see it with the other gifts."

"I know, that is the elf in me!" She smiles.

The family returns home after a lovely service at St. Andrews. "Katarina, Nicholas is so cute. Here sit down, I want to run the train for him." Katarina sits on the sofa; Nicholas' eyes immediately go to the lights on the tree. The train is running under the tree. Karl sounds the whistle on the train and Nicholas quickly turns his head toward the sound and gives a little smile.

"Karl look, he likes that." Christmas morning continues. Karl sings the first day of the twelve days of Christmas to Katarina; and will continue each verse every day until January 5.

"Katarina, time to open our gifts."

"Let's wait for ours, we will open Angie's first, then open the ones for Nicholas, like those will be a surprise." She giggles.

"I love your giggle, Katarina." She giggles again.

"Karl, this is precious, Angie got Nicholas a jumpsuit and a matching blanket." They open Nicholas' gifts, and Katarina places the teddy bear next to Nicholas. He snuggles up to it. "Ah look Karl, he likes it." Karl is playing with the Buddy-L toys, making noises like the real trucks do. "Okay my silly little man, time to open our gifts." Karl hands Katarina her card. She turns it over to open it; and sees he has written three x's and three o's across the flap, symbolizing kisses, and hugs. "Karl, the kisses and hugs are precious. One for each of us."

Katarina reads the Hallmark card. 'For my Beautiful Wife at Christmas. The first time I saw you, I somehow knew you would be important in my life. In my eyes, you were beautiful, in so many ways, there was no doubt that I wanted to spend forever with you. And when we got married, things were every bit as good as I could have dreamed. I did not want anything to change.' Tears begin to run down Katarina's face, then Karl's. 'However, life is full of changes. Just as I thought our life together could never be better, it has, it has become better with you, every minute of every day. Together we have embraced each other in our love and in our journey together. The miracle is, you are even more beautiful than I ever imagined. You are the woman of my dreams, my best friend, and as time passes, I fall more deeply in love with you. Merry Christmas.' Katarina is sobbing, Karl hugs her and kisses her forehead. "Karl, this is the most beautiful card I have ever read, it is us; thank you. How did you find a card with perfect words?"

"Of all the cards, this one was calling me. I saw the cover, opened it, and began reading it. The words were amazing, so perfect. I could not have penned them better myself. I have these for you and Nicholas."

"Karl, these are adorable, a Santa ornament for me, and a snowman ornament for little Nicholas. I love you."

"I know Christmas tree ornaments are special to you. I want to begin a tradition," Karl says with a huge smile.

"Hold Nicholas while I put them on the tree. Katarina places them next to her parent's ornaments. Now it is my turn." Katarina gets a box from under the tree. ·

"Katarina, let's open ours together." Karl gets Katarina's gift from under the tree.

"Look Karl they are the same size, that's odd."

"Yes, odd indeed."

"We will open them together Karl." They each open their gifts and burst into laughter. Katarina gives Karl ice skates, and Karl gives Katarina ice skates. "This is so perfect; we could not have planned this any better."

"I know Katarina, so wonderful."

"Karl; the snow has slowed down; it is so beautiful outside. I will ask Ruth and Ed if they will watch Nicholas this evening. I want to ice skate at the gristmill pond under the moonlight. We can take their gifts over and ask them." Christmas day ends with a moonlight skate at the old Birmingham Gristmill pond.

December 30 arrives. Katarina, Karl, Ruth, and Ed arrive at St. Andrews. Nicholas is wearing his little white outfit, his booties and hat. Katarina has him wrapped in the white blanket. Katarina is wearing her wedding dress, and Karl is wearing his wedding suit. Ruth, these were my parent's clothes Karl and I wore at our wedding, my mother's favorite dress and my father's favorite suit. Katarina leans over to Karl, "Karl my dress, your suit, we wore when we started our life together, now we wear them to begin Nicholas' life." She kisses his cheek. Baby Nicholas is baptized. Ruth and Katarina exchange taking pictures of each couple and Nicholas. "Ruth, Ed, I am hungry, would you like to go to lunch, our treat. After lunch, we all will have a malt. I saw a soda fountain at Gower's Drug Store."

"We haven't had a malt in years. That will be fun Katarina."

A NEW ARRIVAL - THE WAR ENDS

January 1945 arrives. The war goes on. Karl returns to his office on Base. Karl receives a telegram from England, a message from Hans. 'Karl, Merry Christmas and Happy New Year. Say hello to Katarina. How is Nicholas doing? Give him a kiss for me. I wanted to share this news. The year is starting nice. The Third Reich continues to weaken. The concentration camp here in Aurich was closed on December 23, the Germans abandoned it. Our town is getting back to normal.' Karl arrives home that evening and shares the news with Katarina.

"Katarina, I received a note from Hans today. First Hans says hello and to give Nicholas a kiss from him. The concentration camp in Aurich was closed on December 23 and the Germans abandoned it. The town is getting back to normal. That was a very nice Christmas gift for the town. I am happy for them, such an ordeal they went through, we all went through." Katarina begins to cry thinking of her parents. Karl holds her.

Nicholas is growing. Karl awakes to Katarina singing in the kitchen. January 15. Karl walks to her from behind, hugs her. "Happy Anniversary, my Love."

"Happy Anniversary and Happy Birthday to you." Katarina turns, they kiss. Karl begins to sing.

"Happy anniversareee, happy anniversareee, happy anniversareee, happy anniversary. Happy happy happy happy happy anniversareee; happy happy happy happy happy anniversareeee; happy happy happy happy happy anniversareee; happy anniversary to you."

"Karl, that is sweet; you are so silly, that is why I love you so much." January 31, Katarina's, and Karl's anniversary of the day they met. Katarina, Karl, and baby Nicholas go into town for a night out.

Karl's work continues at the Base. Weeks have passed. The war is beginning to turn for the Allies. Germany is becoming desperate. Karl hears from Hans; 'Karl, your operatives all have gathered remarkable intelligence, your plan to protect them against the Nazi fingerprint verification has worked, their cover is safe.'

Valentine's Day is approaching. Katarina asks Karl to take the day off. Karl awakes with Katarina in his arms. "Good morning, my Love."

"Good morning, Karl." Katarina sits up and turns toward Karl. "Do you know why I asked you to stay home today?"

"Valentine's Day?"

"Well that is part of the reason." Katarina holds his face; and looks into his eyes.

"Karl, we are expecting."

"Katarina, that is wonderful. Are you sure? How far along are you," Katarina places her two fingers on Karl's lips; giggles and smiles at Karl.

"I am sure, I know. I am about nine weeks I think; the night we put the tree up. Laying at the fireplace was very romantic, it was a wonderful evening. I have an appointment with Doctor Grabb next week on Friday the twenty-third. I am guessing you will come with me." Karl hugs Katarina. Baby Nicholas wakes up, he is hungry. Katarina feeds Nicholas, he is eating on his own. He uses Katarina's bowl, her fork and spoon, the ones she used when she was a baby. Karl drives to town and brings flowers home.

"Katarina, I have something for you."

"Karl they are beautiful, you know my favorites, red roses and white lilies."

"I want to celebrate tonight; we can ask Ruth and Ed to watch Nicholas."

"I would love that." Katarina and Karl dine at their favorite restaurant in town and go to Gower's Drug Store for a malt afterwards.

Katarina's visit with Doctor Grabb goes very well. "Katarina, congratulations to you and Karl. You are about nine weeks, give or take a week. Your due date will be the middle to the end of September. You and your baby are doing fine."

Katarina looks at Karl, "Doctor Grabb, it would be wonderful if the baby was born on Nicholas' birthday."

"Stranger things have happened. I'll see you in a month for a checkup. We will do the same routine as we did for Nicholas."

"Thank you, Doctor, that worked well for Nicholas." When they arrive home, Katarina sees a heart on their bed, made from dried roses and lilies she had saved.

The days turn into weeks. Winter ends, spring is in full bloom. "Katarina, tomorrow is Easter. Did you know the Easter bunny first arrived in America in the 1700s with German immigrants?"

"I did not know that, yet I know of Osterhase or Oschter Haws."

Sunday morning, April 1, Nicholas' first Easter. Katarina and Karl are playing with Nicholas in bed. They give Nicholas a stuffed bunny. Nicholas immediately cuddles up to it. "Look Karl, he likes the bunny." They have breakfast and attend Easter service at St. Andrews. Katarina spends most of April planting a garden. Karl and Katarina celebrate their first kiss day, April 19. They enjoy playing with Nicholas in the back yard. The evenings are filled with walks in the neighborhood, Katarina, Karl, and baby Nicholas in his carriage.

Hans sends a message. 'Karl; how are Katarina and the baby doing? I have more good news, on the 28 of April 1945, the Canadian First Army captured Emden and Wilhelmshaven and took the surrender of the entire garrison, including some two hundred ships of the Kriegsmarine. The Allies continue to gain ground. The tide is turning.'

"Patrick, send this back to England, have it routed to Hans in Germany." 'Hans, great to hear from you and great to hear the good news. I have news from you. Katarina and I are having another baby, in September. Someday my friend, someday we will see each other again.'

A few days later Karl is at his desk. Patrick storms into Karl's office. "Forgive me, lieutenant, for barging in."

"Quite alright Patrick, what is it?"

"It's Hitler, Sir. He is dead. He committed suicide yesterday afternoon to avoid capture by the Soviet Red Army. It's being broadcast he and his wife's corpses were burned." Karl thinks to himself, *cremated, that seems odd.*

"Sergeant, that is wonderful news, we knew the Third Reich was nearing its end. The war will not last much longer without Hitler, many of the Heer's soldiers were against Hitler and his Third Reich.

Karl arrives home early, "Katarina, I have wonderful news. Hitler is dead, the war will end soon."

"Karl, that is wonderful news, this war has been horrible."

May 8, Patrick storms into Karl's office, again. "Forgive me for barging in."

"No problem, quite alright Patrick, what is it?"

"The war has ended; the Germans have surrendered. Our troops are coming home."

Captain Harris comes to Karl's office. "Karl; I want to let you know all of your operatives are in London, they are safe. You did an excellent job in preparing them, well done."

Karl hurries home. Katarina can see he is happy. "Katarina, I have more wonderful news. The war is over, Germany surrendered today."

"Karl, that is better news than last week, this war has been terrible, look what it did to my family. It did bring us together though, a ray of sunlight for so many gloomy days."

Karl's role, responsibilities, and position changes in the Army Air Force. He is focusing on the transition from war. The summer is hot in Coffeyville. Katarina's pregnancy is progressing. She has her last monthly visit May 23. Karl and Katarina arrive at Doctor Grabb's office. "Good morning Doctor Grabb."

"Good morning Katarina, how are you feeling?"

"I am doing well."

"Karl, wonderful news of the war ending."

"Yes Doctor, it was a brutal and ugly war."

"Let me take your vitals my dear. Everything seems good, now lay back so I can examine you. Everything is fine with the baby. Let's begin two-week visits, I'll see you in two weeks."

"Thank you, Doctor."

The weeks go by, then months. The summer continues to be hot. Katarina, Karl, and Nicholas enjoy the porch swing in the evenings. Nicholas always falls asleep on the swing with Katarina. Katarina enters her final trimester. Katarina's doctor visits continue to go well. It is August 15. Katarina and Karl are lying in bed listening to a severe thunderstorm roll through. The thunder shakes the house. Nicholas sleeps through it. Katarina cuddles close with Karl.

"Katarina, I love storms like this, the thunder is intense, and the lightning is extreme. Tomorrow is your birthday." Thursday morning, August 16. Karl and Katarina lay in bed. Katarina wakes to Karl singing to her. "Happy birthday to you. Happy birthday to you. Happy birthday to Katarina. Happy birthday to you my Love."

Katarina smiles and giggles. "My silly man, you are so sweet. That is what I love about you, thank you." Katarina takes Karl's hand and rests it on her belly. "Karl, do you feel the baby."

"Yes, I do, a restless little one."

"It is a calming restless Karl; I feel we are having a girl."

"I have something for you. Here, open it."

"Karl, the pendant is beautiful, what is the stone?"

"It is a blue sapphire, to match your beautiful eyes."

"Thank you, my Love." Katarina rests through the weekend.

The weeks go by quickly. Tuesday is a restless day for Katarina. The baby is moving more and more. August 28, 11:15 at night, Katarina's water breaks. "Karl, wake up, it is time to go."

Karl sits up immediately. "Time? You are three weeks early."

"I know, but it is time to go to Mercy Hospital, my water has broken." Karl jumps out of bed in a nervous panic, again.

"Karl, calm down, the baby is ready. Will you let Ruth and Ed know the baby is early so they can watch Nicholas? Knowing Ruth, she has been ready for this night for a while. While you do that, I will get him ready. Will you also call the hospital so they can let Doctor Grabb know we will be arriving soon?" Karl gets Katarina's bag ready for the hospital. Ruth takes the baby; they leave for the hospital at midnight.

Katarina and Karl arrive just past midnight. The nurses get Katarina checked in. The wee hours of the morning seem endless. Minutes turn to hours. Karl is at Katarina's bedside, comforting her and getting her water, rubbing her back, her legs, anything that will comfort her. Her contractions are beginning to increase. Karl keeps a vigilant check of his watch. The nurses are helping Katarina be as comfortable as possible. Karl keeps a cool compress on Katarina's forehead as he kisses her.

Doctor Grabb stops in, it's just before six in the morning. "How are you feeling Katarina?"

"I am doing well, just the pain is starting to get worse, the baby is kicking more, and is very restless."

"Let me examine you."

"Everything looks fine, you're just early; you have a way to go though. You're still in early labor Katarina, you are just beginning to dilate. Are your contractions regular yet?"

"No Doctor, they are not."

"Just stay relaxed. I'll be back in a few hours to check on you."

"Doctor Grabb, is there anything I can do for Katarina and the baby?"

"As with Nicholas, just stay with her and keep her relaxed."

Doctor Grabb returns at 9:00 in the morning. "Hello Katarina, have your contractions begun to increase?"

"Yes, they are more regular."

"Good, let me have a look."

"You're moving into your second stage. You have dilated to six centimeters. Your contractions will begin to pick up now. Everything is looking good though. I'll have the nurse give you something for your pain."

"No thank you Doctor, remember from Nicholas, I want this experience to be natural. I can endure a little pain."

"Yes, I do remember. Very good, just relax and breathe steady. I'll check back with you in a few more hours."

"May I get you anything?"

"I would like lemon ice chips, thank you Karl."

Doctor Grabb returns just before 11:00. "Hello Katarina, the nurse tells me your contractions are closer together and lasting longer."

"Yes, Doctor, they are becoming more intense."

"Let me take a look. You're in the last stage of active labor, you are seven centimeters dilated, and everything is looking good. It seems like this baby wants to see her mother. Can we get you anything?"

"No Doctor, I am fine. Thank you."

"I'll be back soon, stay rested the best you can. I'll see you in a little while, remember, stay relaxed, and breathe steady during your contractions." Just after noon, 12:30. Katarina's contractions and pain are increasing. Doctor Grabb returns. "The nurse tells me your contractions have been very regular."

"Yes Doctor, regular and more painful."

"Let's see how the little one is progressing. You are nearly nine centimeters; it shouldn't be much longer. Stay relaxed my dear."

Doctor Grabb holds her hand. "I'll see you in a bit." By early afternoon, Katarina's pain is becoming intolerable. Her contractions are lasting upwards of two minutes. Doctor Grabb returns. "Katarina let's check you again. We are ready my dear, you are ten centimeters. Let's get you to the delivery room. Karl, you will need to wait in the waiting room."

"I know, I would love to be with Katarina though. I understand." Karl leans down and kisses Katarina, and her belly. "I love you both. Be strong my Love."

Katarina looks into Karl's eyes, squeezes his hand, and smiles, "I love you Karl." As Karl watches Katarina get wheeled to the delivery, he checks his watch, 1:45. As before, Katarina looks back one more time, waves to Karl and blows him a kiss. An hour passes. Karl is prancing back and forth in the waiting room. He keeps looking at the clock, seemingly every minute.

Karl notices a nurse walk by. "Hello, I'm Betty, I remember you from your first baby, may I get you anything Mr. Schellenberg?"

"I remember you too. No thank you Betty, I am fine, just nervous." The minutes seem like hours. Karl looks at the time, 3:50.

Betty comes into the waiting room. "Mr. Schellenberg, I have good news. Would you like to see your wife and baby?"

"Yes Betty, how is she, the baby, is it a boy or girl?"

"Mrs. Schellenberg wants to tell you herself." Karl glances up and sees the room number, NSY1, as he walks toward the delivery room. He remembers this is the same room Nicholas was delivered in. He hears the little one crying. He enters the delivery room and sees their little baby laying on Katarina's breast, swaddled in a blanket. Katarina smiles at him.

"Karl my Love, look, look at your baby daughter. We have a baby girl, Caroline Nichole."

Karl walks over to them, "Katarina, Caroline is beautiful, you are beautiful."

"Karl her eyes are brown like yours." He leans down, kisses Caroline on her forehead, and kisses Katarina.

"Again, you have made me the happiest man on earth." He then turns to Doctor Grabb. "Did everything go well?"

"Yes Karl. Your little girl is healthy. She was born at 3:33, she is 5 pounds 11 ounces and 17.3 inches long. Just a little squirt. Katarina did very well also."

"When will they come home?"

"Let's see how Caroline's weight gain is, but I would expect in three or four days, Karl. Just as before with Nicholas." Karl stays with Katarina the rest of the afternoon, into early evening. Katarina is feeding Caroline as Betty comes into the room.

"Mr. Schellenberg, Katarina and the baby need their rest, they have had a long day. You all did. You'll need to leave for the night."

Karl chuckles, "That is exactly what you told me with our first baby Betty." Betty smiles. Karl kisses Katarina and the baby. "Katarina, I need to stop by the Base in the morning, I will see you later in the morning, perhaps early afternoon. Good night my Love, and good night little Caroline, I love you both."

"Good night Karl, we love you."

Karl gets home and walks over to Ruth and Ed's to get Nicholas and share the news. They hear his car; and meet him on the porch.

"Karl, how is Katarina? Did she have her baby?"

"Yes, we have a little girl, Caroline Nichole; she was born at 3:33 this afternoon; she is 5 pounds 11 ounces and 17.3 inches long."

"She is just a little thing."

"How is Nicholas, Ruth?"

"He is fine Karl; he is a good little boy."

"Thank you, Ruth, and you Ed as well. You are such good friends."

"We very much enjoy watching little Nicholas."

"I can take him now."

"Karl, I changed his diaper, gave him a bath, and just fed him, he should be good for a while."

"Thank you both, I will see you in the morning."

"We cannot wait to have him again."

Karl sits with Nicholas in the rocker for an hour or so. Nicholas keeps looking at Karl and smiling. He is playing with Karl's finger. Karl gets Nicholas settled in his crib. At that moment it dawns on Karl, he and Katarina were going to buy a crib for the baby this weekend. The little guy falls asleep within minutes. Karl is asleep nearly as quick.

Thursday morning arrives quickly. Karl awakes to hear Nicholas; he is playing in his crib. Karl gets Nicholas up, changes his diaper, feeds him, and takes him to Ruth. Karl goes to his office. "Patrick, thank you for covering for me yesterday, and I am sorry for calling you at midnight. Patrick, I am a proud father again. The baby came three weeks early."

"Congratulations, Karl! How are Katarina and the baby doing?" Captain Harris comes into the room.

"Congratulations, Karl! I overheard. How are Katarina and the baby doing? I hear the baby was early?"

"Yes, three weeks. Katarina and the baby are doing very well indeed, we had a little baby girl yesterday afternoon, her name is Caroline, Caroline Nichole."

"Karl, go and be with your wife and baby. You deserve some time off; help get them settled in. Katarina will need help with Nicholas, also."

"Thank you, sir." Karl drives into town for flowers.

Karl returns to the hospital that afternoon. He sees Katarina staring into Caroline's eyes. Karl walks over and kisses Katarina and Caroline. "I brought flowers for my girls."

"Karl, the flowers are beautiful, thank you. Did Captain Harris give you time off again?"

"Yes, as before, he said take some time off to help you and the baby get home and settled, and to help with Nicholas."

"That was very nice of him, he is a sweet man. How is Nicholas? I miss him."

"He is fine, Ruth and Ed are taking good care of him, as if he was their own."

"I knew they would."

"Nicholas and I had some quiet time last evening, just sitting on the rocker. You taught me well how to change diapers." Katarina laughs. "Katarina, let me get a picture of you and Caroline, I brought our camera."

"Let me fix my hair. Karl, I thought of something we need."

"Yes, my dear, a crib for Caroline. I realized that last night. We were going to shop this weekend for one. I plan on picking one up today." They spend the remainder of the day together. The day comes to an end.

"Mr. Schellenberg, it's time."

"Yes Betty." Karl hugs and kisses them.

"Good night my Loves, I love you both."

"Good night Karl, I love you. Give Nicholas a kiss for me."

Karl gets home and gets Nicholas. He plays with Nicholas for a while, and gets him settled in. Karl lays down, trying to sleep yet he is restless, thinking of Katarina and Caroline. Karl wakes early Friday morning and gets Nicholas ready for the Franklins, Ruth, and Ed, and returns to the hospital. As he walks in the room, Katarina is feeding Caroline.

"Good morning my Love, did you and Caroline sleep well?" Karl leans down and kisses Katarina and Caroline.

"Yes, I did, Caroline slept well also."

"And you?"

"I was restless, thinking of you and baby Caroline."

"How is Nicholas?"

"He is good, he loves Ruth and Ed, I can tell. He slept well also, I heard him a few times, but he went right back to sleep. He misses his Mommy. I picked up the crib last evening on my way home."

"Good, thank you. Look at her Karl, she is so precious." Karl sits next to the bed and holds Katarina's hand.

"Let me hold Caroline. She is so little." Katarina places the baby in Karl's arms.

"Doctor Grabb just left, he says everything is going well.

Caroline lost a few ounces, but he said that was normal, especially with a little tot like her. He will be in tomorrow morning, at 9:00." Karl and Caroline make immediate eye contact. "See Karl, she knows you."

"Katarina, she is so beautiful, so precious, and so little." A tear runs down Karl's cheek. Karl holds her little hand. He rubs his finger over her hand, she clenches his finger.

Saturday morning, Karl gets Nicholas up, and drops him at the Franklins. He is at the hospital early. Doctor Grabb arrives a few minutes early. "Good morning Katarina, Karl. How are you feeling?"

"I feel good today."

"Good, let me check you and the baby. Everything is looking fine. The nurses tell me Caroline has been sleeping well and is feeding on a regular cycle."

"Yes, she is a good baby, just like Nicholas."

"Katarina, I was hoping Caroline would have gained more weight. I'd like to keep you both a few extra days. Let's plan for Wednesday."

Katarina looks at Karl. "I understand Doctor Grabb. We need to be careful and be sure Caroline stays healthy. A few days will be fine."

Karl anxiously waits, the days seem slow to pass. He spends every day with his girls. Tuesday afternoon arrives. Karl is sitting at Katarina's bedside. Doctor Grabb comes into the room. "Hello everyone. Betty tells me you both are doing well, and Caroline has gained nine ounces. How would you like to go home tomorrow?"

"We would love that, thank you."

"Good, I'll make the arrangements with the nurses, let's say around noon. You can get a couple of feedings in, the nurses can get you ready, and check out afterwards."

"Karl, I am anxious to take Caroline home, I miss Nicholas." They spend the rest of the day together. Katarina finishes dinner, 7:30 approaches.

Betty enters the room. "I know, Betty, time to leave." Betty smiles.

"I hear you're going home tomorrow Miss Katarina."

"Yes Betty, that will be nice, I miss Nicholas."

"We're going to miss you."

Karl says his good nights and gives kisses. Wednesday morning, Karl is at the hospital bright and early. Katarina is feeding Caroline. "Good morning Katarina, good morning Caroline."

"Good morning Daddy."

Karl kisses them. "How are you feeling today?"

"I am good Karl; I am ready to go home." The nurse comes in and checks Katarina's and Caroline's vitals.

"Are you ready to go home Mrs. Schellenberg?"

"Yes, I am."

"Good, I'll go and get the paperwork ready, we will have you on your way very soon."

"Karl, would you get my things ready? I want to take our flowers." The nurse returns with a wheelchair.

"Ready Mrs. Schellenberg?"

"Yes." Karl holds Caroline while the nurse gets Katarina in the chair.

"Let's get you up and into the chair. Take my arm, Mrs. Schellenberg." Karl lays Caroline in Katarina's arms. The nurse wheels Katarina out.

"I will get the car and meet you at the front entrance." Karl scurries to the car.

Karl, Katarina, and Caroline arrive home, it's early afternoon. Karl gets them in the house, and settled in. "It is nice to be home Karl." Ruth and Ed knock on the door. Karl motions for them to come in. Ruth immediately takes Nicholas to his mother. "Nicholas, I missed you."

"Katarina, let me see little Caroline, she is so precious, so little."

"Ruth, come hold her, I want to give Nicholas a big hug."

Katarina looks into Nicholas' eyes. "Nicholas, Mommy missed you. You have a little sister. Her name is Caroline."

"Katarina, can we do or help with anything?"

"No, we are fine; thank you."

"We brought a little present for her." Katarina opens the gift.

"Look Karl, it is a matching blanket, like they got for Nicholas."

"Thank you both, she will love to snuggle with this just as Nicholas did."

"Katarina, we'll let you go now; you both need your rest. I fed Nicholas and changed him for you. I made you and Karl dinner. It's on the table in the kitchen. We are so happy for you and Karl."

"Thank you both, very much, and thank you for watching Nicholas."

"He is a joy, thank you for allowing us."

Karl is up early the next morning, tending to Katarina, Nicholas, and Caroline. He prepares breakfast for Katarina, and she feeds Nicholas and Caroline. Karl hears a car door. He looks out the window, it's Angie. "Good morning, Angie."

"Hey, how is Katarina and the baby? I saw your neighbor Ed at the store yesterday, he told me the good news."

"Come in Angie, Katarina is up. She just finished feeding the babies. Come see Caroline."

"Caroline is a nice name."

"Katarina, Angie is here."

"Bring her back Karl."

"Hello Angie."

"Hey Katarina, I heard the news. Oh my, she is a cutie patootie. Look how little."

"Yes, our little bundle of joy came early, about three weeks."

"Did everything go well?"

"Yes, she is strong. She was born Wednesday the twenty-ninth, at 3:33. She weighed 5 pounds 11 ounces and was 17.3 inches long. We had to stay in the hospital a few extra days while she gained weight."

"She has dark hair, just like you, Karl and Nicholas. Hey, I won't keep you. I just wanted to stop by. I have a little something for her." Katarina opens the gift. "Angie this is so cute, look Karl, a little pajama outfit and socks. Thank you, Angie. These will keep her warm."

"This is the same set I got for Nicholas, only in pink."

"Yes, I recognized that. I love it."

"If you two need anything call me, any time."

"Thank you again Angie."

"Katarina, I do have some news for you."

"What is it Angie?"

"I've been dating a fellow for a while, his name is Al, he is very nice."

"I am so happy for you Angie. Is it serious?"

"Yes, it is becoming serious, we're engaged. He proposed a week ago."

"Angie, that is wonderful news." Karl walks her to the door and chats for a few minutes. Karl returns to the bedroom, Katarina, Nicholas, and Caroline are sleeping. Katarina has her doll baby, Christie, from Germany, snuggled next to baby Caroline. Karl snaps a picture. Both babies are cuddled in Katarina's nightgown. He kisses them.

Nicholas' birthday is rapidly approaching. "Karl; next week is the little guy's birthday. What should we get him?"

"Well, he needs a highchair. You have been feeding him in your lap, and he is getting bigger."

"Yes, that would be nice. I was thinking of a wagon, we can pull him around in it. Caroline will need the carriage. I had a red Radio Flyer when I was little and loved it." Katarina and Karl have a party for Nicholas, and invite Ruth, Ed, Angie, and Al. Ruth and Ed are in the living room when Angie and Al arrive, Karl and Katarina greet them.

"Katarina and Karl, I want you to meet Al."

"Very nice to meet you Al, we have heard many nice things about you. Angie is very special to us."

"Very nice to meet you as well, Angie speaks very highly of you."

Nicholas' first birthday party was low key yet special. Nicholas loved squeezing the cake's icing in his little hands. The smile on his face was precious. After cake and ice cream for all, the party ends. Ruth and Ed leave first. "Angie and Al, we have something to ask of you. We are planning to have Caroline baptized in three weeks and we would love it if you and Al would stand for her."

"Katarina, we would be honored, thank you very much."

October 7 arrives. Katarina and Karl are at St. Andrews with the children. Angie, Al, Ruth, and Ed arrive. Ruth and Ed are seated in the first pew, they have Nicholas. Caroline is wearing her little white baptism outfit, her booties, and her hat. Katarina bought them the week before at Gables Department store. Caroline is wrapped in a white blanket, as was Nicholas. Katarina is wearing her wedding dress, and Karl is wearing his wedding suit.

"Karl remember at Nicholas' baptism, when I said my dress, your suit, are what we wore when we started our life together, now we wear them again to begin Caroline's life." She kisses his cheek, just as before. Baby Caroline is baptized. Ruth takes pictures of each couple with Caroline. Katarina turns to the group. "Who is hungry, let's all go to lunch, our treat. We can get a malt afterwards at Gower's."

A cool Halloween night arrives. Fall is in the air. As they did last year, Katarina and Karl finish carving their pumpkins. Karl's Mr. Pumpkin again has a top hat and a bow tie; Katarina's Mrs. Pumpkin has her same vail, pearls and flowers, Nicholas' baby pumpkin has a blue ball cap, and little Caroline's baby pumpkin has a pink bonnet. The ghosts Karl hung in the trees are blowing in the breeze. Karl sits on the steps ready to hand out treats to the little goblins. Katarina and the babies are on the swing, wrapped up in blankets. The Halloweener's begin trick-or-treating. Karl has fun with the trick-or-treaters.

Winter approaches. Caroline is growing. It appears to be heading for another cold winter in Coffeyville. Katarina is busy with babies, and Karl gets the family ready for Thanksgiving. This year they have invited Ruth, Ed, Angie, and Al to join them.

It is snowing on Thanksgiving Day. Ruth, Ed, Angie, and Al arrive at the same time. Karl hears the car doors and meets them at the front door. "Good morning, Happy Thanksgiving. Come in. Katarina will be right out. She is getting the children ready. I will get a fire started. Make yourselves comfortable."

"Karl, the turkey smells wonderful."

"Thank you, Angie, we are having our traditional turkey meal; turkey, stuffing, mashed potatoes, fresh corn, cranberry, and gravy."

"Karl, Ed and I brought a pumpkin pie."

"I baked fresh bread."

"It smells good Angie, thank you all." Katarina comes with the babies. The day ends with everyone sitting at the fireplace. Nicholas is curled up in Ruth's arms, Caroline in Angie's.

Just over two weeks until Christmas, Saturday the eighth of December. The Schellenberg family heads off to the gristmill for their tree. "Karl, I love being here. It is so pretty in the winter." It's a cold and snowy day, Katarina and the babies stay in the car while Karl hikes to get the tree. That evening Katarina and Karl finish decorating the tree and relaxing by the fireplace. "Can we do our Christmas shopping tomorrow? I will ask Ruth if she can watch the little ones."

"I would like that Katarina."

"Our tree is beautiful again this year. Look at Nicholas and Caroline, they are enjoying the tree lights. I am enjoying the fireplace. We have had many fun nights here." Sunday morning, Katarina feeds the babies, and gets them ready for a day with the Franklins. Katarina and Karl arrive in town just before eleven. "Karl, after church let's have lunch, then we can shop. Maybe get a malt at Gowers when we are finished." They get seated in the diner. It is starting to snow. "Have you thought about any gifts for Caroline and Nicholas, or should I say you?"

Karl chuckles. "I have, have you?"

"Yes, I was thinking of some new outfits for the babies, Nicholas is outgrowing his, and a doll baby for Caroline."

"I would like to get Nicholas a swing set. We can get baby seats; he would love that, they both would. I see how much they enjoy swinging on the porch with you Katarina."

Christmas eve, Karl finishes the outside lights and wreaths, and comes in to get the train and village set up. Katarina has the mistletoe hung. Christmas morning, Katarina feels a nudge and awakes to both babies with her. *Karl did that.* She smells the fireplace and hears Christmas music.

"Good morning Karl, Merry Christmas. I love your traditions." She gives him a kiss.

"Good morning my Love, Merry Christmas to you."

"I will feed Nicholas and Caroline; and get them ready for church." Katarina returns with both babies in little red Santa outfits.

"Katarina, the little ones are so precious."

After church service the family settles in front of the Christmas tree. Karl continues his tradition of ornaments. "Katarina, I have these for you, Nicholas, and Caroline, a reindeer for you, to go with Santa from last year, a Christmas tree for Nicholas, and an angel for our little angel."

"Karl, I want to continue our tradition; I want to ice skate at the gristmill pond under the moonlight tonight. We can take Nicholas and Caroline to Ruth and Ed's." Christmas day ends with a moonlight skate at the Birmingham Gristmill pond.

A few days pass as the family enjoys the gifts of Christmas. Katarina and Karl spend a quiet New Year's Eve at home, Ruth and Ed join them, enjoying the fireplace.

January 15, Katarina wakes up to Karl singing. "Happy anniversareee, happy anniversareee, happy anniversareee; happy anniversareee. Happy happy happy happy happy anniversareee; happy happy happy happy happy anniversareee; happy happy happy happy happy anniversareee; happy anniversary."

"Karl, I so love when you do that, it puts a smile on my face every time. You are so sweet; and so silly. I love you very much. Happy anniversary and happy birthday to you. I was thinking, our special anniversary, the day we met, it is coming up."

"I know, our special day."

The thirty-first is a Thursday. "Karl we can have date night, just the two of us. I am sure the Franklins will watch our little ones; they will love that. We will be right next door if they need us. We can ice skate at the gristmill, at night when you get home. We can have dinner and a malt in town, and spend the evening here, alone." Katarina giggles.

"I love your idea Katarina; it is a date. I will take Friday off; we can cuddle and play all night and into the morning."

Caroline is growing and eating on her own. As with Nicholas, Katarina has Caroline using the bowl, fork, and spoon that she used when she was a baby. It is the night before Valentine's Day. Karl runs into town on his way home from the Base and picks up a bouquet of red roses and white lilies for Katarina, a red and white ribbon for Caroline's hair, and red outfits for the babies. He also stops in the jewelry store to pick up his surprise he ordered three weeks ago for Katarina. When he gets home, Katarina is playing with Nicholas and Caroline on the floor.

"Katarina, the fire is nice."

"Yes, I thought I would surprise you?" He gives them all a kiss.

"Katarina, these are for you."

"Karl, my favorite flowers, thank you."

"I picked these up for the little ones."

"Karl, these outfits are so adorable, and the ribbon is tender." Katarina places the ribbon in Caroline's hair, although she does not have much hair yet.

"I will get the camera and snap a picture on the three of you." Katarina and Karl have dinner.

"Karl, we need a playpen, Nicholas is starting to get around on his own pretty good and it is hard to keep track of him sometimes."

"Yes, I noticed that too. We can pick one up this weekend."

"I will feed the babies, and we can go to bed."

Karl wakes up the next morning and hears Katarina in the baby's room. Katarina returns. "I was feeding Caroline. Happy Valentine's day, Karl."

"And to you my Love." Katarina lays down and feels something under her pillow.

"Karl what is this?"

"Open it my Love, it is for you."

"Karl it is beautiful, what made you think of a pearl necklace?"

"Well, I had this planned for a while, but I did your presents in reverse. I wanted you to have your blue Sapphire pendant for your birthday, now you have something to wear it with."

"I love you Karl, you are so good to me."

Spring has arrived, it is Good Friday morning, Karl and Katarina lay in bed. "This is Caroline's first Easter; and, happy first kiss day, Katarina."

"To you as well my Love." Easter Sunday morning, April 21, Caroline gets her own stuffed toy bunny. She has been playing with Nicholas' stuffed toys. Caroline immediately cuddles up to it. "She likes the bunny, Karl." Nicholas gets a stuffed toy puppy. He names it Burruss. They both have new Easter outfits. "Karl, after church we can take a walk along the river and have lunch in town." As with last year, Katarina spends most of April planting a garden. They enjoy playing with Nicholas and Caroline in the backyard on the swing set. The evenings are getting longer, and the Schellenberg's are enjoying walks in the neighborhood.

THE PLOT [1946]

May 1946, it's mid-morning. Karl is working in the front yard. Katarina has the babies on the porch swing. He notices a gentleman walking down the sidewalk. The man stops and introduces himself. "Hello, my name is Jim Baxter, I just rented a home down the street, the address is 140 Sycamore Avenue."

"Good morning, I am Karl Schellenberg. On the porch is my wife Katarina and our two children, Nicholas, and Caroline. Katarina, this is Jim. He just moved in down the street." Katarina smiles and waves.

"Jim, I detect a slight German accent."

"Yes; my parents were from Germany."

"What part?"

"They were from Frankfurt."

"Small world, mine and Katarina's parents were from Germany as well. My parents were from Bavaria, the towns of Kriestorf and Walchsing. Katarina is from Aurich, in Northern Germany."

"Yes, I have heard of Aurich, but not Kriestorf and Walchsing."

"They are very small towns. We are so happy the war has ended."

"I as well, it was terrible."

"Jim, we will need to catch up on our ancestry someday."

"Yes, I would like that."

"Tell me, what brings you here?"

"I lost my wife last month, in a horrible car accident." Jim gets choked up.

"I am so sorry."

"Thank you. I was not coping with it well, I needed to get away, start a new chapter in my life."

"I am so sorry."

Katarina can barely make out the conversation but can tell it is hard for Jim to talk. Karl continues to inquire, "Where did you live Jim?"

"I came from Kansas City. I like Kansas, and I thought Coffeyville would be a nice change, small town."

"What kind of work do you do?"

"I am in commercial real estate, a developer."

"What do you do Karl?"

"I am in the Army Air Force, stationed here at the Third Army Air Force Base, I am a lieutenant."

"I will be on my way now, nice to meet you Karl." Jim waves to Katarina.

Karl finishes his yard work and sits on the swing with Katarina.

"Jim seems like a nice man, what were you two talking about?"

"The poor man, he lost his wife last month in a terrible car accident. He was having trouble coping with his loss, so he moved here to get a new start. He is from Kansas City."

"That is sad Karl. I detected a German accent."

"Yes, his parents were from Germany, Frankfurt."

"We should have him over for dinner some evening, I am sure he is lonely. What does he do?"

"He is a developer, in commercial real estate."

Overtime, Jim becomes a close friend with Karl. They begin playing golf together. Katarina has him over for dinner, usually every Sunday. Jim gets attached to Nicholas, and Nicholas to him. Another hot summer in Coffeyville. Karl is teaching Katarina to drive. The babies are growing. Jim is becoming a regular at the Schellenberg's home. The middle of July, Karl is working in the yard. He can see what appears to be a severe storm rolling in. The wind is picking up. The thunder and lightning are intensifying. Suddenly the tornado sirens sound. Katarina runs from the house.

"Karl please come in, hurry."

Karl sees Jim running toward his house. "Jim, come with us. We have a shelter in the basement." Karl knows Jim's house has no shelter. Katarina has Caroline, Karl gets Nicholas, and they head to the basement. They hear the storm, the wind, and debris hitting their house. They lose power.

"Karl, I am frightened." This is the first tornado warning they have had.

"We will be fine Katarina." Karl no sooner says that, and the thunder roars, and a lightning bolt strikes, seemingly in the backyard. The littles ones are screaming. Katarina tries to comfort them. Finally, after two hours the storm passes. "You and the children stay here; I will go out and check for damage." Jim goes with him. Karl returns after ten minutes, "Katarina, you can come up, everything is fine, just a lot of limbs and trees down. The swing set has tipped over."

"Karl, I am going to check my house. I will be back and help you clean up." The power comes back on in an hour. Ed and Ruth stop over to check on them. Jim returns and helps clean up the debris.

"How is your place Jim?"

"I have no power; and looks like it will be that way for some time. A tree fell in my yard and took down the service line into the house."

Katarina hears that. "Jim, you can stay with us. We can put the children together; you can use Nicholas' room."

"Thank you, Katarina, I will take you up on that." Jim spends two days with Karl and Katarina.

"Karl, I am glad we met Jim, he is such a nice man, and is so good with the children."

"Yes, I like him, he is a good friend."

Katarina's and Caroline's birthdays are approaching. It's early Friday morning August 16. Katarina returns to bed after feeding Caroline. Nicholas is sound asleep. She snuggles in next to Karl. "Happy birthday to you. Happy birthday to you, happy birthday to Katarina, happy birthday to you; happy birthday to you my Love." Katarina smiles and giggles.

"You are a very silly man. I love when you sing to me. I have always loved that about you, thank you. The flowers you brought me last night are beautiful."

"I have something else for you, here open it."

"Karl, I love it, how did you think of a peridot? My birthstone, the ring is beautiful. I love the deep green color." Katarina kisses Karl, a passionate kiss.

"I have one more present for you."

"What is it Karl?" Katarina asks with a gleam in her eye, and her special promiscuous smile.

"Exactly, meet me under the sheets."

The end of August approaches. "Karl, Caroline's birthday is tomorrow. It is hard to believe our precious little girl is one year old. She is so cute now that she is walking."

"Yes, I love how she chases Nicholas around. The other day I heard Nicholas scolding her for running after him. 'No baby Caroline, no baby Caroline.' She gave it right back to him in her gibberish. It was so cute."

"I am planning a little party for her Saturday. I have invited Ruth and Ed, Angie and Al, and Jim."

"That will be nice Katarina. Angie is still single though, well technically, maybe we can convince Angie and Al to actually marry."

"Ha, I do not think she will ever marry. She has been engaged for a while. I will say she and Al are a thing though. Karl, will you have time to pick-up balloons tomorrow?" Caroline's party lasts the afternoon. Caroline was the life of the party, everyone had fun.

Labor Day, late summer. Katarina and Karl take the children on a picnic to the gristmill. "Karl, will you lay the blanket here? The stream sounds nice flowing into the pond. This reminds me of the Kettle. Look at Nicholas and Caroline playing, they are so cute." Katarina and Karl lay back and stare into the blue sky. "This is just like being at the Kettle in Germany, I love you."

"I was just thinking that, I love you Katarina."

"Karl, Nicholas' birthday is in fifteen days. These two years went by so fast."

"I thought of getting him a pedal car. I saw one at Gables Department store, a little fire truck with ladders."

"He would like that Karl. I will plan a party for him, like we did for Caroline, everyone had a good time."

"Yes, they did."

Nicholas' party is memorable for him. Everyone enjoyed the day and had fun in the yard. October arrives in Coffeyville. Saturday evening, Katarina and Karl are on the porch swing, the little ones are playing in the front yard. "It did not take Nicholas long to master the pedal car. I love how you created a hitch for the car. Nicholas loves pulling Caroline in the wagon. Karl, I love October, I love the smell of fall." Karl kisses her forehead.

"Katarina, Jim was over the other day. Out of the blue he asked if I was ever in Germany, for the war. I thought that was a strange question."

"I would not think anything of it, you are in the Army Air Force. What did you tell him?"

"I have never talked with anyone about Germany, you know, with my assignment. I skirted the question and said no. I told him I was assigned to various bases here in the U.S. Come to think of it, in all the time we have known him, he has never asked how we met, or how you got to the States. Do you think is strange? That was it."

"Karl you worry too much."

Tuesday October 15, a full moon. Karl and Katarina are sitting on the front porch swing. It's late, the little ones are sleeping. Jim walks up the sidewalk. "Hey, you two love birds."

"Hello Jim, how are you tonight, it is a lovely evening."

"Katarina, I need a favor."

"Sure Jim, anything."

"I have an appointment tomorrow, actually I want to talk with Karl about that as well. Anyway, Katarina, my stove is not working. I have a repair man coming over, and they cannot give me an exact time for the repairs. Would you wait at the house for him?"

"I would be glad to Jim."

"Karl, that brings me to my appointment. I thought I heard you were off this week."

"Yes, taking little vacation."

"I am looking at a warehouse in town on the corner of East Ninth Street and Maple, to develop it into flats possibly. I wondered if you would come with me, I would like your ideas, a fresh look."

"I know the building, yet, I know nothing about real estate development."

"That is why I ask, sometimes my head gets into the weeds too much, I need a fresh and independent look."

"Karl, that will be fun, go with him," Katarina says with encouragement.

"Katarina, my appointment in town is at 9:30, will that work for you?"

"Yes Jim, that will give me time to get the littles ones up and ready."

"Good, I will pick you up at 9:00, Karl."

In the morning, Katarina heads to Jim's house with the little ones. Jim picks Karl up and they head to the warehouse. "Karl, I really appreciate this, you have no idea what this means to me, for you and me to be together today."

"I am happy to help Jim, I may learn something today."

"I have been waiting for this a long time."

"Why do you say that? It was only yesterday you asked for me to join you."

"I know Karl, I am just anxious, this is very important to me."

Karl thinks to himself, *that is odd.* They arrive at the warehouse shortly after 9:30. "Karl, we can go to the second floor, that is where my challenges are." On the second floor Karl is looking around; he walks toward the window to see the view. He hears something metal hit the floor; and from the corner of his eye he sees dog tags slide by his feet. He immediately stops, still facing forward. He hears a jaw clicking, a very distinct but familiar sound. Astonished he thinks to himself; *it can't be, yet I know that sound, can it be Wilhelm? No, he says.*

"Lieutenant Pfisterer?" Karl turns and sees Jim staring directly at him.

"Do you know me?" he says to Karl.

Karl simply says, "Yes, of course I do, you are Jim, Jim Baxter."

Jim laughs, "You stupid fool, I am Wilhelm," and pulls out a gun. "I have been waiting a long time for this moment, get on your knees. Pick up your dog tags, yes they are yours." Karl stands for a moment; he recognizes this person as Jim but does not know why he says he is Wilhelm. How does this man even know who Wilhelm is? Karl does not fully understand what is going on. He is taken off guard. Karl knows what Wilhelm looks like and knows his voice. "Get on your knees, I said." Karl kneels and picks up the dog tags, they are his. Wilhelm hits Karl over his back with a piece of lumber. Karl falls to the floor, unconscious. Wilhelm ties Karl to a beam. Karl regains consciousness, he finds himself hanging from a beam, his arms above his head, his feet tied to a column. Wilhelm clicks his jaw again. "Karl, listen to me, I am Wilhelm." Wilhelm begins to tell the story. "I found your dog tags in the barn you were hiding in, on the farm. You Americans are so stupid, the information you put on your tags. It took me a while, yet I was able to track you down, and find you." Wilhelm hits Karl in his stomach with the end of the board. Karl lets out loud a groan. "You made a fool of me in Germany, you embarrassed me. The information you gave the Allies helped them win the war."

"You are wrong, it helped you and Hitler lose the war, Wilhelm,"

Karl mumbles. Wilhelm hits Karl again in the stomach with the board.

"I killed a good man needlessly, for no reason. I vowed to find you and kill you, I was patient, now here we are."

Karl looks Wilhelm directly in the eyes, "I would say there was a good reason for you killing Webber, he was a Nazi." Wilhelm punches Karl. The torturing continues. "Jim, or Wilhelm," Karl says in a muffled voice, "Why did you wait so long, we met you six months ago."

"I am a patient man." Wilhelm hits Karl again in his stomach. Karl wonders to himself, *when were you ever patient?* "I wanted to play with your head, get to know you, your habits, and gain your trust. I developed this plan a long time ago, I have had plenty of time to think about it, and you and Katarina."

"Do whatever you want with me, please do not hurt Katarina or the children."

Wilhelm laughs, "I believe this was your bad leg, your right leg, am I correct? You used to walk with a limp, however it has gone away. Maybe this will bring it back." He whacks Karl's leg with the piece of lumber. Karl screams with pain. "When the Allies captured Emden and Wilhelmshaven, in April of last year, virtually paralyzing the Kriegsmarine, Hitler knew then it was just a matter of time before the Third Reich would fall. He only confided with us, his inner circle. His campaign and propaganda continued to the German Army and the people of Germany; it was flawless.

"Toward the end of 1944, Hitler began to sense the morale of the German Army was faltering. Hitler re-established the Volkssturm, a national militia that had existed, on paper, since around 1925. It seemed like an infallible plan at the time with all of us. Hitler ordered Martin Bormann to recruit six million men for this militia, ages 16 to 60. To control his propaganda, Hitler ordered it would be controlled by the Nazi Party and part of the Nazi endeavor to overcome their enemies' military strength through force of will. However, the intended strength of six million members was never attained. Joseph Goebbels and other propagandists depicted the Volkssturm as an outburst of enthusiasm and the will to resist.

"While it had some marginal effect on morale, it was undermined by the recruits' visible lack of uniforms and weaponry. The new Volkssturm was also to become a nationwide organization, with Heinrich Himmler, as commander. To further inflict the evidence of pending failure, there was no standardization of any kind and the Volkssturm units were issued only what equipment was available. This resulted in the units looking very ragged and, instead of boosting civilian morale, it often reminded people of Germany's and the Third Reich's desperate state. In hindsight these actions further impacted Hitler's ability to calm the German people and promote his propaganda that the Nazi Party was winning the war. It was evident he was losing credibility. This failure was viewed by the German people as a last-ditch effort by Hitler to save his Third Reich and the Nazi Party."

"Why do you not look like Wilhelm?"

"I am getting to that." He punches Karl in the stomach. "Knowing Germany would fall; Hitler developed an elaborate escape plan for himself and his most trusted disciples. Myself, Himmler, Funk, Ribbentroy, Speer, Donitz, Raeder, Bormann, Goebbels, and Goring. We all accumulated wealth, millions, from what the Third Reich stole, mostly from France, England, and Poland. The plan, a year in the making, was we all would have plastic surgery, voice augmentation to disguise us, and new identities to allow us to escape Germany. Just like your false identity, Lieutenant Pfisterer." This time he hits Karl in the ribs. Karl perseveres through the pain. "Hitler engaged the services of a trusted surgeon and a very loyal medical assistant, they both were sworn to, and committed to secrecy. A state-of-the-art operating room and recovery wing was established in the Fuhrerbunker. The Fuhrerbunker was a subterranean bunker, air raid shelter located near the Reich Chancellery in Berlin, Germany. It was built to protect Hitler. Hitler requested me to be the first for the surgery and voice augmentation. That is why you did not recognize me. It obviously worked." He hits Karl again; blood is oozing from Karl's mouth. Karl is slumped over in a hanging position.

"Once my procedure was a success, Hitler and Eva Braun followed. We all learned English, although I already could speak it from my parents. Hitler recruited other loyalists to pose for us once the surgeries were completed, one by one, as body doubles, including himself and Eva. We all were sworn to secrecy, in the name of Hitler. We vowed to take the secret to our grave. The body doubles were to be mirror images of us, our Doppelgangers. It was an ingenious plan. We all put our lives up for Hitler, and the Third Reich. The loyalists were our most trusted. The plan was ingenious. The doubles would be in the limelight, with our troops, the people, while we were in the Fuhrerbunker. Hitler ran the war and Germany for over a year from the Fuhrerbunker after his and my surgeries. I was at his side while our doubles were being prepped for their new roles, by our directives. Hitler's and my double would routinely be seen in public to test the plan, and it worked perfectly. Unfortunately, the Third Reich fell before the others could have the surgery."

It is noon, Katarina is at Jim's house. No sign of the repairman, she continues to wait. *Jim never gave me the name of the shop. If he did, I could call them.*

At the warehouse Wilhelm continues his torture of Karl, and his meticulous story. "In the final weeks of the war, we put our plan in place. We had to make things look real, to be convincing." Karl passes out. Wilhelm slaps his face. "Wake up you bastard, you need to listen." Karl lifts his head, he is groggy. "It was apparent going into April 1945 the end was nearing. Hitler was in denial about the dire situation and placed his hopes on the units commanded by Waffen-SS General Felix Steiner. On April 21, Hitler ordered Steiner to attack the northern flank of the encircling Soviet salient and ordered the German Ninth Army, south-east of Berlin, to attack northward in a pincer attack. That evening, Red Army tanks reached the outskirts of Berlin. Hitler was told at his afternoon situation conference on April 22 that Steiner's forces had not moved, and he fell into a tearful rage when he realized the attack was not going to be carried out. He openly declared for the first time the war was lost and he blamed his generals. Hitler told us he and Eva Braun would stay in Berlin as long as they could, but ultimately would flee to Brazil.

"The Red Army had consolidated their attack on Berlin by April 25, despite the commands being issued from the Fuhrerbunker. There was no prospect the German defense could do anything but delay the city's capture. On April 28, Hitler learned that Heinrich Himmler was trying to discuss surrender terms with the Western Allies and Hitler considered this treason. He was a coward. Hitler ordered Himmler's arrest. Hitler learned the foreign press was reporting fresh acts of treason from the German Army. In a rage, Hitler demanded, without exception, we commit our unquestionable and undeniable loyalty to the Fuhrer. That evening, Hitler ordered the Luftwaffe to attack the Soviet forces that had just reached Potsdamerplatz, one city block from the Fuhrerbunker. During the night of April 28, Hitler learned his Twelfth Army had been forced back along the entire front and it was no longer possible for it to relieve Berlin. The Luftwaffe attack never happened. Hitler married Eva Braun after midnight, the early morning hours of April 29 in Fuhrerbunker.

"In the early morning of April 30, Hitler was updated, the Nazi's Twelfth Army was unable to continue the attack of the Red Army in Berlin and the bulk of Nazi's Ninth Army surrounded. SS Commander Mohnke informed Hitler during the morning of April 30 that he would only be able to hold Berlin for less than two days. Later that morning, he informed Hitler his troops would probably exhaust their ammunition that night and again asked him for permission to retreat. Mohnke received permission at about 13:00 that afternoon. Hitler orders his plan to commence. He witnesses his body double consume a cyanide capsule and shoot himself after taking the life of the young lady, Eva's double. He also witnessed the death of his trusted surgeon and his assistant. Hitler and Eva left the

Fuhrerbunker that afternoon for Brazil through an escape tunnel. In compliance with Hitler's instructions, the bodies of Hitler's and Eva's doubles were burned in the garden behind the Reich Chancellery. A public announcement was released at 15:15 later that day announcing Adolf Hitler and Eva Braun had committed suicide by Hitler consuming a cyanide capsule, then shooting himself, Eva dies by cyanide, and their bodies were publicly burned in the garden. As I said, to convince the world, Hitler had complete alliance from his inner circle, except for Heinrich Himmler's. He surrendered to the Allies. Joseph Goebbels' committed suicide a few days prior, Goebbels himself poisoned his own wife and six children with Cyanide.

"Hitler had commitments from us there would be no chance of anyone testifying. Martin Bormann committed suicide before capture. Heinrich Himmler committed suicide while in British custody. Like you Lieutenant Pfisterer." Wilhelm pokes Karl with his luger. "We had spies as well. Himmler was given cyanide. The remaining members of Hitler's inner circle were captured. No one disclosed the secret, loyalty Karl, loyalty. In the Nuremberg War Crimes Trials, Walther Funk was convicted and sentenced to life in prison. Joachim von Ribbentroy was convicted and sentenced to execution by hanging, which is to be carried out today. Albert Speer was convicted and sentenced to twenty years in prison. Karl Donitz was convicted and sentenced to ten years in prison. Erich Raeder was convicted and sentenced to life in prison. Hermann Goring was convicted and sentenced to execution by hanging, also scheduled for today. I learned he committed suicide yesterday. My double was captured, convicted, and sentenced to execution by hanging, which is scheduled for today also, but he kept the secret. Before leaving the Fuhrerbunker, we killed our remaining chosen loyalists, our direct reporting officers, and our closest advisors, for fear they would be captured and interrogated. Hitler made us swear, we would never contact one another after leaving Berlin. We scattered throughout the world. Hitler and I are the only ones to escape capture. You see Karl, we are the superior race."

Wilhelm hits Karl again, this time on the side of his head. Karl slumps over. Again, Wilhelm slaps his face. "Stay with me Karl. I have left a note for your beloved wife, my dear sister Katarina, to meet us here. I expect she will be here soon." Karl stares at Wilhelm,

"I promise you, if you hurt her." Wilhelm hits him again.

"Promise what, you are in no position to promise anything. You will watch your beloved wife die, then you will die."

Katarina waits until 4:00; and places a note on Jim's front door for the repairman to come to 320 Sycamore, then returns home to find a note on her door. *'Mrs. Schellenberg, if you want to see your husband alive, come to the warehouse on the corner of West Ninth Street and Maple. Come by yourself.'* She immediately thinks something terrible has happened to Karl and Jim. Katarina frantically screams. She runs to Ruth and Ed's and pounds on the door. Ed is not home. Ruth sees Katarina is frantic.

"Katarina, what is it, what happened?"

"Ruth, I cannot talk right now, it is Karl, something happened. Will you watch the babies?" Katarina takes the car and arrives at the warehouse at 4:30. She carefully enters and sees nothing on the first floor but hears a noise on the second floor. She runs up the ramp and sees Karl slumped over, bound, and beaten, hanging from the beam.

She screams, "Karl, what has happened, what is going on?" She runs to Karl, holds him, and begins to untie him. At that moment, from the corner of her eye, she sees a shadow of a man step out from behind a column. Katarina turns and gasps. "Jim, it is you, thank God. Please help Karl. What happened?" She has untied Karl. He lay motionless on the floor.

"Do you know who I am?"

"Why are you asking me that Jim, we need to help Karl, who did this?"

"I did."

She gasps, "What? Why?" She hears his jaw click. She listens intently, Wilhelm clicks his jaw again. Katarina screams. She knows of only one person that makes that distinct noise; and she is petrified.

"I am Wilhelm Katarina; I am your brother."

"Wilhelm? But what, who, where is Jim?"

"I am Jim. I had to get to you, to gain your trust. Hitler protected his inner circle, Katarina. Hitler and I had plastic surgery and voice augmentation to escape Germany."

Katarina is in disbelief. "We took you in as a friend. You played with our children; you held my babies. How could you?"

"That meant nothing to me, all part of my plan to find you and Karl." Karl regains consciousness, he sees Katarina. He struggles to get up. Wilhelm looks over at Karl. Katarina lunges toward Wilhelm, a scuffle occurs. By this time Karl is up and coming at them. A gunshot sounds, Katarina drops to the floor. Karl, lunges at Wilhelm, a fight occurs with them. Wilhelm has Karl pinned to the wall, his hand around Karl's throat. Karl is very weak and in unbearable pain. Their eyes lock on one another's. Another gunshot erupts, Wilhelm drops to the floor, he is slumped against the wall. Karl sees Katarina holding the gun, and rushes to her. As she falls to the floor, the gun falls and slides toward Wilhelm.

Karl is screaming. "Katarina do not die. Help me someone, help me," he screams. He holds her in his arms. "Please do not die my Love." Katarina is bleeding from her abdomen; Karl can see she has lost a lot of blood. "I need to get help stay with me Katarina."

Katarina opens her eyes. She looks up at Karl. "Karl, just hold me."

They look into each other's eyes, "I love you Katarina, stay with me, I will get help."

In a muffled voice, "I love you Karl." Katarina is coughing blood up. Her eyes are weakening. She passes out.

Wilhelm is mocking Karl. "Your precious Katarina is dying. I took her from you." Karl looks over at Wilhelm and sees him reaching for the gun. Karl lunges and gets the gun. He stands over Wilhelm. Karl stares into Wilhelm's eyes. He can tell Wilhelm is dying. Karl stands over Wilhelm, he kicks in his groin.

"That is for hitting Katarina at the farm. You deserve to die you bastard." Wilhelm stares back at Karl, and smiles, blood is running from his mouth. He laughs at Karl. "I recall you once saying you would take a bullet for Hitler. Your wish has just come true. Katarina will have her wish also. As you did to Gerhardt and Anna," Karl raises the gun. Wilhelm stares at him, a cold stare, and laughs. "Today is the day you die." Karl shoots Wilhelm between the eyes.

Karl rushes back to Katarina, he is screaming frantically and crying uncontrollably. "Katarina my Love, please do not die, stay with me, you do not deserve to die. Wilhelm is dead. He cannot hurt anyone anymore." Katarina slowly closes her eyes, her head rolls to the side of Karl's arm. Karl is holding her, crying deliriously. He hears someone coming up the ramp. "Help me, my wife has been shot, she is dying, she has lost a lot of blood, please help me." Karl turns and sees a police officer with his gun drawn.

"What happened, what is going on here? I heard gunshots. Don't move," as he points his gun to Karl. He quickly ascertains the situation. He sees Wilhelm slumped over in the corner; he can tell Karl has been beaten. He runs to Katarina, places his fingers on Katarina's neck. "She has a pulse, a very weak pulse, but I feel a pulse. I'll be right back, there is a call box right down the street." The officer leaves for help. Karl helps Katarina, the best he can, to keep her alive. Minutes pass: they seem like hours to Karl. Help arrives. Katarina and Karl are placed in the ambulance and are rushed to the hospital. Karl is holding Katarina's hand. He can barely sit up. The attendants are trying to stabilize her. Two blocks from the hospital, Katarina goes into full cardiac arrest.

The attendants are working to revive her, Karl is screaming, "Do not die Katarina, please do not leave me and the children." Katarina is quickly wheeled into the emergency room.

Karl is wheeled to another treatment room. "No, let me stay with her, I want to stay with my wife," pleads Karl. Hours pass. Ruth and Ed are frantic. They finally call the police and learn of the ordeal. They call Angie and Al and rush to the hospital with the little ones. Karl is in recovery from his injuries. Ruth stays with the children in the waiting room, Ed comes to Karl's room.

"Karl, oh my Lord, what has happened? How are you?" Karl can barely talk.

"It is Katarina, she is dying. How are the children?"

"Ruth has the children, they are fine."

"Thank you. Ed, how is Katarina? No one will tell me anything," Karl asks in mumbled voice.

"I don't know Karl, she is still in the emergency room, in surgery. The nurses won't tell us anything either." Karl nods off. Ed stays with him.

Angie and Al arrive at the hospital and see Ruth. "Ruth, what has happened? How are Katarina and Karl?"

"We don't know a whole lot other than something horrible happened at a warehouse in town. Katarina was shot."

"Oh, my Lord, what happened?" Angie is trembling.

"The police won't say. Karl was severely beaten; he is in recovery. Ed is with him. Another person was shot also."

"How are the children?"

"They are fine, they don't understand. Ed and I are keeping them calm for now."

"Ruth may I help, what can I do?"

"We're fine Angie, just a nervous wreck. I am so worried about Katarina."

It's after midnight, a nurse comes in. "Sir, we're going to sedate Mr. Schellenberg so he can rest through the night, you'll need to leave."

Ruth, Ed, Angie, and Al leave for the night with the children.

They are back first thing in the morning. It's October 17. The nurse takes Ruth and Ed to Karl's room. Angie and Al stay with Nicholas and Caroline. Karl is in better shape today; and is cleaned up. He has stitches on his forehead.

"Ruth, are the children with you?"

"Yes, Angie is here, she has them in the waiting room Karl."

"I would like to see them." Ruth turns to the nurse, she nods ok.

As soon as Nicholas sees Karl, he shouts, "Daddy, Daddy, where is Mommy?" Karl begins to weep. Karl holds his babies.

"Mommy is sleeping." He nods to Ruth to take the children back to the waiting room.

The Doctor enters, "Hello Mr. Schellenberg, I'm Doctor Bailor."

"Doctor, how is my wife, is she alive?"

"Yes Mr. Schellenberg. She has had a rough go of it. She lost a lot of blood, and the bullet did a lot of severe damage to her lower organs." Karl is weeping uncontrollably. Ed is holding his hand, trying to comfort him. "She went into cardiac arrest three times. She was in surgery for nine hours. She will need at least three more surgeries. There is a lot of reconstruction we need to do. We need to get her stabilized first. We have a great team of doctors and surgeons here at Mercy Hospital. Initially it was doubtful if she would pull through. We still are not out of the woods; the next few days will tell us a lot. I'll be honest, at this juncture, with her injuries, I cannot promise anything. She is in God's hands now. I hope the worst is behind us though. If she gets through the next few days, the next week, she will have a long and slow recovery. We have her in an induced coma. You have a strong lady here; she is a fighter."

"I only ask you to save her life Doctor Bailor, for the babies we have. Thank you for all you and your team have done for her. I want to see her, when can I see her?"

"Not for a while, I'm sorry, she is in the intensive care unit and will be for a while."

"I need to see my wife; I need to be with her."

"Well, I think we can arrange that, although you need to stay at a distance."

"Thank you, Doctor. How long will she be in the coma?"

"Three to four weeks." The nurse wheels Karl to Katarina's room. He can barely recognize her. She has oxygen tubes, IVs, bottles, and so many machines supporting her. She seems to be resting though. Karl is crying like a baby.

Seven days pass. Katarina seems to be stabilizing, her vitals are improving. Ruth and Ed have been by every day with the children. Karl is discharged. Weeks go by. Karl is with Katarina every day, and the children every night. Because of Karl's stellar service in Germany, Captain Harris has arranged for Karl to have as much time off as he needs. The week before Thanksgiving, November 15. Karl is at Katarina's bed side early. Doctor Bailor comes in the room.

"Mr. Schellenberg, I have good news. We are taking your wife out of the coma today."

"When? That is great news."

"Shortly. If all goes well, she should be awake in a few hours. I must warn you, more than likely she will not remember anything, she will be groggy and confused. Keep her calm. We will have her sedated a bit though to help." 11:30, Katarina begins to awake. She opens her eyes and immediately sees Karl. She stares at him for a few minutes. Karl can see she's trying to gather her thoughts. Karl holds her hands.

"Karl, where am I? What happened? I feel like I have been in a dream forever. I dreamed of us in Germany."

"Katarina, welcome back. You had a terrible accident. You are doing much better now. I missed you so much Katarina, I love you."

"Accident, what happened? How are the children?"

"Shh, the important thing is you are here. The children have been fine. They miss their Mommy. Ruth and Ed have been an immense help. We all have been praying for you."

"What happened? When can I see Nicholas and Caroline?"

"We can talk about what happened later, that is not important right now. The important thing is you are here my Love. Ruth and Ed are bringing Nicholas and Caroline by later this afternoon. Angie and Al have been by often; they always ask about you. She helps Ruth with the children when she can."

"They all are sweet and special friends." Katarina's eyes are drawn to Karl's lapel. "Karl, you are wearing my butterfly pin."

THE RECOVERY

Winterlike weather has arrived. It's snowing. Karl meets Ruth and Ed in the hospital lobby, the afternoon of November 15. He wants to prepare the children, knowing though Caroline is too little to realize anything. "Nicholas and Caroline. Your mother has a booboo. The doctors fixed her all up. She is resting and will be home soon. Would you like to see her?"

"Daddy, I want to see Mommy, let's go, let's go now" says little Nicholas. When they enter Katarina's room, she has fallen asleep. Karl sits with the children. Ruth goes to the gift shop and gets them a coloring book to pass the time. An hour passes, Katarina wakes up. She sees the little ones, smiles, and begins to weep. Nicholas runs over to her and holds her hand. Karl is holding Caroline at the bedside.

Katarina looks into their little faces, and in a weak and groggy voice, "Hello Nicholas. Hello Caroline. I missed you very much. I am happy to see you. I love you very, very much." Karl picks them up to kiss Katarina.

Nicholas holds Katarina's cheeks with his little hands. "I love you Mommy and I missed you too. Daddy says you have a booboo." Katarina laughs. A tear comes to Karl's eye. Karl leans down and kisses Katarina.

"Katarina look outside. It is snowing."

"It is beautiful Karl; I love the snow. I remember us playing in the snow at the farm, in Germany."

The nurse comes in. "Hello Karl," she greets Ruth and Ed, and the little ones. "Hello Nicholas and Caroline. I have heard a lot about you. Are you happy to see Mommy?" Caroline is nodding her head and saying something with Mama, Mama in the mix, in baby talk, a hundred miles an hour. Nicholas gets right into a conversation.

"Yes, I am happy to see her. I missed Mommy. My Daddy is not a good cook." The room erupts in laughter.

"How are you feeling today Katarina?"

"Much better now."

The nurse turns to Karl and whispers, "You all will need to leave shortly. I need to tend to Ms. Katarina, and she needs her rest." Karl nods. "Karl, Doctor Bailor will be here in the morning; he would like to see you at 9:00 sharp."

"I will be here, thank you."

Karl wakes Nicholas and Caroline; gets them up and ready; and takes them to Ruth's. He arrives at the hospital at 8:00. Katarina is sleeping. Doctor Bailor arrives promptly at 9:00. "Good morning Karl, I need to talk with you but first let me check on Ms. Katarina. She is doing fine, her healing is progressing, she is sleeping better." Doctor Bailor pulls a chair next to Karl. "Katarina's recovery is progressing remarkably well for what she went through. We are very lucky to have her with us." Karl gets choked up. "I wanted to see you about a few things. First, and this is difficult, I do need to tell you she will not be able to have any more babies, there was just too much damage." Karl lets out a loud cry. He gathers himself. "I do have good news for you. If she continues as she has, Katarina should be able to go home by Christmas. Things will be different though."

"That will be a wonderful Christmas present Doctor."

"She will need daily care. Her dressings will need to be changed, she will need constant attention, probably for three months or so." Karl smiles. "What is it Karl?"

"It is a long story, about how we met. I was in Germany, a pilot for the Army Air Force. My plane experienced some type of mechanical issue and it lost power. I parachuted. My chute failed and I was severely injured in occupied Germany. Katarina found me a few days later, in the woods. She and her mother Anna took me to safety. Katarina bandaged me up, changed my dressings, and gave me constant care for months. In addition to cuts and bruises, I had a punctured abdomen, a ruptured spleen, a compound fracture of my right leg, broken ribs, a broken left forearm, and I could not see from my left eye. She saved my life; we fell in love." A tear runs down Karl's cheek. "Now it is my turn to care for her. I will arrange for her care. Thank you very much."

"Karl, I had no idea what you went through. As I said, let's pray her recovery continues as it has."

Angie stops by that afternoon. Katarina is awake. She pops her head in the door, "hey, do you have a minute for an old friend?"

Katarina looks up, in a weak voice, "Angie please come in. It is so nice to see you."

"I'm glad you're feeling better Katarina." Angie stays with Katarina for an hour. Karl walks Angie out when they leave.

"Angie, I need to get someone to help Katarina and the children, a nanny. Do you know anyone?"

"I do have a few people in mind. I will let you know."

"Good, I would like to talk with them."

"Karl, I've been meaning to tell you something. The warehouse where all this happened, this terrible ordeal, it was never for sale. It has been vacant for years but has never been for sale. Something else. I remember one day Jim, or Wilhelm, and I were talking, and he said something to me. I thought nothing of it until now." Karl looks at Angie. "He told me he had a surprise for you and Katarina, but it was the way he said it though. I asked him what it was. He just stared at me and had a smirky smile. He said, you need to be patient Angie, you will see, you will see very soon. I thought it odd yet thought nothing more of it. We all thought he was so nice." Angie begins to cry. "I wish I would have mentioned it."

"Angie please do not think that. He loved to play with our heads, he played us all."

Ruth and Ed have Karl, the children, Angie, and Al for Thanksgiving. Nicholas and Caroline are playing with Angie. Everyone gets seated at the table for the Thanksgiving meal. The children are hungry. The others can see Karl is doing his best to keep an upbeat attitude for them, yet they can see, and know, his mind is elsewhere, with Katarina. After dinner Karl leaves for the hospital. He arrives at 3:30. As he enters her room Katarina is sitting up. She looks over to Karl.

"Hello, my Love, I am happy to see you up. You look good today."

She adorns a big smile. "I do feel good today. The Doctor will be in soon, he may have news on when I can go home." Karl kisses Katarina and sits next to her.

"Today is Thanksgiving."

"I know Karl."

"Today was hard for me Katarina, I did okay in front of the little ones."

Doctor Bailor arrives. "Good afternoon Katarina, Karl. How are you feeling today Katarina?"

"I am feeling much better."

"I have news for you, good news actually. If you continue as you have, I think we can get you home by Christmas, no promises though. The next couple of weeks will tell us a lot."

Katarina has a big smile, "Thank you, Doctor Bailor. This is wonderful news."

Two weeks pass, December 12. Karl is at Katarina's side; she is sitting in a chair. Christmas music is playing throughout the hospital. A tap on the door.

"Good morning Katarina, Karl."

"Good morning Doctor Bailor."

"How are you feeling today? I see you are up and in the chair; that is good."

"I am feeling better, still extremely sore though."

"That is to be expected. Let's get you in bed. I'll lay the bed down. Now lay back slowly so I can examine you. The nurse and I will help you." Doctor Bailor takes his time with Katarina. "Katarina, you're healing well." The Doctor holds Katarina's hand. "Young lady, you will be home for Christmas."

Katarina's eyes light up. "That is wonderful news, Karl, I can come home."

"Let's plan on the twentieth, next Friday. There will be some changes at home, I have gone over them with Karl. I will see you tomorrow." Doctor Bailor leaves.

"Karl what changes does he mean?"

"We will need to have help for you, someone to be with you, to change your dressings, help around the house, and to help with Nicholas and Caroline, at least during the day. I have been interviewing a few girls, Angie recommended them. The one I like best is a nurse, she works at night here at Mercy, in pediatrics. She will be perfect for you and the children. Her name is Nichole Dianes. Something unique, she spells her name with an 'h', like my name, and Nicholas' and Caroline's. She said she can make her schedule work fine for you."

"Karl, what happened to me that horrible day? What kind of accident did I have? Why did this happen? I cannot remember anything. I just know it was bad."

"The doctor told me your memory would block it, although now may the time, you need to know."

"Where can I begin? We almost lost you my Love, you had very bad injuries." Karl gathers himself. "Do you remember Jim, Jim Baxter?"

"Yes, I do. That lovely man down the street. He is a good friend."

"Well," Karl gets choked up. "He was not who we thought he was."

"What does that mean Karl?" Karl pauses, and holds Katarina's hands.

"This is very bizarre and hard to believe. I will go slow. He was your brother, Wilhelm." Katarina is speechless. She stares at Karl. "Hitler and Wilhelm changed themselves. I mean, they had plastic surgery to change their looks and had their voices changed, so they could escape Germany. In fact, Hitler's entire inner circle was to have plastic surgery, voice augmentation, and body doubles. Hitler engaged the services of a trusted surgeon and a very loyal assistant, they both were sworn to, and committed to secrecy. A state-of-the-art operating room and recovery wing was established in the Fuhrerbunker. Thankfully the war ended before the entire plan was carried out. They all were cowards." Katarina's hands are trembling. Karl holds her hands tighter. "Maybe I should stop."

"No Karl, please continue, I will be fine, I need to know."

"Remember when I lost my dog tags, I thought we lost them in the barn? When I looked there and did not find them, I assumed they fell off when Hans helped us escape on the motorcycle." Katarina nods her head. "As it turned out, I did lose them in the barn. Wilhelm found them. He tracked us here. He set up this elaborate scheme to befriend us, to get close to us," Karl hesitates a moment, collects himself, "to kill us, both of us. He said I embarrassed him in the Third Reich." Tears are running down Katarina's cheeks.

"Karl I am having trouble understanding this. The war ended eighteen months ago."

"I know my Love; it is a nightmare. The war never ended for him. He lured me to a warehouse in town, asking for my advice for development ideas. You know the warehouse, we walked by it many times in town. He told us he was a real estate developer."

"I vaguely remember that."

"Once we arrived, I was walking around. I had my back to him. I heard something metal hit the floor. I looked down and saw dog tags slide by my feet. As it turned out, they were mine. I then heard a jaw clicking. I thought to myself, I know that sound. I turned, he called me Lieutenant Pfisterer. He pointed a gun at me. He had me get to my knees. He attacked me, hit me with a piece of lumber, tied me up, told me his story in explicit detail, and tortured me for hours upon hours. He kept saying I made a fool of him in Germany, that I embarrassed him. He said the information I gave the Allies helped the Allies win the war." Karl chuckles.

"What is it Karl?"

"I told him the information helped Hitler and the Third Reich lose the war. He did not like that, he hit me again. He set you up as well." Katarina is astonished and continues to stare at Karl. Her mind is trying to remember, to recreate what happened, to comprehend this nightmare. "He told you a repair man was coming to his house that day and did not know when. He asked you to wait at his house. He knew you would eventually go home when no repairmen came. It was a lie to lure me, and you to the warehouse. Wilhelm left a note for you, at our house, for you to come to the warehouse. When you arrived, he was hiding. Wilhelm told me I would watch you die first, then he would kill me.

"You found me, untied me, and that is when he appeared. He told you who he was, and how his transition came to be. I remember you were in disbelief. His jaw was clicking. You finally realized it was Wilhelm. I made a move, he turned toward me, and you lunged at him." Karl begins weeping more. "A struggle occurred. He," Karl is crying uncontrollably, "he shot you. I attacked him, we struggled. His gun fell to the ground. He was choking me. You gathered enough strength, and you shot him. As I was tending to you, he tried to get to his gun. I killed him." Katarina cannot talk, she is just staring and trembling.

Finally, as she is trying to process everything she says, "Karl, thank you for telling me, I still am having trouble comprehending everything. I am glad it is finally over with him. He finally got what he deserved."

"I reminded him of that." They weep in each other's arms. Karl chooses not to tell Katarina, due to her injuries, that she cannot have babies. Another time for that conversation. A nurse overhears the story; and allows Karl to continue.

"Excuse me." Karl turns and walks toward her. "I heard everything; I think it was good you told her. I know it was extremely difficult for both of you, she will heal better knowing. I'll give her a sedative to relax her, to help her sleep."

"Thank you, I decided not to tell her that she cannot have more children."

"That is wise at this point Mr. Schellenberg, she has a lot to cope with. Poor thing, you two have been through so much, remember you have each other." Karl stays with Katarina until she falls asleep.

Saturday morning, Karl gets the little ones up. "Mommy is coming home in a few days. Nicholas, do you want to get Mommy a Christmas tree today. Will you help?"

"Yes Daddy, let's go." Karl takes Caroline to Ruth's and heads to the gristmill. Karl puts Nicholas on his shoulders, and they head into the woods. As he passes the gristmill pond and stream, he reflects on the nights ice skating and picnics at the stream. *Katarina and I will skate here again.* Karl spots a tree; yet wants Nicholas to pick it.

"Nicholas do you like this tree?" Nicholas looks up, the tree seems like a giant sequoia to him. His head is tilted back so far, he falls over backwards into the snow. Karl laughs, picks him up and dusts him off.

"I like this tree for Mommy." Karl cuts it down. He and Nicholas drag it back to the car. Once home, Karl sets the tree in the middle of the living room. He takes Nicholas to Ruth and Ed's and heads over to Mercy Hospital. As he approaches the room, he sees Katarina sleeping. He quietly enters the room and sits in the chair. Katarina sleeps for hours.

She wakes up at 5:30 and sees Karl. "Hi Karl," and smiles.

"Hi to you my Love." Karl leans over and gives her a kiss. "How are you feeling today?"

"I am doing well; I was tired today."

"Yes, I have been here nearly three hours, you were sleeping well. Nicholas and I went and picked our tree today. It will be ready when you get home."

"I will like that." Karl stays until 9:30. "I need to get home and get the little ones settled for the night." He leans over the bed, gives Katarina a kiss, and whispers "Only six more sleeps."

Katarina looks confused, she thinks for a minute, "Yes Karl, six more sleeps until I go home," she smiles.

Sunday morning, Karl is up with Nicholas and Caroline. He gets them ready and takes Caroline to Ruth and Ed's. Karl strings the lights on the tree and Nicholas helps with the trimming. When they are finished Karl holds Nicholas up to place their special ornaments and the angel on the top.

"Good job Nicholas." Nicholas scurries around the room, he is happy. Karl drops Nicholas off at Ruth's and heads to the hospital.

Karl arrives as Katarina is finishing eating, she looks up at Karl. "Hello my Love."

"Hello to you my Love. How are you doing today?"

"Today is a good day."

"Nicholas helped me trim the tree today. He did most of the lower ornaments and he did a good job. He was very focused. I held him up, he placed our special ornaments and the angel on top. When I put him down, he started running, ninety miles an hour around the tree. He was proud of himself."

"He is a special little man, just like his Daddy."

"I am going to wait until Christmas Eve to set up the train." Karl spends the remainder of the day with Katarina and leaves later that evening. He leans down, gives Katarina a kiss, and whispers, "Only five more sleeps my Love." Katarina smiles. When Karl gets home, he gets the children ready for bed and lays them down. He sets the Nativity crib up on the fireplace mantel, then goes outside and decorates the porch with the wreaths and lights.

Monday morning, Karl has a final interview with Katarina's

nanny. She arrives promptly at 9:00. "Good morning Mr. Schellenberg."

"Good morning Nichole. Have a seat. "May I get you anything?"

"No sir, I'm fine."

"Nichole, there is something I never shared with you. My middle name is Nicholas, spelled with an 'h' like yours. That's an uncommon spelling. Most are spelled Nicole."

"That's cool Mr. Schellenberg. My parents wanted to name their child after Saint Nicholas, so either way, a boy or a girl, their baby's name was going to have the 'h'."

"That is so amazing you said that, my parents had the same plan. Our son, Nicholas has the same spelling, as does Caroline's middle name. Her name is Caroline Nichole. I wanted to let you know I talked with Katarina; we would love to have you help us."

"That is great news Mr. Schellenberg. I had a good feeling this would work out."

"Please call me Karl, and the Mrs., Katarina."

"Thank you, Karl. When is Katarina coming home?"

"Friday."

"Perfect I will be here."

Karl writes a note to Hans. 'My dearest Hans. It is Christmas week. First, Nicholas and Caroline are growing like weeds. I have enclosed pictures of them for you. The purpose of my note, it is with great sadness I write to you. I do not know where to begin. Katarina had a horrible accident, we almost lost her. It happened in October. We met a man in our neighborhood, he said his name was Jim Baxter. He was a real estate developer. His parents were of German descent, he told us, and that he had just lost his wife in a terrible car accident. Katarina and I took him in, we became close friends. Our children loved him. However, he was not who we thought he was. This is where it gets unbelievable and bizarre. He was Wilhelm. Yes, I said Wilhelm.

'Hitler devised a plan when he knew the Third Reich was falling. Hitler arranged for himself and his inner circle to have plastic surgery to change their looks, and to have their voices changed with augmentation. Hitler engaged the services of a trusted surgeon and a very loyal assistant, they both were sworn to, and committed to secrecy. A state-of-the-art operating room and recovery wing was established in the Fuhrerbunker. This was Hitler's plan of escape. They all were cowards. The plan was to have body doubles created in their likeness, including himself, so Hitler could continue his mockery of the German people. Hitler's reign, from his bunker, went on for a year after his surgery. His double was the one seen in public. No one from the outside world knew. Fortunately, only Hitler and Wilhelm had the surgery. The war ended before the remaining members of the inner circle could have the procedure. Hitler had their stand-ins killed, along with his surgeon and assistant in the days leading to Germany's surrender. All the propaganda you heard of Hitler and his wife committing suicide, was just that, lies. Hitler's body double shot the lady they claimed to be Eva, he then took cyanide and shot himself. The reason the bodies were burned was for further assurance Hitler could escape.

'The day you helped Katarina and I escape from the barn on your motorcycle, the day Wilhelm raided the village and murdered Anna and Gerhardt, I lost my dog tags in the barn. I guess I snagged them on something in my scurry to get out of the basement. Wilhelm found them and tracked us here to Coffeyville. He set up an elaborate scheme to befriend us. He spent months getting close to us, his ultimate plan was to kill us, both of us. He said I embarrassed him in the Third Reich. The war never ended for him. Wilhelm lured me to a warehouse in town. Once we arrived, I was walking around observing the building as he requested. I had my back to him. He threw my dog tags to me, they slid by my feet. Then I heard a jaw clicking. Wilhelm had a very distinct clicking of his jaw when he was agitated. I first heard it in the barn, the day he nearly found us. He called me Lieutenant Pfisterer and pointed a gun at me. He forced me to my knees and attacked me, hitting me with a piece of lumber. Wilhelm tied me up, told me his story, and tortured me for hours. He kept saying I made a fool of him in Germany, that I embarrassed him. We did a good job Hans. Wilhelm said the information I gave the Allies helped the Allies win the war. I told him it helped the Third Reich and Hitler lose the war.

'He had a plan to lure Katarina to the warehouse as well. Wilhelm told me I would watch Katarina die, then he would kill me. Later in the afternoon, from a note left at our home stating 'if you want to see your husband alive, come to the warehouse.' When Katarina arrived, Wilhelm was hiding, waiting for her. Katarina found me and untied me. Wilhelm appeared from behind a column and told Katarina who he was, and how his transition came to be. Katarina was in disbelief. Then she heard his jaw clicking and finally realized it was Wilhelm. I had regained some sort of consciousness by then, my adrenalin kicked in. I saw Katarina and made a move toward Wilhelm.

'When he turned toward me Katarina lunged at him. A struggle occurred. His gun went off, he shot Katarina. I attacked him, we struggled. Katarina saw the fight. She had enough strength to get his gun and shoot Wilhelm. As I was tending to Katarina, Wilhelm tried to get to his gun. I killed him. This is where this horrible story turns somewhat good if you will. Wilhelm finally got what he deserved. I reminded him of that before he died. Katarina was seriously injured; she lost a lot of blood. She went into cardiac arrest three times as the doctors were operating and trying to stabilize her. She spent weeks in intensive care, and many additional surgeries. After months in the hospital we brought her home in time for Christmas. She has been recovering well since.' Karl's note to Hans ends.

Karl is with Katarina. "Katarina, tomorrow is the day."

"I know Karl, I cannot wait. This has been a long journey."

"I best be going, it is getting late, I need to get the children. Tomorrow will be here soon. It will be a big day for you, you need your rest. Oh, I sent Hans a note today, about this ordeal."

"Thank you, Karl, he will appreciate that. I miss him."

Karl leans down, kisses Katarina, "One more sleep my Love."

December 20 arrives. Karl is at Mercy Hospital at 7:00 in the morning. Katarina prepares to come home.

Nichole knocks on the door and pops her head in. "Good morning."

"Good morning Nichole, come in. Katarina, this is Nichole. She will be helping you and the children."

"Good morning Nichole, it is very nice to meet you. I have heard a lot of good things about you."

"Thank you, Mrs. Schellenberg, I'm looking forward to helping you."

"Please call me Katarina. Karl tells me you work here at Mercy."

"Yes, my shift just finished, and I wanted to stop by to meet you."

"Thank you, Nichole, will I see you later today?"

"Yes, I'll see you at your home and help you get settled in."

Doctor Bailor arrives at 10:00. "Good morning Katarina, good morning Karl. How are you doing today?"

"I am feeling very good today, Doctor Bailor. Going home is far overcoming the pain."

"Very good, don't let your guard down with your injuries."

"I know Doctor, I am just so excited."

"Well, let's get you on your way. Katarina, it is very remarkable you have come this far in two months, God watched over you. I'll sign the discharge papers. I do want to see you weekly for a while."

Katarina smiles and looks directly into Dr. Bailor's eyes, "Thank you for all you and your team has done for me." The nurse helps Katarina get ready to leave.

Tears run down Katarina's cheeks, happy tears though. "Karl, I so much want to go home and be with Nicholas and Caroline. This all happened right after Caroline turned one, and Nicholas two. Nicholas, I bet he is toddling around good now."

"Yes, he is all over the house, and Caroline is getting around as well. She controls the house and Nicholas knows she is in charge."

Katarina laughs, "My little girl. What can we get them for Christmas?"

"I have been thinking of that as well. Your coming home is the best gift of all."

"You are sweet Karl, yet they will not understand that."

"I know. I thought of a tricycle for Nicholas, Caroline is so little, I am struggling thinking of something for her."

"I like the idea of a tricycle, Nicholas loves his pedal car, and he will have fun with a tricycle. Caroline loves her doll baby, we can get her a doll house, and doll clothes. She needs new outfits. They both do for that matter." Katarina is ready to go. The nurse brings a wheelchair. Katarina thanks everyone she sees that has helped her. Karl gets the car.

Karl and Katarina arrive home, it begins to snow. Five days until Christmas. The outside Christmas lights are on. Katarina sees the children on the porch holding a banner, 'Welcome Home Mommy!' She instantly begins to weep. "Karl, I am home." Nicholas and Caroline are jumping up and down with joy. Ruth, Ed, Angie, Al, and Nichole are on the porch to greet them. Angie has balloons. They are fluttering in the wind. Karl and Nichole help Katarina from the car and onto the porch. The little ones are hugging Katarina's legs. She is overwhelmed with joy. Karl picks Katarina up in his arms and carries her through the door.

Katarina looks into his eyes, "Karl, you did this one other time at this door," and smiles. Ruth and Angie gather the children, so they do not hurt Katarina. Katarina pauses and looks around the room. "Karl the tree is gorgeous, thank you for having the fireplace burning, I missed the smell. I love to hear the wood crackling, it comforts me. The Nativity crib makes me feel good, thank you for setting that up too. It is beautiful. I love the stockings Karl, especially with our names on them. I see Nichole has one also. Nicholas, did you help Daddy with the tree?"

Nicholas is jumping up and down, "I did Mommy!" Nicholas begins to point out the ornaments he hung.

Karl and Nichole help Katarina to the bedroom. Katarina spots the mistletoe. When she is under it, she says, "Wait Karl," and gives him a kiss. Nichole gets Katarina settled in bed. Katarina notices flowers on the dresser. "Karl, I love the flowers, thank you. They make me happy. Nichole, my favorite flowers are those, red roses and white lilies."

"That is a unique combination Katarina."

"Yes, both the rose and the lily are often associated with love. However, the rose in all its colors, especially red, is usually thought of as the flower of romantic love. The lily conveys the idea of purity. It is often associated with ideal love, or a purely innocent and true love."

"I didn't know that. I see why you like them. They are beautiful."

Ruth, Ed, Angie, and Al spend the remainder the day, playing with the children. Ruth and Angie make dinner. The snow is accumulating. Nichole is keeping Katarina comfortable.

The Franklin's, Angie, and Al leave for the night. "Karl, unless you need us tomorrow, Katarina should rest."

"Ruth, I do need a little help tomorrow if you would not mind. I need to Christmas shop. I could use your help watching Nicholas and Caroline."

"Of course, I will."

"Nichole."

"Yes Karl."

"I need to do some shopping tomorrow; Ruth will watch the little ones. I just wanted to give you a heads up."

"No worries Karl, I'll be here at 8:00 in the morning."

Karl is up early. Katarina slept well through the night. "Good morning Karl. Merry Christmas Eve."

Karl turns his head toward Katarina. "Good morning my Love. Merry Christmas Eve to you. How are you feeling?"

"I am good, will you hold me. It has been so long."

"I would love that; it has been too long my Love." Karl carefully and gently slides over to Katarina, she places her head in the crease of his shoulder, on his neck. She snuggles in closer.

"I love when you do that Katarina, snuggle in my neck. It is my favorite feeling." Karl gently holds the back of her head. Katarina doses off. An hour later a knock on the door.

Karl gently gets up, Katarina stays asleep. "Good morning Nichole."

"Hello Karl. The snow is pretty. How is Ms. Katarina?"

"She slept well; she is sleeping now."

"Oh, okay. I hear the little ones. I'll get them up and fed."

"Thank you, Nichole, I told Ruth I would drop them off at 10:00."

"After I get the children tended to, I'll change Katarina's dressings and get her some breakfast."

Karl arrives in town with his Christmas list. He hears Christmas music coming from the stores. He first gets the ornaments, his traditional ornaments. He picks up the tricycle for Nicholas; a doll house, and doll clothes for Caroline's doll, and outfits for both. He has something special in mind for Katarina. *I want to do something special for Ruth and Ed, and Angie for all they have done. How can I ever repay them? I want to make Nichole feel at home as well.* Karl has heard Ruth and Ed mention they have always wanted a mantel clock for their fireplace. Karl goes to the clock shop and finds the perfect clock. He decides a scarf, mittens, and a wool hat for Angie, she is always cold. For Nichole, Karl gets a nice box of chocolates.

Karl arrives home later that afternoon. "Karl, Katarina is resting comfortably." Nichole prepares dinner for them. "The children are ready for bed. I told them they had to go to bed early, Santa is coming tonight." Nichole leaves for the day. Karl has a fire going. He gives the little ones a goodnight kiss. Nicholas is awake.

"Nicholas, Santa is coming tonight with toys. He will not stop if you are awake."

"Ok Daddy, I'm sleeping Daddy, see," as he cuddles in his blanket. Karl gives Katarina a kiss on her forehead. He goes to the living room and gets the train and village setup under the tree. He sits at the fireplace, thinking of the evenings he and Katarina enjoyed listening to the fire, and smelling the burning wood. He falls asleep.

Christmas morning. Karl is lying in bed with Katarina, thinking how blessed they are, *Katarina may not have been here this Christmas with us.* Katarina awakes and looks over at Karl, "Merry Christmas Karl."

"Merry Christmas, my Love." They exchange Christmas kisses.

"I hear our little elves are awake."

"I will get them; Nichole will be here soon." Karl gets Nicholas and Caroline and brings them to Katarina.

Excited and scurrying around the room Nicholas asks, "Mommy, Daddy, did Santa come, did he bring me toys?"

"We need to wait for Nichole, then we will go see. Stay with Mommy for a while." Nichole arrives and walks to the bedroom.

"Merry Christmas everyone, Nicholas, did Santa bring you toys?"

"We were waiting for you Nichole. Let's go, let's go see." Nicholas is pulling Nichole.

"I will take the children in their room for a few minutes while you help Katarina get up."

"Thank you, Karl."

"Nichole, will you help me to the living room, I want to be there for the children."

"Absolutely Katarina, I was planning on that. How are you feeling today?"

"Every day is a better day." Nichole gets Katarina's dressings changed and dressed. She helps her to the tree. Karl has the tree lit, the train is running, and the fireplace is burning. Karl releases the little ones. Nichole is taking pictures as they run down the hall. Nicholas is running as fast as he can, Caroline is working hard to keep up. She is carrying her doll baby, Lily. As Caroline runs into the room, Katarina reflects, *I always loved that Caroline on her own, named her doll after one of my favorite flowers.* Nicholas and Caroline both see the tricycle and make a dash for it. Caroline then sees her doll house and redirects her path. Karl maintains the peace. Caroline wants to ride the tricycle. They each take turns.

Karl helps Caroline sit next to Katarina. "Caroline look, Mommy has these presents for you." Caroline unwraps her doll baby clothes, and immediately wants to dress Lily. "Nicholas, look under the tree, there is another present for you." Nicholas scurries and unwraps it.

"Mommy it's a truck, look."

"Looks like Daddy got himself another Buddy-L toy." She turns to Karl, Karl grins. Nichole prepares a tray of cookies for everyone, hot tea for Katarina, and coffee for Karl. "Nichole, the cookies you baked are amazing."

"Thank you, Katarina." The children are playing with Nichole. Caroline is fascinated with the train. She loves the whistle just as Nicholas does. Karl sits with Katarina.

"I love you dearly Katarina, Merry Christmas. We had a big scare."

"Shh," Katarina places her two fingers over Karl's lips. "Thank you, I love you dearly, Merry Christmas."

Karl hands Katarina her Hallmark card. Katarina intently reads it. 'Katarina, For My Wonderful Wife. You add a touch of magic to the happy times we share, and it is always Christmas in my heart; for you and your love are always there. Merry Christmas My Love.'

"Karl, this is a lovely Card." Katarina hands Karl her card to him, a home-made card, with love. 'More and more, I realize the miracle of God's love because He has given me you. I never take for granted how much you care, how lucky I am, the love we share. Every day of my life, I realize a new beginning, the wonder of us, the miracle of you. Merry Christmas, Karl.'

"Katarina, the card is beautiful, thank you. Here my Love I have these for you and the children." Katarina opens the presents, their ornaments.

"Karl, a sleigh for me."

"Yes, to go with your Santa and Reindeer."

"You are sweet. Karl these are so cute, a miniature sled for Nicholas, just like his real one; and another angel for Caroline."

"Yes, I thought we would start a collection of angels for her."

Nichole comments, "That is very thoughtful."

"Nichole, I brought my parents' and my own special ornaments from Germany, and Karl has continued our tradition from those."

"Katarina, close your eyes."

"Why Karl?"

"You will see." Karl gets up. Katarina hears a cuckoo clock. Before Karl can say open your eyes, Katarina's eyes are surprisingly wide open, she sees the clock hanging on the wall.

"Karl how did you know I have always wanted a cuckoo clock?"

"You mentioned it once in Germany, at the Kettle, the day we were at the stream and were caught in the thunderstorm." Katarina smiles at Karl.

"I loved that day Karl."

"This is an authentic German Cuckoo Clock, it is an Anton Schneider, made in the village of Schonach."

"I know of those; that town is in the Black Forest Region."

"I found it in town, at the clock shop when I was getting Ruth and Ed's mantle clock. Just as I was entering the shop, it began to cuckoo. That is when I remembered you telling me you loved the sound of a cuckoo clock. It was singing to me. This was the only German clock in the shop."

"Karl, I love it, thank you, you are so thoughtful."

"I have something else for you my Love." Katarina opens her gift.

"Karl this is absolutely beautiful." She turns to him, "Did you make this?"

"I used the flower petals from our wedding, you dried them and brought them with us, remember?" Nichole enters the room from the kitchen.

"Nichole, look. Karl framed a heart he made from our dried flower petals from our wedding. He is so creative; it is two tiered from our red rose petals and white lily petals. The perimeter is red roses and the interior is white lilies."

"Very beautiful Katarina, Karl you did a fantastic job." Karl sits next to Katarina; they hug each other and give a kiss to one other.

"Nichole, we have a little something for you." Nichole opens her gift.

"Thank you, I love chocolates, you're going to spoil me." They spend the morning together. Katarina is enjoying watching Nicholas and Caroline play.

After lunch, Ruth and Ed stop in. "Merry Christmas everyone." The children run to them and give them hugs. "How are you feeling today, Katarina?"

"I feel good. Christmas makes me happy. Have a seat and stay a while. Nichole, would you mind getting them refreshments?" They all talk for a while. Ruth is startled by the cuckoo clock.

"That is my gift from Karl, I have always wanted a cuckoo clock. It is an authentic German clock. I love the sound of the cuckoo."

"I love the sound as well Katarina, it just startled me. I wasn't expecting it."

"The children love it too, especially Caroline. Karl, give Ruth and Ed our gift please."

"You do not need to give us anything. We are grateful for our time with you and the children."

"Stop it Ruth, we wanted to, after all you have done for us, we can never repay you."

"That is what friends are for Katarina. My goodness this is heavy, here feel it Ed. Oh, my Lord, a mantle clock, we have always wanted one, thank you very much. We have something for you and the children." Nicholas and Caroline get right into their presents.

"Thank you both, Nicholas and Caroline love stuffed toys."

"Here Katarina, this is for you and Karl."

"Ruth, this is precious. Look Karl, two framed pictures of Nicholas and Caroline, one with them under the tree, and look at this one with Santa, this is darling. Look at their little elf outfits. Where did you have this taken Ruth?"

"It was at Gables Department store, the Saturday before you

came home. Here are the outfits we had them in, we wanted to surprise you."

"Karl, please place the pictures on the fireplace mantel, next to the Nativity crib."

Another knock on the door, Angie, and Al pop in. "Hey everyone, Merry Christmas."

"Merry Christmas Angie, Merry Christmas Al, please sit with us."

"How are you today Katarina?"

"As I mentioned to Ruth, I feel good today. It is Christmas day; this day always makes me happy."

Nichole is at the window. "Look Katarina, it's beginning to snow."

"It is, I love the snow."

"Katarina, Ed and I need to be going. Thank you for the wonderful clock."

"Thank you both, I love the pictures of the children, and look, they love their stuffed toys."

"Angie, Al, may we get you anything? Nichole made the most amazing cookies."

"I cannot turn down cookies, thank you. We wanted to stop by and see how you are doing, and the little ones. We are not going to stay. It appears you had a big day so far and need your rest. I do have some gifts for you all. These are for Nicholas and Caroline."

"Angie, these outfits are perfect. The little ones are growing so quick it is hard to keep them in their outfits."

"We have this for you and Karl."

"Thank you, Angie, thank you Al. Karl, your turn to open. Angie, how did you know?"

"A little birdie told me."

"We need a comforter. The winters are a bit chilly here. This will keep me nice and toasty, thank you. Angie, thank you very much for recommending Nichole, she has been a God send. Karl, will you get Angie's gift please."

Angie opens her gift. "Katarina, Karl; speaking of keeping warm, thank you for the scarf, mittens and wool hat, they match. I love them." Christmas evening draws to an end. Nichole gets Nicholas and Caroline ready for bed. She tends to Katarina and gets her in bed, says good night, and leaves.

Karl slides in bed next to Katarina. "We had a wonderful Christmas Karl, I love you."

"We did Katarina. Nicholas and Caroline had a nice Christmas, Christmas is all about the little ones, I love you. Sweet dreams my Love."

LIFE IN COFFEYVILLE
[1947]

Katarina, Karl, and the children spend a quiet New Year's Eve with Nichole. News Year's Day, the children are up early. Nichole arrives. "Nichole, we have pork and sauerkraut in the refrigerator, Karl picked it up yesterday. Would you mind making that for dinner, it is a German tradition for New Year's Day."

"What does it represent Katarina?"

"If you eat pork and sauerkraut on New Year's Day, your money will not run out."

"Wow, I will make a big pot."

"Ya ya."

Karl brings a box in from the garage. "Who wants a ride?" Nicholas and Caroline run to Karl, Caroline beats Nicholas.

"I do Daddy, I do."

"Ok, we need to take turns. Little ladies first." He pulls the kids around the house in a cardboard box, seemingly for hours.

"Do it again Daddy, do it again, they keep saying." Karl is having as much fun as the children.

"Karl, you are so silly, so funny. You make me laugh so hard you bring tears to my eyes."

Nichole leans over to Katarina. "He really loves the children."

1947, another cold winter in Coffeyville. Katarina's doctor visits continue, she is getting healthier by the day. January rolls on. Katarina and Karl celebrate their wedding anniversary. January 15, Katarina wakes up to Karl singing. "Happy anniversareee, happy anniversareee, happy anniversareee, happy anniversareee. Happy happy happy happy happy anniversareee; happy happy happy happy happy anniversareee; happy happy happy happy happy anniversareee; happy anniversary."

"Karl, I so love when you do that. You have never forgotten; this always puts a smile on my face. You are sweet; but I maintain, so silly. I love you so much. Happy anniversary and happy birthday to you."

The morning of January 31. Katarina is lying in bed. "Karl, our special anniversary is today, the day we met. I was thinking, for our special anniversary, do you think you could drive me to the gristmill? I would love to see the pond."

"I would very much like that. Nichole will be here soon." Karl and Katarina head to the gristmill. As they leave town it begins to snow, a heavy snow.

"Karl, the pond is so beautiful." The pond is mostly frozen, except for where the stream enters, at the waterfall.

"Karl, I want to sit on the rocks with you. I want to watch and feel the snow."

"Yes, let me help you." Karl carries Katarina through the snow. He sits her on the rock and wraps her in a blanket. He sits next to her, they hold hands.

"Karl, may I ask you a question."

"Yes, my Love, anything."

"We are not going to be able to have children, is that right?" She looks into his eyes, he into hers. Karl is choked up; a tear runs down his cheek. "Karl do not cry; your tears will freeze." Karl chuckles, Katarina chuckles.

"No, my Love, your injuries were too severe, they caused too much damage."

"I thought that; and felt that. I am very thankful for Nicholas and Caroline, and thankful to be alive, to be here with you."

"Katarina, I do not know how I would have lived without you."

"Shh, we will not talk about that anymore. Let us enjoy the day. It is nice to be out and get some fresh air. Someday, someday soon we will skate here." Katarina makes a snowball and tosses it at Karl.

"Just like in Germany my Love." They spend the remainder of the day at the pond. Karl builds a fire to keep them warm.

Hans responds to Karl's note in utter disbelief, disbelief of Hitler's plan, but more so of Wilhelm's plan to kill Katarina and Karl. He is grateful Katarina is recovering, and the monster Wilhelm is gone. Hans also tells Katarina and Karl of his good news. He and Lieselotte, his childhood sweetheart and Katarina's childhood friend, are going to be married on March 15 1947.

Karl's career continues to advance. In early 1947 Karl shared his knowledge of Hitler's plot for himself and his inner circle's doubles, and their planned escapes from Germany with his superiors. Detail by detail as Wilhelm bragged about. The United States, British, French, and German Governments launch an intensive global manhunt through the Interpol for Hitler. Karl is promoted to captain, responsible for training young recruits for Officer Training. The United States Army Air Force becomes United States Air Force on September 18 1947, its own branch of the armed forces.

Katarina continues to heal. Days turn into weeks, weeks into months, months into years. Nicholas and Caroline are growing up. Katarina injuries are healed. Nichole stops by at least once a week to see the children. She has been engaged for a year. It's early evening June 4 1949. Katarina and Karl are on the porch swing. The children are playing in the yard.

Suddenly Caroline runs down the sidewalk, "Nichole is here." Katarina sees Nichole and her fiancée Kevin walking toward the porch.

"Hello Nichole and Kevin, how are you two love birds."

"We are doing well. Katarina, do you and Karl have a few minutes? Kevin and I have something to tell you."

"Yes, always for you two love birds."

"Kevin and I have picked a wedding day, it's Saturday September 17, this year. We wanted to tell you first."

"That is Nicholas' birthday, how sweet."

"Yes Katarina, it's pretty cool how that worked out. We wanted a September wedding, and that was the only Saturday the church had available."

"That is wonderful, a fall wedding will be nice." Katarina and Karl give them both a hug.

Nichole's wedding day is here. Karl and Katarina get the children ready. They arrive at St. Andrews. Nichole has a reserved pew for them. The organ begins playing, Katarina and Karl turn and see Nichole walking down the aisle.

"Karl, look at Kevin, he seems nervous, he is so cute." As Nichole passes by Katarina and Karl she turns and smiles. "Karl, she is beautiful." Her gown is white lace, and the train seems to go on forever. Nichole and Kevin are married. Katarina, Karl, and the children stay for pictures. Nichole wants them to be in some of her wedding pictures. Afterwards they leave for the reception.

September 5 1950, Nicholas' first day of school. Katarina and Karl walk Nicholas to school, Caroline rides her bicycle. "Karl, our little boy is growing up."

A year goes by. September 4 1951. Caroline's first day of school. Katarina and Karl walk the children to school, this year with their new puppy, Keilah. "Karl, our little angel is growing up."

Katarina and Karl stay in touch with Hans regularly. Karl keeps Hans informed of Katarina's recovery and of the children growing up. Hans and Lieselotte are married on March 15 1947. Ruth and Ed adopt a little boy on April 27 1951. He is two. His name is Peter. Angie finally gets married on July 2 1955 to her long-time boyfriend, Al. Angie and Al make their own fireworks that weekend! Nicholas' and Caroline's childhood years in Coffeyville are filled with happiness. They picnic in the summertime, swing on the porch, take walks in the woods in the fall, and ice skate at the gristmill pond in the winters. The elementary school years pass, the middle school years pass, Nicholas and Caroline are in High School. Nicholas is wrestling and Caroline is cheerleading. They both are in the marching band and orchestra. Nicholas plays trumpet and Caroline plays the clarinet and piano.

June 1 1962, Nicholas' graduation day arrives. At seventeen, he graduates with honors. Katarina, Karl, Caroline, the Franklin's, Angie and Al, Nichole and her husband Kevin attend the ceremony. "Karl, I cannot believe Nicholas is graduating, he is so handsome." Katarina and Karl have a reception for everyone afterwards at their home. On September 20, three days after turning eighteen, Nicholas enlists in the Air Force. He is assigned to Randolph Air Force Base in San Antonio for his eight and one-half weeks of basic training, beginning October 15. October 13, Karl, and Katarina take Nicholas to the bus station for San Antonio. Karl is reflecting, *my son is assigned to the base where I began my flight training.* Katarina cannot stop crying. "Karl, our boy is leaving us."

"Karl holds Katarina. "It is all good Katarina, he is a man now, serving our country."

Nicholas looks into Karl's eyes, "I will make you proud Father." A tear comes to Karl's eye. Nicholas finishes basic training, December 12. He is assigned to the Third Air Force Base in Coffeyville Kansas. Karl had something to do with this.

May 31 1963 Caroline's graduation day arrives. Caroline graduates with honors, at seventeen, following her brother's footsteps. Katarina, Nicholas, the Franklin's, Angie and Al, Nichole and her husband Kevin attend the ceremony, as they did with Nicholas' graduation.

"Karl, I know I said this last year about Nicholas, I cannot believe Caroline is graduating, she is beautiful. Our children have grown up." After the ceremony, Katarina and Karl have a reception for everyone at their home. The summer evening ends. Karl and

Katarina are on the front porch swing watching the sun set. Nicholas and Caroline are out with friends. "I will be right back Karl." Katarina returns to the doorway and knocks three times. "Karl." Karl turns and sees Katarina in her white silk slip, lace panties, thigh high nylons, and high heels. She has her promiscuous look in her eyes. Karl smells her perfume in the gentle breeze.

"There is my Katarina. You are beautiful. The three knocks, just as you did at the barn when you came to see me." He sees the silhouette and sensuality of her breasts through her slip. Her breasts are accentuated by the low-cut neckline. Karl walks towards her. Katarina slowly unbuttons his shirt. They embrace in a passionate kiss.

"Come with me Karl, I am going to be a naughty girl tonight."

RETURN TO GERMANY [1964]

January 15 1964. Katarina wakes to Karl singing. "Happy anniversareee, happy anniversareee, happy anniversareee, happy anniversary. Happy happy happy happy happy anniversareee; happy happy happy happy happy anniversareee; happy happy happy happy happy anniversareee; happy anniversary. Happy Anniversary my Love."

"Happy Anniversary and Happy Birthday to you." Karl turns forty-two. "Karl, you have done this every year since we married, you are so sweet, that is why I love you so much." They kiss and enjoy their day. January 31, Katarina's, and Karl's anniversary of the day they met.

"Karl, you are going to be late for the Base today. This is our twentieth-first special anniversary. The day God sent you to me."

"Katarina, it is a nice winter day. I took the day off; we can play all day."

Katarina and Karl celebrate their first kiss day, twenty-one years ago today, April 19, the smell of spring is in the air. "Karl, every day of every year, I fall more in love with you."

"As do I my Love."

The summer of 1964 is another record for heat. August 16, Katarina wakes to red roses and white lilies, and Karl singing. "Happy birthday to you. Happy birthday to you." Katarina smiles and giggles. "Happy birthday to Katarina. Happy birthday to you my Love."

"You are silly and so sweet; you always make me giggle. I love you Karl, thank you." Katarina turns forty-four. Karl has flowers for her. "Thank you, Karl; you have given me flowers every year, you have never forgotten, and you always sing to me, you are a special man."

"Katarina; I was thinking about planning a trip to Germany, to see Hans and Lieselotte."

"Karl, I would so love to go back to Germany to see Hans and Lieselotte. When were you thinking of going?"

"I was thinking next spring."

Caroline has a job at Gowers, at the malt counter. She celebrates her nineteenth birthday. Nicholas is busy at the airbase. His rank is Airman Third Class. His actions do not go unnoticed. He is placed in Karl's Officer Training Group. Nicholas celebrates his twentieth birthday.

Karl is in his office, October 28, a knock on the door. "Come in?" Karl stands and salutes. "General Davis."

"As you were captain." Private First-Class Baker, General Davis' administrative assistant is with him. "Have a seat. Captain Schellenberg, may I call you Karl?" Karl nods. "Karl, your twenty-five years of service in the Air Force; your dedication, your actions have been stellar. Karl, over the years, since the war ended, our Intel has confirmed that your efforts in Neuengamme, your disruption to the German's Western Front immensely helped in ending the war. Your distraction took enough of the Third Reich's focus off the Eastern Russian Front, the Russians were able to defeat Germany. The information you provided about Hitler and his inner circle and their body double scheme, although we have not located Hitler, yet, has proved invaluable information.

"This has been Interpol's top priority. The world accepted the fact Hitler was dead, until you learned the apparent body of Hitler was an imposter, and the real Hitler is in hiding. One thing for certain, one of his inner circle's henchmen, Wilhelm is gone, thanks to you Karl. We will find Hitler. Since you provided the information, Interpol has had hundreds of leads, even leads that Hitler may be hiding in Brazil as you mentioned. I also want to mention your leadership in developing a counter plan to the Nazi's plan to suddenly implement fingerprint verification program, keeping our five operatives in place in Berlin, your recruits Karl. Their training and their success stemmed from your ability to infiltrate the Nazi Regime. In very short order you ascertained the situation and developed a plan to, once again, foil the Nazi's plan and protect our young men, your boys Karl. The reason for my visit today. Please stand captain. It is with my utmost honor to promote you to Major, congratulations."

"Thank you very much General Davis. I am honored."

"I have one other piece of news. You are being transferred to Germany, to our Air Force Base; Ramstein Air Base in Rhineland-Palatinate Germany. You will report to the Third Air Force Group."

"Sir, that is wonderful news."

"Major Schellenberg," *Karl thinks to himself, that has a nice ring to it,* "as you know, the United States has been involved in the Vietnam War since February 28 1961. We began advising and accompanying South Vietnamese troops in their operations. As you know, the war's start was formally established as August 5 1964. That stemmed from an attack on August 2. The USS Maddox was attacked by North Vietnamese patrol torpedo boats in the Gulf of Tonkin. Those attacks spurred Congress to pass the Gulf of Tonkin Resolution, which authorized the President to take all necessary measures, including the use of armed force, against any aggressor in the conflict. President Johnson called for air strikes on North Vietnamese patrol boat bases. Two U.S. aircraft were shot down and one U.S. pilot, Everett Alvarez, Jr., became the first U.S. airman to be taken prisoner by North Vietnam. The tensions have been escalating since. We need to supplement our forces in Europe to support our bases in South Vietnam. You will oversee the Vietnam Offensive Initiative, and the training of our cadets, our new pilots. You will report to Air Base Ramstein in January."

"Thank you, sir."

"By the way Karl, I hear your son is following in your footsteps, he is being reassigned to Ramstein as well."

Karl heads home to tell Katarina of the news. *How will she take the news? Will she be happy, excited? How will she feel about leaving our American friends?* Karl arrives and sees Katarina on the porch swing. He walks to the porch and sits down next to her. He takes Katarina's hands, with a smile so she doesn't get nervous.

"Katarina, I have some news."

"What is it my Love?"

"I have been promoted." Katarina's eyes light up. "Katarina, I so love your smile. I have been promoted to Major."

"Karl, that is wonderful, I am so proud of you." Katarina kisses him.

"I have more news." Karl holds her hands tighter. "We will be going to Germany sooner than we planned."

"That is good news, when will we be going to see Hans and Lieselotte?" Karl takes a deep breath.

"I have been transferred." Katarina has a puzzled look in her eye.

"To Germany?"

"Yes, to Germany my Love." Katarina hesitates, then hugs Karl.

"Karl, that is wonderful news, we are going back to Germany. Where?"

"To Ramstein Air Base."

"I know Ramstein, it is in a beautiful part of Germany. It is in the heart of wine country; and is very close to the Black Forest."

"Katarina, I was not sure how you would take the news, and I am happy to see you so excited."

"Karl, I will go anywhere with you." She cups Karl's face with her hands. "We are going back to Germany. I am very happy about that. Let me think, I believe Ramstein is about six hundred kilometers from Aurich."

"You are correct, I have already checked."

"Katarina, when we go back to Germany, we will plan to drive to Aurich and visit with Hans and Lieselotte as we originally planned. I will call Hans and give him the news."

"I would love that Karl. When are we going?"

"January, I do not have an exact date yet."

"It will be wonderful if we can celebrate our anniversary there. We will be so far away from Nicholas though."

"Celebrating our anniversary in Germany would be very nice. I have one last piece of news. Nicholas is being reassigned to Ramstein as well."

"Karl the news did just get better, this could not have worked out more perfectly."

That evening Katarina and Karl share the news with Caroline. Although she will miss her friends, Carolina is looking forward to moving to Germany. Nicholas is ecstatic as well. Karl was able to share the news personally with him earlier in the day. The next day they walk over to see Ruth and Ed. Peter is playing catch in the front yard with Ed, Ruth is on the porch. "Ruth, Ed, we have some news for you."

"Here come sit Katarina, what is it?"

"Ruth, I do not know how to say this, Karl is being transferred to Germany." Ruth is taken back and begins to weep.

"Katarina, I am happy for you, for you to go back to Germany, yet I'm being selfish. I am sad for us. You and Karl have been very special to us, we have been through so much together."

"I know Ruth, we feel the same. You and Ed have been very special to us as well. You are Nicholas' God parents. The children love you both very much, as do we."

Ruth holds Katarina's hand. "Ed and I knew this day may come, with Karl being in the Air Force, a transfer is always a possibility. But on the good side, you have been here twenty years. We are happy for you. When will you be leaving?"

"January, Karl does not have a date yet."

"Katarina, wouldn't it be nice if you could be there for your anniversary?"

"We said the same thing."

They call Angie and Al that evening and share the news with them. Angie breaks into tears; yet calms down and is happy.

"Katarina, I will miss you, Karl, and the children, especially with us being Caroline's Godparents."

"Well, you will just have to come and visit us."

"We would love that; I have never been to Germany."

"Angie, we will need to get the house ready to sell, will you help us?" Angie begins crying again.

Halloween night is upon them. A nice fall evening. Katarina and Karl are sitting on the front porch waiting for the trick-or-treaters. As they have done every year, except the year Katarina was injured, they have decorated their pumpkins. As always, Mister the groom with his top hat and bow tie; Mrs. with her bridal vail, pearls and flowers; and the two children pumpkins, one with Karl's Air Force hat, and one with a dress. Karl's ghosts are blowing from the trees.

"Karl, our children grew up in this house."

"Yes Katarina, we have many great memories here. I called Hans today, he and Lieselotte were very happy and excited to hear we are coming back to Germany. They are anxious for us to see Little Karl and Katarina."

"I always thought that was very touching, they named their children after us."

"We were very close to Hans, as were your parents."

"So, Han's Karl is what, fifteen, and his Katarina is thirteen?"

"Yes, I believe that is right Katarina."

The holidays arrive. It is Thanksgiving Day. Katarina prepares the meal. Ruth, Ed and Peter, Angie and Al, and Nicholas and Caroline. Katarina and Karl make the best of the last holiday season in Coffeyville. November 26, Karl receives his orders. He is to be at Ramstein by Monday January 6. He shares the date with Katarina.

"Karl, how ironic, that is the day you came home to me, it will be twenty-one years ago. I was waiting for you that evening at the barn, that night we conceived Nicholas."

"Yes, I vividly remember that night at the barn, it was wonderful." Katarina and Karl get the house ready for market. December 10, Katarina, Karl, and Caroline head for the gristmill for their Christmas tree. Nicholas arrives later. It's a cold Saturday and has snowed the night before. Again, they find a perfect tree. It's beginning to get dark as they exit the woods.

"Karl, I brought our skates. I thought we could ice skate one last time. It will be a clear sky tonight; the pond will be pretty under the moonlight." Nicholas and Caroline go back to the house, Katarina and Karl stay. They all decorate the tree the next day. Katarina hangs the mistletoe, as she has every year. Katarina decides to have their Christmas meal on Christmas Eve, something Anna and Gerhardt always did in Germany. After attending church at St. Andrews, Christmas Day is spent with Ruth and Ed and Angie and Al.

"Karl, the best thing to do is sell our furniture, hopefully with the house."

"I agree, we will take our personal things." The Schellenberg's spend the next week packing. Katarina packs Christie, her doll from Germany, her Christmas cards from Karl, their ornaments. She runs across her reindeer and reminisces. *Karl, after he gave me my Santa and Santa's sleigh, our first two Christmas' in this home, he gave me one of Santa's eight reindeers the next eight years, such a sweet man. He always has a plan.* Katarina gently packs her cuckoo clock, her framed flower petals, the children's ornaments, the mistletoe from Germany and their letters from when Karl was in Neuengamme; she reflects on Karl's tradition every Christmas; tears come to her eyes.

"Karl, remember when we left Germany, we had very little with us. It was January 31, our special anniversary, almost twenty-one years ago. That was the last we saw Hans. I am anxious to see him."

"I always knew in my heart we would see him again. Katarina, we should pack a few days of clothes, and we will need our winter coats with us. It will be cold when we land." The Air Force plans to pick up their personal belongings on December 30. The Schellenberg family plans to leave December 31 to be in Ramstein by January 6. December 31, a very emotional day. Ruth and Ed, Angie, and Al, are with Katarina and Karl. Many tears shed, tears of sadness and tears of joy. The staff car arrives. Katarina, Karl, Nicholas, and Caroline get in.

Katarina rolls the window down, "We will stay in touch with you, I promise. We love you all." As they drive off to the airfield, Katarina turns and looks out the back window, as she did in Aurich with Hans, she has one last wave to their friends.

GERMANY, A NEW CHAPTER [1965]

Katarina, Karl, and the children fly through the night and arrive in London the morning of January 1. The plane touches down at the Eighth Air Force Bomber Command in Kettering, Northamptonshire, England.

"Happy New Year Karl." Katarina leans over and kisses him.

"Happy New Year to you my Love. Katarina, this is the Base we landed when we left Germany."

"Things look so different since I was last here. I am tired Karl, with the time change and not sleeping well on the plane, I am ready for bed." They spend the night and leave for Ramstein the next morning. The Air Force plane descends to the Base. "Karl, look out the window. That is the Black Forest Mountain Region. The evergreens are so beautiful. I love how the snow clings to them, I missed those." The Schellenberg family arrive at Ramstein Air Base on Thursday January 2 1965, 11:00 local time. There is a skiff of snow on the ground, and the temperature is a cold minus four Celsius. A staff car awaits them on the tarmac. As they exit the plane a Staff Sergeant greets them. They solute.

"Major Schellenberg, welcome to the Third Air Force and

Ramstein Air Base. I am Staff Sergeant Arrington. I have been assigned to you as your assistant."

Karl solutes, "Nice to meet you sergeant. This is my wife Katarina, my son Airman Third Class Nicholas, and our lovely daughter Caroline."

"Welcome all of you. I'll get your luggage and we will be off. You will be staying in our officer's village, just off Base. Your house is ready for you. Your personal items have been delivered from the States. Airman, you will be staying on Base."

"I know sergeant, that is the requirement for non-commissioned officers."

"I can show you to your quarters when you have time."

"Thank you, sergeant."

Sergeant Arrington drives them to their house. The officer's homes are in a special neighborhood in the town of Ramstein-Miesenbach.

"Karl this house is lovely. The whole neighborhood is lovely. I love the Timber Framed homes."

Sergeant Arrington helps them in.

"Mrs. Schellenberg, I hope the furnishings are to your liking."

"They are lovely sergeant."

"If you need anything, anything at all, please let me know. Major Schellenberg, I'll meet you at 0600 hours Monday morning to meet General Powell, the Base Commander. He is expecting you."

"Thank you, sergeant."

"Katarina, you mentioned timber framed homes, what does that mean? Is it a style?

"They are the typical home here, very common in southern Germany. Unlike where I lived in Northern Germany. These are very quaint and to the period architecture here in Germany. Half Timbered Homes are also common."

They tour their new home. The first floor has a parlor. "Karl, I love the dark wood floors and the dark wood trim. It has a fireplace," she squeezes his arm. "The high ceilings are very nice with the plastered molding." They continue through to the dining room, kitchen, a small half bath, and laundry room. The second floor has the master bedroom in the back of the home, with a fireplace. Katarina squeezes Karl's arm again, looks at him and smiles. The two guest bedrooms flank each other at the front of the house. They spend the weekend unpacking and getting settled in. Caroline gets her room ready. She places her doll Lily on a shelf in the room.

"Karl would you hang my heart of dried flower petals you made me above our bed. I would like my cuckoo clock in the parlor, at the bottom of the stairs. It will echo through the house nicely."

"I will my Love."

Karl calls Hans to let them know he, Katarina, Nicholas, and Caroline have arrived in Germany. "This is wonderful Karl, when can we meet?"

"I need to get my schedule tied down. I will talk with Katarina and let you know. Soon though my friend, soon we will be together. Give Lieselotte and your children our love. Hans, Katarina, and I are so looking forward to seeing you. I told you we would have a beer together some day."

"Likewise, the same to you Karl, to Katarina, and your children. I will have the beer ready."

Sergeant Arrington picks Nicholas up Sunday evening and takes him to the Base. Katarina and Karl are lying in bed Sunday evening.

"Karl, I am very happy we are back in Germany." She slides under the covers and nibbles his belly. With soft nibbles, she works her way to his neck, then his lips. They kiss very intensely and christen their home.

The next morning, 6:00, Karl is ready for Sergeant Arrington. The sergeant is prompt. They arrive at General Powell's office at 0700 hours.

"Good morning General Powell," Karl salutes.

"Have a seat Major, I have heard many good things about you. As General Davis outlined, you will take command of and oversee our Vietnam Offensive Initiative, and the training of our cadets, our new pilots. In recent years, and most noticeably since 1961, our principal role in Southeast Asia was to advise the Vietnamese Air Force in its struggle against insurgents seeking the collapse of the Saigon government. In order to combat these insurgents, we must have supreme air power. With an insurgency like we have, the most effective way to advise a foreign ally is to work side by side with them and train them. The challenges and issues we have, which is unique to the Vietnamese conflict, is how to coordinate a centralized, technological modern Air Force with a feudal, decentralized, indigenous one without overwhelming it. We are up against Russian technology with their MIG fighter jets as well. North Vietnam is being aided by both their Soviet and Chinese Allies. Our internal challenge is how best we can adapt our fighters, our reconnaissance, our airlifts, and our liaison planes to a jungle environment. Over the past several months the Vietnamese conflict has escalated. We are getting closer to a full engagement with North Vietnam. That is where you come in Major.

"Your history of piloting aircraft, your proven ability to effectively train our cadets, coupled with your uncanny ability to understand the enemy is exactly what we need. I heard what you did in Germany, and of your training program in Coffeyville. You have the liberty to develop and conduct the training as you see fit. Our new pilots must adapt to this new type of warfare. One more thing Major, I must say this is unusual in the Air Force, we are assigning your son to your group. Your son has high regard from General Davis."

"General, he will be treated equally, like all the other cadets, well perhaps a bit more stringent." Karl chuckles. Karl gets settled in his work. He spends the next week meeting with other officers and gathering information.

"Karl, this is January 6, the day we conceived Nicholas at the barn, the day you came home to me. We are back in Germany, twenty-one years later, how amazing. Karl, tomorrow is twenty-one years since my parents died." Karl holds Katarina. "I want to visit their graves when we go to Aurich."

"We will do that my Love."

"Karl, I was walking through town yesterday and found a lovely church. Guess what the name is?"

"I have no idea."

"Katholische Kirche St. Nikolaus, St. Nicholas, how wonderful. Can you believe that? The inside is simply gorgeous, very old world."

January 15, a snowy Wednesday in Ramstein. Katarina awakes to fresh flowers, red roses, and white lilies. "Karl, you are amazing, you never forget." Karl slides over and snuggles Katarina.

"Happy anniversaree, happy anniversaree, happy anniversaree, happy anniversary. Happy happy happy happy happy anniversaree; happy happy happy happy happy anniversaree; happy happy happy happy happy anniversaree; happy anniversary."

"Please never stop doing this. Happy anniversary and happy birthday to you my Love. As always, you are sweet; and as always you are so silly, I love you so much. Karl it is early, you do not need to leave for the Base for two hours, I have a special present for you. It is playtime."

The following weeks have Karl very busy. Nicholas is settled in on the Base. He continues his Officer Training. Katarina and Karl's teaching of German to Nicholas and Caroline over the years has paid off. Even though the Base speaks primarily English, most of the town does not.

"Karl; I thought it will nice to visit Hans, Lieselotte, and their Karl and Katarina on our special anniversary. I would love to go back to Aurich for that."

"I would like that as well. The thirty-first is a Friday. I will put in for a long weekend. I will request Monday and Tuesday off as well. I will call Hans and let him know."

"Will Nicholas be able to join us?"

"I think I can arrange that."

"Hello Hans, it is Karl. We are planning to drive to Aurich Friday the thirty-first and spend a long weekend with you. Will that work with you, Lieselotte, and the kids?"

"Great Karl, we are all excited and look forward to seeing you. It has been so long. What time can we expect you?"

"It looks like a seven hour or so drive. We will plan to leave early. We should see you around noon."

"We will be watching for you, drive safe Karl."

Friday morning, Karl packs the car, and they leave for Aurich. They arrive at Hans' just after noon. Hans, Lieselotte, and their Karl and Katarina are sitting on the porch. Hans jumps up and runs to the car. Karl no sooner gets out and Hans embraces him. "Karl, it has been so long, I missed you my friend."

"I know Hans, it is hard to believe twenty-one years have passed."

Katarina and Lieselotte give each other hugs, and kisses on the cheeks. "Katarina, it is so nice to see you, it has been so long. When I went to University we grew apart, then the war came. Now look, we have been brought back together."

"Lieselotte, it is good to see you, my goodness, I remember when we were little, we were inseparable."

Lieselotte takes Katarina's hands, "Katarina, I am so very sorry about Anna and Gerhardt. Hans told me what that awful brother of yours did, their own son. How could someone do that?"

"He was a monster Lieselotte, he got what he deserved, and for that I am happy."

"Hans told me of your horrific injuries, I am glad you recovered." The children hang back.

"Hans, Lieselotte, this is our Nicholas and Caroline."

"These are our precious children, Karl and Katarina. We will need nicknames this weekend."

"Karl, Katarina, come, let us all go in the house. Even though it is a nice sunny day, it is January, and it is cold."

They spend the rest of the day catching up. Hans has beer for everyone, a nice cozy warm fire burns in the fireplace. The children are getting to know one another.

"Katarina, Hans told me how you and Karl met, that was so special and so sweet. A charming story"

"Yes, Lieselotte, my darling Karl came to me from Heaven. As a matter of fact, today is our anniversary, the day we met twenty-two years ago."

"That is special you two celebrate that anniversary."

"Had it not been for that day, we would not have our wedding day. Tell me Lieselotte, how did you and Hans meet?"

"After University I stayed in Belgium for a while. I decided to come back to Aurich to be with my parents, the war was still ongoing. You and Karl had already left. I went to Hans' market one day. I have been in the market hundreds of times. That day though we struck up a different kind of conversation, more than small talk. We fell in love that day, and here we are."

"That is a special story as well, when things are meant to be, they will happen. It just takes a while sometimes. Hans, I remember the day Karl and I left Aurich. I remember turning, looking out the back window of the car, and waving to you. I knew we would see you again someday." They all settle in for the evening.

They awake to a freshly fallen snow, about three inches. Lieselotte has breakfast ready. "Hans, I realize it will be hard for me, yet I want to visit my parent's graves, and I would like to see the remains of our farm."

"Katarina, we will go to the cemetery first, then walk over to the farm. It is a shame what the Nazis did, what Wilhelm did. You came into town from the other direction yesterday, so you did not see it. It is open fields now. After the war ended the German concentration camp was torn down and the property reverted to the church. Saint Ludger has not done anything with it. They are trying to sell it but have not had any offers."

"How is Father Root?"

"He is doing fine, he has grown old, and is still active in the church."

"We want to see him also." Katarina turns to Karl, "Karl, I want to take a walk to the Kettle while we are here."

"The Kettle, what is the Kettle Katarina?"

She giggles.

"Hans, the Kettle is a special place in the woods Karl, and I would go to. It is by the stream on the north side of the farm. There is a rock shaped like a kettle. The stream fills it up and the water spills over, back into the stream. Karl and I had some very special times there. Remember Karl?"

Karl smiles. "Yes, I think of those days often."

"I will get breakfast cleaned up and we can head out."

"I will help you Lieselotte."

"No, you will not Katarina, you are our guests. My Katarina will help me."

"Karl and Katarina, after the cemetery, we can visit Father Root, then go to the farm if that works. We will pass the church on our way to the farm."

"That will be fine. I will need time to prepare myself. Hans, do you have flowers at your market? I would like to take some to the cemetery, even though it is cold. I want to give my parents flowers."

"I do, we can stop by and get them. Afterwards we see the farm, we will walk into the village for Kaffee and Kuchen."

"That will be fun, I remember doing that with my parents."

"Tomorrow evening we have planned to go to the Kneipe for dinner."

As they walk to the cemetery, they pass the spot where Anna and Gerhardt were murdered. Katarina stares as they walk by but says nothing.

"Katarina let us go to the market and get your flowers. I have roses, carnations, and just in, Edelweiss."

"The Edelweiss, they are perfect. My mother loved those. I would like two red roses also, to complement the white Edelweiss in the snow."

When they arrive at the grave, the clouds part and a ray of sun adorns the head stone. Katarina and Karl kneel, and pray. *Hello Mother, hello Father, I so miss you. Karl has brought me back to Germany.* Katarina places the flowers at the base of the headstone, she is weeping. Hans, Lieselotte, and their children stand behind them. Nicholas and Caroline at their sides. "I am ready Hans," Katarina says weeping. "I am ready to see Father Root."

With a brisk thirty walk they arrive at Saint Ludger Church. A young priest greets them, "Hello Hans, Lieselotte, Karl, and Katarina, may I help you?"

"Yes, we are here to see Father Root. These are the Schellenberg's; Karl, Katarina, Nicholas, and Caroline." The young priest takes a double take, *same names as Hans' children, odd.* "Father Root married Karl and Katarina in this church, twenty-one years ago."

"I will get him for you, have a seat." Katarina reflects hiding in the bell tower, and the damage the church suffered from Wilhelm's henchman. The night the soldiers were raiding the town looking for Karl. The night Wilhelm killed my mother and father. A tear runs down her cheek.

"What is wrong Mother?" as she wipes the tear from her mother's face.

"Nothing Caroline, just memories. Nicholas, Caroline, this is the church I attended in my childhood. My parent's, your grandparent's funeral services were here. Your father and I were married here."

Father Root sees Katarina and Karl and scurries over to them. "My goodness, it is so nice to see you after all these years. Hans told me you were visiting. How have you both been?"

"We have been very well Father, Karl has been transferred to Germany, to Ramstein."

"That is wonderful."

"These are our children, Nicholas and Caroline."

"Very nice to meet you both."

"We are going to see the farm today."

"How so very sad with what happened. We had a family staying at the farmhouse when the Germans evicted them and took the farm."

"Yes Father, we heard. Hans kept Karl and I filled in over the years." They spend another hour at the church.

The group heads to the farm. As they round the curve in the road Katarina becomes very distraught, she is in shock. She falls to her knees, crying. Caroline comforts her mother. Karl helps her up.

"I thought I was prepared for this, yet it is so devastating. The home I grew up in is gone." Karl helps her through the snow. "Karl, the farmhouse used to be there, and the main barn over there." At the crest of the hill, Katarina can see the remains of the stone barn, where her and Karl's little stone barn once stood. She sees the burnt barn doors, the ones she would knock on three times on, laying in the opening. She weeps more. "Karl, our barn, they did not completely destroy it." The construction of the concentration camp stopped short of the barn. "Nicholas, Caroline, that is what is left of the stone barn, the one I always talk about. Where I cared for your father." Katarina leans over to Nicholas and whispers, "You were conceived there. Karl, I am ready to go, this is difficult for me. The farm, our farm has changed so much. I hardly recognize anything. It is just flat, barren land. You and I will come back tomorrow and walk to the Kettle. Time to go to the café and have Kaffee and Kuchen. Aurich is such a nice village."

After a brisk forty-minute walk into town, they all have a great time at the café. They spend hours reminiscing, laughing together, and often crying together. They return to Hans' and Lieselotte's home for dinner and a relaxing evening. Hans has the fireplace stoked, Lieselotte and Karl's Katarina prepare dinner. The evening concludes at the fireplace, with the families enjoying beer. That evening Katarina and Karl lay in bed together.

"Karl."

"Yes, my Love."

"I want to buy the farm from the church. We can come back here someday when you retire."

"I love that idea Katarina; we can rebuild the farmhouse, just like it was. We can rebuild the barn, and best of all, we can rebuild the stone barn."

"I want to talk with Father Root tomorrow, we can see him after our walk to the Kettle. Karl, today was difficult for me, although it was good for me. It brought back some horrible memories. More good memories than bad though. It was good to come home and bring closure. I love you, thank you for bringing me here."

"I am glad we came here as well. I love you my dear."

Sunday morning, the families attend church service together at St. Ludgers. Afterwards, they mingle with other parishioners outside the church. The sun is out, and the day is a bit warmer.

"Katarina, you mentioned you and Karl wanted to walk to your Kettle place today."

"Yes Hans."

"We will take Nicholas and Caroline into town, we can shop, and spend the day. You and Karl, take your walk and enjoy the nice day. We will meet you for dinner at the Kneipe."

"Thank you, Hans. Karl, I am ready for our walk, but first, we need to talk with Father Root. I would like to talk with him before our walk." Katarina and Karl remain at the church. Father Root is at the altar. "Father Root, may we have a word with you?"

"Yes, by all means Katarina."

"Father, Karl and I were talking. We love Aurich, and someday want to come back, and live here. Hans mentioned you want to sell the farm."

"Yes Katarina, Saint Ludger would like the property to go to someone who will enjoy it; and make something of it again. We do not have the funds to maintain it or improve it."

"Father, Karl and I want to buy it." Father Root pauses for a moment. He takes Katarina's hand.

"My girl, we will simply return the farm to its rightful owner. I will see to it the papers are drawn for you and Karl."

"No Father, we want to buy it from the church."

"Katarina, I will have no such thing. You were very gracious to give your farm to the church, now you shall have it back." Katarina begins to speak. "Shh Katarina."

"Thank you, Father. Please bless the land for us, remove the evil that came upon it." Katarina looks at Karl and begins weeping. Karl and Katarina head to the Kettle.

"Karl, we need to stop by the car. I brought our ice skates and a blanket."

"I did not know you did that."

"I know you did not, it is a surprise." Katarina smiles at Karl and flutters her blue eyes. "We can clear the snow, build a fire, and skate on the pond." They arrive at the Kettle. Karl gathers wood for the fire. Katarina clears the snow and lays the blanket out. "Karl, hold me for a while, hold me tight. I love this place. It is just how I remember it and imagined it through the years. I want to enjoy it again, in your arms, just as we did so many years ago." Katarina and Karl spend a very memorable day at the Kettle. They lay by the fire and gaze up to the blue German sky. "Karl, we have the farm back, I am so happy, my parents are happy. I can feel it. We are coming home, Spinnaker."

"Katarina, we will make a sizable donation to the church, we can help Saint Ludgers that way." Katarina stands, gathers a snowball, and throws it at Karl. They have fun playing in the snow.

"I want to make snow angels." They ice skate on the pond the rest of the day. "Karl, we have been here for hours. I had so much fun, thank you. We better head back. The sun is going down, and we need to meet everyone at the Kneipe. I want to share the news with Hans about the farm."

Katarina and Karl arrive at the Kneipe just before six. Hans, Lieselotte, and the children are seated. Hans has beer for everyone. "Katarina, Karl, come, sit, join us, I have beers for you. How was your day at the Kettle?"

"Always Sehr Gut with Herr Schellenberg. The day was very nice. It brought back so many good memories, I needed that. We built a fire, played in the snow, and ice skated on the pond Father built. Karl and I have news for you."

"I am listening Katarina."

"Karl and I talked with Father Root this morning. We are getting our farm back; we will be coming home someday; home to Aurich. We will rebuild the farm, the farmhouse, the barns, just like before. We even have something to start with at the stone barn."

"Katarina, Karl, we are so hoppy for you, that is wonderful news."

"How was your day?"

Caroline chimes in. "Mother, we had a great time. Katarina and I have a lot in common. Nicholas and Karl enjoyed their time together also. I love this village. I had a strange but good feeling walking around town, that I would like to live here someday. Then you bring us this news."

The families enjoy dinner, and each other. Katarina has Sauerbraten with red cabbage and potato dumplings, Caroline and Lieselotte each share Schweinshaxe with potatoes and cabbage. Karl has Rouladen with mashed potatoes, pickled red cabbage, and gravy. Hans has Wiener Schnitzel, coated in breadcrumbs with cheese and ham sandwiched within, a green salad, and potatoes. His children both order German sausages, Katarina has Munchner Weisswurst with sauerkraut and mustard and Karl has bratwurst with sauerkraut and mustard. As they walk home, a light snow begins to fall. They all retire for the evening.

Monday is a day of relaxing. Hans has a fire going. The ladies are busy in the kitchen. The men are relaxing in the parlor. After lunch, the children walk to the village. Katarina, Karl, Hans, and Lieselotte spend the afternoon reminiscing.

"Hans, we have many memories together."

"We do Karl. I remember when Anna and Katarina came to the church, Dr. Vandenburg was with them. Katarina told me she found the pilot the Germans were looking for. She told me of your injuries, and that she was caring for you. Do you remember that Katarina?"

"Like it was yesterday Hans."

"Karl, I remember the first time we met. It was late in the evening, June of 1943, at the farmhouse. We had to be careful, the German patrols were in town looking for you. Katarina brought you from the stone barn. The scheme Gerhardt developed; it was ingenious. For you to become a spy; and infiltrate the Army Group's North Command. You played them all, you were masterful Karl. You were able to instill a new focus and a sense of urgency within the German High Command on the European Front. To take Germany's focus off enough and distract them from the Russian aggression. This ultimately helped Russia conquer the Third Reich and defeat them, bringing the Nazis to their knees. Your actions were key in bringing Hitler and the Third Reich down."

"We made a great team Hans. You and your Underground were always spot on. Remember the fingerprint verification ordeal?"

"Oh, my yes. I remember it very well Karl. It caught us completely off guard. As always though, you developed a masterful plan in short order."

"Hans, as always, you and your team executed the plan flawlessly. Hans, I have a question."

"Yes Karl, what is it?"

"The night Katarina and I escaped when we flew to London from Egmond aan Zee. Was Rudolf captured?"

"Yes, Karl he was. However, the German patrol left their guard down, stupid Nazis. As they were driving over a bridge, over the Markermeer Sea, you and Katarina drove over that bridge that day. Rudolf disrupted their attention. He distracted the two soldiers and managed to jump from the car, into the water. He escaped."

"I am happy to hear that Hans. He was a good man. I thought he may have been captured. He risked his life for us that day. I was concerned what the Germans would do to him, you know, torture him for information about the plane or worse. I always wondered."

"Karl, let me show you something." Hans returns with a picture. "This is Katarina and Nicholas when Nicholas was born. And this, a picture of Nicholas and Caroline when they were little, look Katarina. You sent them to me Karl. I have something for you Katarina."

"What do you have Hans?"

"Here Katarina," Hans hands her a book. Katarina begins to weep.

"Hans, my mother's cookbook. How did you get this, where did you get this?"

"Henrich told me you forgot it the day you left Germany. When you came back to get it, you saw a German convoy in town. That was Wilhelm, he came back, I guess for a surprise visit. Katarina and Karl, your timing was so precise and fortunate that morning. Had Wilhelm been fifteen minutes earlier, or you fifteen minutes later leaving, you would have been captured. Wilhelm first drove through the cemetery and then to the farmhouse. Anyway, I went and got your mother's cookbook afterwards. I meant to send it to you, but with the distraction of the war, it slipped my mind."

"Hans, thank you so much. I have often thought of her cookbook. Look, Mother would make special notes on the pages, the recipes she liked best." Katarina and Karl lie in bed. Katarina's head in on Karl's chest.

"Karl, this was a good trip, I had such a good time. I enjoyed spending time with Hans, Lieselotte, and their children. We need to do this often. I wish we did not have to leave tomorrow." Katarina falls asleep. An emotional Tuesday morning arrives early. The Houseman's and Schellenberg's say their goodbyes. Karl, Katarina, Nicholas, and Caroline head back to Ramstein.

Karl is at his desk, February 5, Katarina calls. "Karl, we have a telegram from Angie. We have an offer on our home."

"That is great news, what is the offer?"

"It is a full price offer, a young couple. They are moving from central Pennsylvania. They have requested the furniture be included rather than purchased separately."

"Well, I think that is a fair request. We had a little buffer built in thinking we would need to negotiate. We will still be whole, and we can move on. I think it is an easy decision my Love."

"Great, I will telegram Angie back and let her know we will accept the offer."

Nicholas is busy in officer's training. February 7 1965. President Johnson orders the bombing of targets in North Vietnam in Operation Flaming Dart in retaliation for a Viet Cong raid at the U.S. Base in the city of Pleiku and at a nearby helicopter base at Camp Holloway.

Thursday February 13. Karl stops by the florists on his way home. When he arrives home, Katarina and Caroline are sitting in the parlor. Karl has the flowers behind his back. "Flowers for my valentines." Katarina gets her red roses and white lilies; Caroline gets her red and white carnations.

The next morning, Karl wakes to Katarina snuggled in his arms. He kisses her forehead. "Happy Valentine's day my Love."

"And to you Karl."

"Katarina, would you like to go out for dinner?"

"How about we have a quiet evening at home tonight. Since Caroline and her girlfriends are not dating, they are going out tonight. We can have date night." Karl gets home at 18:30, Katarina has dinner ready. Katarina is in her white lace robe.

"You are beautiful my Love." He gives Katarina a kiss and begins to go upstairs.

"You cannot go upstairs?"

"Why Katarina." She only smiles at him and tugs him off the stairs.

"We will have dinner first, I have it ready. Then it is date night." Katarina has candles at the table, and soft music in the background. Katarina and Karl finish their lovely dinner together. "Come with me Karl, now is time to go upstairs." Katarina has her promiscuous look. As Karl approaches their bedroom, he sees the mistletoe hanging from the doorway, and notices an orange glow, a flickering reflection coming from beneath the door. He can smell the fireplace. "I have a surprise for you Karl." Katarina opens the door slightly and kisses Karl beneath the mistletoe. She pulls Karl into the bedroom. He sees Katarina has made a heart from fresh rose and lily petals. She has it carefully placed on the bed sheets.

"Katarina, I love the petals, and the fire is perfect for tonight."

"Close your eyes big boy. Ok my Love, open your eyes." Karl opens his eyes to Katarina in a red bra and red lace panties. Her silhouette from the fireplace is dancing on the wall.

"Oh, my Katarina, you have my lederhosen in a bunch."

"Happy Valentine's Day Karl. It is time to play in the flower garden." Katarina and Karl make inexhaustible love in the rose and lily petals. The cuckoo clock chimes midnight.

THE PREPARATION

The Vietnam War begins in earnest on March 2 1965 with Operation Rolling Thunder. This attack sends U.S. aircraft on strikes against targets in North Vietnam. President Johnson launches a three-year campaign of sustained bombing of targets in North Vietnam and the Ho Chi Minh Trail. U.S. and Allied ground forces join the campaign. On the morning of March 8, 9.03, thirty-five hundred U.S. Marines land on beaches near Da Nang, South Vietnam as the first American combat troops to enter Vietnam.

Katarina and Karl celebrate their first kiss day on April 19. Caroline is working at a café in town. The tensions in Vietnam are escalating even more. Nicholas has graduated officer training as a lieutenant; and is assigned to the 86th Air Base Group in Ramstein, under Karl's leadership. The Air Force Command has Nicholas and selected others on a fast track accelerated program, mentoring under Karl and military leaders. In February of 1964, the 516th Fighter Squadron equipped with fifteen Douglas A-1 Skyraiders are moved to Da Nang Air Base from Nha Trang Air Base. Nicholas' group's flight training is on the Douglas A-1 Skyraider, a single-seat, long-range, high performance attack aircraft.

On August 12, four days before Katarina's birthday, Nicholas' squadron is assigned to the 516th Fighter Squadron, Da Nang Air

Base Vietnam. At twenty-one years old, Nicholas is promoted to captain, Squadron Commander. The youngest ever in the Air Force. He has twenty-four aircraft under his command. Karl presides over the promotion with Katarina and Caroline at his side. "A very proud day for me Nicholas, congratulations my son. Nicholas, take this, and keep it with you. Your mother gave me this butterfly pin in Germany. It will protect you."

Nicholas squadron ships out to South Vietnam. He will miss celebrating his mother's birthday, Caroline's, and his own with his family. Nicholas' squadron fly sorties into North Vietnam. The Air Force fly their initial combat missions in late 1964. Nearly a year later Nicholas' squadron continues those missions.

"Karl, October in the Black Forest is absolutely breathtaking. I love how the maple and elm trees are sprinkled within the evergreens. I want to take a hike this weekend."

"I would love that Katarina. I have enjoyed our hikes this summer in the forest, the fall will be beautiful."

"I wish Nicholas could be with us."

"I know Katarina, I do too." The family routinely hikes in the Black Forest. Katarina, Karl, and Caroline return to the forest for a late October hike. Katarina finds a pond in a secluded ravine.

"Karl look, we can ice skate here in the winter." On one of their last hikes in the fall, Katarina and Karl are lying in a clearing in the forest, next to the pond. A cool autumn breeze is descending from the mountain top. The pine needles are rustling in the breeze. Caroline takes a walk to enjoy the forest, and to have quiet time. She misses Nicholas. "Karl, smell the evergreens, smell the fall air. The holidays are approaching, it will be so different without Nicholas. I want to celebrate Thanksgiving here. We will keep the tradition going in Germany." The Schellenberg's have their Thanksgiving in Germany, Christmas is approaching.

November brings the Soviet Union increasing its support to North Vietnam, sending aircraft, artillery, ammunition, small arms, radar, air defense systems, food, and medical supplies. Meanwhile,

China sends several engineering troops to North Vietnam to assist in building their critical defense infrastructure. During the war in Vietnam, U.S. Air Force fighter pilots and crewmen are repeatedly challenged by enemy MIG's in the skies over North Vietnam. The air battles which ensue are unique as U.S. fighter and strike forces are mandated to operate under stringent rules of engagement. The Soviet MIG bases could not be struck. The rules forbade bombing or strafing of military and industrial targets in and around the Vietnamese heartland which includes the capital of Hanoi and the port city of Haiphong. These restrictions give the North Vietnamese a substantial military advantage. North Vietnam constructs one of the most formidable anti-aircraft defenses to date. These include MIG forces, surface-to-air missile (SAM) batteries, heavy concentrations of antiaircraft artillery (AAA) units, and an array of early warning radar systems. These elements sought to interdict and defeat the U.S. bombing campaign against North Vietnam's lines of communication and its military and industrial bases. The primary mission of U.S. fighter pilots is to prevent the North Vietnamese MIG's from interfering with U.S. strike operations.

"Katarina, Caroline, it is Saturday morning, already the fifth of December. Do you want to find a Christmas tree today? This is our first Christmas in Germany."

"That will be fun Father, where do you have in mind?"

"The Black Forest."

"Karl, I will get our ice skates, we can skate like we did at the gristmill. Just as we did when we would get our tree in Coffeyville." The three head off to the mountains. They find the perfect tree, and skate in the moonlit night. They arrive home late, have dinner, and go to bed. "Karl, I loved today, I had so much fun in the forest."

Sunday morning, Karl has a fire going in the fireplace in the parlor. They set the tree up in the middle of the room; and begin decorating it. Katarina places their special ornaments, and Caroline places the angel on top. "The tree is beautiful Mother and Father." Karl decorates the outside of their home.

Karl is busy at the Base. The Vietnam initiatives and tensions are growing. Christmas morning, Katarina and Caroline are making breakfast, Karl has the tree lit and stokes the fire. Caroline brings hot chocolate in for the family. Karl has Christmas music playing. It begins to snow. "Look Katarina, Caroline, it's snowing. Perfect for Christmas morning!"

Katarina, Caroline, and Karl return from Katholische Kirche St. Nikolaus. They gather around the tree to exchange gifts. "Karl, I miss the sound of the train set." "Yes, I do too. Nicholas and Caroline loved it as well. You must miss your toy trucks Karl," Katarina giggles.

Caroline looks at her father, "Toy trucks, what is Mother talking about?"

"It's a joke between your mother and I, I loved buying Nicholas toy trucks, just as I had when I was a little boy. Your mother always teased me that I was really getting them for myself."

"Karl, I have been thinking of Nicholas. I miss him, I hope he is okay."

"We all do Katarina." Katarina hugs Karl and Caroline. They continue to exchange gifts. Karl gives Caroline and Katarina each a stocking. In it they find a small box. The girls open their traditional ornaments. Karl gets them both a miniature German Chalet. They each get a Christmas card.

"Caroline, this is from your father and I." Caroline opens her gift. It is a pendent necklace.

"It is beautiful, thank you."

"It is your birthstone, our birthstone, Caroline. It is a Peridot."

Katarina hands Karl his gift. He opens it. "Katarina, when did you have this made?"

"In Coffeyville, I had the photographer blend photos from Nicholas' and Caroline's births, special times in their lives, and Nicholas' enlistment. I nursed it through our trip."

"I have never seen anything like this. It is beautiful, thank you very much." Karl kisses Katarina.

"Now Katarina, your turn. Close your eyes." Katarina hears Karl moving something heavy. "You can look." Katarina opens her eyes to a large, rectangular gift on the floor, next to the tree. "Go ahead my Love, open it." As Katarina begins to open her gift, she can see it's made of wood.

"Karl it is a hope chest. I have always thought of having one. I love the inlaid hearts. I have never seen that before, they are beautiful. It smells, oh it has a cedar lining. I love this, thank you Karl."

"Yes, my Love, for your special things, and our memories. I have one more gift for you Katarina." Katarina opens a box, about the size of a shoe box.

"Karl this is beautiful, I have never had a music box. I love the picture on the front, and sailboat with a kiss, of red lips on the sail."

"I had that custom painted. Remember I told you my code name on my first mission into German was Spinnaker? The lead sail on a sailboat."

"Yes, I do Karl."

"Do you remember you sent me a lily petal with your kiss on it, red lipstick, when I was in Neuengamme?" Katarina begins to cry. "Open the lid my Love." Katarina opens it. It begins to play Edelweiss.

The holiday's come and go. Katarina, Karl, and Caroline are settled in Germany. New Year's Day arrives, 1966. For several months, Nicholas' squadron has been dispatched to provide air support for U.S. troops in North Vietnam. The squadron continues to fly sorties into North Vietnam, searching for anti-aircraft installations, but most importantly to prevent the North Vietnamese MIG's from interfering with U.S. strike operations. To date his group has flown one thousand five hundred thirteen missions with no loss of aircraft.

THE RETURN

Nicholas's flight plan has him on a southern heading out of North Vietnam, piloting his Douglas A1 Skyraider.

"Command, crossing into South Vietnam now."

"Roger that Captain Schellenberg, welcome home." There is slight turbulence. The plane rocks to the left. Nicholas corrects the roll and adjusts the flight path as planned, he eases the controls to correct the yaw of the plane. The plane corrects itself to the planned flight path. He settles back and continues his focus on the mission. He focuses his vision to the horizon. He sees the enemy's artillery fire in the westerly sky.

Suddenly, a severe flash of bright light encompasses the sky.

"Command, an unusually bright light has just enveloped the sky around me. I lost track of the earth for a moment. A type of flash I have never experienced before."

"Captain Schellenberg, we have no reports of any abnormal issue in your area."

Nicholas grasps his mother's butterfly pin on his lapel. "Command, I feel vertigo. I have dizziness. It feels as the sky is moving abnormally, like it's spinning. I'm having a problem focusing, my eyes are blurry. My hearing, I cannot hear. I have a severe ringing in the ears. My balance is off. I'm beginning to sweat profusely. I feel nauseous. Something from the flash of light." The young pilot passes out. Three minutes pass with no communication from Nicholas.

"Captain Schellenberg, we have lost you on the radar, please respond Captain Schellenberg, do you read me? Come in captain." Five more minutes pass with no communication from Nicholas. "Captain Schellenberg, do you read me? Come in captain." Radio silence seems to be forever. "Captain Schellenberg, do you read me, come in? We are scrambling jets. Your radio transmission is breaking up. It's cutting in and out, with very much static. Come in captain."

REWIND

The young pilot regains consciousness. He hears static on the radio, crackling, the transmission is going in and out. "Bogey, this is Spinnaker, do you read me over? I see heavy bombing from coalition forces on the horizon with heavy ground fire, do you copy? Crossing the German Border now."

"Roger that Spinnaker."

"Bogey, I see the city of Wilhelmshaven with heavy bombardment. Explosions and heavy fires erupting. An unusually bright light has just enveloped the sky around me. I lost track of the earth for a moment. A type of flash I have never experienced before."

"Spinnaker, we have no reports of any abnormal issue in your area."

"Bogey, I feel vertigo. I have dizziness. It feels as the sky is moving abnormally, like it is spinning. I have a problem focusing, my eyes are blurry. My hearing, I cannot hear. I have severe ringing in my ears. My balance is off. I am beginning to sweat profusely. I feel nauseous. Something from the flash of light." The young pilot passes out momentarily.

"Spinnaker; try to collect yourself."

The radio is silent.

"Spinnaker, do you read me? Come in Spinnaker."

A few minutes pass. "Bogey, yes I read you. I must have passed out briefly. The symptoms are subsiding, that was very strange."

"Glad you're back with us Spinnaker."

"Bogie, I am experiencing electrical problems. Karl reaches for his dog-tags, where he has always carried his mother's locket. "Bogie, my electronics are failing, my engines are failing. I am aborting the aircraft."